Being a Ship's Log Kept By Richard Jacob, Third Viscount Keld

Donovan M. Reves

Springfield, Oregon

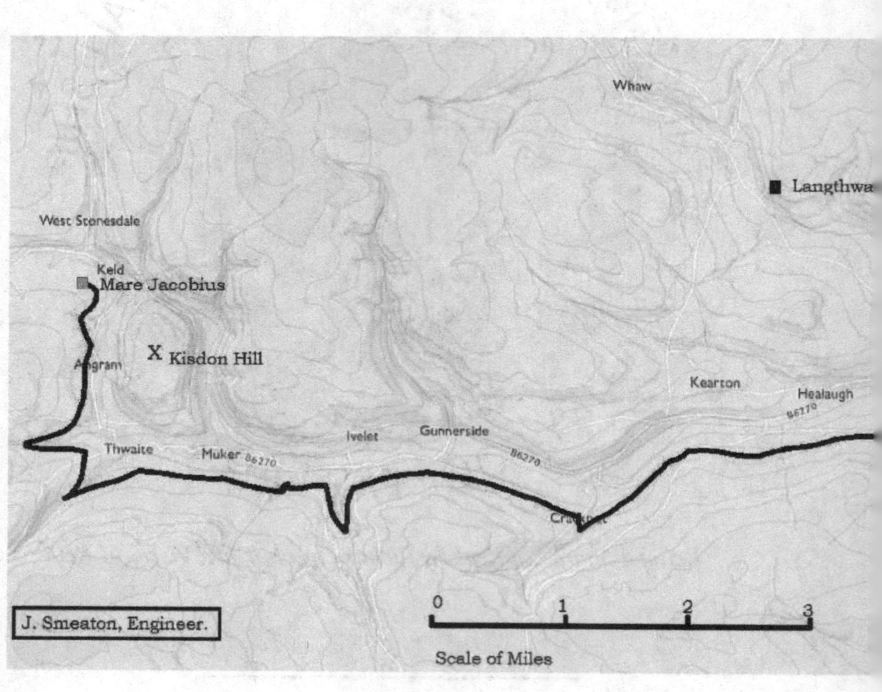

Whaw
Langthwa
West Stonesdale
Keld
Mare Jacobius
X Kisdon Hill
Angram
Kearton
Healaugh
B6270
Thwaite
Muker B6270
Ivelet
Gunnerside
B6270
Crackpot
J. Smeaton, Engineer.
0
1
2
3
Scale of Miles

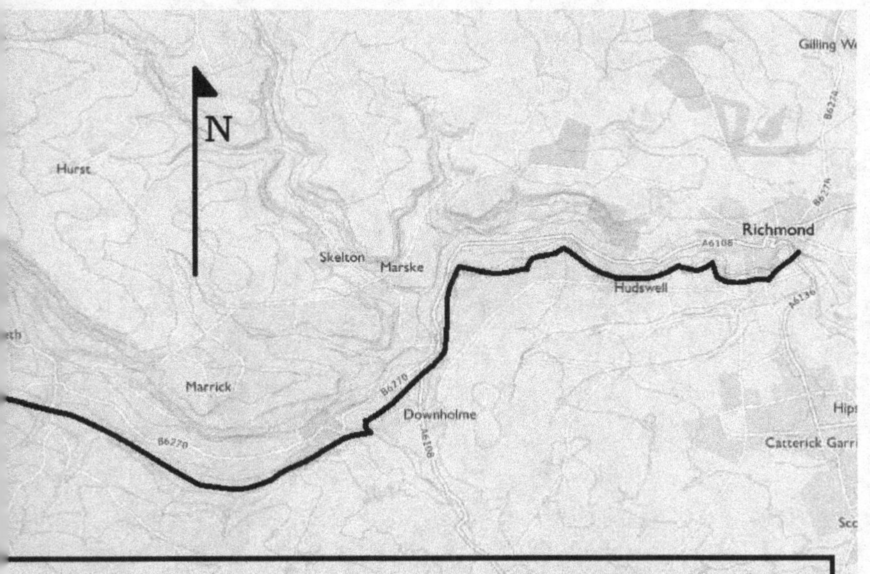

N
Hurst
Skelton
Marske
Richmond
Gilling W
Marrick
Downholme
Hudswell
Hips
Catterick Garri
Scc
B6270
B6270
A6108
A6108
A6136
B6274
B6271
eth

ute of the Swaledale Turn-pike Yorkshire, Eng. 1795

For Rima

Friday, May 15, 1795

I may now commence my ship's log. Late yesterday evening saw my magnificent vessel completed at last, as some of the most skilled woodworkers in Yorkshire put the finishing touches on my *Mean Fish* by lantern light. This morning as the sun began his journey across the heavens, I fell out of bed and hastened to the window of my chamber, from whence I witnessed glorious rays of sunlight strike the crows' nest atop the mighty mainmast, the grassy slopes of Great Shunner Fell rising into blue sky beyond.

The *Mean Fish* must surely be the loveliest ship ever built by human hands. Patterned after third-rate ships-of-the-line built for His Majesty's Royal Navy, the *Mean Fish* has an overall length of one hundred sixty-six feet, a keel length of one hundred thirty-five, a beam of forty-seven, and a draught of twenty-eight. When fully armed she shall carry sixteen cannons (eighteen-pound long-guns), although as we still await delivery from Newcastle, her armaments currently consist of a musket tied to a post.

It is not her size which constitutes her true beauty, however; nor her incipient prowess which caused me to shed tears of joy this morning as I gazed from my chamber window. The *Mean Fish* has been designed by none other than myself to far surpass any vessel of HM's Royal Navy in the grace of her lines and the luxury of her appointments. I am particularly pleased with the captain's quarters, where rich woods from around the world are accented with gold filigree and a sumptuous captain's privy awaits my exclusive use. The apogee of my elegant design is the magnificent figurehead from which the ship's name derives—a writhing, scowling fish with great fangs. This symbol came to me in a dream and it is a thing of sublime beauty.

The single element which my mighty vessel lacks at this point, is water in which to float. However, that deficiency is to be remedied this very day. Crews have labored diligently for over a year, constructing the marvelous ditch of nearly a mile in length which, once its gates are opened, shall bring water from Sleddale Beck into the dry dock. In less than twenty-four hours, the pool shall be full and the *Mean Fish* afloat.

Nelson is of the opinion that never in the history of the world has a ship of such note been built and floated so far from the sea, and I readily concur. By my reckoning it is a riverine distance of one hundred thirty-one miles from Stonesthrow Hall to the mouth of the river Ouse, then another thirty-nine miles of the Humber estuary before one reaches the open sea.

Although my villagers in Keld have been and continue to be enthusiastic supporters of my project, not everyone in the neighborhood is as accepting of my vision as they. There are great idiots in Swaledale, two of whom in particular I shall refrain from mentioning by name, who scoff at the possibility of my splendid *Mean Fish* ever reaching the sea. But in good time they shall be shewn how stupid they are.

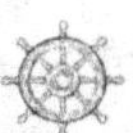

May 15; In the Evening

Today as planned, the gate up-valley was opened and our ditch conveyed the clear, cold waters of Sleddale Beck into the dry dock. Nelson, Whitehand, and I enjoyed a cold luncheon adjacent to the hall, at a spot from whence we could observe as the rising water cradled my *Mean Fish* in its aquatic arms. We watched the markings on the sides of the dry dock. Five feet of water. Ten feet. Fifteen feet. Nelson and Whitehand shewed clear signs of impatience as the hours passed, our good vicar going so far as to suggest that he had important business elsewhere. But I did not allow either of them to leave. The moment was too historic for that. Historic moments must be witnessed. Never mind that the moment lasted nearly nine hours. I have sat through enough of Whitehand's dull sermons that he owed me this.

Twenty feet. Twenty-five feet. I could scarcely breathe as the waters reached this level. At what point would my *Mean Fish* rise free of her timber cradle and float? Would her balance be true, or would she list? Worse yet, would she capsize before moving an inch, her shapely masts dashed into matchsticks by the flagstones edging the pool? The tension was excruciating. I paced. I chewed my fingernails. I moaned. Nelson admonished me to stop moaning as it was not befitting a ship's captain and I agreed with him.

Finally, I directed Rugby to find some distraction for me, as the uncertainty had become extremely vexing. Rugby did this admirably by reading to me from a very ludicrous novel by someone named Fielding. I became so absorbed in mocking this silly piece of so-called literature, that I must have missed the crucial moment at which my *Mean Fish* finally lifted from her cradle and floated free. My attention was pulled away from Rugby's reading by Nelson releasing the signal balloon, by which means we informed the villagers up-valley to close

the gate, lest further water flowing through our ditch cause the pool to overflow. At this point I saw that the *Mean Fish* was drifting, straining against her mooring ropes, which meant that she was afloat—heaven be praised, her masts entirely perpendicular and her balance true.

I thoroughly berated Rugby for having caused me to miss the most auspicious moment of my life with his perverse novel. Then it was time for dinner. The tall windows of the dining hall provided me with a marvelous view of my magnificent vessel, now fully deserving of the appellation "ship" as she lay in harbour, as it were, at over twelve hundred feet elevation above the sea, in the Pennines of Yorkshire. Nelson asked me if I had a notion to name the pool in which my ship now sailed. I pointed out to him that the *Mean Fish* was hardly sailing as of yet, but then I added that the pool shall be named Mare Jacobum. From his nod and indulgent smile, I could tell that my uncle thoroughly approved.

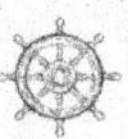

Saturday, May 16, 1795

Late last night, I shewed yesterday's entries in my ships' log to Nelson. He asked me for whom this log is intended. I replied that the *Mean Fish* is a ship, and I am a ship captain, and therefore I am obliged to keep a ships' log. Nelson said that this would be true enough were I captain in a navy, or a merchant captain, but as I am captain of a ship which is presently sitting in an excavated pool high in the Pennines, I am under no such obligation.

I disagree. It is in fact the unique situation of my ship which makes it historically important for me to document my career as captain of the *Mean Fish* and the various adventures which befall us. I explained this to Nelson and he nodded slowly, tapping his pipe stem against his temple as he is wont to do when in thought.

He said, "Richard, you have a point. Many wonderful adventures must inevitably befall the crew of a ship perched in a tiny pool far from the sea. At the very least it is, as you say, a situation unique in the annals of naval history. It is well that you have begun a ships' log. However, there is one thing I suggest. You toss about names such as Nelson, Keld, Rugby, Swaledale, and so on, as if anyone who may pick up this log in three hundred years' time shall somehow have knowledge of those persons and places. Your log needs more of an introduction."

Of course, my uncle is right. This was an oversight on my part. So today, as servants move furnishings and personal effects from my chambers in Stonesthrow Hall to my captain's quarters aboard the *Mean Fish*, I take the time to provide future readers of this account with an introduction.

My name is Richard Jacob. I am the Third Viscount Keld, and a mature gentleman of eight and twenty. Keld is a village in the upper

reach of Swaledale, one of the great valleys penetrating the Pennine Mountains in Western Yorkshire.

I was born in and dwell at Stonesthrow Hall, our manor perched upon the verdant slopes above Keld. I share the hall with my maternal uncle, Sir James Nelson. I am master of the house, my parents both having departed this world at tragically young ages. Portions of Stonesthrow are recent, having been built by my grandfather when this viscountcy was created for him. However, other portions are quite ancient, dating back at least three centuries to a noble family whose title has been lost to local memory. Villagers of Keld and others in this corner of Swaledale refer to these bygone aristocrats as "the old ones," and sundry strange legends are associated with them, although there is no call to describe those here.

Aside from our servants, two others dwell upon the grounds of Stonesthrow Hall, although not in the main building. Paul Whitehand is vicar of Keld and attends to the chapel in the ancient portion of the hall. Otto Converse is our family physician and may always be relied upon to furnish morose company. These worthies did their best for my parents; of that I have no doubts. When heaven wills that a human being is not long for this world, there is nothing a mortal man may do.

Rugby is our chief steward, in charge of our household staff. He hails from Cornwall and his language can be difficult to understand at the best of times; when he upbraids an underling he often lapses into Cornish and no one within five hundred miles can make heads or tails of it. Rugby can be a rather disagreeable fellow, at times, but difficulty of finding an adequate replacement, together with his undeniable competency, has thus far prevented me from sacking him.

The villagers of Keld are an upstanding lot whose lives revolve around sheep and lead. The former graze Swaledale's grassy slopes in great flocks; the latter is mined from numerous pits and transported

elsewhere for smelting and manufacturing. Both commodities provide comfortable and steady incomes to both my family and the commoners of Keld. The villagers appreciate the beneficence shewn to them by our family over the generations, so that a bucolic mood reigns over Keld and its environs. I cannot say the same for certain villages farther east.

The East—in that direction my destiny lies. This ship, the *Mean Fish,* shall one day sail upon the sea, and I shall be her captain. Nelson may be right about finding adventures in a tiny pool, but the sea is the Odyssey, the sea is Lord Howard smashing the armada, the sea is adventure writ large. One day I shall have more to describe in this log than ditches, landscapes, and ill-humored servants.

Sunday, May 17, 1795

It has been an exhausting yet rewarding past couple of days. I have been too busy inspecting the ship and supervising the arrangement of my captain's quarters to write. I was also too busy to attend chapel this morning. Whitehand was not pleased and said something about imperiling my soul. I cannot believe that he spends as much time as it would seem, from his speech, worrying about my soul, as it would leave him precious little time to worry about his own. But then I suppose that he and God must have an understanding.

I should write a few words about my marvelous *Mean Fish*, whose decks I trod yesterday for the first time. She is not only beautiful and strong, but also designed with an eye to the comfort of her officers and crew, to an extent which has never before been seen on this globe. It is my belief that a ship should be a home, seeing as how those serving aboard her are often confined thereon for months, if not years. How medieval we remain if we fail to provide even the barest amenities to hardworking officers and sailors. Such shall not be the case aboard my ship.

As one example, consider the forecastle. This portion of a ship typically suffers an evil reputation, as a foul hole where sailors bunk in squalor and indecency. Aboard the *Mean Fish*, by contrast, the forecastle on deck one is an open, well-illuminated area furnished with chairs, tables, and artwork, where the crew may pass their time with such wholesome activities as lying and gambling. On Sundays the furnishings may be arranged to make the space function as a chapel, and there is a gangway leading to the crew's mess hall, directly below.

Also on deck one, below the poop deck, we have a spacious officers' mess which shall double as a meeting place or strategy room. Gangways lead directly from the strategy room down to my quarters and the first mate's.

Deck two includes all of the mates' and officers' quarters, along with some crew quarters, the general mess hall, the galley, and storage areas.

Deck three consists largely of crew quarters but includes several specialized rooms. First amongst these is the library, which is being filled with volumes even as I write, drawn from the family library in Stonesthrow Hall and focused upon such subjects as navigation, natural sciences, and philosophy. This collection is not for direct use of the crew, many of whom I anticipate shall be unable to read, and very few of whom I would deem trustworthy enough to handle volumes that have been in my family for generations. Rather, the crew shall be indirectly edified by the enlightened officers which the library must surely produce.

Next door to the library is a pub. It shall serve a limited selection of food produced in the galley, and also beer. The pub has a stage for the performance of music and production of morally appropriate dramas to educate and inspire the crew. Whitehand has made it clear that he objects to having a pub onboard, but why should Englishmen be expected to cheerfully relinquish access to a clean and friendly local? Such a place has at least as much to do with a community's contentment, in my opinion, as does a church.

Across from the pub is a sick bay. This is to serve as a place where Dr. Converse may treat the injuries or ailments which must inevitably arise, and hopefully also as a quarantine of sorts for his perpetual gloom, as the darker a spot he has in which to sit and sulk on his own, the less his moods should infect the rest of the ship.

Adjacent to the sick bay is a brig, consisting of a gaoler's office and five cells. Sadly, even the leadership of enlightened officers and the delightful environment aboard the *Mean Fish* may not suffice to avert all trouble and vice. As the brig shall hopefully not receive

much use, I expect the corridor outside of the cells to function most of the time as a nine-pin bowls lane for the officers.

Deck four is the general cargo hold, although it also includes workspaces for carpentry and whatnot, and one section has been walled off for use as my wine cellar.

Thus ends a brief tour of the *Mean Fish*, the most humanely and insightfully planned ship ever to sail the sea. I have no doubt that my parents would be proud of the pains I have taken to make her a true home to those who serve aboard her.

Late this afternoon, as I made small but important adjustments to the arrangement of my things in the captain's quarters, there came a knock at the door. This startled me more than a little, as I had not been aware that anyone else was aboard the *Mean Fish*. It was my Uncle Nelson, looking a tad sheepish.

"I suppose that, according to the law of the sea," said he, "I should have asked the captain's permission to come aboard. However, the gangplank looked welcoming, and I gave in to temptation."

With that, he gently pushed his way past me—Nelson is certainly the only human being on Earth from whom I would tolerate such a gesture—and stood in the middle of my quarters, having a look around. I must say that the room looked especially pleasant at that point, with the afternoon sun slanting in through the large windows at the stern and my monogrammed silk pillows freshly arranged upon the bed.

"Hmmm. Yes. Hmmm. Yes," said Nelson. "Everything as it should be. Only I see that you have mounted the chronometer and the barometer here instead of in the strategy room, as we discussed. I take it that longitude and incoming weather are to be privileged information aboard the *Mean Fish*?"

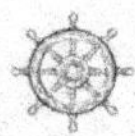

I reminded Nelson that the strategy room was only a few paces from where the instruments had been mounted, thanks to the connecting gangway.

He raised his eyebrows. "Still, there's plenty of room for them up there. Autocratic tendencies, Richard, autocratic tendencies."

Autocratic tendencies are something Nelson has been warning me against ever since I can remember, in spite of the fact that he himself exhibits no dearth of such tendencies.

Nelson made a slow circuit round the cabin, examining my decor and furnishings, giving a little nod here, a little "hmmpf" there. How well I know this penchant of his, to give his approval or disapproval of anything which I have had a hand in, and for the most part I am glad to indulge it. I am certain that his situation is not altogether agreeable, being the eldest man in the hall and yet not in charge, by dint of not being the viscount.

Finally, Nelson stopped at my bed. This is the only furnishing in the place which has not been moved from my chambers in the hall, as it is new and freshly delivered from Richmond.

"I say, nephew, same old bedclothes but a new bed, eh? Out here away from the house, perhaps you've a mind to make it a *flower* bed?"

Nelson had not named any names, but there was no mistaking the prurient leer on his face.

"How dare you speak of Thistle in that manner!" I thundered.

Nelson gave a sarcastic bow. "My apologies, nephew, for daring to presume that your interest in Keld's comeliest shepherdess could be anything but platonic and intellectual."

"I far prefer Aristotle, thank you very much! And now if you would be so kind as to leave my cabin, before I order you out of it!"

Nelson adopted a falsely pensive air. "It is tempting, Richard. I have here the opportunity to be on the receiving end of the very first order you give aboard this ship. But, I leave it for another time.

Ta-ta, I am off across the corridor to inspect my own cabin, which shall be, I daresay, hardly half the size of yours." And with that, he was off, closing the door gently behind him.

I am certain that my uncle meant no actual insult. It is his way to tease anyone and everyone around him. Still, he should know better than to make light of some subjects, amongst which is my admiration for the incomparable Thistle . . . The Darling of the Dell, the Flower of the Fell, the Sweet of all Swaledale.

Monday, May 18, 1795

How delightful to awaken this morning in my luxurious new bed, surrounded by my new cabin, aromatic with the sweet odor of freshly hewn wood! Early light flooded in through the windows, and the *Mean Fish* gently swayed beneath me (wind pushing the ship against her mooring ropes, I expect, as there is very little chop on the Mare Jacobum). I lay there for some time savoring these various sensations. Then I fell out of bed and began my morning ablutions, in expectation of a busy and fruitful day.

Today's main order of business was the recruitment of two additional officers. My first mate, of course, is my uncle, Nelson. This he is qualified for not only because of his advantage in being my uncle, but also due to his nautical experience as a commander in His Majesty's Royal Navy. Although Nelson's naval experience took place somewhat prior to the dawn of time, he speaks of it constantly, and thus kept fresh in his thoughts, I trust that his wisdom shall be undiminished by the intervening centuries. Jesting aside, Nelson is modest about his achievements, readily admitting that there was not a great deal of glamour in the command of a supply sloop based at the obscure Royal Navy dockyard at Sinkhole-On-Sea. Still, he has first-hand knowledge of sailing, the sea, and the particulars of command—certainly more so than anyone else in our part of Yorkshire—and I anticipate that I shall rely upon him a good deal, at least at the outset.

Second and third mates remained to be chosen. To this end, I had placed advertisements in sundry periodicals, and had the same posted at various ports, to the effect that interested parties should report to Stonesthrow Hall by noon on this day.

We could have held our interviews at a less remote, and possibly more congenial, location. For example, the Town House in Richmond which the duke has graciously allowed me to utilize for business on occasion, would probably have been available. However, it was of great importance to me that all of our applicants have the opportunity to see not only the ship on which they would be serving, but also its unique geographical situation. This, I hoped, would enable us to easily eliminate any whose preconceptions would render them unfit.

In this I was proved exactly correct. The dozen or so estimable sailors who were shewn into the great room of the hall at noon, had all gotten a good look at my ship, as its gleaming hull and tall masts are in full view of all the country roundabout Keld. The question was, would they one and all regard it as a curiosity unworthy of their nautical experience? Or were any there disposed to recognize the rare opportunity presented?

"Gentlemen," I began, in my most capitainly tones, "no doubt you have all noticed the magnificent ship moored beside Stonesthrow Hall. I must make it plain from the outset that this is the very ship upon which two of you shall have the good fortune to serve as second and third mates. I can assure you that …"

My speech became drowned out by loud expressions of incredulity, not unmixed with laughter, from nearly all of the applicants. Voila, the *Mean Fish* had done her part! The majority, who met her land-locked condition with derision, were politely shewn back to their conveyances by Rugby. Only two applicants remained in the great hall.

One of these gentlemen looked as if he had come straight from a seaside pub, after having roundly trounced every other customer inside, and the proprietor as well. This is not to say that he bore marks of a fresh fight, but rather looked as if he had won a great many in his time and meant to win a great many more. When asked to introduce himself, he gave his name as Michael Bridger and his occupation as "sailor, and leader of sailors, though never captain of a ship." From his accent I took Mr. Bridger for a Liverpudlian, but

when I enquired, he growlingly replied that he is from Blackpool and hates Liverpool more than any other thing on Earth. He went on to add that he also hates kittens, ice, and musical notes more than any other thing on Earth. I asked Mr. Bridger his opinion of my *Mean Fish*, to which he answered that she was the sweetest vessel he had ever laid eyes upon, and that any man standing between him and an officers' berth on such a ship, was asking in plain terms to have his everlasting soul separated from his body. I noted Mr. Bridger's enthusiasm and turned to the next remaining applicant.

This young fellow, in contrast to the sea dog beside him, looked as if he might never have set foot in a pub, let alone found himself in a fistfight. He also looked familiar, and after squinting at him for a few moments, I realized why. It was John Lampson, youngest son of Charles Lampson, a worthy if somewhat choleric wool merchant in Richmond who does business with my family and others in Swaledale. I had not seen John for some years, not since a holiday fete at Goodwood House, when he had been about to depart for university in Cambridge. I greeted John and asked after his father.

"My father is very well, thank you, sir."

"And how was your time at university?"

"Very enlightening, thank you, sir. I have graduated with a degree in botany."

"Well, well. Botany. I daresay our Jacob family sheep know a thing or two on the subject, although they may not be competent to sit for examinations!"

Nelson laughed at my jest. Mr. Lampson gave a nervous little chuckle and said, "Very good, sir, very good. Sheep know botany indeed, sir."

"They could lecture, if only they had the facility of speech!" I went on.

"Yes, indeed they could, sir. Only they might cause the lecture halls to smell poorly. Their excrement, you know."

"Well, it is a fascinating thought experiment, which we shall likely come back to, as I feel that we've barely nicked it. But tell me, young Mr. Lampson …" and here I paused, as an idea had occurred to me. "I say," I went on, "would you happen to be here representing your father on business? Or are you here for …" I motioned with my head in the direction of the ship.

"Oh, I'm here for the ship, sir," said Mr. Lampson.

"Ah, well, I thought you might've come here about wool, you know, and only happened to arrive when the sailors did. So tell me, what is it about an officership aboard my vessel which appeals to you?"

"Why, the going to sea, sir," said Lampson, with a kind of brightness exclusive to the young. "It's the best way to botanize in distant lands. Great Britain is crawling with botanists, sir; in order to make any real discoveries, one must get out and about, as you might say."

I regarded him narrowly. "You *are* quite aware that the *Mean Fish* is currently afloat in a pool measuring one-hundred by two-hundred feet."

"I am, sir. But I am not one of the naysayers, sir. I believe wholeheartedly that the *Mean Fish* shall sail upon the sea one day, and I hope to be aboard when she does—if not as an officer, for I don't take it for granted that I shall qualify, then at least as a common sailor who may have the opportunity to botanize."

Asking our applicants to wait in the great hall, I took Nelson aside into the drawing room. He agreed with me that Mr. Bridger and Mr. Lampson would make fine second and third mates, respectively. "Bridger has the sea in his veins," Nelson told me. "Rarely have I seen such a man, even in the Navy. Mark my words, nephew, he will share with our crew an understanding, if not an authority, which neither you nor I shall be able to match. Mr. Lampson, on the other

hand, should serve nicely as a counterbalance of sorts to Mr. Bridger. Neither has been a ship captain, as our advertisements specified. That fits our purpose perfectly. It would be a very difficult thing for us to ask of any man who *has* held that position, to be content answering to the likes of us."

We retained Bridger and Lampson on the spot. The *Mean Fish* now has a full complement of officers. May our voyage, as Lampson anticipates, lead to botanizing as well as adventure.

Tuesday, May 19, 1795

This morning I breakfasted for the first time in the officers' mess aboard the *Mean Fish*. The ship's galley is now fully functional and capable of duplicating anything the kitchens in Stonesthrow can produce. For the time being the galley is staffed by Gertrude and her staunch underlings, but once our crew is in place, I anticipate that some of our newly hired sailors shall serve as cooks.

I had the mess hall to myself this morning. It shall probably be the only such occasion, for my officers reported to their posts today and are forthwith required to dwell, dine, and sleep on board. As I sat there partaking of sausage and eggs it was rewarding to imagine the camaraderie, the animated intellectual discourse, the discussions of triumph and discovery, to which this handsome room shall surely bear witness over the years to come.

After breakfast I examined the ship's library to make certain that the correct volumes had been moved from the hall and were properly organized on the shelves. I became so distracted leafing through the revised Linnaeus, and reflecting upon how greatly young Mr. Lampson shall surely appreciate having that volume at his disposal, that I quite lost track of time. The ship's central chronometer striking nine o'clock brought me out of my reverie, and at once I hurried up to the strategy room, for this was the appointed time for our first officers' meeting.

I was gratified to find all of my officers already assembled around the large oaken table. I was also gratified when they stood to their feet as I entered the room, a gesture befitting my stature as captain.

I was a good deal less gratified to note that my uncle had apparently been sitting in the large ornate chair at the head of the table which, given its position and dignity, no one of sound mind could have failed to recognize as the captain's chair. At the sight of this, so many

indignant words strove to leave my mouth at the same instant, that no one of them could overpower every other and victoriously pass my lips; to wit, I was momentarily struck speechless. Before I could gather myself, Nelson stepped aside with a slight bow and pulled out the chair for me in a most gracious gesture of acquiescence. "I was but tending your spot for you, nephew," said he, his expression carefully neutral, though I could hardly mistake the mischievous note in his voice.

I took my seat and Nelson took his. Looking down the long table I had my uncle, young Mr. Lampson, and Dr. Converse on my right, Mr. Bridger and Paul Whitehand on my left. All watched me expectantly.

This was beyond any doubt an auspicious moment. Such moments are uncommon in life and must be savoured. To that end, I prolonged the moment by inaction. I sat perfectly still and looked straight ahead, feeling very much, I am certain, as King Arthur must have when he first sat to table with his magnificent knights. To their credit, my officers must also have sensed grandeur in the air, as no one stirred or said a word.

Five minutes seemed to me a sufficient length of time for savouring this particular moment. Once I judged that five minutes had passed, I stood up and descended the gangway to check the marine clock in my cabin. It was in fact only three minutes past nine o'clock, so I returned to the table and resumed my seat.

I was just settling back in to continue savouring the auspicious moment, when Nelson said, "Really, Richard. We would indulge the King thus for fifteen minutes, a duke for perhaps ten, but for a viscount more than two minutes of such nonsense is unbearable. Begin the meeting, or I for one shall take my leave and go do something useful."

I considered whether I should upbraid my first mate for this outburst of insubordination, but decided against it. Everyone at table

was well aware that my first mate is also my uncle, and therefore more entitled to speak his mind than the average first mate. Also, I judged the moment to have been adequately savoured. So before Nelson could have gone on to say anything about autocratic tendencies in front of his fellow officers, I opened the meeting by welcoming everyone aboard the *Mean Fish* and asking if the ship's accommodations and features shall meet the needs of their various professions.

On this, agreement was nearly unanimous. Mr. Bridger did complain about his cabin having been equipped with bed rather than hammock, but I assured him that this oversight would be corrected immediately. Mr. Whitehand thanked me for having provided a chapel space aboard the *Mean Fish*; the lack of such an amenity on sailing vessels in general had been a topic of concerned discussion between him and myself during the ship's design. (I may not always concur with his unwaveringly dogmatic approach to the betterment of humanity, but though our means may differ, our ends are often harmoniously aligned.)

I felt especially anxious that Dr. Converse be pleased with sick bay, and with the shadowy corner of the officers' quarters which has been prepared especially for him, as he is more particular about his surroundings than any other man I have ever known. So particular, in fact, that this eccentricity has contributed to very strange and irresponsible rumors about his person.

I began to hear these rumors myself about three years ago, although I am assured that they had been circulating at Stonesthrow, in Keld, and indeed as far afield as Richmond, for some time before then. The smoldering embers of this gossip had been fanned into flame, I dare say, when Dr. Converse had every window of his cottage on the hall grounds covered over with black paint. The local response to this unconventional but harmless improvement was so foul and widespread that I felt it necessary to issue a public statement

of refutation. What fair-minded Englishman, I wrote, could ever imagine that a physician who practices bloodletting for the benefit of his patients, who shuns daylight, and who happens to hail from the Bavarian Alps, might be a vampyre? The notion is ridiculous in the extreme. Any advanced scholar of science, I pointed out, would certify that vampyres spring from the hot-blooded Mediterranean races, are not so sensitive to sunlight as is often supposed by the unlearned, and are by nature too recklessly passionate to succeed in any course of study at a university.

In the wake of my published epistle the unkind rumors about Dr. Converse all but ceased. Clearly my appeal to reason had a salubrious and educational effect upon the good people of Swaledale and their understanding of vampyres. Still, this incident involving the good doctor had made me sensitive to his sensitivities, as it were, and so today I asked him specifically if he found the sick bay and its accoutrements to his liking.

"Yes," said Dr. Converse, with that baleful gaze of his which never quite meets your own.

"And your berth in the officers' quarters? Are there any adjustments which you would like made?"

"No," said Dr. Converse.

This was encouraging, so I moved the meeting along to our main order of business—the recruitment of our crew. The details of this are too dull for my ships' log, and were also recorded by young Mr. Lampson, who takes the minutes of our meetings, so I shall dispense with them here. Suffice it to say that the effort has already been underway, in a manner similar to the solicitation of our officers, and that if all goes well the process should come to a successful conclusion two days' hence.

One conversation which is more worthy of inclusion in a ships' log, began with Nelson trotting out one of his musty nautical tales. I

had heard this particular yarn just short of three thousand times, but since at least two of his audience today had never had the pleasure, I indulged my uncle.

This sordid story involved an ill-fated romance between an officer of Nelson's sloop, the *Hedgehog*, and a young lady of Sinkhole-On-Sea. It ended, as do an inordinate number of Nelson's navy stories, with someone being brutally stabbed, in this case a lad of the town who had also fancied the young lady. As Nelson finished his tale with a gory description of the crime, I was quite surprised—as was everyone at the table, I would wager—to hear a subtle but unmistakable chuckle from young Mr. Lampson.

Nelson stopped short in the midst of a sentence. He turned to glare at the young man next to him. "I beg your pardon, Mr. Lampson, have I said something which strikes you as amusing? Because I can assure you that there is nothing whatsoever amusing about a brutal stabbing when …"

Nelson stopped again when Mr. Lampson let out a mild guffaw. The young man was, it appeared, losing a concerted battle to rein in his merriment.

Nelson was about to say something else, which probably would not have qualified as friendly, when Mr. Lampson held up a placating hand and said, "I am so sorry, Sir James, I do apologize. In no way do I wish to make sport of your tragic and fascinating tale. It's just that you have inadvertently touched upon a subject which was a bit of a private joke amongst my friends and myself at university, and I have failed to master my reaction. Please, do continue."

Nelson would not have it. His arms now folded upon his chest, my uncle said, "No, Mr. Lampson, my tale is done. But by the King's Colours, I would very much like to hear exactly which grim ingredient in my tale of woe furnished so much entertainment for you and your Cambridge classmates."

Lampson looked to me as if in appeal. "Well, er, I actually don't know if this would be the proper time to elaborate," he said.

"Nonsense, Mr. Lampson," said I. "This table is a democracy, with me as its King. All insights are welcome and I'm certain that my uncle does not speak in a spirit of confrontation when he says that he would like to learn about your university experience."

Lampson did not appear much reassured, and hesitated for a moment or two, looking round the table. When he saw that he was now the undisputed centre of attention, the young man visibly swallowed and said, "Well, I fear that your expectations of a genuinely witty anecdote are bound to be dashed. This was only my companions and I mincing words in a way which provided passing amusement. But if you must hear of it, then the gist is this. One of us, I forget whom exactly, observed that the phrase 'brutally stabbed,' which one hears frequently in connection with such an incident, is perhaps burdened with an unnecessary adverb. How, this person posed, could a stabbing *not* be brutal? And if stabbing by its nature is inevitably brutal, why not leave off the modifier 'brutal' and stick with simply 'stabbed'?

"At this point, some wag amongst us, probably addled by too many hours of study at the expense of sleep, suggested that perhaps all stabbings need not be brutal. Might it be possible, he suggested, to be delicately stabbed, courteously stabbed, magnificently stabbed, or even charmingly stabbed? Well, young and flippant as we were, we found this line of thought amusing and others contributed their own variations. It became a recurring theme of jest for our group over the passing months, which by its sheer absurdity never failed to lighten the mood."

Here young Lampson paused and looked round the table with a rather sheepish air. All was quiet for a moment, until Mr. Whitehand said, "One could be *accidentally* stabbed. That would not in most cases qualify as brutal."

"One could be half-heartedly stabbed by a hesitant assailant," I said.

"A bloke could be stabbed in the eye," said Mr. Bridger, a remark which did not strike me as contributing to the drift of the conversation, although it did adhere to the general topic of stabbing.

Nelson sat there regarding young Mr. Lampson with a dour expression, his arms still crossed. No one ventured a further word until my uncle cleared his throat and said, "Thank you, Mr. Lampson, for this insight into the sort of intelligent and mature discourse which takes place at our universities. It is heartening to know that our young men find such novel ways to edify themselves, since learning a legitimate profession no longer does the trick." Nelson rose to his feet and went on. "I am sure we all of us here thank the heavens for the privilege of having you onboard. Should our ship ever be assailed by pirates, or trapped in the crushing embrace of ice floes, or drifting and bereft of water in the tropical doldrums, I feel certain that your learned pleasantries and knowledge of plants shall prove invaluable."

My uncle turned to me with the slightest of bows and said, "Captain, I feel that my contributions to this meeting have been made, so I shall now excuse myself to profitable tasks elsewhere."

He made as if to leave, but then spun about upon his heel and thrust a finger in Mr. Lampson's direction. The young man, already looking quite miserable, appeared to almost jump out of his chair at this swift and menacing gesture. "And as for *you*, Mr. Lampson," thundered Nelson, "don't you dare, don't you *ever dare* …" and here his expression melted from fierce outrage, into a broad, sly grin. When he resumed speaking, it was with his most clement voice. "Don't you ever dare take my stories or my ranting too seriously, young man." With this, Nelson gave the youngster a solid swat upon the shoulder, then turned and left the room.

I had seen this coming, but then I know my uncle. I daresay that Whitehand and Converse had not been too terribly startled, either. However, the effect of this mercurial behaviour upon young Mr. Lampson was amusing to behold. He sat there in what appeared a state of perfect and utter awe, looking like a man nearly consumed by a raging tyger who has seen the onrushing beast transform at the last possible second into a cloying waft of lavender-scented air.

Mr. Bridger was the only one of us who laughed out loud at poor Mr. Lampson, adding something about shite and britches which I didn't entirely fathom. And thus ended the first meeting of the officers of the *Mean Fish*.

I now await what is certain to be a more vexing meeting, set for tomorrow. I have wavered between hosting it aboard the *Mean Fish*, or in Stonesthrow Hall, and even now am not entirely decided. Visitors from York are ever troublesome, but the inquiries of this Turn-pike Commission shall need to be dealt with most delicately, if my aims are to be achieved.

Wednesday, May 20, 1795

Upon falling out of bed this morning, I remained undecided as to the location for my meeting with the Turn-pike Commission. On the one hand, I am anxious for my *Mean Fish* to host her first visitors. On the other, bringing these particular gentlemen onboard the ship would almost certainly raise uncomfortable questions regarding my intentions for it. On the third hand, there is no way to cut the ship out of the picture entirely, unless we were to convey the commission to Stonesthrow wearing blindfolds, and I cannot imagine a convincing pretext for such an eccentric welcome.

During breakfast in the officers' mess I at last reached an irrevocable decision that our guests should be hosted in the Great hall. Since there is no hiding the ship from them entirely, they may as well experience the magnificent view of her which that room affords. To this end, I had Rugby and our staff beautify the Great Room with five gigantic pot plants which were brought out of the orangery especially for this occasion. These are varieties of mimosa and all of them happen to be blooming at present, forming a wonderful and fragrant spectacle. Furthermore, the pots themselves are amongst those which my late cousin Theodore shipped here from Bengal and their craftsmanship is remarkable.

By the end of my meal, however, I had misgivings about this hasty choice. Surely if the Turn-pike Commission is to be charmed today, there can be no more charming spot in all of Swaledale than the main deck of my marvelous *Mean Fish*, with its sweeping views of Stonesthrow Hall and the grassy fells all around. So I reached a second irrevocable decision, summoned Rugby to the mess, and ordered that the pot plants be immediately moved from the Great hall to the ship. Rugby made an unpleasant face, but he departed forthwith to do my bidding.

After breakfast I ascended to the main deck to see what progress had been made. Less than two hours remained before the arrival of our guests. One of the mimosas had been emplaced, and our cargo crane was swinging the second aboard. Owing to the fact that each of these pots, the soil they contain, and the trees growing within them, weigh at least a hundred stone, moving them anywhere is no mean feat and the crane was an absolute necessity to get them aboard ship.

As each pot was secured by the crane on the land side, carried across the water, and brought to rest on board, I gave instructions as to where exactly each one should be placed. My household staff—for the *Mean Fish* still lacks sailors—laboured heroically to position each tree, heaving in unison against the elephantine stone vessels and their tropical contents. Once all five pots were aboard, my staff went right on working to reposition each tree, as I compared several different arrangements for aesthetic effect. I then made a third irrevocable decision that the pot plants were to be moved back to the Great hall, as no conceivable pattern of mimosas formed a harmonious constellation with the ship's masts. In addition, I suddenly felt a good deal of misgiving about my chance of success in this meeting with the commission, should our conversation occur atop the very object I wish to divert their attentions away from, however proud I am of her.

Although Rugby was visibly displeased with this decision, the man knows his place; he mustered his troops at once and the crane swung back into action. Less than one hour remained until our guests were to arrive.

I went to the great hall. As the gigantic pots were returned to the chamber one by one through the herculean efforts of my staff, I walked in circles round the pianoforte, rehearsing in my head the likely course of the upcoming interview. As the second pot arrived, I sat at the instrument and dabbled on a Mozart sonata, in order to calm myself. Alas, this only increased my agitation. As the fourth pot arrived, Nelson dropped in to say hello; I was not in the mood for frivolous discussions and dismissed him immediately.

As the fifth pot was heaved into place, I made a fourth irrevocable decision to hold my meeting in the orangery and ordered that the pot plants be moved back to their original locations. At this Rugby snapped in twain across his knee, the stick which he uses to encourage good behaviour amongst the staff, but he quickly mastered his over-enthusiasm and set his men to moving the pot plants yet again, this time with a copious dose of that baffling Cornish tongue peppering his language.

Less than one-half an hour remained. I was beside myself. I could hardly think, so largely did the importance of this meeting loom in my mind. I strode back and forth between the Great Room and the orangery, observing as the mimosas gradually resumed their customary places amidst our other tropical plants.

Just as the hall clock struck ten, its chimes echoing through the corridors, my tenacious staff heaved the fifth and final pot into position. Rugby declared to me that, unless I now wished for the bloody mimosas to be moved into the village of bloody Keld, he and his staff would go break their fast. I graciously declined his thoughtful if oddly profane offer, and dismissed the pot movers.

Here was the crucial moment. Any second would bring the sound of the Turn-pike Commission's carriage rattling up the road from Keld. And yet each second, each minute, remained silent. Was the commission already in the hall, their arrival perhaps unannounced due to Rugby's preoccupation with the mimosas, the sounds of coach and horses drowned out by the cacophony of moving the pots? At ten minutes past, I could stay in place no longer; I checked the Great Room, the old parlour, and the entrance hall. Empty. On my way back to the orangery I ran into Nelson, who asked me what I was doing.

"Looking for our guests, if you must know," I retorted. "It is quite possible that they are already here and were misdirected in the confusion." Then a terrible thought struck me, and I dashed off at once, calling back over my shoulder. "The ship! Good lord, Uncle, what if the turn-pike commission went directly to the ship! I must intercept them at once!"

I have dwelt in Stonesthrow Hall every day of my life. I know it intimately, every nook and cranny, every creaking step and floorboard, every eccentricity. So I should have recognized that the moment was ripe for the Loose Stone of the Hall to make an appearance. But alas, my distraction was too great. So when I sprinted around a corner into the west corridor, and there sat the Stone, directly in my path, I was utterly unprepared for this development. I made an attempt at evasion, but was running too fast. My right foot clipped the top of the Stone, and I went sprawling into the far wall, my head striking with enough force that it hosted a brief display of fireworks.

I recovered my senses within moments, but my left knee was hurt from my slide into the wall, and I remained prone when Nelson came strolling around the corner, at a maddeningly casual pace, and asked me why I was writhing about on the floor.

"Because I have injured myself, you great oaf!" I said respectfully. "It was the bloody Loose Stone! I came flying round the corner and there it was, the devilish thing!"

My uncle has not lived in the hall so long as I, but he has encountered the Stone himself, on more than one occasion, so he clearly did not think it in any way strange, that the capricious object which had caused my accident was now nowhere to be seen. He merely reached down to help me up and said, "You really mustn't round corners in this house in such haste, Nephew."

"But the Turn-pike Commission! The ship! Uncle, I beg of you, speed at once to the pool and see if anyone is there! I shall be lamed up for a few after that spill, I daresay, but I'll follow as quickly as I can!"

"My dear nephew, if you had been willing to spare three seconds to listen to your benevolent uncle, when I approached you an hour ago in the Great hall, then you would know that our visitors have been delayed. They lost an axle down valley. Somewhere around Reeth, according to the messenger. Heaven forbid that these city folk should straddle a horse, so they're casting about for another coach in that neighbourhood and they'll be here as soon as they're able."

My relief must have been plainly writ, for Nelson appeared pleased by the effect of this news. I allowed him to help me up off of the floor, and rather gingerly tried a bit of weight on my left leg. My knee was in pain, but it supported me.

"It is a stroke of luck, Richard," my uncle went on. "The detestable, axle-eating state of the road around Reeth is sure to make our visitors more enthused about a new road in Swaledale. Put that together with the progress they shall see all the way up valley, plus their lust for tolls to swell the county coffers, and I daresay that your meeting with them has just become a good deal easier."

This was a very astute point, and I said so. Thanking Nelson for his assistance, I went upstairs to the comforts of the drawing room—with a bit of a limp but nothing intolerable—to await the arrival of the Turn-pike Commission.

Surprisingly, I hadn't long to wait. It was barely half-past ten when I heard a coach coming up the drive. How, thought I, had they so quickly procured another halfway-respectable coach in such a place as Reeth? Perhaps news of the broken axle had been exaggerated.

Peering through a window, I received a nasty shock. There could be no mistaking the horrid heavy coach of the Rector of Reeth, looking like a storm cloud on wheels, slowing to a stop before Stonesthrow

Hall. Few men on Earth would have been less welcome in my home at that moment than his gracelessness. Thankfully, when the rector's slovenly excuse for a coachman opened the door, it was not the rector himself who alighted, but Mr. Archibald Shildon, known to me from previous meetings as chairman of the Turn-pike Commission. He was followed by his two equally nearsighted and decrepit colleagues, all three of whom were shewn inside by Rugby.

Here it was, then. In spite of Nelson's optimistic homily, my nerves returned. The outcome of this meeting could make, or break, so many years' worth of careful planning, and building, and yes, a certain amount of necessary duplicity. By the time Rugby entered the room to announce that our guests awaited me in the orangery, my anxiety was nearly as great as it had been a half-hour prior. But there was nothing for it. Composing myself as best I could, I limped downstairs to face my fate.

No supplicant in all of history could have seen his fortune resting in the hands of less impressive judges. Mr. Shildon and his companions are so clearly hair balls coughed up from the depths of the county administration, that had they not wielded such power over my project, I would scarcely have deigned to give them the time of day. As it was, I greeted each of them with the utmost politeness, expressed my hope that their journey from Northallerton had not been too arduous, and listened to their tales of horse-drawn woe as my servants brought tea and biscuits.

I was especially interested to learn how the commission had so quickly secured the use of the rector's coach. It turns out that the rector had also been traveling up valley, to visit an ailing parishioner in Gunnerside, and had run across the hobbled coach mere minutes after its axle had broken. He had offered the commission the use of his coach, and had himself continued up valley on horseback.

Although the Turn-pike Commission saw nothing to be leery of in this turn of events, and had naught but praise for the rector's conduct, I found the entire thing suspicious in the extreme. Firstly, the rector is not known for being overly attentive to his parishioners, unless they happen to tithe exceptionally well. Secondly, the timing of his coach following so closely behind that of our visitors could have been mere coincidence, but given his interest in the commission's work, I had my doubts. I found myself hoping that the rector's shabby coachman had been properly detained in the stables, rather than allowed into our servants' quarters or left to skulk about and possibly spy. My choice of the orangery over the Great hall suddenly seemed cunning, as anyone loitering about outside of its glass walls would easily be seen.

This disturbing pleasantry dispensed with, I trusted that we would get down to the business at hand. But instead one of Mr. Shildon's colleagues (I did not retain either of their names), a droopy old fellow whose oddly high voice might have suggested a eunuch in some other milieu, came out with: "Lord Keld, I must say that we are all of us bowled over by ship in yonder pool. There's no missing her as you drive up road. Magnificent sight! I wonder what chance there be, of quick tour whilst we are here?"

"Oh, ha ha, nothing much to see there," said I, "just an eccentric whim on my uncle's part, and quite ugly, really, up close. Dangerous, in fact. Overrun with, er, stoats. Rabid ones. We shan't go near." There was no mistaking the disappointment on High Voice's face, and something like revulsion on those of his companions. Encouraged by the ease with which I had deflected that parry, I cleared my throat and went on, "So, shall we discuss the new road? You would've gotten a rather good look at our progress, I daresay, on your way up from Richmond."

Finally the discussion swung round the right way. I was elated to find that the Turn-pike Commission were in fact highly enthused about what our years of work have produced: twenty-five miles of uniquely engineered, all-weather road up Swaledale from Richmond, soon to provide a boon to shepherd, miner, and merchant alike. The increase in ease with which people and products shall move up and down our valley can hardly be overstated, I pointed out, especially in winter, and I added that we consider it entirely feasible to extend the road over the hill to Edendale and Kirkby Stephen, should we bring the Cumbrians in on it. I added that the new road's position well up on the south slopes of the valley shall spare it from the flooding which not infrequently blocks or washes out sections of the old road.

At this, High Voice referred to the current road up Swaledale as a 'godforsaken axle-buster'. Mr. Shildon nodded in agreement, then mentioned the tolls which a bustling new road shall inevitably produce, and from the edge of avarice in his voice, I considered our quarry positioned squarely within the trap, and yanking upon the bait.

"The road's constant grade is remarkable," Mr. Shildon went on. "We have seen a great many turn-pikes, but never one in a mountainous area, with so gradual a climb. This shall be, by far, the most clement crossing of the Pennines north of Leeds, not to mention the most scientific and modern turn-pike in all of England. To my knowledge, nothing to match it has even been contemplated in the south." He took a sip of tea and went on, "The assistant engineer was very helpful yesterday and this morning, but I say, Lord Keld, our commission must have the opportunity to meet your chief engineer and congratulate him on his outstanding achievement, which we would very much like to see duplicated elsewhere in the county—although not anywhere which would draw traffic away from Swaledale's turn-pike, of course."

I assured the commission that, although our chief engineer was currently away overseeing a bridge project near Lancaster, he is anxious to have the honour of meeting them as soon as opportunity allows.

High Voice remarked on how the bedrock and gravel surface of the new road, together with its deeply sunken cut following the contours of the valley slope, and the partial roof of timber which shall be built over its entire length, will make it almost tunnel-like and impervious to the worst weather our corner of Yorkshire may hurl at it. "I daresay theren't be drop one of water find its way onto entire course of new road," he finished, with as much satisfaction as if the enterprise had been his own idea.

"Oh yes," I agreed. "Nary a drop. We wouldn't want any water on it, now would we?"

Mr. Shildon wagged a bony finger and said, "One thing puzzles me, Lord Keld, and that is the number of tollgates. Sixty-two in twenty-five miles is a large number, even for a turn-pike in a populous area. Swaledale is, and I assure you that I mean this in the most complimentary way, not exactly Buckinghamshire. I expect that we shall rely heavily on through traffic, especially if we extend to Edendale, so why more than five dozen gates between Keld and Richmond alone? The cost of manning so many must inevitably cut into profits."

I explained to the commission, and not for the first time over the years, how numerous entrances shall be dug to provide ingress to the sunken, roofed-over grade of the new road, thus making it convenient for shepherds and miners to access from the many remote parts of the valley in which they ply their trades. The great number of gates shall provide users the opportunity to pay for only that exact portion of the road which they have actually trod, and thus encourage local use as well as through traffic. "The highest individual payments shall, of course, come from long-distance use," I reminded them, "but

a great deal more profit is to be accumulated if locals come to rely on the new road for their countless daily movements up and down Swaledale." As for the cost of manning so many gates, I assured the commission that I was prepared to cover that personally and that the language of our final contract shall say as much.

The commission seemed well satisfied at this point, and bade me good day with the assurance that their report shall be wholly supportive of the North Riding's involvement, and that contracts would be drawn up forthwith, in the expectation that the new road, or Swaledale turn-pike, shall handle its first traffic prior to September of this year. When I saw them out to their coach, it was with hearty handshakes and congratulations all around, and as the rector's turnout vanished in the direction of Keld, I experienced a rush of overwhelming relief, of a magnitude I have rarely known.

At the same time it came home to me how very exhausted the day's events had left me. Although the clock had yet to strike noon, the drama of this crucial meeting, along with the exertion of moving the mimosas, and the trauma of my fall, had left me feeling poorly. I sent a servant to Nelson with a message that all was well with the commission, but that I would retire to my cabin aboard the *Mean Fish* for the remainder of the day and was not to be disturbed.

Only when I reached the cheerful confines of my cabin, with the pleasant prospect of a restful afternoon and evening ahead, did it occur to me: the third commission member, although seemingly polite and in good spirits throughout our interview, had never during that time spoken a single solitary word.

Was the man painfully shy? A mute? A former Benedictine from the continent still honouring his monastic vows?

Or could his silence signify that he has divined the true purpose of our so-called turn-pike?

Thursday, May 21, 1795

Today has been a marvelous day. As I write these words, my *Mean Fish* thrums with activity. A multitude of boots tread upon her decks. Orders are shouted and received. Aromas of delicious food waft from the forecastle. Our crew is aboard.

Granted, their arrival did not play out quite as planned, yet I hope that this shall be for the best.

My strategy in recruiting a crew, was essentially the same as my strategy for recruiting officers, but writ large. We had run advertisements in the dailies of coastal cities, and had bills posted near docks and wharves, indicating our need for able-bodied seamen. My uncle and I had not the ability to seek potential hires in person at the multitude of maritime locations, and as Swaledale is a tolerably central meeting place when one is recruiting from the entire isle of Great Britain, my expectation was that interested sailors would make their way to Stonesthrow Hall, at which point the peculiar nature of the ship's situation would again serve as a litmus test, as the alchemists would say, to weed out those unfit to sail with us.

As a result of this campaign, I had expected news to trickle in over the previous day or two, to the effect that nearby villages found themselves awash with sailors seeking room and board on their way to Keld. (This would cause a significant stir in Swaledale, where our interaction with the nautical world is limited to the occasional young man hankering after a life at sea, and the occasional old salt retiring from such a vocation.) As of yesterday no such news had reached my ears, and yet so much else has diverted my attentions, that I thought little of it.

At breakfast with my officers this morning, I mentioned this lack of tidings and inquired if anyone had heard anything. Bridger instantly cleared his throat and said, "You may's well have saved yer

breath, sir, nobody here will have heard anything yet about sailors in Swaledale."

When I asked Mr. Bridger how he could be so certain of that, he said, "Because I've seen to the whole affair by my own self. It'll come off well, you've nothing to vex about. You'll see what I mean in about an hours' time."

Just forty-eight hours before, my officers and I had discussed this very matter, including the advertisement strategy which Nelson and I had deployed, and Bridger had raised no objections, nor had he said anything about seeing to the affair 'by his own self.' In fact, to the best of my recollection, he had said nothing at all, which I had taken as tacit agreement. So I was gobsmacked by this casual declaration that our ordained plan had been subverted, and I told my second mate, with an edge in my voice which no man could possibly have mistaken, that I would very much appreciate it if he were to explain himself further.

If Bridger heard the ice in my words, he gave no sign. He went right on cutting his bacon and spooning up his beans as he said, in the most matter-of-fact manner, "Well, no offense to you, Cap'n, or to your esteemed uncle here, but I'll be dipped in tar if the two of you haven't gone about this thing all wrong. In fact, you went about the officer recruitment all wrong, too. You're unaccountably lucky—damned lucky, if the priest'll pardon my saying so—that after the rest of that lot laughed themselves out of a job, there was a sailor left in that room with my skill and experience, and a botanyizer of Mr. Lampson's … er … enthusiasm. You'd never see a second roll of the dice like that 'un, nay, not with a hundred rooms full of officers, and not with a thousand rooms full of common sailors, for the wind blows a different way there."

I opened my mouth to say something about an ill wind for Mr. Bridger, and heard Mr. Whitehand making the point that he was not

a priest, thank you very much, but Bridger kept on talking over the both of us as he munched his toast. "First, would-be officers are far more likely to have the means and motive to follow a job prospect to the middle of the country, about as far from saltwater as you can get. Common sailors readin' your invitation to Swaledale are sure to laugh out loud and never give it a first thought, let alone a second, and I've it on good authority that a great many men in our port cities have done just that.

"Second, not a one amongst the common seamen, even *if* they'd hoofed or hitched it all the way here, would've reacted the way Mr. Lampson and I did to your lovely ship a-plugged up in a bottle. When you put that quandary in front of a man, you're asking him to take a leap *up here*," and he wagged his fork at his cranium, "which the common sailor is not wont to take, nor should he be. Believe you me, Cap'n, you've no need, nor no want neither, of a crew filled with men of ideas. You want a crew what shuts their bloody fly traps and follows orders. If I may ask, Cap'n, do you take suggestions from your household staff on how Stonesthrow should be run?"

I assured Mr. Bridger that I most certainly do not. Bridger gave a solid nod whilst chewing a large bite of egg. "Well, there ye have it, then."

In that moment, I was unable to consider Mr. Bridger's words, or weigh his intentions, in a thoughtful manner. I heard only gross insubordination, flippantly trotted out in plain view of my assembled officers. During his speech I felt welling up within me, a seething indignation akin to the atmospheric charge let loose in a lightning bolt. But before I could play the role of petty Zeus, I chanced to glance at my uncle, who met my eye and gave a slight but unmistakable shake of his head. This check enabled me to subdue my rage somewhat, so that when I opened my mouth not thunder rolled out, but rather the blustery words, "Mr. Bridger, if you would be so kind as to

elaborate on the steps you have seen fit to take, in lieu of those I explicitly wished, your captain and your fellow officers would very much benefit from this knowledge, seeing as how it affects all of us greatly."

Again, Bridger seemed wholly nonplussed. Still shoveling breakfast into his mouth—although by this time the rest of us had entirely ceased to eat—my second mate said, "Cap'n, it'll be my pleasure to elaborate. Now, aside from my sharing your vision fer this here ship, you hired me on fer my history and my know-how. I can honestly say that, through good fortune and cultivation of acquaintanceships, I have hauled in a greater catch of trustworthy colleagues in twenty years at sea than many men would amass in ninety. From Dunvegan to Dover, from Perth to Penzance, I call a legion of salty dogs 'friend', from ship captains on down to drunken good-fer-nothing barnacles what sleep under piers. If it be a wicked boastfulness for me to say so, I beg the priest's pardon."

"I am not a priest," Whitehand reiterated.

Bridger went right on, "When you brought me on board, Cap'n, the first thing I did was to send messengers to nearby ports. Before I answered yer call for officers, I'd seen your sailor advertisements and knew how worthless they'd be. I hadn't time to draw men from all over the isle, as you reckoned on, but there's no need fer it. Scots, southerners …" here he gave an indifferent shrug, "… we've no need fer 'em. Piles of good solid sailors in England's beauteous north, by Neptune's beard! I sent to Blackpool and Southport. I sent to Scarborough, Newcastle, and Hull. All close enough fer a quick response. I sent fer men I personally know to be able sailors, and asked 'em to bring along any of the like they'd vouch fer. I made sure they know full well ahead of time what sea they're divin' into, and are at peace with it, so not a one of 'em'll shew up here and get knocked on his arse by the sight of a tall ship sittin' in a pond."

Bridger had cleaned his plate by this time. Wiping his mouth on his sleeve, he concluded, "They're all here, Cap'n, well over two hundred of 'em, just down the valley at the camp fer turn-pike builders. Had 'em stay there so they'd excite no local interest, seein' as how you seem a mite bashful about this here beautiful ship, which you've built in plain sight, in the middle of a valley as treeless as the sea. They've instructions to report here within the hour."

To say that my angels of propriety and iniquity warred within me, would be a towering understatement. My heart thrilled at the prospect of what Bridger's tactics might produce, with regards to a quality crew, and yet his manner of going about it had been sly if not seditious, and the nonchalant way in which he presented this *fait accompli*, with his fellow officers witness to explicit criticisms of my authority, bordered on mutinous.

It was all terribly confusing, and in fact I became so very agitated, that I have no memory of my own reaction to Bridger's news. I learnt of that later, from Nelson, when the two of us discussed the matter in private. According to my uncle, after Bridger had finished speaking I stood, crushed a fried egg in my fist, and roared, "Thank you, Mr. Bridger! But bloody hell, man, how divine must be the ends which would justify such diabolical means? And yet I appreciate so very much the generous application of your knowledge and connexions to this issue!! Which is to say, why in the bloody blazes did you not approach me for approval at once, instead of acting in a manner which violates every tenant of shipboard hierarchy and *requires your captain to reprimand you for your thoroughly commendable actions!!!*" At that point, I apparently uttered a cry of dismay, tore at my hair with both hands, and quit the mess for my cabin, knocking over my chair in the process.

I am wont to believe this account of my uncle's, as it explains the sticky mass of cooked egg which I discovered in my hair a short time later.

It pleases me to report that order was quickly restored. My uncle served as messenger between myself and Bridger, and within ten minutes of my outburst I was back in the mess, with all of my officers present as before, hearing an articulate and public apology from my second mate.

Bridger expressed surprise at the violence of my reaction, but allowed that reflection on the cause of it shewed me to be entirely in the right, and himself deserving of censure, for behaviour ill-fitting a sailor of his experience, however good his intentions. He should have brought his plan to me, and very much regretted not having done so. "I confess to all present," he went on, "that I am not accustomed to having a man of our Lord Keld's caliber as my cap'n, and I did us all a disservice in puttin' my expertise ahead of his authority. I swear to never do so again, or may I be whipped fer it."

I graciously accepted Mr. Bridger's *mea culpa*, then informed him that whilst no whipping of officers would ever occur aboard the *Mean Fish*, punishment was still necessary in order to set an example. Therefore I announced that the ship's second mate would be confined to his cabin until such time as the recruits he spoke of should arrive at the ship, and furthermore, he would receive no sweet with his dinner for one day. Bridger accepted these germane judgments with a respectful bow, and took his leave. It was at that very moment when I was puzzled to discover the egg in my hair.

Bridger's confinement did not last long. Scarcely had I removed the egg from my person, and had a few words with Nelson in my cabin about my handling of the situation, when there came a knock upon the door. It was Lampson, there to inform us that a large body of men were approaching the ship on foot, from the direction of the turn-pike-builders' camp. Surely this was the very crew whose imminent arrival Bridger had foretold.

Nelson, Lampson, and myself went upstairs to the strategy room, the windows of which afforded an excellent view. It would be entirely untrue, were I to claim that the sight which met my eyes did not produce a wondrous thrill of excitement.

Call it intuition, if you will, but in spite of my dearth of nautical knowledge, I felt convinced at first sight of this crew, that Bridger had done well. Their attire was by and large tidy, their faces mostly honest, if not uniformly handsome. Most carried small bundles of personal belongings. Nearly all of these men wore on their faces, a clear look of admiration and wonder, which could only have been excited by the lovely ship rising before them.

In that moment I fully recognized the wisdom of my second mate's policy, that only sailors with a prior understanding of my ship's peculiar location should be brought here to man her. If we had invited any and all sailors to Swaledale without first adjusting their expectations, as Nelson and I had planned, what percentage would have been willing to stay on? Would we have ended with fifty willing and able sailors? Thirty? Ten? Not enough to have manned the *Mean Fish*, that is nearly certain; and the majority of applicants, who would have likely found our project worthy of ridicule, would have returned to their maritime haunts and very soon made my ship and myself the laughing stock of the seafaring community. I literally shudder to think of the likely consequences, had not Mr. Bridger taken it upon himself to correct our course.

With this uppermost in my mind, I dispatched Nelson to retrieve Bridger from his cabin and have him join myself and the rest of my officers on deck.

The crew—for so I thought of them already—had been well instructed. Without urging from anyone aboard the *Mean Fish*, or

any visible guidance from a leader amongst themselves, the men fell into neat ranks facing the pool, about two rods distant from it. There they remained as if at attention, looking like a sort of ragamuffin army, as my officers and myself gathered along the main deck railing facing them.

Bridger, immediately to my left, leaned in close and quietly said, "If I may, Cap'n, I've a few words to say to this here assembly, to finish the recruitment process. Any men still here when I'm through, may be considered provisionally engaged, at Your Lordship's pleasure, of course."

I had no objections to Bridger bringing his scheme to completion. He took one step forward so as to be right against the railing, cleared his throat, and addressed the crowd of sailors in a far different voice than any I had heard him use thus far.

During the few days I'd known him, Mr. Bridger's manner of speech had been uniformly rough and unpolished, albeit comprehensible, although occasionally he would lapse into mutterings, or jargon beyond my understanding. In all of this he seemed to differ little from other workingmen of his age, say, an old shepherd of Keld or a freehold farmer at the Richmond market.

This, however, was a voice of command, with a rhythm, a vocabulary, and a sort of snarl which put me in mind of a pirate treading the boards in a gothic play. What follows is both a summary, as Bridger carried on for what seemed much longer than necessary, and an approximation, for I would be unable to reproduce perfectly the language he used, without further exposure to it.

Bridger began by welcoming the sailors to Swaledale, and thanking them for taking pains to make the journey, which he hoped had not been unpleasant. So in substance, if not in style, his opening remarks would not have been out of place at a corn merchants' convention in York. From there, however, things took a more colourful turn.

Bridger exalted the *Mean Fish* as the most magnificent seagoing vessel to have been built this far removed from the sea since Noah's famed ark; but no, he corrected himself, our ship was more magnificent, for anyone could see from Bible pictures that the ark had been a sorry old tub in comparison. Like the ark, however, the *Mean Fish* had been born of inspiration—whether divine or not, it was not his place to say, that being a question for the priest.

"Not a priest," said Whitehand, with a terse shake of his head.

"I trust ye'll all recall from yer schoolin' days," Bridger went on, as best as I may translate, "how folk far and wide ridiculed old Noah for buildin' that there ark on dry land. But when the rain fell fer forty days 'n forty nights, and the blessed sea submerged every speck o' soil on this globe, I ask ye, who was laughin' then? I reckon that old Noah and his kin had a mighty guffaw at the expense o' them damn fools what hadn't listened. So us here today, we too may pity them who fail to understand, 'cause we know what evil befell them what scoffed at old Noah. And while the Lord tells us, with every rainbow in the sky, that no man need fear no second great flood, still the good book shews us that it ain't seemly to mock a ship built on dry land, fer no mortal may see what lies o'er the horizon."

Bridger's audience appeared thoroughly captivated. Every sailor's eye fixed upon him, every face shewed the strain of keen attention, and a great many nodded in agreement with his interpretation of Noah's tale. I daresay that Whitehand would have given his left hand to inspire such rapt engrossment at even a single sermon.

"Now this ol' jaw's flapped long enough. One more thing I've to say to ye, and that is, at this very minute every one of ye faces a reckoning. Look around ye and think well. And if the men you see standin' there ain't yer mates ... or if this here stout-hearted viscount ain't yer cap'n ... or if this here graceful three-master ain't yer ship ... or if this here wee basin ain't yer ocean, then by God you'd best

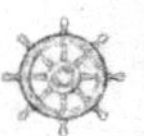

make yerself scarce this very second an' welcome to it, fer the rest of us are damn well pleased to serve here."

Given this opportunity, I expected at least a few sailors to break ranks and return the way they had come. However well-informed they had been ahead of time, surely the sight of our landlocked ship would cause some to reconsider. But not one man so much as batted an eye.

Looking satisfied with this result, Bridger concluded, "Aye, an' one last thing. If any of you scurvy dogs happen to hail from the heaping alp o' shite which goes by the name Liverpool, then you may serve at our cap'ns pleasure, should he allow it, but you'll needs work twice as hard as everybody else, to have any hope of curryin' *this* officer's favour. Anyone findin' themselves in that category would do well to slink along home."

Again, my expectations were upturned. Where before not one sailor had moved when I thought several would, now when I expected none to leave for such a fatuous reason, one man hung his head, shouldered his bag, and left the formation.

For a long moment I debated whether to order the fellow back in line. If his heart were in it, why on earth would it matter where he hailed from? Yet Bridger's nautical knowledge so outweighed my own, that I could not bring myself to countermand his judgment. Since he strongly disapproved of Liverpool and its inhabitants, surely he had perfectly defensible reasons for it. But again, that city is famed around the world for its maritime commerce, and how could it be so were there anything intrinsically flawed in its sailing men?

Tangled in this conundrum, I glanced at Nelson for guidance. Perhaps I could meet his eye and find there some clew. But my uncle stood immobile, watching the Liverpudlian go, his face impassive.

Bridger stood back from the railing. I was not certain as to what would happen next, as there had been no rehearsal for this drama.

I did nothing for several long moments, until a subtle kick from my uncle informed me that it was my turn to address the sailors.

Only at that point did it occur to me, that with the wrenching change in strategy which had taken place within the previous hour, I had nothing prepared to say. The speech which I had intended to give the sailors, was to have been very brief and along the same lines as the one I had given to our prospective officers some days before. Now that the process had been so altered, that I found myself standing before not a crowd of skeptics, but an orderly array of believers, words failed me utterly.

Yet something had to be said by the captain on such an occasion. I suppose that I must have fallen back upon my many years' experience as master of Stonesthrow Hall, for after a couple of false starts, I found myself giving a slight bow, indicating the gangplank with a sweep of my arm, and in a tone I might have used to welcome a duke, calling to the sailors: "Please, make yourselves at home!"

Bridger clearly disapproved of this performance. He gazed at me for a moment with what I shall call a sneer of astonishment (however, he quickly recovered himself and muttered what may have been an apology). My uncle openly laughed at my folly, as he inevitably shall. Notwithstanding the merit of my speech, at the conclusion of it a sort of puzzled, uncertain cheer went up from the assembled sailors and they at once began to ascend the gangplank.

A movement away from the ship caught my eye. It was the expelled sailor from Liverpool. Whereas I had expected him to head back towards the road-builders' camp, or perhaps down the hill towards Keld, he had instead struck off uphill, south-southwest over the grassy shoulder of Great Shunner Fell. It occurred to me that this was likely a direct bearing towards his home city: across Wensleydale, over Pen-y-ghent and through the Bowland forest before reaching

the lowlands. I would not have supposed it true, but mayhap men of the sea even *walk* on rhumb lines.

Such fancies aside … as I reported at the start of today's entry, the *Mean Fish* has become a perfect hive of activity. Bridger's recruitment, I have learnt, was not merely aimed at procuring talented sailors agreeable to our situation, but also to provide the ship with a full complement of specialists at the outset. Therefore we have cooks, and our galley has awakened. We have a barkeep for our pub. We have a brigmaster. We have riggers although no sails as yet, and gunners with no guns to service save our single musket on a post.

To savor this marvelous activity from a perfect vantage point, and because the uppermost parts of this ship shall soon enough (and properly so) be more the domain of my crew than of myself, I climbed up the rigging to the crow's nest shortly before sunset. I had been up there a couple of times before, as the view is tremendous.

From the crow's nest Swaledale curves off down-valley to the southeast, and up-valley to the west merges into Birkdale. To the south, through the Gap of Angram, one may make out the village of Thwaite. The noble green fells rise all around: Water Crag, Lovely Seat, Great Shunner. Stonesthrow Hall resembles a doll's house (albeit a rather grand one) from that great height, and one may peer over its venerable roofs and right down the hill to the cottages of Keld.

Looking in that direction tonight, a movement caught my eye—a lone figure ascending the verdant slope above the village. Even at that distance, which must have been a half mile, there was no mistaking this person's graceful, resolute walk. Still, I employed my spyglass to be certain.

It was she. My incomparable Thistle. Heading in that direction at that hour, she must have been en route to relieve one of her brothers watching the family flock, over around Gunnerside Beck.

The scene in the spyglass was too picturesque for words, yet I must attempt it. The golden light of eldest evening burnished the gently waving grasses, making her seem an angel mounting to heaven through elysian fields. Her simple woolen shepherdess' cloak drawn around her against the oncoming chill of night, she appeared to float unhurried up the slope with the measured pace natural to those born amongst these hills, a perfect balance between too little speed and too much exertion. Her hood was up, and a lock of her long raven hair fell out on the side, framing her face, whose lovely profile I could see quite clearly. How serene she looked, a strong woman with seemingly no care in the world—even though as everyone knows the business of sheep husbandry is fraught with peril and is devilish hard work besides.

As I watched Thistle glide uphill, the sun set behind Tailbridge Hill, whose dusky umbra pursued her up the grassy slope with surprising swiftness. She reached the ridgetop just before this shadow, and although she was now farther away, I saw her turn for just a moment, sunlit still at that height, and look back in my direction.

She could hardly have discerned me from across that distance unless she carried a spyglass of her own. I would've appeared as the merest speck in the crow's nest. Far more likely, she had spared a glance for the ship, or Stonesthrow Hall, or perhaps the village. Even so, her turn sent a thrill through every atom of my being. Had the object of her gaze been the *Mean Fish*, or the hall, then surely I myself must have been in the background of her thoughts, as she like all of the locals thoroughly equates my person with those things, even though my family are still considered newcomers to Stonesthrow.

The moment passed, and was gone. Thistle vanished below the ridge into the swale of Gunnerside. The shadows of high fells to the west completed their conquest of the landscape, allowing the sun to linger for only a few moments more on the heights of Water Crag.

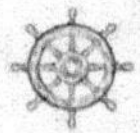

How much more worthy of admiration is she—this Darling of the Dell, Flower of the Fell, Sweet of all Swaledale—than a royal carriage full of earls' daughters.

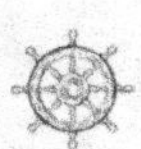

Friday, May 22, 1795

How satisfying to rise this morning to the sounds of bustle aboard my ship, which for all her beauty, formerly lay silent as a tomb. As the galley has only just begun to operate, and I consider its staff to be in a trial period, breakfast was again delivered to the officer's mess from Gertrude's kitchen in Stonesthrow Hall. Once Bridger judges that the galley is up to snuff, I shall rely upon it exclusively.

I spent an enjoyable early morning in the company of my officers, going round the ship on a tour led by Bridger, who introduced us to the several crewmen personally known to him. How delightful it was to see the galley, the pub, and the brig fully staffed, and the good manners shewn by every sailor we encountered, as opposed to the surly nature typically attributed to seafaring men, was both a credit to Bridger's recruitment stratagem, and a hopeful omen for the future.

Later this morning, at our officers' meeting, Mr. Bridger informed me that the crew had selected a spokesman, a fellow by the name of Mr. Bigg. I expressed my admiration for the crew's initiative in taking such a step, and then put to Bridger the entirely reasonable questions as to why in blazes the crew *require* a spokesman, and whether or not this unauthorized plebeian election might presage trouble.

Bridger assured me that it is not unusual for the crew of a large non-naval vessel such as ours, to select a relatively articulate individual for the purpose of presenting collective concerns to their officers. When I pressed the issue of whether this might be an unnecessary or even dangerous overreach of democracy aboard the *Mean Fish*, and this on our first full day, Bridger replied that there was nothing seditious in it, and that he could be relied upon to quell with the utmost alacrity anything inappropriate brewing in the crews' quarters.

Satisfied on that point, I was led to expect that Bigg would request an audience with me before evening, and I told Bridger that this was acceptable.

During early afternoon I busied myself studying a crew roster which Lampson has compiled, listing names, places of origin, and special nautical abilities for each man aboard. The roster is alphabetized by last name, so I rather quickly came across the entry for Mr. Bigg. His given name turns out to be Edward, his hometown Whitehaven, and his specialty the rigging and repairing of sails. My thoughts being thus returned to this elected worthy, I began to speculate on whether his physique might match his name. More specifically, it occurred to me that it would be a natural source of jest, were Bigg a large man, in which case his moniker would be amusingly appropriate, or a rather small man, in which case it would be amusingly ironic. Either way his name and his person promised to be an excellent source of witticisms with which I could both entertain the crew, and perhaps somewhat reduce Bigg's stature in their eyes by rendering him slightly ridiculous. One must watch these democratically elected fellows and not allow them to get Bigg-headed! (I congratulated myself on that one; already the puns rolled from my tongue.)

I carried on looking over the roster until about three bells, at which time there came a knock upon my cabin door. Fully expecting that only one of my officers would thus intrude upon my sanctum, I opened the door and was utterly astonished to find a fellow whom I had never knowingly laid eyes on before, standing there with such composure that one would think he has knocked at captains' cabin doors every day of his life.

In my perplexity I leaned out into the corridor, and looked both ways along it, expecting to see an officer here or there or somewhere, but none were to be seen. This fellow was inexplicably on his own. "Hello," I said to him with as much courtesy as I could muster in

my flustered state, "I am certain that there has been some mistake. Perhaps you are looking for the pub?"

The fellow, a smart-looking sailor a few years my junior, introduced himself as Mr. Bigg and added that Mr. Bridger had led him to believe that I expected his visit.

There was simply no precedent in my experience for this method of greeting. It was as if a gardener or groom had taken it upon himself to barge into my private chambers in Stonesthrow—which is to say, an event only slightly less unexpected than meeting a sheep with wings. More than that, it was as if this impertinently forward gardener or groom was so new in my service that they and I had not yet even been properly introduced. The situation was simply outrageous.

Mixed with my astonishment at his method of approaching me, were dashed hopes on account of Mr. Bigg's appearance. I was crestfallen to find that Bigg, far from being notably large or small, instead seemed of entirely average size and demeanor, with nothing whatever about him which could be termed amusing or even remarkable. Given the vast potential for jest at the man's expense which I had envisioned, I found this bitterly disappointing and immediately formed the opinion that if Bigg were considerate of others, he would change his name so as not to mislead those who had not yet met him.

A moment passed before I gathered myself sufficiently to reply; then I said to Bigg, "God's blood, man, surely you haven't shewn up here intending to invite yourself into my cabin."

"Certainly not, sir," said Bigg, "but I was told to find you here. I'm entirely at your service as to when and where we meet, Captain."

"That's what you were told, eh?" Said I, anticipating a discussion with Bridger on this matter before the day was out. "Well, here you are, and I could use a respite from the exhausting and important

work I have undertaken on behalf of this ship and her crew. So, I suppose that I may spare a few minutes for you. Be in the strategy room in five minutes. Do you know where to find it?"

Bigg replied that he did, gave a bow, and then departed. Thus did I learn that one aspect of shipboard living which I had not anticipated, is the oddity of not having a steward to properly evaluate and present petitioners. (I could bring Rugby aboard to serve in that capacity, as he has so well for many years, but his knowledge and authority are needed for keeping things in good order at Stonesthrow.)

After five minutes (plus three more, for good measure) regaining my composure, I ascended the gangway to the strategy room. Bigg sat at one of the small tables; I took my seat at the head of the long table used for officers' meetings, and indicated that Bigg should take a chair near the far end of it.

"Well," said I, as Bigg moved to the long table, "it is a pleasure to meet the man upon whom the crew have bestowed such an honour. Have you been spokesman before, on some other ship?"

Bigg replied that he had not. "I see. As you are no doubt aware, I have not previously been a ship captain, so we are each of us new to our roles. That puts the two of us on the same boat, eh? Ha ha!"

"Your observation is most amusing, sir," said Bigg, although he looked about as amused as a sheep watching grass grow.

"Now, as I am, of course, an exceedingly busy man, and no doubt you are as well, let us broach the business at hand. What have you to say to me on behalf of the crew, this fine day?"

Bigg cleared his throat. "Firstly sir, I am to say that we are most grateful to find employment upon such a lovely ship as this, and one so new to boot that many blokes onboard have remarked that one could eat off the decks. We seamen don't often find ourselves in such luxurious surroundings, sir. I mean, the wonderful clean airy fo'c'stle, the pub . . . We've none of us seen the likes of her, sir."

"Very good, but let us back up for a moment. Do I understand you to say that men are eating their food off of the floors?"

"Oh, no, sir, it's a figure of speech. As in, aboard a vessel this clean it would be *possible* to eat off the decks without contracting some horrid sickness."

"Well, I wish you to understand, Bigg, that you are not only a conduit for the crew's words to me, but that your function hereby includes the reverse. And in fact, I believe that you may make yourself far more useful to everyone, by conveying my wishes to the crew, rather than the other way round."

"I see, sir."

"So let us begin by making sure the crew fully understand, that no one is to eat their food off of the decks at any time, or for any reason. There is no place on this ship for such culinary skylarking."

"I understand, sir. I will make this rule known to all, and if I happen to see any man eating off a deck, I'll give 'em what for."

"No Bigg, you may be spokesman, but it is not your place to give anyone 'what for'. That would be an officer's job, preferably Mr. Bridger's. Please refer to him any cases involving deck eating."

Bigg blinked. "Meaning, the eating of food off a deck, sir? Or the eating of a deck?"

"Either one, for heaven's sake! Although I daresay that my meaning was perfectly clear!"

"Very good, sir. Understood."

"Right. Well, have you anything else of such great import?"

"Yes, sir. The crew were provided with a number of rules last night, read off for us by Mr. Nelson. We got the impression, sir, that once we are fully provisioned the gangplank will be drawn in, and at that point no one may go ashore without leave. Is that so?"

"It is most certainly so. How could it be otherwise? Would you expect to go ashore from any other ship, whenever the fancy struck

you? I say, what a strange sight that would be! Skiffs all over the ocean, pulling hither and yon like so many pleasure boats on the Serpentine."

"That would in fact be a strange sight, sir. But I'm sure I needn't point out that from this particular ship, the shore is only about three strokes away for a strong swimmer."

"Indeed you needn't point that out, and so I find it rather vexing that you have seen fit to do so. The *Mean Fish* is on a voyage, Mr. Bigg. You have all signed up for shipboard service, not a holiday. I may grant shore leave under certain circumstances, and there shall, of necessity, be some resupplying via the gangplank, but except for those times no one is to go ashore without my permission, either by swimming, flying, or any other method. Is that understood?"

"Yes it is, sir. Very good, sir."

"Good. Now, is there anything else? I must return to my captainly tasks."

"One more thing, sir," said Bigg. He leaned towards me, a gesture which seemed ridiculous given the large distance between us, and in a stage whisper went on, "the crew would very much like to know, sir, if it is true, that you intend to take the *Mean Fish* to sea?"

The question took me aback. It has always been my belief that the crew of this ship need not see the larger picture, and that opinion had been reenforced by Bridger's warning against sailors who are men of ideas. Yet something in Bigg's voice, or his earnest look, gave me pause. How fair was this approach, given that these are men of the sea, possibly as out of sorts here in Swaledale as a cod in a fountain? I hesitated for a few moments before deciding upon a middle way.

"More than any other man could, Mr. Bigg, I desire that the *Mean Fish* someday see shores and waters other than these. The difficulties are considerable. Lord willing, it may one day come to pass."

Bigg waited a few moments more, as if to ensure that I had finished speaking. Then, he gave a slight nod, as if of approval or comprehension, and rose to his feet. "Thank you, sir, for your candid replies. I understand that you may not be at liberty to divulge details, and I shall make certain that the entire crew are aware of this. And now, with your permission, I shall retire to the crew quarters."

I assured Bigg that he had my permission, whereupon he went to the door, and with a slight bow and the rather pretentious parting words, "The crew have spoken," he was off.

I must admit that I find this fellow more likeable than not, and can see why the crew have elected him to such a lofty post.

The rest of the afternoon and evening passed without notable events, which is not to say that I was in any way idle. The business of being a captain involves a not insubstantial amount of work and thought. But the next incident I wish to record here, began at ten bells, when only a faint blush of dusk remained in the northwest. I left my cabin dressed for riding, descended the gangplank, and took up a position beneath a certain plane tree between the hall and the stables. From that shadowy spot, I watched for the approach of my accomplice.

Unfortunately, I watched in the wrong direction. I had not yet been under the tree for three minutes when a wholly unexpected voice from behind caused me to cry out and very nearly jump into the branches. "Ahoy there, Nephew," said the cheery voice.

"I say, Nelson, what sly business is this? I thought you had not yet left the ship. Did you come from the hall?"

"Where I've been, Nephew, is my own lookout, but since I have nothing to conceal, I shall tell you freely that I *have* come from my chambers in the hall. And as for what sly business this is, you know very well—as we are in it together." With that, my uncle strode towards the stables and I followed. "Oh, and Richard," he spake low, back

over his shoulder, "next time you are startled in a moment which calls for stealth, do *try* to not shriek like a silly chambermaid when some village-playhouse Macbeth slays his Duncan."

I had shrieked in no such way, but I held my tongue, as there was no use getting into a tiff at that moment, and at any rate we were indeed aiming for some degree of stealth.

In the stables, we saddled our own horses—I my Arabian, Restlicht, and Nelson his jet-black palfrey, Fitzroy. We then took off at a smart trot across the downs.

We made our course over the shoulder of Great Shunner Fell—in fact just a few degrees to port from the bearing our Liverpudlian sailor had taken the previous day—for the purpose of reaching Buttertubs Pass without using roads. The sky was clear and the moon well towards first quarter, giving light enough to navigate by without the revealing glare which a fuller moon would have cast over the fells. A half-hours' ride, during which time we fortunately saw no one and spoke nary a word, brought us to an ancient stone cottage on the high moor within earshot of Cliff Beck's rushing waters. Although long without regular inhabitants, this place is fitted with sturdy door and shutters, and generally prevented from falling down, so that it may serve as a retreat for shepherds or travelers caught by ill weather astride the pass.

Nelson and I hobbled our mounts behind this lonesome haven and stole within. We closed the door and shutters, though we kindled no fire in the dusty hearth, nor did we light lanterns. Chinks in the shutters might have admitted a stray gleam to the road below, and we had no sentry posted as yet.

With moonglow shut out, that place was dark as a cave—and likely quieter, there being no drip of water into subterranean pools or rustle of bats. Only our breathing and the faint murmur of the Beck broke the silence for a good ten minutes.

Then my ears, no doubt sharper to every nuance due to the dearth of sound, picked out the stealthy approach of two riders from the direction of Wensleydale. Over heather and gorse they came, one halting a short way off, whilst the other continued right up to the cottage. That first would be the sentry, now surveying the road below and the surrounding slopes; the second would be the singular individual we were there to meet.

I heard our horses' low nicker of greeting to the newcomer's animal, then footsteps circled the old stone walls to the cottage door. The portal opened with a creak which seemed to resound like a cannonade in that silent spot. My eyes had grown so accustomed to the stygian blackness of the room, that the figure in the door appeared silhouetted against twilight by comparison.

The door was closed, a lantern lit. Our visitor placed it upon the cottage's rough wooden table and pushed back the cowl of their traveling cloak.

As the face of Miss Jane Smeaton emerged into the lantern light, I could not help but notice my uncle's features soften. She favoured us both with nods of greeting, and then, as is her wont, got straight to business.

"Lord Keld, I received your letter. The news is promising," she said in her brisk, no-nonsense way. "But, extending as far as Stonesthrow before September shall be tricky indeed. One advantage is that we've no wintry weather to contend with between now and then. Also, the uppermost stretch shall require less excavation. Of course, we'll need to also start straight away on our Trojan horse sections, both upper and lower." She fixed me with her large, dark eyes and said, "Your Lordship should realize that I use the term at your request, not because I find the metaphor apt. It's not as though we're sneaking spies into a foreign court in some novel."

I thanked Miss Smeaton for thus indulging me, and assured her that had my project involved spies and continental courts, I should have engaged a well-connected fellow member of the landed peerage, rather than an engineer.

She smiled at this, and pulled from the satchel at her side two rolled papers. These she spread out upon the table, using rocks to weigh down the corners. The papers bore detailed schematics prepared by Miss Smeaton, depicting the uppermost and lowermost portions of our project, each of which is designed to disguise our true intent until the last possible moment.

At this point, it is conceivable that readers of this log may be inclined to dismiss as the most brazen of fiction, any or all of what I have previously written, on account of the sudden appearance in my narrative of a female engineer. For some who have thus far amiably chosen to accredit my marvelous *Mean Fish*, the mystery of the Loose Stone, and the incredible fact that such an eligible viscount as myself lives as a bachelor, such an unconventional thing may simply be beyond their ability to accept.

Unfortunately, I cannot say that I blame readers for any such reaction they may experience, and the problem is not so much their own receptivity or lack thereof, as it is the regrettable and pervasive view held by our society at large, of women as little more than the detached rib of a man, as they are so condescendingly described in the Pentateuch. For that archaic reason (as if such a fairy tale had anything whatsoever to do with a given individual's abilities), Nelson and I had of necessity convened with Miss Smeaton in secret throughout all the years of our project, and I had been obliged to deflect numerous requests by the Turn-pike Commission to meet our brilliant chief engineer in person.

Also, the majority of the 'road-building' crew have been kept entirely ignorant of the architect whose vision they fulfill, as we may certainly not reply upon every single one of them to remain silent on the matter. Only a handful of trusted supervisors know that they follow a woman's lead, and even they are unaware of her identity. The sensation which would be caused by the public announcement of a female engineer in charge of so vast a work, would bring a wave of unwanted attention to our project, and sadly I feel certain that Miss Smeaton herself would become subject to ridicule or even animosity—and not only from men, but also from unenlightened women, who regrettably comprise the majority of her own sex.

By the time anyone peruses this log, however, the project shall be complete, and either a success heretofore undreamed of in British engineering, or else a colossal failure. Either way, after the fact I may safely name herein as our chief engineer Miss Jane Smeaton of Leeds. She is daughter of the great John Smeaton, a famous builder of innumerable bridges, canals, and lighthouses all around England. She shares his predilections and his talents, and studied at her father's knee since, of course, university would have been impossible. She also follows the late Mr. Smeaton's lead in styling herself a civil engineer, which is to say, that her work focuses upon projects benefiting the nation's civilian commonweal.

Before we enlisted Miss Smeaton to design and oversee our project, she had already assisted her father in designing a number of public works. In addition, she had acted as principal designer on a few of her own projects. In all such cases she had been obliged to take no credit, due to the likelihood (to give just one possible example) that a great many oafs would have refused to entrust their coaches, teams, and lives to a bridge designed by a woman.

My uncle was fortunate to have learnt about Miss Smeaton through an acquaintance from his navy days, who had been privy to her design of a breakwater for the harbour at Sinkhole-On-Sea. The breakwater was a great success, replacing an earlier one which had

failed to adequately protect the harbour. Once Nelson and myself had seen the body of work she has completed, and heard the very low rate which she was compelled to charge for her services, we had no doubts that here was our chief engineer, and we hired her on at rather a higher rate than that she had modestly suggested.

I am inclined to believe that, in my uncle's case, Miss Smeaton's natural charms may have had some bearing on the decision, as well. She is a handsome as well as intelligent woman, and about my uncle's age. In spite of his protestations that the adjective lonely never be appended to his unfortunate title of widower, I am certain that Nelson is hardly immune to the attraction of womanly grace in general, and I suspect that he may fancy Miss Smeaton, in particular.

In sum, there may well be many skeptics amongst my readers now where before there were few; yet all have my word as a gentleman, that Jane Smeaton and her intellectual abilities are every bit as unfeigned as the mighty ship which now floats in the pool beside Stonesthrow Hall. May there soon be many more like her in every department of expertise proper to the exercise of womanly acumen.

After we had spent an enlightening quarter-hour or so discussing the upper and lower Trojan horse sections of our project, I heard the peculiar whistle from without the cottage, which the sentry gave to signal that our allotted time was up. Miss Smeaton returned the rolled papers to her satchel, and we made our goodbyes by lantern light. Again, it was eminently clear to me in the expression on my uncle's face, and the gravity of his bow to our engineer, that his regard for her exceeds merely professional admiration.

The lantern was extinguished, plunging us into deep darkness. The sentry opened the door from without, as otherwise the three of us should not easily have located it. Upon the moonlit moor outside, we wordlessly mounted our horses and went our separate ways; Miss

Smeaton and her sentry down the south approach to Buttertubs, my uncle and I down the north.

Thus ended another shrouded visit with our chief engineer upon the high moors of Swaledale, hopefully witnessed by none but the night-jars.

Saturday, May 23, 1795

Very busy day provisioning the ship. During the past weeks and months, a great many deliveries were scheduled for this particular date, in anticipation of our crew being aboard by this time. I am pleased to say that nearly everything arrived as expected. Casks of wine and barrels of fine whiskey for the officers, beer and grog for the crew, a bewildering variety of foodstuffs for the galley, gunpowder and ammunition for the cannons (which we still lack), and even a custom-made ninepin set all the way from London were amongst the goods lifted aboard by the crane or rolled up the gangplank between dawn and dusk. Most of these items were then lowered down the main hatch into the hold.

The single shipment I am most pleased to see, consists of several thousand square yards of sailcloth—the finest cotton-duck from Ghent, every inch of it dyed a purple of the richest, most royal hue imaginable. When my ship's keel touches the waters of the North Sea, it shall be with unfurled sails fashioned from this marvelous material.

Why others have not seen fit to use colour to add majesty and distinctiveness to the sails of their vessels is incomprehensible to me. Instead sails are white, white, white, from pole to pole and along every line of longitude. From an aesthetic viewpoint, one may as well rig with undergarments. I suppose that in far China one may find ships with brown or tan sails, but that is hardly better. For truly artistic sail designs, it seems that one must look back to the marauding Danes of centuries past; they may not have known the use of cutlery, but when it came to making their boats beautiful or sacking villages, they had few peers in their time or since.

One notable occurrence took place midafternoon today, as I stood at the great steering wheel atop the poop watching the crane

bring over bundled rolls of sailcloth. I found myself approached by none other than Mr. Bigg, who asked if he might have a word.

"I say," said I, "is some missive from the crew to be a daily event? Perhaps I should ensure that my schedule is clear every afternoon at about this time, in order to hear what their spokesman has to say."

Bigg apologized for interrupting. He assured me that he could speak at some other time were that more convenient, and that he did not anticipate thus approaching me on a daily basis. I gave a sigh, of the feeling and duration proper to such a moment, and bade him go on with what he had to say.

"The crew wish it to be known, sir, that in their collective opinion the pub aboard this ship deserves the advantage of a name. At present it appears that the place is known by no particular title. There is no sign above its entrance, and we have only heard of it referred to as 'the pub'."

"I see. Perhaps the crew is concerned that unless this oversight is corrected, they may confuse that pub with one of the many other public houses aboard this vessel."

"No sir, that is not a concern, seeing as how no other public houses appear to exist here, although you know better on that score than we."

"There *are* no other pubs aboard, Bigg, and there you have it. There is no more point in giving our pub a particular name, than there is in giving our sun a particular name, seeing as how we have but a single one to keep track of. I suppose that the crew are going to come back tomorrow, suggesting that we provide the sun with the 'advantage of a name'. I don't know—perhaps a good Christian moniker such as Arthur or William might enable us to differentiate our usual sun from others which might at any time wander across the heavens causing confusion."

Bigg shifted his feet and went on, "that is a very good point about the sun, sir, but if I may persist, the feeling amongst the crew is that a proper local should have a name befitting an English public house, as such institutions have had since time immemorial. If the reason for the pub is to foster a sense of community aboard the *Mean Fish*, and I have been informed by Mr. Bridger that this is the case, then it would be well for the pub's title to support this goal."

Confound that Bridger, thought I—first giving Bigg leave to approach me directly, and now this. Just how chummy is he getting with the crew's spokesman? However, this point of Bigg's I felt was worth addressing. "All right, then, how about christening our pub the *Mean Fish*, after the ship? We could have a sign carved for over the entrance, which mimics our figurehead. Surely that would lay this goose to rest."

"Begging your pardon, sir, as that is a most excellent proposal, but the crew themselves have come up with a number of names worth considering, and would like to know if the matter might be put to a vote."

"A vote? A *vote*? Two days ago they elected you, and now they wish to hold a referendum on the name of our pub? Are we in England or the United bloody States?"

"I am sure there is nothing radical or American about it, sir. The men merely wish to give input on the name of the friendly local where they tip a pint with their fellows. The outcome need not be binding—no one on board is under the illusion that you are anything but our absolute ruler. These are men of the sea, sir, not colonial farmers."

When Bigg expressed it thusly, it seemed a potentially amusing undertaking. I must admit to curiosity about what names the crew would suggest for a seagoing pub. So I gave Bigg my approval for

the scheme and informed him that Mr. Lampson would be in charge of conducting the vote on the morrow.

Bigg thanked me, bowed, repeated his apparent motto 'The crew have spoken', and was off. God help me if he is going to say that every single time.

Sunday, May 24, 1795

This Sabbath day saw Paul Whitehand move his ecclesiastical musings from the chapel in Stonesthrow Hall, to the large space in the ship's forecastle which may be arranged for the purpose of worship. I am pleased to say that things generally went well, save a bit of tribulation, if I may so term it, during the musical portion of the service.

When I approached him years ago about attending to the spiritual needs of my future crew, Mr. Whitehand from the first was loath to give up entirely the gracious and historic chapel in the hall, and I was equally opposed to the idea of my ship sitting empty at least once per week whilst our officers and crew attended worship elsewhere. Thus, my vicar and I hit upon the idea of his conducting two services on Sundays and appropriate holy-days: an early one onboard ship, and a later one in the hall for my household staff.

Yet a second difficulty soon presented itself. Nelson and I were reluctant to make adherence to the Church of England a requirement for serving aboard the *Mean Fish*, as we both support the right of free worship for nonconformists—and yet bringing in additional men of the cloth to serve those with varied beliefs would have stirred up more trouble than Aaron casting the golden calf. A compromise on this point was difficult to reach with Whitehand, as he exhibits a low tolerance for dogmatic differences. In the end, he agreed to minister to any and all Christians who would pledge to worship communally through the Book of Common Prayer, with any additional or diverging rites to be conducted in private.

Although we did not enquire as to the religious persuasions of any sailor as part of the hiring process, Bridger informed me privately that to his knowledge we have at least six Methodists and two Catholics on board, along with a significant number of what he

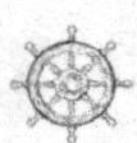

termed 'nautical agnostics', whom he assured us would be tolerably good Anglicans in appearance if not practice. (In that respect they sound very much like the majority of our local population, whom I suppose may be called Terrestrial Agnostics.)

Today's difficulty during service stemmed from an agreement which Whitehand made yesterday with Mr. Bigg, in order to accommodate a small but vocal group of nonconformist sailors. The intention was to add an extra hymn to the service set forth in the book, which would be chosen by this group, and performed by one of their number. Our vicar agreed beforehand that *Row the Holy Oars*, a pleasant (albeit non-Anglican) tune popular with sailors, would be acceptable.

When it came time to insert this hymn into the order of service, I was surprised to see a gangly sailor stride to the front of the chapel (for such I may call our forecastle on Sabbath mornings) holding, of all things, a guitar. He sat on a stool facing the assembly and made a few fumbling attempts to tune his instrument, then cocked his head to one side in a strange, birdlike sort of way and announced, "I'm from Chelsea!"—As if that detail was in any way relevant. Then he started into a surprisingly delicate, if not entirely on-key, rendition of the hymn.

I watched Whitehand's face closely. Whilst he appeared to be more or less satisfied with the music, a shadow stole over his features shortly after the guitarist began to sing:

Row the holy oars on the Sea of Galilee
Row the holy oars on the Sea of Galilee
Row James, row Andrew
Row John, row Pilate
Row the holy oars on the sea

Before this verse had quite ended, Whitehand leapt to his feet and sputtered, "Peter. Peter! Peter!!"

Three sailors (whom I later learnt share the name Peter) shot to their feet as if called by the very trumpet of the Lord, but our vicar's wrath was not meant for them. Instead, addressing the guitarist, he bellowed, "Row *Peter*, you fool! Not Pilate! Peter!"

The guitarist grinned rather idiotically, nodding in agreement. "Oh! Yes! I see your point and all! You know, I always did find that a rather strange lyric!"

"A blasphemous lyric, you mean," fumed Whitehand. "Now sing it correctly!"

Not seeming to hear the vicar, the guitarist went on, "Always did wonder if that was a mite inappropriate, and all. I mean, what would Pilate, being the Roman governor and all, be up to out on the Sea of Galilee? Not fishing, that's for sure! You can't tell me that Roman governors had time to go fishing and all! Let alone go fishing with apostles! Quite unlikely all around!

"And, being the Roman governor and all, I can't picture the bloke pitching in on an oar himself! He'd have slaves and all for work like that! Now, as a Roman he'd also be a pagan bloke, which makes it a bit surprising that . . ."

During this speech I observed Whitehand's complexion progress from its natural pasty colour, through various shades of pink, to a livid red. I have witnessed his anger innumerable times over the years, and fully expected one of his customary volcanic outbursts, but to my surprise when he interrupted the guitarist his tone was even, civil, and almost mild.

"You will kindly sit down now and play the hymn correctly, or I shall personally see to it that you are cast into the fires of perdition," said our vicar.

This subtle promise got the fellow's attention. Swallowing hard, he gave a curt nod, and resumed the hymn, this time giving due credit to Simon Peter. Aside from an odd pronunciation of 'Mount

Hermon' (he made it sound more like mouth vermin), I noted no further errors in the song.

Not surprisingly, Whitehand was in a mood after that incident, and his sermon, drawn from Paul's Epistle to the Ephesians, was spat forth in a way which shewed him to still be quite vexed. Happily, by the time we reached the benediction he seemed to have regained his usual serenity.

Even so, he made an announcement following the service which I wager we would not have heard, if not for the hymn debacle. Mr. Whitehand informed us that he had reversed his earlier decision, about a vote being allowable on the Sabbath, meaning that the crew's opportunity to select a name for our pub was to be delayed until at least Monday. This news was received with several groans of disappointment—which were swiftly stifled by a disapproving look from our vicar.

So, with no provisioning or other physical work to do on this Lord's Day, and with the gangplank still down, the crew, officers, and myself have enjoyed pursuits edifying to the mind and spirit. Many of the sailors took this opportunity to stroll about the grassy fells of Swaledale, becoming somewhat more familiar with their surroundings. As for myself, I retired to my cabin with Wordsworth's descriptive sketches.

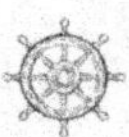

Monday, May 25, 1795

Today we resumed the crucial work of provisioning the *Mean Fish*, and as dusk falls I am pleased to report that this is nearly complete. However, the day's chief matter of import was the start of construction on the upper Trojan horse section of our project.

A contingent of road-builders appeared at around nine bells this morning, on the grassy slopes above Stonesthrow Hall, taking sights with a theodolite and pounding in survey stakes. We wish to give the impression that our 'turn-pike' is to be extended beyond the vicinity of Keld, at a steady grade which would allow it to clear the summit towards Kirkby Stephen. None of this will ever be excavated—I would hardly tolerate the rear-facing windows of the hall overlooking a nasty gash in the fells—but it must *look* as though such work shall soon commence.

And then, of course, there was the matter of the vote. Lampson compiled a ballot using input from both officers and crew. Voters were able to select from a list of twelve options for the name of our pub. These included six submitted by the crew, which ranged from appallingly bad (Rock & Stick) to clever (I appreciate the winking irony of naming a social establishment St. James's Palace). Also on the ballot were names submitted by myself (*Mean Fish*), Nelson (Sinkhole-At-Sea, a nod to his navy days), Bridger (the Drunken Mermaid), Lampson (Anvil & Butterfly), and Whitehand (the Tobes of Hades). Rounding out the lot was an inexplicably weird suggestion from Dr. Converse (Flirtations) which supports my opinion that although his grasp of Latin is impeccable, his understanding of the English language remains suspect.

Votes were cast during the noon meal. Lampson collected ballots in the crew's mess, then tallied the results in his quarters. At two bells, he presented them to me.

At once I searched for my contribution, and was crestfallen to find *Mean Fish* at the very bottom of the list, having earned zero votes. It had fared more poorly than Rock & Stick (which had one vote) and Flirtations (which had two). The winner, with eighty-eight votes, was Cat & Cabbage, a crew suggestion which I had found too pedestrian to take notice of.

My initial reaction was to exercise my God-given veto of this democratic nonsense, and require our carpenters to immediately prepare a *Mean Fish* sign to grace the pub entrance. But then my own words about fostering a sense of community onboard returned to me, and the wisdom of such an approach is undeniable. After all, throughout history Bread & Circuses have pacified more peoples than the Romans only. I therefore gave Lampson leave to announce the result to the crew, and to commission a sign of the winning name for the pub. This loaf of bread today; perhaps some form of circus next week.

Tuesday, May 26, 1795

This day brought an event which I never, in all my years of imaginings, expected aboard the *Mean Fish*—at least not before she even reached the sea. A stowaway has been discovered on board.

Things began ordinarily enough. The last of the provisioning was completed by ten bells this morning, and what was to be the day's great occasion commenced at noon, to wit: the drawing in of the gangplank to signify that our voyage has officially begun.

Originally my plan had been to have Rugby, Gertrude, and the rest of the Stonesthrow Hall staff assemble at the edge of the Mare Jacobum, near the foot of the gangplank, to give us a sending-off, as it were. I had pictured banners waving, a hurrah going up from the small crowd, the scullery maid shedding tears, perhaps even a band of sorts cobbled together from some of our neighbourhood musicians. The more I contemplated, however, how ludicrous such a scene was bound to appear, the more I favoured a subtler approach. After all, Rugby and company could have stood there and waved until their arms had fallen off; the *Mean Fish* was not actually going anywhere. Not yet. Such a *fete* must wait until another day.

In casting about for a replacement ceremony, it occurred to me that the *Mean Fish* had never been properly christened. Nelson had mentioned something about this oversight, shortly after the filling of the pool, as that event had been our land-locked equivalent of a launch and would have been the moment for it. Given their well-known penchant for superstition, it is possible that many of the sailors, and even Bridger, would feel less comfortable should they ever learn that a christening of the ship had never taken place.

So, I chose to incorporate a christening into our festivities today. At noon, my officers joined me on the poop, looking out over our full crew, who had assembled on the main deck in response to a call

from Bridger's bosun-pipe (a curious form of communication, with which I have gradually become more familiar over the past few days). Bridger then gave another pipe-call signifying that an announcement was to be made. I cleared my throat and stepped to the railing.

After my poor display inviting the crew aboard some days before, I was determined to make up for it in this, my first official address to all hands. I had rehearsed my speech fifty-four times before the looking glass in my cabin and had confidence in my ability to deliver it. I cleared my throat and opened my mouth to speak.

At that very moment, there came from some indeterminate location a pounding sound. I paused; the crew looked about uncertainly. After a moment, the sound came again. This time several sailors turned towards the main hatch, and peered into it. We heard the sound a third time.

Bridger growled, "What see ye down there? Let's have it, now!"

"See nothing, sir," replied one of the peering sailors, "but sure enough that noise is coming from the hold."

After this was said, the sound came again, more insistent this time. There was nothing for it; I would never be able to deliver my speech with such a vexing distraction nipping at my heels. I ordered that three sailors descend into the hold immediately, find the source of this obnoxious rapping, and cause it to cease.

These men adroitly descended the rigging along the side of the cargo hatch, and the other sailors clustered around the opening, jostling for a view down into the hold. For a few minutes, I heard vague sounds of movement and the shifting of heavy objects from down below, as the pounding or rapping continued sporadically, becoming ever louder. Finally, there came a noise which over the past few days I have come to know very well as the cracking screech of a crate being pried open. This was followed by a few seconds of utter silence.

Then an unfamiliar voice boomed out from the hold—a fine voice, nearly aristocratic, but with an accent unmistakably southern—possibly of Kent, or even London: "Good heavens, boys, you jolly well took your time, didn't you? Well, my thanks just the same. You may put those pry-bars down, by the bye."

This was followed by a sailor's cry: "Captain! We have a stowaway!"

"A stowaway!" Called several of the sailors on deck at once, sounding every bit as gobsmacked as I felt.

"Yes! I am a stowaway!" came the unfamiliar voice. "And I demand an immediate audience with your captain!"

I so dearly wished to go ahead with my meticulously prepared speech at that moment, for still its opening words danced upon the tip of my tongue, longing to leap out into the world, but it would have been folly. The attention rightfully mine at this august occasion, the christening of my beloved ship, had been usurped entirely by this sensational development in the hold.

Feeling the bile rise in my throat at the execrable timing of this interruption, I bellowed in reply, "Villain! You are in a position to demand nothing! However, as it happens to be my pleasure that we two confer this very instant, you shall indeed have the honour of meeting me! Men, bring this miscreant to the strategy room, on the double!" I then turned to my officers and required their presence at this interview.

Mere moments later, my officers and I sat around the long table as two husky sailors escorted our uninvited guest into the room. I must say that this fellow instantly confounded my expectations as to the likely appearance of a stowaway. Far from the unkempt mien I had anticipated, this man was richly dressed, immaculately groomed, carried himself well, and even smelled of *eau de cologne*. The impression of a Londoner which I had divined from his voice

was reinforced by all of this, and also by a certain cosmopolitan aura which he undeniably radiated.

"What a blessed relief to be free of that crate!" said the stowaway as he was led in. "I was well-watered and well-victualed in there, but I had run out of dried meat. It was high time to emerge from my cocoon!"

This fellow spoke not as an offender being brought before the victim of his offence, but as an old acquaintance run into on a street corner. I was not to be diverted by such false pleasantries. "You shall hold your tongue until you are given leave to speak, or you shall be cast back into that crate for however long I wish, dried meat or no!" I barked. "You have stolen aboard a vessel illegally, not ducked into the *foyer* of some Pall Mall gentlemen's club to dodge a passing shower! This is a breach of law most grave, and you shall answer for it! Now, furnish me with your name, and such reasons as you may wish to give for your egregious trespass!"

The stowaway plucked from his head the feathered tri-corner he wore, and executed a caliber of deep, practiced bow which might have pleased a prince. "Lord Keld, I beg your forgiveness. I have forgotten myself," said he. Drawing back up to his full height and clasping his hat in both hands upon his chest, he went on, "You see before you Augustus Wheelwright, adventuring librarian, entirely at your service, and your mercy. I regret any inconvenience I might have caused by boarding your ship in this way. It is not in my nature to approach any undertaking in a non-adventurous manner, hence this unorthodox mode of presenting myself for employment."

"You certainly *shall* regret having caused inconvenience, to myself and the entire crew of this ship!" I shot back. "And as for . . . Er . . . Did I hear you say *employment?*"

"Yes, Captain, that is my reason for seeking you out, at considerable danger and expense to myself."

"And what sort of *employment* shall be the reward for sly villainy and the disruption of an important ceremony? Perhaps you may dwell in the bilge compartment and keep things tidy down there!"

"Although that may qualify as an adventure, Captain, it is not what I have had in mind."

"I see. So what adventure, pray tell, have you reckoned to meet with aboard the *Mean Fish*? I should like to better understand your misguided expectations before graciously providing you with the very considerable adventure of being tarred and feathered!"

"Why, naturally, I aspire to the management and protection of your fine onboard library, Lord Keld! I don't believe I failed to mention that I am an adventuring *librarian*. Adventure for its own sake would mean little to me, were there not a collection of books and maps involved."

This motivation, like the man's appearance and bearing, was so far removed from what one would anticipate from a stowaway, that I was again taken aback. I could only sputter, "What qualifications could a blackguard like yourself possibly have, for such a position?"

"Lord Keld, my qualifications are legion," returned our stowaway, with marked enthusiasm. "I have overseen priceless collections from Lima to Kyoto, from Arkhangelsk to Cape Town! I have wandered the wilderness of Central Asia acquiring the love-poetry of Kublai Khan, which I catalogued at the Great Library in Petra, a wondrous building carved from a single gigantic stone! I have worked alongside Hottentots and Incas at the ancient bibliotheke of Prester John in far, fabled Abyssinia's Gondar! I have even plied my trade at the Great Library of Alexandria!"

"Ha!" I cried. "Here at least, your tongue outruns the truth! Every person on Earth knows that the Alexandrian library was burned to the ground by Julius Caesar, at a time when Paul of Tarsus still knocked about the Mediterranean visiting churches! You have a remarkably sprightly look about you, for a fellow far in excess of a thousand years old!"

The stowaway bowed his head. "Here you catch me in an exaggeration, Captain. I labored at a tiny *remnant* of the Alexandrian library, saved from the ancient flames you speak of by some courageous devotee of knowledge, and kept now behind a stocking shop in a side street of that Egyptian city. It consists of taxation and civil lawsuit records from the age of the Ptolemies. Not overtly thrilling, I grant you." Abruptly regaining his former exhilaration, the fellow went on: "But just think of it, Lord Keld! These mundane memorandums predate the revelations of our Christian faith, and their great antiquity gives them such worth! Cleopatra herself may have handled some with her own exquisite hands!"

I am too familiar with the burdens of leadership, to doubt that a queen of Egypt might in fact have had occasion to leaf through dull documentation—her daily world would not likely have been all palm fans, pet asps, and romantic interludes with strapping Romans, as we are shewn upon the stage. I was better impressed by our stowaway's grasp of this, than by any of the other more or less dubious things which had come spouting from his mouth, and perhaps for this reason I tempered my wrath somewhat when I spoke.

"Sir, your resumé, or your imagination, or to some extent both, are admittedly impressive. For the moment, I know not how much of your speech to believe, and until I do, you shall certainly not be allowed anywhere near our library. However, your words and your comportment shew you to be more than a common man, and therefore I shall for now reserve judgment, and commit you to the ship's brig, until such time as I have decided whether you should be commended to the county authorities, or keelhauled, or hired."

I made a decisive motion with my hands, which I hoped would be understood by my sailors as a sign to haul the stowaway to the

brig. When this failed to elicit any response, I gave a verbal order to that effect, which was followed immediately. As our stowaway was led from the room I heard him exclaim, "Lord Keld, your mercy outshines the stars even as seen from Ararat, highest mountain on Earth!" Then the door closed, and he was gone.

"Well," said Nelson straightaway, "I am sure that there is no question of entrusting the library to such a charlatan as that!"

"We've not enough feathers," said Bridger.

I turned to my third mate. "Your thoughts, Mr. Lampson?"

"Well, Captain," said our young botanist, "a charlatan he must surely be, yet I admit that he seems to have more wit than one or two professors I have known."

Bridger had fixed Lampson with a rigid stare. "Feathers," said my second mate.

Lampson gave me a nervous grimace. "Er . . . I'm afraid that I have absolutely no inkling how many feathers might be required for a tarring . . . So I shall defer to Mr. Bridger's educated opinion on that matter."

"I for one," said Whitehand, "would like to examine the crate from which our visitor has emerged. Whatever one's opinion of his motives, character, or deserved fate, one must admit that he *did* chuse a truly adventurous method by which to come aboard——one which few of us would willingly endure, unless the prize glittered very brightly, indeed."

I too found interest in examining the stowaway's cocoon, as he had termed it, if only to ascertain the amount of hardship he had endured, and to learn what manner of shipment he had arrived in. So I led the way down to the hold, where a short search sufficed to discover the opened container which Mr. Wheelwright had occupied. It was a crate, marked with the insignia of the Galton Works, Birmingham, which had supposedly contained twenty-four sea service muskets.

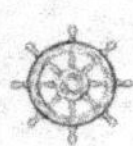

Instead of weapons, it now held various sumptuous furs which I suppose had been used as bedding, along with several ceramic jugs and leather pouches which had probably served as our stowaway's larder. How the stowaway had managed to answer or avoid nature's call whilst sealed within a crate for days I have no idea, but in any event there was nothing soiled or foul to be found, including within the jugs.

I spied the corner of some object protruding from folds of ermine; on closer examination this turned out to be one of several very ancient-looking books. These were written in languages which even Whitehand and Lampson could not identify, let alone read, and one included curious illustrations which appeared to depict fairy legends of some remote land.

"The presence of these does lend credence to his tales," said Lampson, leafing gingerly through one of the tomes. "Such works are not to be found in the average bookshop, that is for certain."

"Nonsense," retorted Nelson. "Their presence proves nothing. He could easily have pilfered these from the last nobleman's library he wormed his way into, before setting his sights on ours. As far as I am concerned, these only shew our stowaway to be a likely book thief, as well as a liar of gigantic proportions."

It is good that no one asked for my opinion in that moment, because I found it wavering between Lampson's view of the matter, and my uncle's. Whilst I trust the latter implicitly on most subjects, and his viewpoint in this case seemed entirely sensible and justified, still for reasons I could not have explained I was not altogether inclined to agree with it.

Before I had time to sort things out, however, I was brought out of my reveries by a pragmatic remark from Bridger: "Well, Cap'n, there'll be time for this rat bastard and his toys later. Fer now, I advise

we get back to our christening ceremony, as the day's general work is held up on account of it."

The christening! I had forgotten it entirely. Worse, I had forgotten my meticulously prepared speech. Half-an-hour prior, I had known every word; intervening events had erased them from my memory, except for a bit about otters which I had been going to work in somehow, but which would now sound rather strange if presented *per ipsum*.

Still, Bridger was right—the ceremony must go forward, and quickly, as the crew's routine was disrupted. Given this urgency and my lapse in memory, I chose to have done with the whole thing as rapidly as possible.

I had the crew summoned back to the main deck. This time my officers and I assembled atop the forecastle, as there was no time for the procession I had originally planned. Whitehand made the sign of the cross with holy water. Nelson adroitly smashed a bottle of champagne upon the bow. I declared that the ship formerly known as the *Mean Fish* was now officially christened *Mean Fish*. Bridger and his bosun-pipe blew a sign to shove off, and the gangway was drawn in. He blew a sign to dismiss, and the affair was duly wrapped up.

I found the need to give this matter of the stowaway much thought, so I retreated to my cabin for the remainder of the day. I remain undecided on how to proceed. However, behind this vexing problem, of a sort only known to those in command, lies the pleasant knowledge that my marvelous ship is now properly christened and that her voyage has commenced, at least insofar as we are no longer in direct contact with dry land. We remain at anchor, it is true— both fore and aft, to prevent our drifting into the flagstone shores of the Mare Jacobum—and yet the umbilicus, represented by the gangplank, has been cut.

Wednesday, May 27, 1795

Events transpired this day, which would stretch the boundaries of credulity in even the most outlandish species of novel.

My first order of business was a private dialogue with Mr. Wheelwright. I expected that an overnight stay in our brig should have reduced his bluster, making a meaningful conversation more likely, and I wished to converse with him sans the input of others.

Directly after breakfast I paid a visit to our brigmaster, who is called Selfridge. It was my first meeting with this fellow, and my initial impression is that he lacks both the warts and the ill temper one might expect in a gaoler. Selfridge very clemently accepted my request that he leave his office (which doubles as his cabin) whilst I spoke to our prisoner, as I wished for perfect privacy. He unlocked the inner door, announced my arrival in a fitting manner, then made a point of stepping out into the main corridor, leaving me entirely alone with our stowaway.

Mr. Wheelwright, housed in the cell nearest the brig office, looked none the worse for a night spent behind bars. In fact, before I could utter a single word he greeted me heartily and praised the worth of his cell, which he deemed a 'luxurious accommodation'.

"More times than I can recall, My Lord Keld, have I been confined to a cell of one sort of another," he said, "Not through nefarious actions on my part, you understand, but through ending up on the losing side in some horrific battle, or offending some potentate with my dedication to truth and the written word. Surely the worst was the fortress of Mehrangarh, where I was obliged to share a subterranean enclosure with a pair of Rajasthani tygers! I assure Your Lordship that only my command of Upanishad poetry allowed me to soothe the voracious beasts and survive to tell the tale!"

It seemed that our stowaway's bluster had survived the night quite intact. In spite of this, I was determined to glean at least a few solid facts about his history and character. I began by demanding to know how he had managed to embed himself into a crate meant to contain muskets, and for what amount of time he had been confined there.

"It is most compassionate of Your Lordship to ask," Wheelwright beamed, "and I am pleased to explain, although I hope you shall not hold the Galton Works accountable. A certain foreman employed there owed me a favour, on account of my having saved his life in the steamy boscage of the Kongo some years ago, and he saw to it that my supplies and myself were covertly sealed into crates bound for your ship's hold. You needn't worry about whether or not Galton has shorted you any muskets. The crates where my effects and I reposed were in addition to those you had ordered—I heard crewmen commenting on the extras as they loaded me on board, in fact—so you have exactly the number of firearms you paid for. I am a bonus, as it were!" Here he gave a sort of prancing flourish, before going on. "As for how long I spent in the crate—the shipment came straight here from Birmingham, so little more than three days. No hardship at all, compared to others I have endured! Why, I once spent over a week in a pickle barrel, with only the tiniest air space to sustain me, in order to escape the unspeakably evil court of Abalala-la!"

Feeling little confidence in anything I had so far heard, I nevertheless pressed on, asking about the books we had found amongst his personal effects.

For the first time since meeting Wheelwright, I saw fall away the frivolity which seemed to be his natural state, replaced by a manner most earnest and grave.

"Lord Keld," said he, "the books you mention I value more than the beauteous downs of Sussex, more than the inscrutable heavens, more indeed than my own eyes. Only my unwavering belief in the

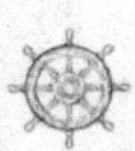

trustworthiness of you and your crew have allowed me to part with them for even the smallest part of a second. I need not ask if they are safe. I know that they are. They have been entrusted to me, Your Lordship. By whom I am not at liberty to say. One day I shall return them to their rightful home, whose location may not be named, on pain of suffering a most terrible curse. I thank you from the bottom of my heart for finding the books and taking care of them for me."

Wheelwright grasped the bars of his cell—not in the aggressive manner often shewn by the incarcerated, but with an air of something like supplication. "Your Lordship," said he, his voice lowered, "we are informed by the Gospel of John that the word was God, and it precedeth all other things. The written word is our portal to the divine. Be it the holy Bible, or the adventures of Don Quixote, or anything in between, the creative and transformative power to be found in books, is the nearest mankind may aspire towards the essence of the everlasting almighty, since our expulsion from the garden."

Such extraordinary words, together with the fervent manner in which they were spoken, could not fail to make a strong impression upon me. I suddenly saw in this man, a genuine and rarefied veneration for books which any library owner would wish for in a librarian. Despite my uncle's belief that Wheelwright must be a fraud, and despite Bridger's determination to wreak corporeal punishment upon the fellow, I understood in that moment what my course of action would be.

No further interaction with Wheelwright was necessary at that time, so I excused myself, wished him a continued pleasant stay in his luxurious cell, and retired to my cabin to rehearse counterarguments against Nelson and Bridger.

An officers' meeting was to commence at ten bells. A few minutes before that time, I crossed the corridor to knock at the door of Nelson's cabin, as I wished to have a few words with him beforehand about

our cargo inventory. There was no reply. At ten bells I ascended the gangway to the strategy room, where I found that everyone save my uncle was already in attendance. When I asked if anyone knew his whereabouts, no one was able to give a definite answer. We waited for three more minutes, before Nelson finally appeared through one of the doors from the main deck, as opposed to the gangway from his cabin, carrying a sheaf of inventory papers and appearing not to realize that he was late.

Under other circumstances I might have enquired about the cause of this delay, but as it seemed reasonable to assume that Nelson had been in the hold checking our stores against the inventory, I said nothing. Also, it was my intention to open the meeting with a decision sure to stir controversy, and I wished to dive straight in, rather than dog paddle about for any amount of time with lesser topics.

So, my uncle's posterior was scarcely settled into his chair when I announced my decision to hire Augustus Wheelwright as our ship's librarian.

As expected, this caused a minor uproar from my first and second officers. Overlapping objections tumbled from their mouths and this went on for a good minute and a half—sounding like a good hearty debate in Commons, I thought, with the difference that both voices held forth on the same side of the issue.

When it seemed that the two of them had emptied their quivers, and paused in order to fetch additional arrows of demurral, I held up a hand to indicate silence, and recounted that morning's interview with Mr. Wheelwright and the impression it had left upon me. I expressed my conviction that, in spite of his obvious inclination for hyperbole, our unexpected guest had been altogether honest with us in at least one particular, to wit, his motivation for joining our crew. I reiterated that it was my firm decision as captain to give the fellow a chance at management of what was, after all, my own library, and I pledged that at the first sign of treachery from Wheelwright, Bridger would be allowed to chuse the punishment meted out.

To this my uncle glowered, "The first sign of treachery, Nephew, shall consist of priceless items pilfered from our collection and this villain nowhere to be found. Mr. Bridger may only mete out punishment upon those foolish enough to be caught. This is a slippery fellow, for my money, and we are hardly far enough from shore to prevent an easy escape. Furthermore, allow me to remind you that whilst the title viscount is undeniably yours, and welcome to it, the Hall and its contents belong to the Jacob family. It is our misfortune that said family has come to consist of only ourselves, but make no mistake, it is entirely proper for me to have a say in the disposition of our heritance, and I shall be heard."

I conceded to Nelson that he was absolutely correct when it came to 'the Hall and its contents', as he put it, but then reminded him that the small portion of our library under discussion was no longer *in* the Hall. It had been handpicked by myself to furnish us with an aid to safe and informed voyaging, and now resided aboard a ship of which I was the undisputed captain. Therefore the rules of familial heritance did not strictly apply in this case, and I would be entirely within my rights, were I to order the entire collection heaved overboard.

"May as well, while you're at it!" growled my uncle.

"Beggin' yer pardon, Cap'n," Bridger interjected at this point, "but does this mean that the stowaway ain't to be tarred and feathered? Or may we still do so afore he officially begins his duties?"

I informed my second mate that no such fate was to befall the man whom I had designated as our librarian, as he was now one of our onboard professionals, in a class with Whitehand and Converse.

"P'haps just the tar part?" Bridger went on, almost beseechingly. "We've plenty of that, although we're still casting about fer feathers enough."

"Absolutely not! Mr. Wheelwright is to be treated with the utmost respect by all present, from this moment forward, as befits a gentleman of his stature! What is more, he is no longer to be referred to as a stowaway. Eccentric he may be, but if this fellow turns out to be a genuine scofflaw, I shall eat my hat! Now, I consider this matter settled and it is time that we ... For heaven's sake, will someone answer the door? It sounds as if some rogue is trying to break it down!"

That last I spoke in response to a persistent knocking on one of the doors, which had been growing steadily louder for the previous minute or so. Normally we paid no heed to such attempted interruptions during our officers' meetings, and the offending knocker would soon realize that his errand was futile, and bring his business to one of us after the meeting. But as this knocker shewed no signs of ceasing to knock, I intended to give him a piece of my mind before sending him away.

Dr. Converse, being nearest the noisy door, rose to his feet and opened it. The sailor on the other side appeared to recoil slightly when he saw who had answered, but his gaze quickly found me and he began, "Cap'n, a thousand pardons for interrupting an officers' meeting, but ..."

"A thousand pardons, indeed!" I cried. "Try ten thousand and you will have made a good start! Now, on pain of serious punishment, be gone this very instant and never ..."

I could not believe my ears when this common sailor dared interrupt me. "Sir, I am terribly sorry," he said, "but we think that you and the officers should be aware that there is a stowaway on board."

This statement was followed by a moment of complete silence, after which I made the entirely reasonable riposte, "But of course there is, you buffoon! We were just discussing that gentleman's case before your extraordinarily rude and unnecessary disruption!"

The sailor looked thoroughly amazed and confused. "Er … *Gentleman,* sir?"

"Mr. Wheelwright is absolutely a gentleman in my estimation, and my officers are in unanimous agreement. I will not hear him disparaged in any way! You shall be very fortunate if he does not see fit to challenge you to a duel in response to such a slight!"

An expression of understanding crossed the sailor's face. "Ah, sir, I see that I have not explained myself well, and I beg your forgiveness. The news I mean to convey, is that we have a *second* stowaway on board."

After another momentary pause, I managed to frame the reply, "What?"

"A second stowaway, sir. I believe you are aware by now that Mr. Wheelwright and his personal belongings came aboard in three crates, all marked from the Galton Works. Well, sir, the second was entirely filled with clothing—it is in fact, sir, the smartest set of apparel I have ever laid eyes on—but in the third we found mixed in with Mr. Wheelwright's papers and some tapestry-like things, a second stowaway. Who I must say, sir, seems far too foul and disheveled to strike anyone as a gentleman."

Another pause. I had become aware that, during this exchange, Dr. Converse and indeed all of my officers had been sitting there looking back and forth between the sailor and I, like so many spectators at a tennis match. As the ball returned to my court, as it were, I demanded to know whether this rapscallion had been brought hither.

The faces turned back to the sailor. "Why yes, Cap'n. We have him right here." With that, the sailor stepped aside, and someone unseen was thrust into the doorway—the sorriest excuse for a man that ever my eyes beheld.

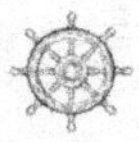

Rag-like objects which may have once been clothing hung over his near-skeletal frame. He held himself in a deplorably slouched manner, head sagging so far forward that a mass of disarranged and hideously yellow hair entirely concealed his face. I became aware of a revolting reek which must have originated from this pathetic scarecrow; several of my officers reflexively covered their noses, although Bridger and Converse appeared impassive.

"Bloody hell!" said Nelson, through his hand. "I shall thank Mr. Wheelwright straightaway for dragging such an appalling slave as this aboard our ship!"

"I'll none of that, Uncle!" I returned. "If our librarian brought such a fellow along deliberately, then I am an Irishman! We'll get to the bottom of this!" Addressing the wretched fellow in the doorway, I said, "You, wretched fellow in the doorway! Do you speak English?"

The fellow nodded, his filthy mane flopping grotesquely.

"For heaven's sake, don't stand before the captain of a ship in such an unmanly way! Draw yourself up! Shew your face!"

The fellow's posture improved, if slightly, and flinging aside matted bangs with a toss of his head, he disclosed a visage most unpleasant—young, homely, pockmarked, smeared with grime, and emblazoned with fear.

"Well! I almost wish you had kept that hidden. Give us your name, boy!"

In a voice so feeble as to barely be heard, the fellow said, "M … M … Mustardhead, sir."

"Well, I shall call you Mustardhead for short. Now, Mustardhead, what exactly do you mean by stowing away in our stowaway's crate?"

"I hid in a box."

"Yes, that's been established. What I'd very much like to know, is how that came to happen."

The stowaway fell to his knees and wailed loudly, in what seemed a sudden fit of despair. "Please, sir, please don't make me eat grass! I was runnin' from Baker's boys! I hid in a box! It got nailed up and I couldn't leave! Now I'm here because I weren't good enough to me mam an' me auntie, an' I stepped on spiders, an' I beg you to have mercy on a poor sinner, sir!"

I was rather at a loss what to say to a supplication of this nature, and the stench was really quite awful, so I resolved to continue my interview with Mustardhead at a later time. I gave orders that he should be confined to the brig, but only after he had been thoroughly washed and provided with some decent clothing. Two sailors pulled the boy back to his feet, and escorted him from the room, closing the door behind them.

During the discussion that followed, it became apparent that the arrival of the second stowaway had had a more salutary effect on attitudes towards the first, than any of the declarations I had made minutes before. The venom previously directed towards the finely dressed, well-mannered Wheelwright instantly swung about to the slovenly scamp Mustardhead. Nelson exclaimed that he had never, even in the navy, set eyes upon such a sorry specimen, who was clearly unfit to lick a cabin boy's boots, and who should be tossed overboard immediately without benefit of either a bath or new garments. Bridger expressed a fervent hope that perhaps the inhabitants of Keld could be prevailed upon to provide feathers, and even our Whiggish young Lampson expressed contempt in a manner which surprised me.

And so, as of this writing, Augustus Wheelwright has been freed from the brig with the unanimous consent of my officers, although I daresay that my uncle in particular shall keep a close eye upon him. He has been provided with a berth in officers' quarters with his fellow professionals, and has already made himself quite at

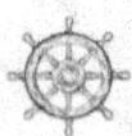

home, hanging up tapestries and using the very crate he had been confined in as a wardrobe.

In the afternoon I gave Wheelwright a personal tour of the ships' library. As we perused my collection of books and maps, his disposition appeared to veer back and forth between that of a child in a sweet shop, and that of a passionate scholar presented with a weighty but exciting responsibility. The two of us delved into deep discussions of a number of items in the library, and whatever misgivings any of us may have about his professed adventures, there can be no doubt that his knowledge of literature, history, and science is real and very extensive. We spent nearly two hours in this pursuit, and I came away thoroughly convinced that I have made the correct decision in designating Wheelwright our librarian.

As for Mustardhead, he resides for now in the brig. I am told that he cleaned up well enough, but refused to have his hair trimmed, and that in sharp contrast to his predecessor has regaled our gaoler with an unceasing cacophony of moans and wails. Again we shall see what effect a night behind bars may have upon a stowaway. I intend for him to be interviewed in the morning, this time by Mr. Whitehand rather than myself. Several of the boy's utterances today convinced me that before we can decide what to do with him, he is in need of evaluation by—and possibly counsel from—a man of the cloth.

Thursday, May 28, 1795

This morning our good vicar cheerfully did his duty to God and man: the forsaken task of paying a visit to the moaning wretch in our brig. Whitehand's report on the matter was uppermost on the agenda of our officers' meeting a short time later.

"It is a most interesting case," he began, with an air of bemused puzzlement. "Upon being freed from the crate yesterday, for reasons not entirely clear to me, Mustardhead believed himself to be in purgatory. Only with much difficulty was I able to persuade him that he is in fact in Yorkshire. Even now I am not certain that he is altogether convinced."

"More the fool, he," said my uncle, "to not recognize heaven-on-earth when he sees it."

"Really, Sir James," said our vicar. "I share your fondness for this land, but let us reserve such lofty language for the Kingdom of Heaven on Earth, which shall follow the return of Our Saviour. Now, as I was saying, the boy's belief in such an aberrant doctrine as purgatory shews that he is either a Catholic, or else his feeble mind has been misled by popish influences. Oddly, though, he seems to have the idea that souls do purgatorial penance by eating grass. *That* is not a feature of the concept I have previously heard tell of."

"Perhaps we should toss the dolt back into his crate and ship him down to Canterbury," said Nelson. "I daresay the ecclesiastical worthies of that city would have a splendid time teasing out the theological implications."

"They could also peel off the tar," said Bridger.

"Mr. Bridger," said Whitehand, "your commitment to maritime justice is commendable, but let us all take a step backwards and have a fresh look at this poor waif. As far as I can tell, he is orphaned and homeless. He is also frightened, and seems to be rather stupid. Is

this not exactly the sort of unfortunate which Christ Our Lord has enjoined us to meet with compassion? Should we not contribute in some way to his improvement, if circumstances allow?"

"Ah, Whitehand, you and your New Testament God," chided my uncle with a shake of his head, although he also shot me a wink to signal that his disapproval was feigned.

Lampson, who had been looking pensive, spoke up. "I must own that I agree with our vicar. I have been too harsh in my judgment of this young fellow, and yesterday I allowed my moral compass to be turned by his repugnant appearance, which was low of me. Mr. Whitehand is right; it is not Christian of us to punish this boy for the misfortunes which have brought him here."

Bridger turned to me. "Cap'n, I feel the spirit of universal brotherhood flappin' its gossamer wings within me, an' I move that we commute the stowaway's sentence from tar an' feather to walkin' the plank. If he don't swim yet, that may encourage such an improvement, and it'll rid our ship of a useless trespasser. I maintain it's what Christ himself would chuse, were he captain of our ship—deferrin' to the priest, of course." Whitehand rolled his eyes, but said nothing.

All present looked to me, their captain. I felt the full weight of this office as never before, acutely aware that the earthly fate of a young soul rested in my hands. And even as Pontius Pilate bowed to the wishes of the multitude, and set Barabbas free, so I agreed that the reduced sanction of walking the plank would justly serve the unlawful actions of our second stowaway (although unlike Pilate, I did not in the same moment allow a more worthy man to be crucified). I put Bridger in charge of the event, and he assured me that a plank would be prepared forthwith, as the *Mean Fish* has not been equipped with such a tool of punishment.

This afternoon saw the first of what I expect shall be a series of regular meetings with Rugby, concerned with the management of Stonesthrow Hall. The worthy Cornishman appeared at the edge of the pool just before three bells, and the gangplank was lowered to admit him on board. We held our meeting at a table in the open air of the forecastle, which affords an excellent view of the hall's rear facades.

I began by expressing my hope that Rugby and the rest of our staff are well, and that the hall and its contents are sound. Rugby assured me that, as it has been only eight days since I set foot in Stonesthrow, the ravages of time have as yet had little effect upon the Hall or its inhabitants. We went on to necessary if mundane discussions of roofing, gardening, horses, news from Keld and farther afield, *et cetera*, with Rugby taking notes of my directions on the various topics.

This business finished with, I was about to bid Rugby good day when he gave me a strange sort of troubled look and said, "Your Lordship should know about one additional thing. It is the Loose Stone, My Lord. It was seen yesterday in the great hall."

"Good heavens, man, why did you not inform me right away? Is anyone hurt? Is anything destroyed? Surely the Stone has not crushed yet another footstool!"

"Indeed no, My Lord, although I almost wish that it had," said Rugby.

"And what, pray tell, do you mean by that? Are all my family's footstools to fall victim to an ancient curse? You might not take such a cavalier attitude, were it your own footstools at risk!"

Rugby replied in a measured and deliberate manner, looking me straight in the eye, clearly keen that I fully appreciate the import of his words. "What I mean, sir, is that *no one* was hurt. *Nothing* was broken. The Stone was seen by several of us, including myself, over

a period of a quarter-hour, sitting in the very middle of the great hall that whole time, and it left no apparent mischief in its wake."

Both Rugby's words and the manner in which he delivered them sent a chill down my spine. My gaze sought out the tall windows of the great hall, as if to penetrate the mystery which suddenly blossomed there. For what Rugby described was an unprecedented sort of behaviour in the Loose Stone of the Hall. Never in memory, to the best of my considerable knowledge, had it appeared in any given location for longer than a few seconds, and never did it manifest without causing injury of some sort to either persons or property. The idea of the Stone persisting for a full fifteen minutes, and wreaking no havoc during that time, seemed disconcertingly sinister.

As Rugby observed my reaction, his mouth set into a grim line and he gave a slight nod. "Aye, My Lord. I'll speak nothing further aloud, as I see we're of the same mind. You may rest assured that we all of us in the Hall shall be on our guard."

With that, my trusty steward went ashore, leaving me to contemplate what I cannot help but interpret as a very bad omen.

Friday, May 29, 1795

This morning Bridger and I met in that portion of the hold used as a carpentry shop, in order to examine the plank. This slab of pine is a scrap left over from construction of the ship, and its length has been trimmed to fifteen feet. I was surprised to find that it has been thoroughly sanded, making it silky to the touch, and bringing out the lovely grain of the wood.

"Our chief carpenter's an experienced sailor," Bridger told me, "an' also a talented furniture maker. This'll be the finest plank ever walked by way of punishment, Cap'n. Normally they're crude, unfinished things."

Later, at our officer's meeting, I mentioned the plank, and recommended that each of my officers devote a few minutes' time to appreciation of its fine qualities. Then I broached the main topic: the arrival of a written request from a delegation of local worthies to visit our ship three days hence. The principal signatories of this letter are His Grace the Duke and the venerable archdeacon, both of Richmond, and more estimable guests we could hardly wish for. I have in fact been looking forward to the time, when one or both of them might honour us with their presence.

However, this ointment contains two disgusting flies, namely, the secondary signatories of the letter: my least favourite ecclesiastical on Earth, the Rector of Reeth, and Henry Fitzhenry, a Bedfordshire boor and former Viscount Luton, who at the pleasure of our betimes-deranged King, is lately allowed to style himself Earl of Arkengarthdale. These idiots have expressed nothing but scorn for my project from the beginning, and I cannot imagine the intention of their visit to be anything other than ridicule of my ship. I would certainly decline their request, were it not hitched to that of the duke and archdeacon. As it is, I cannot refuse two of the signatories whilst welcoming the

others. It simply would not look well (despite my belief that the duke holds Fitzhenry in as much contempt as I), and it would give the earl and rector grounds to complain of me to the duke.

Looking over the letter in our meeting, Nelson shared my exasperation. "I am afraid that it's to be all or nothing, Nephew," he sighed. "We could deny all four of them at this time, say on grounds of not being prepared to entertain, but that would reflect ill on us."

Turning to my second mate, my uncle went on, "Mr. Bridger, I believe you are the only one here not yet acquainted with the earl and the rector, so allow me to enlighten you. Rector Simon Wright is an ass. Henry Fitzhenry is an ass's ass. The rector is at least of the neighbourhood, having grown up around Reeth and Richmond, but Fitzhenry is a southerner installed here by a King—God save him—who created this earldom to bolster the number of Pitt's supporters in Lords. It is generally known that His Majesty was not in his right mind when he did so, but of course, the King would be admitting as much if he dissolved the peerage now, so that is out of the question. It would take something earthshaking, indeed, to get Fitzhenry out of his atrocious so-called cottage at Langthwaite, and being a bigoted, ignorant libertine seems not sufficient."

"Politics," Bridger sneered—shewing, at least to my way of thinking, that he understood the situation perfectly well.

It was decided that we should welcome all four of our would-be guests, and take steps to ensure that the rector's and earl's opportunities for scorn shall be minimized. Seeing as how they are less likely to find fault with the *Mean Fish* herself, as opposed to her geographical situation, the entertainment of our visitors shall take place almost entirely on board, where the ship's cleanliness, comfort, and innovative features can hardly fail to impress.

Mulling things over this afternoon, it became clear to me that I need to know more about the genesis of this proposed social call.

If the idea originated with the duke or archdeacon, and was then naturally enough extended to the earl and rector whose domains lay nearer the ship, then I would not feel overly alarmed by the motives which precipitated it.

If, however, Wright or Fitzhenry hatched the idea, I would find cause for trepidation; in that case their motivations must be not only to denigrate my achievement, but to do so before the duke and archdeacon in such a way as to discredit me. That could easily lead to further disputation over our 'turn-pike' which, in the vicinity of Reeth, is being built across lands belonging to both the earl and rector. Securing their reluctant permission for rights-of-way has been the most herculean task facing me over the past few years—more so even than building the ship—and I have only accomplished it with assistance from the duke, who is a great believer in the Swaledale turn-pike. Even so, construction has been delayed in the section near Reeth, and although the grade is dug there, it remains in a less finished state than the rest of the project.

In order to ascertain the nature of the duke's involvement, I have dispatched Rugby to Goodwood House on the pretext of some errand, which I trust him to invent. There he should be able to subtly sound out His Grace's staff on the matter, and discover what I wish to know. This stratagem has worked splendidly in the past, most notably in the matter of the donkey accident, and I hope that it shall do so again.

Just before sitting down to compose this entry, I knocked upon Nelson's cabin door, intending to acquaint him with Rugby's mission. I heard no response. I conducted a quick search for him in every nook of the ship, but to no avail. Also, no one reported having seen my uncle since supper time. This continues a disconcerting pattern of Nelson not being where he is expected, which began on the night of our clandestine ride to Buttertubs. It bears further looking into.

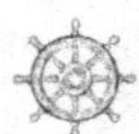

Saturday, May 30, 1795

Upon falling out of bed this morning, I straightaway crossed the corridor to Nelson's cabin door, upon which I knocked loudly for several moments. I heard no reply. I knocked again, with greater force, and for a longer time. Still nothing.

Having made such a colossal effort to announce myself, I felt justified in taking an action which normally, even as captain, I would have been loath to do: I opened my first officer's cabin door without his leave.

I called my uncle's name, but still received no response. The entire cabin was visible from the doorway; unless Nelson had hidden under the bed, he was simply not there.

I made a quick reconnaissance of the entire ship, from bow to stern, keel to crow's nest. No Nelson. Perplexed by where he could have gone at such an hour—the sun had not yet appeared, and my uncle does not normally rise with the roosters—I went for a look at the plank, in hopes that its smooth surfaces and mesmerizing wood grain might have a soothing effect upon me.

I was astonished to discover that during the previous day the plank had been lovingly varnished, to a rich mahogany-like hue, and I found myself not merely soothed, but positively enchanted. Upon further examination I found that elegant patterns of interwoven leaves had been carved around each end of the plank, these indentations untouched by varnish, implying that some other treatment was to occur there.

What magnificent work! It seemed patently unfair that the slovenly Mustardhead, of all persons, was to have the honour of placing his feet upon so lovely a plank. Yet the tarring option still seemed too severe, so I comforted myself with the certainty that the boy's capacity for aesthetic appreciation is so stunted, that he shall derive

no enjoyment from the plank, and therefore, there is nothing for me to envy.

At this morning's officer's meeting, I was intrigued to see Nelson ascend into the room via the gangway from his cabin. Given his glaring absence earlier in the day, the sight was not unlike finding a lost object in the very place where one has, without any doubt, already searched for it fruitlessly several times. My face may have betrayed some confoundment, for as he took his seat, my uncle asked me what was the matter.

"Nothing. Nothing is unusual," I said. Nelson gave me a long look, eyes narrowed. "Everything is normal," I said.

He raised a skeptical eyebrow. "Well, Nephew, I expect that you shall acquaint me later with the *actual* status of nothing and everything, as it is plain to me that *something* is afoot. But now, here is Dr. Converse, looking as usual like the merriest corpse in the morgue, and that gives us a full table. Shall we begin, Captain?"

Although momentarily somewhat shaken by the cumulative effect of Nelson's vanishings and reappearings, my composure quickly returned as I updated my officers on the progress of the plank. It was, I informed them, the most resplendent slab of wood beheld in our hemisphere since the time of Solomon, and I issued an order that anyone who had not yet paid a visit to the hold in order to appreciate it, was to do so immediately following the meeting.

Our subsequent discussions this morning, and my efforts and attention during the remainder of the day, centered around the upcoming arrival of the duke and his retinue. That august occasion is now but two days away, one of those being a Sabbath.

Thankfully, the *Mean Fish* remains in a condition I may call pristinely clean; there is nothing to do in the way of removing dust or grime. However, I wish for our visitors' programme to be optimized; it is of vital importance that every step of the tour, every

tableaux presented, be flattering to our ship, our crew, and myself, and ensuring this shall require a good deal of forethought and practice, if not arduous physical work.

To this end, my officers and I conducted three rehearsals today, beginning at the gangplank where we shall welcome our visitors, and following our projected route through the ship, noting any clutter or eyesores which may serve as sources of contempt or jest for Fitzhenry and the rector. Such niceties as forms of address and proper degrees of bow were reiterated by myself as we went along, for all our benefits but particularly Bridger's, as he has had little experience with clergymen and none at all with dukes. Later I ventured ashore to the kitchens of Stonesthrow Hall, in order to personally discuss our special menu with Gertrude. Although the ship's galley has begun to furnish respectable meals for the officer's mess, it could never meet the standards required for a duke; for that I must rely upon the most formidable cook this side of Paris and her crack staff.

But my thoughts never strayed far from the mystery surrounding my uncle. I watched him closely all day for signs of atypical behaviour. He seemed entirely his usual self. At suppertime we sat together as always, and I casually enquired as to what activities remained on his agenda for the evening. He mentioned a few hands of whist with Lampson, Bridger, and Wheelwright, followed by an attempt to reconcile some outstanding discrepancies between goods paid for and goods received. None of this sounded the least bit suspicious, although I was surprised to hear of him socializing with our librarian, whom he still surmised a possible scoundrel, and I told him so.

"Well, Richard, you know what they say about keeping your enemies close," said my uncle, "and that goes doubly for suspected enemies as opposed to known ones. Besides, I have found that there

are few better insights into a man's nature and intentions, than a cracking good hand of whist."

Fortunately, Nelson seemed to have forgotten what I had said that morning, about nothing and everything—at any rate he did not chuse to pursue the topic further, which I found a relief. At the finish of our meal I bade him good night and retired to my cabin.

At least, that is what I wished him to think. I did go to my cabin, but I did not retire for the evening. Instead, I sat upon the gangway, just below the closed hatch which gives access to the strategy room, and there I listened intently to the cordial conversation and slap of cards which accompanied four hands of whist. My uncle was partnered with Lampson, Bridger with Wheelwright.

I have never been overly fond of cards, although whist being as much an expected passtime in English social circles as excessive whiskey and hurling of axes is for Scots, I have acquired some knowledge of the game and my uncle's style of playing it. It was clear to me that Nelson deliberately diverted Wheelwright's focus by drawing out our adventuring librarian's fantastical stories, and that Bridger tried equally hard to keep his partner's mind on the game with a stream of admonishments which grew steadily more cross as the two of them lost hand after hand. Wheelwright seemed not to realize that he was at the centre of this Lilliputian tempest; his tales hardly ceased the entire time, whilst I never once heard him acknowledge Bridger's increasingly abusive pleas to mind his goddamned cards.

During the first hand of whist, it occurred to me that I had neglected to use my personal lavatory before beginning my vigil. This did not seem problematic at first. During the second hand, my oversight began to cause discomfort. During the third, I began to seriously long for the relief promised by the lavatory only steps away, yet I feared that in leaving my post I might miss some telling remark from my uncle. During the fourth, my misery became acute;

I felt as though I must soon burst, yet I remained unwilling to heed my bladder, instead wriggling my bottom back and forth upon the gangway step in an effort to find some modicum of relief. Finally, during what promised to be the final trick of the hand, with probably moments left until the game was finished, I could simply tolerate it no longer. As quietly as possible, I stumbled down the gangway and hurled myself into the lavatory.

Once my business was finished I returned to the gangway, only to find that—naturally enough—I *had* missed a crucial moment. The sounds of footfalls, chairs pushed in, and doors closing signified that whist was finished. Whilst relieving myself I might even have drowned out the sound of Nelson descending the starboard-side gangway to his cabin, had he done so.

I had to locate my uncle quickly, but without attracting attention. I opened the hatch just a crack, and looked out across the strategy room floor. Luck was with me; I recognized the pair of boots just leaving by way of the portside door as Nelson's, and more than likely to contain Nelson's feet, presumably attached to the rest of him.

I waited until the door was shut and counted off ten seconds. There was no further sound in the strategy room; everyone seemed to have left. I lifted the hatch and stealthily crossed the floor. I opened the door very slightly and peered through.

The main deck of the ship, and Stonesthrow beyond, remained lit by twilight, thanks to the blessedly long days this time of year. The ample illumination shewed clearly my uncle leaving the *Mean Fish*, via the gangplank. Once he was ashore, a couple of sailors heaved the plank back on board.

This time I counted twenty before making a move. It was a delicate business; I did not wish to lose Nelson's trail, yet without darkness to conceal me I dared not follow him too closely. Spotting a tablecloth which had been left behind after supper, I seized upon a plan.

I advanced from the strategy room hooded by the tablecloth, hopefully looking as anonymous and inscrutable as an Arabian in his thwab. Through my makeshift cowl I saw Nelson crossing the grass towards the rear of the Hall. The pair of sailors remained at the railing, apparently watching my uncle go and exchanging comments about it. I strode up to the sailors, rehearsing what witty riposte I would employ when they challenged this mysterious robed figure who had suddenly appeared on their ship. But, to my surprise and disappointment, the duo snapped to attention and one of them, a fellow with a very long beard, said, "Evenin', Cap'n."

My opportunity for wit dissolved, I snapped, "What, you recognize me?"

"Why yes, Cap'n, although I'll own that the tablecloth ain't yer usual rigging."

"I'm from Chelsea," said the second sailor, whom I then recognized as the muddled guitar player from church.

"Not another word from *you*!" I said to the Chelsea-ite. Turning to long-beard, I went on, "Just now you men lowered the gangplank for Sir James. Did he claim to have my explicit permission to go ashore?"

"Why no, sir, but then he don't usually," said the sailor.

"He don't *usually*?" I repeated. "And just how often is the first mate going ashore?"

"Why, every evenin', sir." Long-beard must have seen my displeasure through the cowl, for he added, "If any of the crew thought there was anythin' irregular about the first mate goin' ashore when we're essentially in port, sir, I'm sure it would've been reported. But …"

"But, nothing! My orders are crystal clear! *No one* is to go ashore without my leave! That goes for the officers, it goes for the first mate, it would go for Jesus Christ himself, were he aboard, and I'm quite sure that Our Saviour would have the good manners to respect my

wishes and obtain my permission! Now, put out the gangplank, I am going ashore!"

The two of them hesitated for a moment—why I know not, but this spurred me to follow with, "You dolts, that is an order! I don't require my own leave to go ashore, but if I did, it would be granted to myself instantly! Now put out that gangplank or I'll throw you both into the same cell as Mustardhead!"

This threat, which was anything but idle, certainly lit a fire under long-beard, as he scrambled so fast to get the gangplank down that the Chelsea-ite scarcely had the chance to assist.

Moments later I hurried across the grass towards the Hall's kitchen door, into which Nelson had vanished. My haste may have been a bit excessive, as at one point I trod upon a corner of the tablecloth and this misstep sent me sprawling upon the ground. Undaunted, I gathered myself up and pressed on, this time being more careful with the corners.

Immediately upon setting foot inside the kitchen door, I was greeted by a shrill scream and a clattering, crashing noise. I had startled one of the scullery maids, causing her to drop a tray of tea service.

"Merciful heavens!" exclaimed the girl, eyes wide and slender hand pressed to her heart. "I took 'e for a ghost! A thousand pardons, M'lord!"

"Now look here!" I said. "You know perfectly well there are no ghosts in this house! We have the vicar's word on that!"

The redoubtable Gertrude hove into view, no doubt drawn by the commotion. Having been cook at Stonesthrow Hall for longer than I have been Richard Jacob on Earth, she knows very well the diverse businesses to which a viscount must attend, and seemed entirely nonplussed by the sight of her Lord Keld draped in a tablecloth. She was, however, vexed by the condition of the tea service, and commanded the maid to clean things up at once.

Turning to me, Gertrude said, "P'haps I could fetch a fresh tablecloth for Your Lordship. That un's a mite soiled."

I followed her gaze and noticed for the first time that my disguise was marred by several reddish spots of dried sauce, as well as a grass stain from my fall outside. But there was no time for such niceties; I thanked Gertrude for her kind suggestion and pushed past the servants. Then I stopped short, realizing that I had no idea where Nelson had gone. I asked Gertrude and the maid if either of them had seen Sir James pass by.

"Why yes, M'lord," said Gertrude. "Makin' fer the great hall, 'e was, not fifteen seconds ago."

Popping into the great hall moments later, I spied a flash of movement upstairs—someone, presumably my uncle, rounding the corner en route to the west wing apartments. I followed, thankful for the stealth afforded by the stairs' thick carpeting, and looking down the corridor, I observed in silhouette the unmistakable form of Nelson ducking into his own chambers.

I did not count off any seconds before making my next move. Even as my quarry vanished, I strode straight down the corridor to his door, and for the first time in my life, barged straight in to my uncle's sitting room without so much as a knock, whistle, or how-d'you-do.

Nelson was just getting a lamp lit. His head snapped about to shew me an expression of utter shock—which quickly melted into one of mingled resentment, amusement, and, so I thought, guilt.

"How now Richard," he said, "taking vows as a Benedictine, are we? I daresay the Roman church ought furnish its novices with better togs than that!"

I had momentarily forgotten about the tablecloth, or else I would have divested myself of it before bursting in. Now I flung it upon the floor and said, "Explain yourself, Uncle! You have been coming

ashore without leave! Many times, apparently! For what purpose, I would very much like to know!"

Nelson made no reply, save a movement of his eyes in the direction of his desk.

"What!" I said.

This time Nelson extended his arm towards the desk, and my gaze followed. His great rolltop, normally crowded with bills, receipts, invitations, invoices, and heaven knows what else, was piled even higher than usual—so much so that the desk itself was hardly visible.

"I see that you have been doing some of your work here," I said, "and that helps explain how very tidy your cabin on the *Mean Fish* has remained. Confound it, Uncle, all you had to do was ask! I would've been happy to grant shore leave daily for such important business, although I must say I'd rather you did it aboard ship! We can have your desk moved, you know!"

Nelson still said nothing, but with an expression which I may call sour resignation, he walked to the door of his bed chamber, and indicated with a gesture that I should look within.

Whilst I cannot say that I have ever been exactly familiar with my uncle's bed chamber, none of the furnishings or accoutrements there struck me as odd or out of place. "It's all in order, Nelson. I daresay the maids are doing their jobs well. What of it?"

In a flat voice which sounded as though it were being dragged out of him, my uncle said, "The maids, my dear nephew, are making that bed each and every morning."

"Why, that is very odd, indeed! Why would they do such a thing? Perhaps they require the practice?"

"They are not doing it for practice, they are doing it because someone is sleeping in it."

"Heavens! Who has been sleeping in your bed? Is the culprit known? We must make an example of them, for such a trespass is absolutely unwarrantable, even while you and I are on the ship!"

I had never seen such an expression on my uncle's face, as I saw in that moment. Not only did he still appear to have eaten a lemon, but a faint blush, of all things, had appeared upon his cheeks. With a slight tilt of his head and lift of one eyebrow, he gave me a look which seemed to say, 'Now really, Nephew, *must* I spell it out?'

It took a moment more before the truth dawned upon me. Even then I could scarce believe it. "You … you have been sleeping *here*?" I stammered.

Nelson gave a curt nod.

"But that is absolutely forbidden! I require that all personnel reside aboard the *Mean Fish*, and it is essential for officers to provide a sterling example!"

Nelson heaved a great sigh. "I am not proud of it, Richard, for it does not seem too much that you ask of me, given how much time, effort, and money we have already put into creating our ship and how very pleasant she has turned out to be. And yet, I have found myself unable to resist the temptation of my own cozy chambers here in the Hall, for the purposes of both work and sleep."

I could hardly have felt more shocked and disappointed in that moment, had my uncle informed me that he was a Tory. I knew not what to say. My wit utterly routed, it sounded a general retreat; without a word I turned and retraced my steps to my cabin aboard the *Mean Fish*.

I found myself beset by doubts. It may seem a small thing, this matter of my uncle continuing to sleep in the Hall, and perhaps it may prove so, but as I returned to the ship I could not help but feel that it cast a shadow over the entire enterprise. How many stars needs must align correctly, and how many resolute spirits must wholeheartedly

conspire with my own—my uncle's foremost among them—to push this marvelous ship from the womb into the world, as it were! We have come so far, Nelson and I, but there is farther yet still to go. If he may not be relied upon to give his all, who may be?

Perhaps best now, thought I, to celebrate the significant achievements already accomplished, and leave our final chimerical gambit in the twilit realm of the might-have-been. A skeleton crew would suffice to keep the ship clean and functional in the Mare Jacobum next the Hall; there she could become in fact what my detractors believe her to be—a mere curio, the eccentric and expensive hobbyhorse of a cracked viscount. Our great building project, with a few alterations, could indeed function as the promised Swaledale turn-pike, and why should it not? For it to do so would save me from the baneful necessity of perpetrating a swindle upon my neighbours —our upstanding duke amongst them—in order to realize a selfish and ridiculous dream. Miss Smeaton would be paid in full, and the project would still stand as a testimonial to her prowess and vision, as the most modern turn-pike in all England (should the social *mise-en-scène* ever allow her to take credit).

These dire musings had swirled in my mind for several minutes, here in the suddenly somber confines of my cabin, when activity in the corridor without arrested my attention. It sounded as if a group of sailors were moving something heavy down the corridor and into the first mate's cabin.

A possible identity for the heavy something immediately suggested itself, but I dared not tarnish my gratifyingly doleful mood by jumping to optimistic conclusions. Aiming to discover facts, I opened my cabin door the merest crack. At first my view was entirely blocked by a swath of brown wool inching past my vantage point—the back of a sailor's tunic. A moment later, this strapping fellow had passed by and I was able to ascertain that his hands supported a corner of my uncle's desk, which was indeed being maneuvered, and not without difficulty, into the first mate's cabin.

My heart leapt within me like a salmon jumping a rapid. This could mean only one thing, and given the remarkable speed with which it had occurred, Nelson must have given orders to move the desk before I had even left the Hall. My principled uncle had wasted no time in attempting to make right his acknowledged wrong.

I closed my door but continued to listen with increasing satisfaction as the movers properly situated the desk, Nelson himself giving directions. Additional sailors followed the movers; it sounded as though they conveyed the articles of business customarily heaped atop the desk. After the sailors' departure I clearly discerned a prolonged rustling of papers, opening and closing of drawers, and other signs of Nelson busily organizing things according to some system. Such noises were easily enough heard through the bulkhead separating my cabin from his.

It seemed certain that my uncle's place of business had thus been moved from the Hall to the ship—but where would he sleep? I had made it clear, both in my initial orders and in my remarks this evening, that the paramount issue was where my first mate laid his head, not where he scratched it whilst puzzling over transactions. Surely he would not move the desk without also relocating his nightly *rendez-vous* with Morpheus.

On this point, too, I was ultimately satisfied, albeit only after two hours of further vigil. It sounded as if Nelson worked at the desk for nearly all of that time, given the intermittent scratching of pen and creaking of chair which I was able to make out—but at last I heard him rise, give a great yawn, and stretch with a cracking of his old joints. I went on listening as he undressed, did his nightly regimen of exercise (a holdover from navy days), and finally settled into the comfortable bed furnished for his use.

It may seem improper or even shameful for me to have eavesdropped on my uncle in such a manner, but given the shocking discovery made earlier this evening, I simply had to know whether or not he made his berth upon our ship tonight. Only if certain of that could I have fallen asleep myself; otherwise the tormenting doubts described above would surely have returned.

As for those doubts, I do not now dismiss them lightly or even entirely. Such measures may still prove necessary, should it become clear at some point that no amount of engineering or artifice shall suffice to baptize this landlocked hull in seawater. It is a possibility which, in my enthusiasm, I have failed previously to duly recognize. But by his selfless actions tonight, I must say that my uncle has ultimately upheld my belief in our project and its chance for eventual success. For what prize, however unattainable it might seem, may long elude the combined genius and efforts of two such men as us?

Sunday, May 31, 1795

First thing this morning I paid a visit to the plank. On my way there I paused outside Nelson's cabin door, and listened. I heard his distinctive snore, a gentle rather than grating sound, which has always reminded me of North Sea surf upon the sandy shores of Bridlington. This seemed a good omen indeed; not only was it soothing to find that my uncle had fully cast in his lot with the rest of us, but the coastal location brought to mind is one where the *Mean Fish* may one day lay at anchor.

As for the plank, I was filled with delight to see that it had been further embellished since the previous morning, its carved leaf designs now sporting a rich golden colouring which forms a lovely contrast to its varnished glory. I spent at least half an hour in the hold admiring this vision of luxury, before pressing business finally drew me away.

Later this morning, as we assembled for Sabbath-day service in the forecastle, I congratulated Bridger on his role in this delightful creation. "This breathtaking plank," I told him, "is fit to grace the study of a Raja, and I feel much obliged to you for bringing a worthy furniture maker aboard and allowing him the opportunity to create such a sublime object for us. I have half a mind to include it in the tour when our guests arrive tomorrow."

Seeming uncharacteristically sheepish, Bridger said, "Well, sir, I'm gratified to hear that our man's fine work pleases you. Yet I suggest it ain't proper to distract our visitors with sech a trifle, when there's so much else to shew 'em."

"Nonsense, Mr. Bridger! That plank is easily the most alluring phenomenon aboard the *Mean Fish*; it appeals to every faculty of human perception! Well, at least sight, touch, and scent. I must allow

that I have yet to taste it, nor have I explored what dulcet sounds may be brought forth from it."

Bridger cleared his throat and replied in a low voice, looking more distinctly discomfited than ever had I seen him. "Er … beggin' yer pardon, sir, but if I may speak freely, let's not forget that this here slab o' wood, charmin' as it may now be, remains an instrument of punishment, a form of punishment that ain't strictly legal in this country, as yer doubtless aware. When I set him this task, I'd forgotten that Woodley used to make furniture fer upper-class folk, an' it never occurred to me that he'd slather varnish an' gold leaf on the bugger, fer Christ's sake. To be plain, Cap'n, I fear that he's gone overboard."

"Ha ha! My word, Mr. Bridger, you have made a pun! I daresay that may be a first!"

Bridger gave me a blank look. "I don't foller you, sir."

"Very well, cleverness aside, you cannot seriously expect men of the world such as our visitors to be put off by the plank's intended purpose. The idea is to ceremoniously eject a sorry wretch from our midst, not to relieve the boy of his mortal coil! We are gentlemen, not pirates! The pool's edge is less than a stone's throw from the ship. Walking the plank would put Mustardhead nearly halfway there. Surely even a weakling half-wit such as he could not possibly manage to drown in the Mare Jacobum!"

Bridger gave me a look which I took to be tacit disagreement.

"Well, we shall ensure that nothing tragic occurs, and at any rate the spectacle shall amuse the crew. Now, as for the plank itself, I would like for you and Sir James to confer on how best we may work it into the tour."

Bridger gave a nod but avoided my eye. "Aye, Cap'n, you may rest assured that I'll confer with Mr. Nelson straightaway after church."

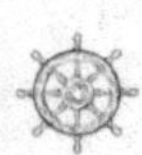

Following the service, which happily proved less eventful than last week's, I paid another satisfying visit to the plank. Then after a fine luncheon in the officers' mess, I met with Wheelwright in the library, in order to discuss what items we might wish to bring to our guests' attention on the morrow. Our librarian suggested a number of particular volumes and maps, owing to the duke's especial interest in isles of the Arctic Region.

"Why yes, that would in fact be highly appropriate, and edifying to our chief guest," I said, "but tell me, Mr. Wheelwright, how is it that you are acquainted with his grace's affection for things boreal? I myself might not be, had I not personally perused his collection of curiosities down at Goodwood House on more than one occasion. Surely your multifarious past has not included a stint in the duke's service?"

"Not at all, sir, but while I spent a winter compiling a lexicon of walrus utterances in the Svalbard Archipelago, for the Prince of Kiev, I came in contact with several agents of His Grace, intent upon collecting some of the very pieces you have probably seen at Goodwood. That was a terribly arduous project, sir, but its most salutary outcome is that I myself may now converse with walruses."

"I see! Well *that* must prove a rather useful and fascinating faculty to possess!"

Wheelwright shrugged. "Useful, certainly, on occasion. Fascinating —I would not say so. Walrus palaver, I have found, consists mainly of commentary on the weather and assertions of sexual prowess."

"Ha! Toss in money, and that sounds very much like the Earl of Arkengarthdale's favourite topics of conversation. Perhaps tomorrow you should endeavour to engage His Loutship with walrus-language!"

We shared a laugh about this, but then I was quick to ensure that Wheelwright understood my remark to be in jest. Seeing as how walrus-language must greet the average human ear as merely

various barks and growls, I should be very much embarrassed were my librarian to launch into such an oratory in the presence of our guests. I also warned him against use of the term "loutship" which I had previously only employed when speaking to my uncle, and which had more or less slipped out on this occasion.

I was about to leave, when I noticed upon one of the more remote bookcases, the spines of several volumes which I did not recognize. Having spent my entire life with the family library of which this ship-board collection is a part, the patterns formed by its book spines, both singles and sets, have become as familiar to me as the faces of old friends. I took a closer look and recognized the mysterious antediluvian tomes which our adventuring librarian brought aboard with him, and whose nature and provenance he is unwilling to divulge. I had previously glimpsed these in the dim light of the hold; here in the library I noted that although their dimensions varied somewhat, they were all bound in identical black leather, of a striking luster which somehow gave them the look of living things.

In place of titles, each spine sported a single arcane symbol in what appeared to be gold leaf. As my eyes slid across this row of motifs, from left to right, I felt myself seized by a sudden and irrational desire to look away from the books; my eyes almost seemed to avert themselves of their own accord.

"I say, Wheelwright," I sputtered, somewhat taken aback by this imagined effect of the black books, "I would expect you to keep these close to your person, say in your dressing-crate, rather than here in plain sight. Have they not been entrusted to you, and are they not of considerable value?"

"They have been, and they are," said Wheelwright, giving me a strange look at once keenly appraising and curiously ominous. "But I believe them to be safer here, amongst your collection, sir, than they would be in the officers' quarters. Not everyone onboard affords my

person—and by extension, my belongings—sufficient respect. Yet I have noted a reluctance on the part of both officers and crew to set foot in this room—excepting yourself and Mr. Lampson, both of whom I deem trustworthy. I daresay that the common sailors find this depository of a learned nobleman's property more than a bit intimidating." Then his face relaxed into an affable smile as he added, "Sometimes things may effectively hide in plain sight, Lord Keld, as you are surely aware."

I am inclined to attribute both my perplexing reaction to Wheelwright's books, and his somewhat forbidding speech about them, to the peculiar intensity which the man may exhibit. Neither is anything for me to feel troubled about, I am sure, and if he wishes to keep these volumes in the ship's library, I do not object. Still, I must admit that I have no desire to further investigate the black books any time soon.

Late this afternoon I met with Rugby in my cabin, to discuss what intelligence he had been able to glean from his fellow servants during his sojourn at Goodwood House. The news is not encouraging. Tomorrow's visit is, as I feared, the brainchild of His Loutship Arkengarthdale; it is he who extended invitations to the duke, archdeacon, and rector, and it is in fact the rector's gloomy coach and suspect coachman engaged to convey the lot of them up-valley. This reenforces my augury of ill will in the visit, making it all the more vital that our best collective foot is put forward, and that sensitive subjects such as the turn-pike are not dwelt upon. I thanked Rugby for his work and awarded him with a horehound candy for his trouble.

Again tonight I hear my uncle going about his business in the adjacent cabin, and find that his mere presence comforts me to no end. As an unusually sensible American is said to have told his fellow insurgents during a time of trial: we must all hang together, or we shall assuredly hang separately.

Sunday, June 21, 1795

Future readers of this ship's log, should any exist, shall note that there are no entries for the period June 1 through June 20, 1795. This is due to a catastrophic event on June 1, which had the effect of plunging me into a well of melancholia and sloth, from which I have only lately begun to emerge.

It is my wish to record the events of that fateful day, as well as some of the more important developments since then. In order to prevent this recollective entry from becoming as long as the *Divine Comedy*, I shall indicate the entries for separate days parenthetically.

(Monday, June 1, 1795)

This figured to be a day of promise and peril for our project, as we prepared to entertain important gentry and clergy from down-valley aboard the *Mean Fish*. And whilst moments of both triumph and disgrace were, as it happened, associated with that visit, the cause for my desolation came from another direction entirely, one unforeseen by myself prior to that day.

The unlooked-for development occurred at half-past ten, thirty minutes before our guests were to arrive. I stood in the hold gazing upon the lovely plank when a sailor informed me that a delegation from Keld had appeared on shore, with the stated intention of greeting the Duke and Archdeacon of Richmond, and asking whether they were to be allowed aboard ship, or if it would be the viscount's pleasure that their salutation be extended on dry land.

This was the first I had heard of a delegation from the village being part of the day's festivities, and I later confirmed with Nelson and Rugby that neither of them had gotten wind of it, either. Still, it was not unusual for locals to pay respects to a visiting dignitary,

particularly the duke, who is well-liked in our corner of Yorkshire. So there seemed nothing out of the ordinary about this delegation and it was with no sense of looming doom that I went on deck to parley with it.

I strode to the ship's railing in order to hail the leader of the delegation, whom I assumed would be a man. I was considerably surprised to find instead a triangular formation of three graceful figures clad in the simple Sunday-dress of village-girls, and bedecked with flowers. "Well, I say," I began, pleasantly struck by this unexpected vision of beauty, "You lot certainly eclipse the average village delegation! Would that more of the world's business be conducted by …"

My voice quit me entirely. The tallest young woman, standing at the front of the triangle, had at first been turned aside, as if speaking to a companion behind her, but as she faced the ship in response to my words it struck me that this was none other than Thistle—Darling of the Dell, Flower of the Fell, Sweet of all Swaledale!

Although my family and I have always cultivated an amicable relationship with the villagers of Keld, our paths do not cross as frequently as a city dweller might suppose, given the proximity of their homes to the Hall. The villagers are quite occupied from dawn until dusk seeing to the details of their daily lives, and the same may be said for the Jacob family. Our social contacts with Keld are generally limited to discussions of lead-mining or wool business with a handful of village elders. So, for the most part, I had previously admired Thistle only from afar, as she moved about on the wide-open slopes of Swaledale tending her family's flocks.

Even Holy-day services did not often bring me into contact with the locals, as mine were normally held in Stonesthrow's chapel and theirs at the church down-valley in Feetham. However, there had been one Easter Day, in the year 1794, when my uncle and I were invited to Feetham Church, as Whitehand conducted the service there due

to the local vicar being ill. The tantalizing glimpses I caught of her there on that day had put the bellows to the smouldering coals of my admiration, and my pet-name for her had also emerged at that time, in the sole embellishment of her Easter dress: a single purple Thistle pinned upon it.

Now our eyes met for the first time, and it was like a ray of sunlight piercing dull cloud. No—it was like the glorious fiery disk of the sun soaring above the horizon on midsummer morning. Again, no—it was like the whole world exploding and falling away, leaving just us two facing one another over a ship's railing and a ribbon of mirror-smooth sea. Her face, nearly fierce in its natural beauty, could on its own have hardly been rivaled in any royal court on Earth; with a wreath of penny-cress and rock-rose gracing her brow, her elegant neck below, and a bouquet of lilies from the village gardens in her hands, the overall effect was utterly breathtaking. Imagine the loveliest portrait ever you have seen, suddenly come to life and breathing before your very eyes, and you may have some faint conception of the experience.

And then Thistle spoke. Something about her voice brought to mind instantly the River Swale tumbling over Kisdon Force. I beg readers' indulgence here, as clearly no human voice literally sounds like a waterfall—I can only attempt to explain that something there suggested to me a river nymph who finds no reason to be demure, whose confidence in her feminine powers is complete and justified. Her words and her tone were respectful enough, yet there was something playfully arch just below the surface, which one would hardly expect from a village maiden addressing a viscount to whom she had not even been formally introduced.

"M'lord," said she, "I am called Mary Ashwood; you know of my father Benjamin, who is a shepherd of Keld. These are my friends Bethany Cartwright and Lucile Smith, daughters of local tradesmen.

We've come to present His Grace the Duke and the venerable Archdeacon of Richmond with flowers and highest regards from the villagers of Keld. We understand that the duke and archdeacon are to arrive shortly. Shall we wait beside the pool, or may we be allowed onboard your ship, in order to enrich your guests' welcome?"

It struck me that her speech sounded at once carefully rehearsed and yet altogether natural, quite the sort of balance which I myself strive for on such occasions. Whilst admiring this, and the entirely proper way in which Thistle had addressed me and my esteemed guests, it occurred to me that I had been asked a question, and therefore a response was expected, and that the lady had been waiting several moments for it, as I had been caught in a sort of reverie.

I began with, "This …" Before catching myself, realizing that I had nearly blurted out my pet-name for her, the significance of which would have been awkward to account for. Thus recovered, I went on, "This is a most charming development, indeed! Miss Ashwood, it is with heartfelt delight that I welcome you today! And your friends. I would be most honoured, as I'm sure our guests shall be, if you were to await their arrival onboard the *Mean Fish*! Along with your friends. Of course."

A few moments passed. I watched, enchanted, as one corner of her lovely mouth turned up ever so slightly, in the most fetching and quizzical manner, and a heartbeat later one of her eyebrows rose as she said, "Are we to swim it, then, M'lord? We're strong girls and up to it, I'm sure, but that'd spoil our dresses."

"Oh! But of course! You could hardly swim in those dresses! Which is not at all to suggest that you swim without them! I mean— of course, I shall order the gangplank lowered at once for you! And your friends." Feeling confusedly exhilarated, or perhaps exhilaratingly confused, I turned to the nearest sailors and barked an order for the ladies to be welcomed aboard.

The gangplank was put out, and the alluring delegation from Keld boarded the *Mean Fish*. How transporting my pleasure, as her beloved feet finally graced the deck of my beloved ship! Countless times had I rehearsed in my imagination how this gladsome event might come to pass (to give a single example: an attack by Spaniards *could* cause Thistle to seek my protection, and she *could* arrive clad as Scheherazade, *if* the onslaught happened to interrupt a village play) and yet the reality was far more enthralling than any gothic-novel fiction I had conjured. *She was here*, and not only that, I felt pleased to discover that her words and conduct shewed a quality of character befitting her great beauty!

I made arrangements at once to ensure the comfort of Thistle and her companions during their wait. At my command, chairs were brought out from the forecastle, and a sun-shade was deployed fresh from its crate in the hold. I found the oldest, homeliest sailor available and charged him on pain of death with personally guarding the ladies—especially the tall one—against any harm, or discomfort, or inconsiderate behaviour on the crew's part. I made it clear that I would not tolerate so much as a fly landing upon the tall one.

And then, with twenty minutes to go until our guests from down-valley were to arrive at the Hall, I found myself pulled between two horses. It struck me that I still had not personally visited the kitchen or any other part of the Hall that morning, to ensure that all was well there, and although I have faith in Rugby and Gertrude one must *always* check the work of one's servants on signal occasions. Yet I was loath to quit the ship whilst Thistle was there, as if turning my back might cause her to vanish, breaking the spell, proving this lovely vision to be just that, a filament of beguiling magic sanctioned by the Gods in order to torture me.

After several moments of excruciating indecision, during which time I could not pry my gaze from the lovesome lady now relaxed

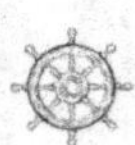

in a chair under the sun-shade, I forced myself to depart for the Hall, and Atlas himself could have found no greater difficulty in shouldering the world.

I came to this decision for two reasons. Firstly, I simply *had* to make a pass through the Hall; no detail could be left to chance with so august a personage as the duke, and such ardent critics as Fitzhenry and the rector, expected within mere minutes. Secondly, although every atom of my being yearned to engage Thistle in amicable and witty conversation, I had no idea whatsoever what I should say. It felt as if a thousand years' worth of amorous yearning swelled within me, clamouring for expression, and yet no words, however amicable or witty, could have done justice to such a sensation.

Idiom thus failing me, I was nearly overcome by an urge to fall upon my knees and kiss her hands, but such a reckless and public shew of admiration would have been blatantly ridiculous, and would have hobbled any chance I might have had, to learn if she might harbour reciprocal admiration for my person.

So, in spite of the teeth-gritting effort it entailed, I approached the delegation and very properly expressed my hope that they were comfortable and content, adding that I was dreadfully sorry to leave them but had pressing affairs to attend to in the Hall—hoping all the while that I did not sound or appear as discomposed as I felt. I finished with, "Please understand that only the most momentous duties could possibly pull me away from my lady. Er, you ladies. But things *are* rather momentous today. Aren't they? Yes. Well. Off I go, then! Ta ta!"

With that, I took my leave, furious with myself for having lapsed into such vapid speech in Thistle's presence, and imagining that the three ladies must be tittering amongst themselves at such silly behaviour in a viscount.

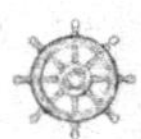

I gained some solace in finding all well at Stonesthrow, both in the kitchen and elsewhere. The great hall and new parlour were tidy, clean, and enhanced by ambrosial odours of the meal being prepared, all elements of which were on schedule. Things were so well in hand, in fact, that I found there was essentially nothing for me to do. I was about to find a window facing the ship, so that I might indulge in further reverence of my lady's fine features, when I heard the sound of a heavy coach coming up the drive. I rushed into the drawing room, from whence I spied the rector's Cimmerian behemoth just looming into view.

They were a full ten minutes early—terrible form indeed, especially in those who must know from experience how often last-minute adjustments are necessary when welcoming guests. I could not imagine that the duke or archdeacon would have knowingly committed such a *faux pas*; surely they would have held back the carriage until they felt certain of not being over-soon. This must have been Fitzhenry's doing—the scoundrel hoped to embarrass my household by catching us unready. I thought of all the meticulous preparations and rehearsals of the previous few days, and assured myself that Richard Jacob and his subordinates were not to be thrown off balance that easily. Thus fortified, I went downstairs to greet our guests.

On the way, I found Rugby hastening to marshal the proper elements of the hall staff and assemble them out front; he too had clearly been shocked to hear the carriage quite so soon. However, all was accomplished within moments, and by the time the rector's turnout slowed to a stop before the main doors, my key servants and myself were all in place, looking as composed as if we had been there awaiting our guests' arrival for several satisfyingly contemplative minutes.

The rector's uncouth coachman dismounted with all the grace of an overripe apple plopping to the ground, then he opened the carriage door in a rather abrupt and surly fashion. To my surprise, the first figure to emerge was not the duke, as would have been proper, but the Archdeacon of Richmond. This worthy-looking more aged and fragile than he had just a few months before, I am sorry to say, met my gaze immediately and came to me with a warm greeting.

"His Grace sends his most heartfelt apologies," said the archdeacon, pressing my hand, "but he was taken rather ill this morning, and had not the time to send word ahead. I feel certain that he shall make the journey himself, as soon as his health and schedule allow."

This news came as a disappointment, and yet immediately I spied the gleam of a silver lining. Whilst I had been anxious to share my ship with His Grace—a wise and moderate man with great curiosity about the world, who has always found my project intriguing rather than ridiculous—on the other hand if Fitzhenry's aim really was to ridicule my accomplishments in the duke's presence, then such unpleasantries would now be postponed until another day, and might never occur at all.

The other occupants of the carriage had by then appeared, and I was taken aback to see that, instead of the three visitors I would have expected in the duke's absence, there were actually four. One was the Rector of Reeth, of course, looking as lithe and cunning as a fox, but behind him Fitzhenry, clad in his customary tawdry manner, was helping someone else alight from the carriage.

Before I could get a good look at this fourth person, the rector pinched my hand in his cold grasp and gave me a perfunctory greeting, his feral grin flashing. Then he stepped aside and the ridiculous bewigged oaf Arkengarthdale, the colour of whose frock suggested nothing to me so much as vomit, came forward to greet me and introduce his companion, who turned out to be a rather striking woman.

"Keld, I would like for you to meet my fiancée," said he, in his lazy southern elocution. "This is Miss Fenny Drayton, of Lamb's Conduit Street, Bloomsbury. Her father is a judge at the law courts, so we had all better watch ourselves in the vicinity of her person, hmm?"

The vulgar remark about his fiancée, made in the presence of two clergymen and one of our housemaids, speaks for itself as regards the earl's character or lack thereof. As for the reference to Miss Drayton's street address, this puzzled me, as I was hardly a hackney-driver on hire to take her home. (Later, after Lamb's Conduit had been mentioned a half-dozen times, I enquired of Lampson and came to understand that the lady hailed from an expensive neighbourhood on the outskirts of London, which fact Fitzhenry was clearly keen to make known.)

As for the young blossom of Bloomsbury, I found her face pretty in a kind sort of way—a softness of feature which I had not observed in any of Fitzhenry's previous fiancées—and yet her mode of dress was very much what I have come to expect from Fitzhenry's ladies, which is to say, rather less than modest. Her figure I may best describe as Rubenesque, of a sort certain to inflame many a lad's ardent interest were it to appear in a painting representing some classical muse, and whilst I am endlessly thankful to the maker that such beauty exists in the world, Miss Drayton's dress showcased her share of it in a way which I found to be highly distracting. Again, two members of the clergy were present, making her style of *accoutrement* even more questionable.

"I say, Keld," continued Fitzhenry. Again he omitted the "Lord" portion of my title, as is his habit. This is surely meant to appear to others as a kind of genial intimacy, yet the man knows full well that I take it as a grating condescension, as he and I are neither genial nor intimate. "Is Stonesthrow Hall one thousand years old, or two thousand? I forget. Either way, it's jolly well fabulous that the place manages to stay standing, as ruddy decrepit as it's become. Why, there's even a stone altogether missing, there by the main entrance. Ha ha! Charming old barn, though, wouldn't you say, Miss Drayton? Perhaps we should have a similar picturesque ruin erected as a folly in our new gardens at Langthwaite."

Miss Drayton gave me a smile which I took to be a sort of desperate apology for her beau's deplorable manners, and which shewed a pair of fetching dimples on her cheeks.

"Sir James seems to be missing, My Lord Keld," said the rector. "I hope that he is not indisposed?"

This observation pricked a hole in my balloon, so to speak, although I hope that my face did not shew it. As a principal inhabitant of the Hall, Nelson should have been there to greet such important visitors, and surely would have been, had they not arrived so damnably early. Fitzhenry's breach of etiquette had caught us out, after all. Fighting back the urge to say something about guests arriving when they are expected, as opposed to whenever they please, I thanked the rector for his kind concern and assured him that my uncle was entirely well. "Sir James shall be part of the welcoming committee aboard the ship herself," I told him, hoping that this would in fact be the case, as I had no idea of Nelson's whereabouts at that moment.

Fitzhenry's prevailing affected smile, so constant as to almost seem painted on, suddenly doubled in size; he looked like an overgrown child who finds all his keenest desires arrayed beneath the Christmas tree. "Yes, the ship! The *Mean Fish*! By God, Keld, we saw her from miles away as we came up-valley! If the archdeacon and rector would indulge me, I wish to ask our host to take us straight there, without any further preliminaries!"

This unexpected enthusiasm from Fitzhenry put me more on my guard, than if he had begun by expressing contempt for the ship. I exchanged a glance with Rugby, whom I believe shared the same

thought, then agreed that our visitors should indeed be taken directly to the *Mean Fish*, and that I myself would lead the way.

An array of refreshments awaited us in the great hall, as it had been my intention to first shew our visitors the view of the ship through that room's tall arched windows, but now we proceeded right past the savouries and mineral waters as I conducted our guests through Stonesthrow by the most direct route, taking care to set a pace comfortable for the archdeacon.

We emerged from the rear of the hall to the grand sight—it overwhelms me still—of the *Mean Fish* in her pool, looking perfect in every particular, the grassy fell rising beyond. Our visitors proved not immune to this dramatic effect; the archdeacon stopped in his tracks, mouth agape at the spectacle, Miss Drayton uttered a soft exclamation of awe, and Fitzhenry, to my continued astonishment, literally clapped with glee. Only the rector shewed no sign of wonderment beyond a slightly raised eyebrow.

It pleased me to find that Nelson did indeed lead the group waiting atop the gangplank; either he had had the presence of mind to gather them together a bit early, or else some intrepid servant had run back to warn him, I have never been sure which. At any rate, Bridger gave a peculiar call on his bosun-pipe and the entire crew, assembled along the railings of the foredeck, main deck, and poop, snapped to attention as our guests boarded the ship. The scene from a few minutes before then more or less played out again, with Nelson standing in for myself, as the archdeacon shared the duke's apologies, the rector bestowed a curt greeting, and Fitzhenry presented Miss Drayton.

Then Fitzhenry retained centre-stage, as it were, as he continued to confound all our expectations by loudly regaling Nelson with gushing esteem for the *Mean Fish*. This behaviour so engaged the attention of all present, that I was not certain if anyone else noticed a most curious

exchange which took place between Miss Fenny Drayton of Lamb's Conduit Street, Bloomsbury, and our own Dr. Otto Converse, who stood in the welcoming line betwixt Whitehand and Wheelwright. For several long moments whilst Fitzhenry droned on, these two gazed at one another in a most fixéd and extraordinary manner, as if each sought with their eyes to bore into the other's very soul. It was, without question, a species of recognition; whether due to a prior acquaintance or something more metaphysical, I could not say.

This peculiar moment passed and the delegation from Keld stepped forward to present themselves. I am proud to say that my fair Thistle appeared entirely undaunted by the constellation of privilege and beauty which formed her primary audience, as she expressed on behalf of her village wishes for His Grace the Duke's better health, followed by highest regards for the worthies who had made the trip. Then she and her companions executed charming (if clearly unpracticed) curtsies, and presented their bouquets of lilies. (Fitzhenry should have doubled his fiancée's share of these, of course, by instantly handing his bouquet to her, but being an ass he did no such thing.)

And then, the tour of our ship officially commenced, according to the plans so carefully laid out during the preceding few days. One slight change took place at the very first: whilst Nelson ushered our visitors into the strategy room, I hung back for long enough to entreat the delegation from Keld to remain onboard for dinner, as I had noticed them preparing to depart. Since I could not possibly have spared any time just then for the object of my admiration, I very much wished for such an opportunity once the tour and meal were finished. After sharing glances of confirmation with her friends, Thistle graciously replied that the delegation would be glad to acquiesce to my kind wishes and remain my guests for dinner; she acknowledged the invitation as very much an honour not only for themselves, but

for the entire village. She concluded with a slight curtsey and a heart-stopping smile which, love-addled as I was, I see in hindsight that I may have taken as more significant than she intended.

As for the tour itself, the enterprise went more smoothly than I could have hoped. Our guests seemed duly impressed with every chamber through which they were led, and each feature of the *Mean Fish* brought to their attention. One of the reasons for this pleasing outcome was surely the preparation which my officers and myself had undertaken for the occasion; we all of us played straight through the score without missing a note, as it were, but equally important was the lack of outright hostility to be dealt with. I had fully expected ill-treatment from Fitzhenry, and possibly from the rector as well, and yet throughout the tour, the earl continued to exhibit an almost child-like wonderment with everything and never asked a single question which seemed calculated to mock or embarrass. Whilst the rector's behaviour was rather less benign, that was hardly surprising; I'll wager that his gracelessness would remain dour and reserved even if presented with the keys of heaven by Saint Peter himself. The rector's lack of enthusiasm, however, never descended into the kind of invective I had feared from him.

Whilst it was impossible to not feel relief at this turn of events, still I found myself subtly and persistently unsettled by the feeling that there was in fact something sinister about it—that this apparent goodwill masked an ominous portent. That alone prevented me from enjoying the tour to the fullest possible extent, as otherwise all went swimmingly, and of course I had been chomping at the bit to share my lovely ship with an appreciative audience.

General success aside, there were a pair of ticklish moments during the tour. The first occurred as we approached the pub. I heard a sort of snicker from Fitzhenry, followed by the remark, "I say, Keld, could this be the public house I have heard rumours of?

A pub aboard a ship, no less! And what do we have here on the sign? Might this establishment be called the Turtle & Tumbleweed?"

I politely corrected Fitzhenry's interpretation of the sign—the elements of which I suspect he had deliberately misidentified, as the cat featured there resembles a turtle no more closely than I resemble a hedgehog, but it was the archdeacon's face I watched anxiously. His expression did indeed fall as we approached the pub, lips hardening into a line of disapproval, and he shared a significant look with Whitehand. Naturally, the clergy were not enthused about this particular amenity, but the archdeacon had been so visibly pleased with the space provided for Sabbath-day services in the forecastle, that I hoped the two facilities might cancel one another out in his mind, as it were.

I halfway expected our men of the cloth to wait outside of the Cat & Cabbage, due to their professional misgivings, yet they graciously stepped inside with the rest of us.

It was my first time there since the pub had begun to function, as its intended purpose would hardly be advanced by the captain's presence, and I must say that Nelson, Bridger, and Lampson had done a fine job fitting the place out to resemble a *bona fide* local. Woodcut-prints depicting various rural scenes graced the walls, and it pleased me to see the Jacob family arms prominently displayed as well. The stage sat empty, as my officers and I had previously dismissed the idea of providing a musical accompaniment to this segment of the tour.

Since the crew remained on deck, the only person in the pub was the barkeep, a doughty fellow by the name of Penywern. As I introduced each of our guests, he bowed respectfully in turn, properly reserving his lowest bow for the comely Miss Drayton.

"A pub aboard ship, no less!" Repeated Fitzhenry, looking about with an air of approval. "You comprehend the common man, Keld,

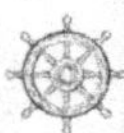

I'll give you that!" Then with a flourish he turned to the bar and said, "A pint of Whitbread, please, should it suit the landlord!"

Fitzhenry must have meant this in jest, for when Penywern promptly nodded, put glass to cask, and poured a draught, the earl looked as though he might have been knocked over with a feather. "Ye Gods!" He exclaimed. "You have Whitbread here! Your ship, Keld, may just be the most civilized spot in this whole howling wilderness called Yorkshire!" Receiving the pint from Penywern, Fitzhenry invited our barkeep to pour one for himself, then sipped contentedly on his porter as we continued our tour.

The second awkward moment took place minutes later, after we had looked in at Dr. Converse's sick-bay and were en route to the library. My officers and I had agreed to exclude the brig from our tour, in spite of innovative features such as its ninepin-lane, due to the presence of Mustardhead, whose unpleasant person could only have cast a pall over the proceedings. As we passed the brig door I held my breath in hopes that none of our guests would think to ask what lay beyond it, as I had not been able to fabricate an especially good answer. I felt relief when this hurdle seemed to have been overcome. But at that very moment, there reached my ears the most dismal wail imaginable, no doubt issuing from the miserable wretch we sought to avoid. Our guests clearly heard this lament, for they all came to a sudden halt.

"Good heavens," said the archdeacon. "What in creation could make such a baleful sound?"

"Er … Someone has stepped upon a cat," I offered.

We all stood perfectly still for a long moment, our guests looking as if half-afraid that the awful noise might repeat itself, and yet wishing in some perverse way that it would. Thankfully, it did not.

"We do have cats onboard, in order to prevent rats," I said, which was perfectly true.

"Well," said Fitzhenry, "I have heard caterwauls before, but that one could have given Lucifer himself the shivers!"

With that, Nelson took a step or two forward by way of example, and mercifully the archdeacon followed suit, unsticking us, as it were, and allowing us to leave the brig behind.

Lampson later informed me that the entire tour took forty-three minutes exactly, satisfyingly close to the forty minutes we had rehearsed for. By the time we re-emerged onto the sun-drenched main deck, a properly lavish banquet had been laid for our visitors, the ships' officers, and the delegation from Keld.

Conversation at the main table continued to exceed my expectations, in that Fitzhenry remained entirely civil with regard to my ship and my person, although he did proceed to dominate the discussion with loud elaborations on his recent improvements to Langthwaite. This 'cottage' as he disingenuously terms it, tucked into the verdant folds of Arkengarthdale some way down-valley, was several times the size of Stonesthrow the last time I saw it, in spite of the fact that its cornerstone was laid a mere seven years ago—and apparently the earl continues to add wings, galleries, towers, and cupolas to this monstrosity as fast as his poor fatigued architects may conjure them up.

Of course such an exceedingly dull topic would hardly have held my attention under normal circumstances; with Thistle dining at an adjacent table, the talk of Langthwaite died away into a droning gnat-like murmur somewhere on the periphery of my world. How gracefully she ate—surprisingly so for a commoner. In twenty minutes' time I observed only one or two slight foibles on her part. With minor corrections she could have held her own dining at Goodwood House—and this coming straight from a shepherd's cottage in Keld. What a remarkable creature, thought I, what God-given adroitness! Rousseau himself could hardly have found a more compelling example of his innately noble natural man (or in this case, woman).

Speaking of woman, the one thing at the main table which continued to engage a modicum of my attention, was ongoing intrigue between Miss Fenny Drayton and Dr. Converse. Since the intense moment betwixt them nearly an hour before, I had observed that throughout the tour these two had taken exceedingly great care to not directly engage each other in any way, to the extent that this pointed lack of acknowledgment became a glaring sort of acknowledgment in itself. It was clear to me by the Byzantine manner in which they carried out this subtle dance around one another that, in spite of their apparent lack of interaction, they were each in fact acutely aware of the others' proximity at every moment.

This had carried over to the banquet table, where Converse had somehow ended up seated beside the earl (an impropriety; I am not sure how it happened), putting him obliquely across table from Miss Drayton. From my place at the head of table, I could hardly have missed the glances which never quite met, the way in which both of them sat in their chairs turned ever-so-slightly towards one another; one could practically see the tension shimmering in the air between them.

I wondered that no one else noticed this extraordinary interplay, but then there had been constant distractions for all, Fitzhenry's loquacious manner not least among them. Still, as the fool rambled on about his deplorable 'cottage' the man seemed entirely blind to this significant something between his fiancée and my physician—a state of affairs which I found most amusing indeed.

After a meal which, I am pleased to say, met my own standards entirely for such an occasion, it was time for our visitors to depart. As myriad good-byes and well-wishes were exchanged on deck amongst my officers and our guests, I watched Converse and Drayton closely and felt a thrill of satisfaction upon catching a second meaningful look between them, far shorter and more furtive than the first, but

unmistakable nonetheless. It was enough to fully convince me that nothing I had noticed before had been merely a product of an overly theatrical imagination.

Nelson and I escorted our visitors back to the rector's carriage, the earl and his fiancée beside me, my uncle walking ahead with the archdeacon to set the pace. As we crossed the grass towards the hall, Fitzhenry cozied up to me and said, "I must say, Keld, you've outdone yourself and all the rest of us with your *Mean Fish*. I won't even try to duplicate her at Langthwaite. As tempting as that might be, I could hardly achieve the same effect, and at any rate mine would suffer as an obvious imitation of your very original attainment. I see now why your ancient pile is so poorly; you've given all your attention to your ship, and understandably so. She really is a wonder. The world hasn't seen the like. 'Tis a pity she'll never taste salt water."

I felt my guard fly up instantly; if the fellow had brandished a rapier at me my reaction could not have been more visceral. Still, his usual blithe façade remained in place and he had given me no pointed look, so I could not tell in exactly what way the remark was intended.

Unsure, I tested the waters with a light laugh and the remark, "It is gratifying to know that a man of Your Lordship's irreproachable taste regards our ship with the same esteem as we. But should we not, as it is said, never say never? I am sure that few expected the Montgolfiers to fly."

Fitzhenry gave a loud, dismissive sort of sniff and said, "The Montgolfiers are French." As if the fact of their nationality had in any way diluted their achievement.

The two of us walked in silence for a few moments, but shortly after we passed into the Hall the earl spoke, and for the first time that day—perhaps for the first time ever in my hearing—his customary flippant inflection was replaced by one a good deal more somber. Amazingly, he even managed to lower his voice. "Speaking of France,

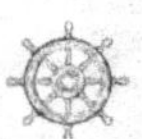

Keld, rumours have reached Langthwaite—and Richmond—to the effect that elections have taken place aboard your vessel. I've no doubt that it's a harmless sort of thing, and having seen the ship myself it hardly strikes me as a hive of Jacobinism, but you surely understand that even hints of such things are enough these days to make men of our class nervous."

I assured Fitzhenry that elections are not uncommon aboard non-naval vessels of our size (for so I am told by Bridger) and that such activity aboard the *Mean Fish* has been limited to selecting a spokesman, and chusing a name for the pub.

"I see. Well, that explains Cat & Cabbage, I suppose. Hmm, well, the duke will be pleased to have my assurance that we've no Republican activity stirring in Swaledale, as he has expressed some concern to me. Our poor noble cousins across the channel, Keld … Men, women, and children fed to a ravenous revolutionary machine, thousands of them. It must not happen here."

I thanked the earl graciously for passing such a good report along to His Grace, whilst simultaneously fending off a strong urge to wring Fitzhenry's nefarious neck. I had little doubt that the earl's 'assurance' in this case would be couched in language calculated to leave uncertainties in the duke's mind, and that this innuendo of radical tendencies aboard my ship is yet another volley in his barrage of slander against me. Fitzhenry's amiable words and conduct had very nearly lulled me to sleep, but this parting shot from him shewed how very unwise it would be to place any confidence whatever in apparent niceties on his part. In hindsight I believe that he had been genuinely entranced by the *Mean Fish* in spite of his inclination to mock her, and having seen this weapon snatched from his arsenal of ridicule, he had switched to a blade even sharper and more insidious.

Thus did I fume internally as we saw our guests back into their carriage. But even then, the outrage was not ended. As Nelson took his leave of the archdeacon, Fitzhenry, and Miss Drayton, the rector pulled me gently aside. "It strikes me that Your Lordship may go in for a bit of boating soon," said he quietly, with a smile icy enough to freeze the fires of hell. "In that case I should remind you, as a concerned friend intimately familiar with conditions down-valley, that the River Swale is especially difficult to navigate in the vicinity of Reeth. It is a rocky stretch, where many a skiff has been dashed to pieces. I wish Your Lordship a most blessed and rewarding day."

With that, the Rector of Reeth followed the others into the carriage and then it was off, leaving me on fire with indignation at the oblique threats, which two of our guests had seen fit to furnish in return for our hospitality. Nelson saw quite clearly the state I was in (he told me later that he feared I might begin to hurl handfuls of driveway-gravel after the departing carriage, as I have, embarrassingly, done in the past) and so he gently took me by the shoulder and guided me back towards the Hall.

"Well, Nephew," said he, "all in all it was a great success. The archdeacon was well pleased, and I daresay that we have given the others no substantial ammunition with which to pelt us. And heavens, Richard, did you note the goings-on between the doctor and Miss Fenny Drayton, of Lamb's Conduit Street, Buxombury? By the King's Colours, I feared that at any moment the two of them might lose all composure and fly together like magnets!"

The image of such a thing taking place in front of Fitzhenry was droll indeed; I felt a wan smile appear on my face in spite of myself. Also, I found it gratifying that eyes other than my own had so interpreted the synergy between those two.

"Never have I seen Converse take any but the most clinical interest in the fair sex," Nelson went on. "Hopefully for his sake she shall not hear any of that vampyre nonsense. But then again, perhaps such a thing might interest a modern young lady from London. And

speaking of young ladies, Nephew, I daresay that you may now have a few words with that comely shepherdess you fancy, but it should be quick. On your behalf I arranged for them to remain here a few minutes more, but if she and her companions aren't back to Keld soon, the village might send out a reconnaissance party."

I must have shewn a strong reaction to this remark, for Nelson laughed, clapped me heavily upon the back, and said, "Richard, over the past year or two this lass has figured all too often in your remarks, circumferential though they have been. There has been no need for you to spell it out for me in posies. What is more, only a man both deaf and sightless could have missed the way you mooned over the girl when she got here today; I have seen subtler swooning upon the comic stage. In fact, between you and the doctor, one might have supposed the lot of us were putting on the second act of love's labours! Ha ha!"

I felt myself colour at this description; until then I had thought my behaviour reasonably decorous, and certainly not that of some lovestruck fool in a play. Knowing, however, my uncle's penchant to tease me with exaggerated accounts of myself, I took his words with a grain of salt. At the same time I hastened my steps towards the *Mean Fish*, for Nelson was at least correct about the delegation having long exceeded their expected stay.

I found Thistle and her companions seated again under the sun-shade, enjoying an early tea. Silently blessing my uncle for thus contriving to keep the ladies onboard for a while longer, I strode right up to the tea table, thanked the delegation for the grace and beauty they had brought to the day's proceedings, and then without wasting one further second upon shallow niceties, asked Miss Ashwood if she would care to take a turn about the fells with me before going home.

Immediately my heart fell, for clearly my invitation caused her discomfort. For the first time I witnessed Thistle's composure waver,

but only for a fleeting moment, teacup paused halfway to her lips and brows knitted with sudden uncertainty. Then she resumed a gracious expression, took a sip of tea, placed the cup into its saucer, and said, "My goodness, M'lord, you surprise and honour me very much. I do love a turn about the fells, and a good thing too, given my family's business. I shall take you up on your kind suggestion, but I must request that Miss Cartwright and Miss Smith accompany us, as it would be only proper to include them."

My heart fell further. Thistle was all too right; given that there was no prior understanding between any of the ladies and myself it would have seemed ungallant on my part to have gone walking with one of them whilst leaving the other two with tea. And yet every particle of my being longed to speak with her alone. As viscount I could have dictated any arrangement I saw fit, of course; it would have been my right to command Thistle to walk with me by herself, but my family have never abused our privileges in such an uncouth way, and I was not about to break with our noble tradition. Also, there was her reputation to consider; heaven knows that these are all too easily besmirched, often in a manner patently unfair to a maiden, and once that white garment is soiled there is no cleansing it.

So I executed a bow. "Miss Ashwood, you are absolutely correct, and I apologize most earnestly to all three of you for being such a lout. My pleasure would, of course, be tripled were this entire charming delegation to trod the grass with me."

Moments later, the four of us had quit the ship and struck out uphill. We quite naturally fell into two pairs, with Thistle and myself in front, and the other two ladies a bit behind—it could hardly have been lost on any of them where my interest lay, and I was pleased to see that Miss Smith and Miss Cartwright did not appear stung by the slight. As we reached the line of stakes which the builders had emplaced across the hillside, outlining a section of so-called turn-

pike which never shall be excavated, we paused and looked back the way we had come.

It may sound strange, but since the *Mean Fish* had been completed, I had never once ventured this short distance up the hillside to take in a view of her and Stonesthrow Hall. There had been too much else pressing for my attention. So the gasp of admiration which escaped my lips at the sight was entirely spontaneous.

My glorious tall ship lay below us, Union Jack fluttering proudly from her mainmast, sunlight glinting from intersecting patterns of ripples which refracted across her flagstone-lined pool. Just beyond, Stonesthrow threw her aged wings wide, embracing the ship and looking rather like an elaborate stage-setting which had been created for it. The outbuildings were visible from that spot as well, including the cottages where Whitehand and Converse formerly dwelt, and the stables. Add to all that the emerald slopes of Swaledale (much of the land visible from that vantage belonging to my family) and also, off to the right, the uppermost end of our magnificent excavated 'turn-pike' which now extends all the way to Richmond—this view encapsulated the entirety of my life in a way which quite literally took my breath away.

It was in such a state of mind that I looked to the captivating lady next me, and saw on her face—in marveling eyes and gently parted lips, in rise and fall of breath which seemed quickened by more than the mere exertion of our walk—there I saw a perfect mirror of my own admiration for this place and the things which human hands have wrought here. The conviction blossomed within me that having this woman by my side would wholly complete the perfection of all that we surveyed, and furthermore that she would without any doubt be the most marvelous, kind, and capable mistress which the denizens of the hall and these lands could wish for, were Mary Ashwood called by the name Mary Jacob.

This ecstatic hope, I would still swear, resounded only within my mind in that blissful instant. However, to my great regret, a good deal of it must have inadvertently escaped my lips in the form of audible words—the import of which was, of course, entirely inappropriate to the moment, and which the lady was utterly unprepared for, given the tenuous nature of our acquaintance.

Not understanding at first that I had actually vocalized any of the feelings which buoyed my heart, I was puzzled when the look of wonder on Thistle's lovely face vanished, replaced by blank shock. I simultaneously heard gasps from her companions, but attributed these to the effects of the view.

Only when Thistle faced me, her eyes averted to some patch of grass near my left foot, her voice trembling, did I begin to grasp the extent of the catastrophe, as she said, "M'lord, unless I have misunderstood you completely, I must beg you to remember to whom you speak, and … and to consider the injustice of such a jest, given our circumstances. I … I would certainly have thought better of you, m'lord, than to toy thus with the heart of a simple shepherdess. Especially when I could certainly never … Oh!"

With a cry of dismay Thistle took off downhill, making a beeline for the clustered cottages of Keld.

After a moments' pause—during which Miss Cartwright and Miss Smith regarded me with the astonishment one might accord some fantastical creature freshly arrived from Mars—they followed their fellow delegate.

Without turning her head, Mary Ashwood called back to me, her words now so choked with emotion that they were difficult to apprehend: "On behalf of the village of Keld, my companions and I thank Your Lordship profusely for your gracious hospitality and your tea, and we wish Your Lordship a most splendid evening and the very best health!"

Thus did I unconsciously let fly the bolt before taking proper aim, and the consequence of this ridiculous blunder, this humiliation, this effective ruin of my fondest hopes, plunged me into a black despair the likes of which I would never wish upon any fellow human being.

Never mind keeping the ship's log; for days afterwards 'twas a burden to breathe.

(Thursday, June 4, 1795)

I have little to say about the two days which followed this inauspicious event. What pittance I ate, I took in my cabin, where I stayed sequestered, seeing no one, curtains drawn against the hateful brightness of day and the empty darkness of night, each of which vexed me in its own cruel manner. That baneful scene played over and over in my memory.

How incomparably lovely she had been in the sunlight, even as her voice had quavered with indignation at my *faux pas*. How very proper and well-chosen her words, even in a state of surprise and agitation. And how fraught with uncertain meaning that phrase, begun but never finished, as she was overcome with emotion: "Especially when I could certainly never ..." Ye Gods, of all points at which to have broken off her speech! Certainly never could what? Never could return my admiration? Never could thrive as the lady of an estate? Never could aspire to marry a viscount, whatever his feelings might be? That interrupted phrase tortured me.

During this time, Nelson did his duty as both my uncle and my first officer, by stepping into the void of command I had left. I did not ask him to do so, nor did I expect that it would be necessary for me to ask—this was, unfortunately, not the first occasion on which melancholia has driven me to isolate myself in this way, and so he was prepared for the possibility. He performed my various captainly duties, including the chairing of our officers' meetings. My good uncle also saw to it that the only knocks upon my door for the first two days were those announcing that a meal had been left for me upon a tray in the corridor; no other business of any kind was allowed to impinge upon my solitude.

That changed on the third day when a peculiar style of knock, coming between meal-times, caused me to realize that my uncle stood without and wished to speak. I went to the door and signified with a word that I was listening.

"Nephew," said Nelson through the door, "there is one order of business today in which you may wish to participate. Mustardhead's unceasing lamentations have set the crew on edge, to the point that a general strike has been discussed. Bigg does not believe that such a radical action would have sufficient votes to go into effect, but the very fact it was brought up shews that we have all had more than enough of that waif sitting in our brig moaning like a lost soul from Dante's Inferno, and so the officers have ruled that Mustardhead shall walk the plank today, at three bells. I thought that you would wish to know."

With that, my uncle left me again alone.

I approved of this decision, and did not resent not having been party to it; on the contrary, I was glad to have been relieved of such concerns. But, Nelson was right to have informed me when he did. In my misery I had all but forgotten about the plank, and the prospect of seeing its lovely surfaces again buoyed my spirits in a way I would have thought impossible five minutes before.

At that point four hours remained until the ceremony. With a break for my noon meal, it took me nearly that long to properly compose myself. I had not bathed or groomed for nearly three days, and in particular my eyebrows were in desperate need of plucking.

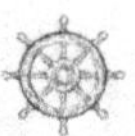

At half past two, I took a deep breath, ascended the gangway to the strategy room, and by that route emerged onto the main deck. Several sailors were there, going about their duties—swabbing the deck, tying knots into a long rigging rope, recording readings from a wind-gauge and a portable barometer. None of them shewed any particular interest in their captain's reapperance above-decks after two days' absence, which came as a relief to me. I was not in the frame of mind to entertain questions from anyone about my frame of mind.

I wondered what story Nelson had concocted in order to explain my truancy. It seemed likely that he had simply told everyone that the captain was feeling unwell, which would have been true enough. (I later learnt that my uncle had indeed given this reason to the officers, but had not seen fit to explain my absence to the crew at all, and to his knowledge none of them had enquired about it.)

As for the scene which had brought on my bout with wretchedness, it had taken place far enough from the ship for me to hope that its embarrassing particulars had not been witnessed. Over the next few days, I gradually determined that this did in fact seem to be the case. Only my uncle had divined the reason for my despondency, and he had been good enough to speak with no one else about it, a shew of tact for which I shall be forever grateful.

Pleased that my resurrection caused no stir, I next made for the hold in order to feast my senses on the captivating plank. There I found a small group of sailors, headed by Bridger, starting the process of moving it into place. Three sailors carried the plank—more beauteous even than I had remembered it—to the main hatch, where it was slid into waiting coils of rope and heaved upwards to the main deck. How its deep lustre glowed as it emerged into daylight; how its gold-leaf ornamentation sparkled in the sun! Never had my eyes beheld a more desirable object. A sense of injustice stirred anew

within my breast, at the prospect of Mustardhead setting foot on this plank fit for an Alexander.

The sailors carried the plank to a spot near the poop, carefully laid it down at a right angle to the ship's main axis, and slid it beneath a pair of iron braces which had been bolted onto the main deck. Simultaneously, one sailor opened an adjacent section of starboard railing which had been turned into a swivel gate. As the plank gradually passed through the braces, its far end reaching out over the water, I enjoined the sailors to take great care, lest the harsh iron mar its exquisite surface. Thankfully no such mishap occurred, and soon the plank was fully deployed—ten feet extended clear of the ship, the remaining five feet held firmly against the braces by the beam's own weight.

By this time a crowd of sailors had assembled upon the forecastle and main deck, as fifteen minutes remained until the entertainment was to ensue. I joined Bridger and Nelson at the corner of the poop, from which we officers could enjoy an excellent view of the proceedings. Lampson politely enquired after my health as he joined us a few minutes later; he was followed by Converse, who muttered something scolding about a gentleman who fails to consult his physician when ill, but aside from these two, none of the officers remarked upon my reappearance.

During the next ten minutes or so, as more and more of the crew gathered, a festival atmosphere suffused the decks of the *Mean Fish*. The sailors' spirits appeared as high as ever I had seen them; their chatter and laughter brought to mind nothing so much as a congenial race crowd at the St. Leger Stakes (albeit without the formal dress and ladies with parasols). One enterprising fellow even contrived to make money from the event, going about through the crowd selling effigies crudely carved from sticks, with a shock of yellow dyed wool glued on as hair. His asking price for these satirical moppets was a

farthing, but when he tossed one up to me at my request, I rewarded his artistry and pluck with a full penny.

At last there came a stir around the gangway leading down to the crew quarters. The chief actor in the day's drama was brought up from below, and a sarcastic sort of cheer went up from the crowd.

Mustardhead cringed visibly as he emerged into sunlight for the first time in over a week. He threw both arms high to shield his face and wailed something—so I interpreted it—about the sky being too large. Led by our stout gaoler Selfridge, whose formidable person cleft the crowd like Moses parting the Red Sea, the boy crossed the deck to the braced end of the plank.

After letting fly a few desultory mockeries in Mustardhead's direction, the crew fell silent and their dozens of expectant faces turned to me.

It is a dear hope of mine that, at some point during my illustrious captaincy, when this entire crew is assembled and looking to me for an articulate and edifying speech, I shall find myself able to oblige. On every occasion some disagreeable development has prevented me. In this case part of the difficulty lay in my lack of preparedness; during the busy days leading up to the archdeacon's visit, and in the pit of despair I had inhabited since, it had simply not occurred to me that I would be called upon to say anything on this occasion.

However, there was also a greater difficulty. Even if the world's most splendid walk-the-plank speech had been writ by God himself, and the heavenly scroll held before my eyes by hovering angels, I would have been unable to read it aloud in that moment, due to an overpowering sensation of dismay. For days, the mere thought of this uncouth Birmingham street urchin setting foot on the wonderous plank had vexed my imagination; seeing the outrage about to unfold was altogether too much for me.

So instead of speaking, I sprang into action, rushing down the gangway to the main deck, elbowing sailors aside. I shoved Mustardhead away just as he raised a foot to take the fateful step; he sprawled off-balance onto the deck with a pathetic yelp.

I stepped onto the plank. Moses himself could have felt no greater satisfaction with his first stride into the Holy Land, after forty years of dull milling about in the wilderness of Sinai.

Only then did I find my voice, and I issued two ringing commands: first, I declared Mustardhead pardoned for his accidental crime and appointed as our cabin boy; second, I ordered that the plank be moved to my cabin immediately, there to be made a permanent fixture.

Twenty minutes later, my living quarters aboard the *Mean Fish* had been enhanced beyond measure, by a stupefyingly beautiful fifteen-foot plank bolted onto the floor, which I was now able to enjoy without fear of its being sullied by unworthy feet. And whilst my excursion above-decks had gone well enough, I was not yet ready to entirely quit the mourning period for my shipwrecked love, and therefore remained the rest of the day cloistered with my prize, walking the plank at my leisure.

(Friday, June 5, 1795)

The next day I also spent mostly in my cabin. I walked the plank whilst reading. I walked the plank smoking my pipe. I walked the plank looking over Lampson's notes from officers' meetings. I found that there was no conceivable upright activity, which was not greatly enhanced when upon the plank in one's stocking feet, and its salutary presence helped to dispel my gloom, albeit gradually.

Also soothing was the news I gleaned from Lampson's notes, and a brief epistle from Nelson. From the former I learnt that excellent progress had been made preparing the sails and rigging,

and that our cannons were finally en route and expected to arrive soon. The latter contained an encouraging account of my uncle's latest clandestine meeting with Miss Smeaton, conducted of necessity without my presence—work on our project had advanced so much faster than forecast that a ready-date in August might be possible, given expected stream flow conditions. Many of the so-called toll gates were in place, and the 'bridge' begun over the Swale below Richmond for our 'turn-pike' had so hornswoggled the townsfolk there, that a blacksmith shop was being relocated to its eastern approach in anticipation of heavy trade.

I had one meeting worthy of note, occurring midmorning, when my first and second mates called to consult upon an urgent matter. Nelson and Bridger took my two most comfortable chairs whilst I remained standing upon the plank. Throughout the interview my uncle seemingly took no notice of the kingly board beneath my feet, whilst in contrast Bridger appeared unable to take his eyes off of it.

"It's this cabin boy business, Richard," Nelson began. "Whilst I've no doubt that your decision to appoint Mustardhead our cabin boy was preceded by a good deal of careful thought on the matter" —and here he gave me a look to shew that his belief was in fact quite the opposite— "even you, in your considerable wisdom, seem to have overlooked the fact that we already have one."

"One what?"

"A cabin boy."

"No, we do not."

"Yes, we do."

"We certainly do not! I'd put a guinea on it."

"Then you'd lose a guinea, Richard. We have a cabin boy and his name is Jimmy Fish."

This struck me as such an obvious jest that I laughed aloud. When my uncle's face remained entirely impassive I said, "But you cannot be serious! I have never seen such a name on the ships' roster; I should remember it."

"His name is not on the crew roster. As cabin boy he is considered a petty officer."

"Then why have I not seen him at officers' meetings?"

Nelson mimed a mute appeal to the heavens for help, before replying, "God's blood, Richard, the cabin boy does not attend them. He works closely with Mr. Bridger and myself on daily nuts-and-bolts aspects of running the ship, which you have repeatedly insinuated are beneath your notice. Your first and second officers assure you that this fellow exists; will you contradict us? Did you require William Herschel to drop by Stonesthrow Hall and personally vouch for the existence of Uranus, a planet none of us have ever seen?"

This comparison did not seem at all apt, but before I could quite work out the problem with it, Bridger spoke up. I inferred from his words that they were directed at me, even though an observer might have thought him speaking to the plank, so fixed was his gaze upon it. "Cap'n," said he, "I vouch fer Mr. Fish as the best English cabin boy outside of His Majesty's Navy; that's how come I brung him aboard. We can ill afford to lose sech a gem, specially if he's to be replaced by a muttonhead wot's afraid of his own shadow. Mr. Fish brings over fifty years' experience; this snot-nosed Mustardhead don't know his arse from an anchor-chain."

I stomped upon the plank. "Wait one moment! Fish has *how* much experience as a cabin boy?"

"Fifty year, if a day."

"Good God, man, just how old *is* this fellow?"

Bridger managed to look away from the plank, tilting his head as if in thought and doing a bit of maths under his breath. Then he resumed staring at the plank and said, "Sixty-four, as I reckon it, though he might tell you a bit diff'nt."

Suddenly I knew of whom they spoke. There was only one person on board who might be even close to such an advanced age. "Ah! This fellow Fish must be the notably decrepit old sailor whom I directed the other day to look after the young ladies from Keld."

"That is he," said Nelson.

"Very well, then," said I, feeling less at a loss and beginning to pace along the plank. "And how is it that this venerable and expert man of the sea remains a mere cabin boy in spite of his knowledge and prowess? Should he not be in the Admiralty by this time? A good many of those worthies began their careers as cabin boys, did they not?"

"Indeed they did," said Nelson, "but in the navy, not on civilian ships, and most of them were of noble birth besides. This fellow of humble origin has made a career of it, as some cabin boys do, and the result is an assistant of great skill. Half the time he knows what we need before we even ask for it, isn't that right, Mr. Bridger?"

Bridger nodded his agreement with this description, although to me it sounded like a confoundedly irritating quality in an underling, rather than one worthy of praise.

"So," said I, "we shall have two cabin boys. Surely that old codger Fish could use a hand, or would welcome an apprentice."

For the first time during this interview, Bridger looked me full in the face, and with such an expression of horror that one might have supposed me a judge committing his family to some terrible doom. "*Two* cabin boys? No, sir, it ain't seemly, it ain't done. Jimmy Fish specially, he'd never stoop to sech an arrangement, he'd jump right off this ship."

"Fine, then perhaps we could promote Mr. Fish? To ... shall we say ... boatswain?"

Bridger glowered at me in a rather unnerving manner, and seemed to chew the very words coming out of his mouth as he said, "Beggin' yer *pardon*, cap'n, but I be the boatswain on this here ship. That's how come I play sech sweet tunes on my bosun-pipe ever' day. If my services ain't adequate, I can easily take 'em elsewhere!"

"Now look here, Mr. Bridger," my uncle intervened, "I'm sure that won't be remotely necessary. We're beyond pleased with your services and those of Mr. Fish. If the captain is a bit muddled about who carries out which duties, I take full responsibility for it, as I have shielded my nephew overmuch from certain aspects of his role."

Bridger gave my uncle a slight but unmistakable bow and said, "I'll give ye that, Mr. Nelson, and I appreciate yer being candid and responsible. I too aim fer candid and responsible, so I must insist that Jimmy Fish remain our sole cabin boy and this Mustardhead feller not be considered even fer an apprenticeship. Near as anyone can tell, the boy don't read, nor cipher. 'Tis not a job for the likes of him. If you've a mind, fer some strange reason, to keep the poor bugger aboard, we can find work fer him, make no mistake about that —but I'll not have him cabin boy, not fer all the gold in El Dorado."

Seeing as how I had rather less gold than that at my disposal, and given Bridger's very earnest opinions on the matter, it was soon settled, Mustardhead was to begin a career with us as the very lowest sort of sailor, which is to say a kind of drudge, and the ancient cabin boy would continue in his indispensable capacity, whatever exactly that consists of.

In the wake of my officers' departure I found myself reflecting upon exactly why I had abruptly chosen to keep Mustardhead aboard the *Mean Fish*, in spite of his obvious lack of any professional qualifications or endearing qualities. I found that the answer lay in Whitehand's words on the day after the boy appeared. Christ's admonition that believers should care for the poor and the outcast, and His proclivity for ministering to such unfortunates Himself, is surely amongst the noblest teachings of our faith. That is the kind

of Christian behaviour which I as a leader of men should like to demonstrate, by way of example, to those around me, as opposed to self-aggrandizing shews of empty piety which benefit no one. Hopefully, as our vicar suggests, Mustardhead's lot in life may be improved by altruistic attentions. Certainly he seems, as they say, to have no-where to go, save up.

(Wednesday, June 10, 1795)

One of the most auspicious things I learnt during the period of my recovery, aside from the excellent progress being made on our ostensible turn-pike, was the way in which day-to-day business aboard the *Mean Fish* had settled into a stable routine. Now that we had officers, and our crew, now that our stores were aboard, our stowaways properly dealt with, and the great occasion of the archdeacon's visit behind us, many days brought few, if any, events worthy of noting in my log. Even if I had consistently kept it during the recuperative weeks following my loss, there would have been many very short entries.

Hence the jump in this retrospective portion of my log, from June 5 to June 10. There was simply little to report from those days, except for my gradual return towards full captainly duties, spending less time in my cabin and more about the ship. During this time I also resumed chairing officers' meetings.

On the day noted above, an event occurred which I do wish to record. I sat at a reading table in the library consulting a Royal Navy pamphlet of bosun-pipe signals, in order to better understand the whistling language with which Bridger directs the crew. Wheelwright had earlier stopped by to regale me with one of his tales, cheerfully relating how the Caliph of Istanbul once issued a fatwah against him (which presumably still stands), enjoining all devout Mohammedans to hasten Wheelwright's death, this as the result of a regrettable

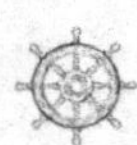

bookbinding accident. Then our librarian had left me to keep an appointment in the pub, and I was alone in the library.

The pamphlet necessarily used words to describe the various calls, making it a challenge to connect what I was reading with what I had heard from the pipe; doing so required a good deal of concentration. Thus I remained unaware that anyone else had entered the library, until a sudden sound close at hand nearly sent me toppling from the stool on which I perched. There stood Dr. Converse, at a shelf not five steps away, calmly leafing through a Latin medical text, one of several such tomes which he has petitioned be kept in the sick bay, but which I see fit to leave in the library, where they are less likely to be bled (or vomited) upon.

In response to my abrupt movement, or perhaps a sound of surprise which I might have uttered, Converse gave me an odd sideways look without moving his head, then resumed his reading. In anyone else, such a disrespectful lack of notice would have been infuriating. My long acquaintance with this learned man and his eccentric ways allows me to overlook such behaviour as acceptably foreign, or perhaps acceptably Catholic, if not exactly pleasing.

"Why, greetings, Doctor," said I, "I must own that you have given me a bit of a shock just now. Quite the stealthy physician, as always. Ha ha! I daresay you could sneak up on your own shadow!" When the doctor failed to shew mirth or any other reaction to this worthy jest, I went on, "If I may ask, what marvelous aspect of human physiology engages your scholarly attention this fine day?"

"Pus," said Dr. Converse, without looking up from the book.

"Ah, pus," said I. "Heaven knows we could hardly live without it! At least, I expect it must be rather important or else we shouldn't have any. Hmm."

There the conversation seemed poised to naturally expire, but as often occurs when confronted by the doctor's aloof mood, I felt

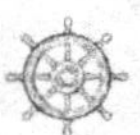

compelled to draw him out a bit. And on this occasion, I struck upon an especially intriguing topic with which to bait him.

"I say— I don't know about you, Doctor, but I found the archdeacon's visit the other day to be a rousing success! We all of us acquitted ourselves well, and our guests appeared greatly impressed by all we had to shew them. Wouldn't you agree?"

Still not looking up, Converse gave a characteristically teutonic sort of terse shrug and muttered something which could have been, "*Ja, es war gut.*"

"And as for our visitors—well! I would have to say that none of us were prepared for the advent of Miss Fenny Dayton of Bloomsbury! What an uncommonly striking young lady! 'Twould be quite impossible to hold a croquet match with her nearby; the shots would all veer in her direction from sheer force of allure!"

This panegyric seized the doctor's attention. Looking first over the top of his book, then aside at me with a quizzical expression he said, "Herr Lordship, I am sure that you are not forgetting, the lady under question is betrothed to an earl of royal appointment. Which makes her not a proper topic of lurid *gespräch* between those of us who are not the earl."

I felt positively gleeful to have gotten so much English verbiage out of Converse—about a week's worth under normal conditions. I was about to see if he could be goaded further, by a protestation that there was nothing *lurid* about my praise, when without warning the doctor's gaze shifted over my shoulder and his face melted at once into a perfect mask of horrified awe.

Reflexively, I looked behind me, half expecting to find some heinous ghoul hovering over my person. But I saw nothing which might explain the doctor's terrified expression. Before I could demand that he explain himself, he blurted out, in the most emotive voice ever I had heard him use: "*Groß gott! Die schwarzenbücher!*"

I looked over my shoulder again, and realized that Converse had caught sight of Wheelwright's mysterious books, their spines forming an ominous rectangle of ebony on one of the shelves behind me.

When I turned back to Converse, I caught only a glimpse of him, walking rapidly out the library door, tome on pus tucked beneath one arm. He has still not returned it to the library as of this writing. By which I mean the tome, not his arm.

Although on this occasion I experienced no strange sensation related to the books, the doctor's reaction had made a very strong impression upon me, and I found myself unwilling to remain alone in the library with them. I resumed my study of bosun-pipe signals in my own cabin.

Thus far I have not screwed up the courage to seek further enlightenment about the books from either Wheelwright or Converse. I find my curiosity countered by an irrational sense that knowing little about these books and their contents may not be a regrettable thing—indeed, that it may be positively salutary.

(Thursday, June 11, 1795)

For this uneventful day, I chuse for the first time to create a log entry describing it as such. Nothing of note occurred on this day!

(Friday, June 12, 1795)

Idem.

(Saturday, June 13, 1795)

My uncle, whose knowledge of things nautical I naturally respect, informs me that most ships' logs consist largely of notes upon the topics of navigation, weather, and crew discipline, and that my log,

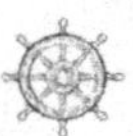

having little to nothing to say upon these subjects, might better be termed a diary than a log. If considered a log, he regards it as possibly the strangest such document ever produced in the history of ship captaincy. So he said upon a recent occasion, when I shewed him a portion of my log and requested his opinion of its quality.

Although I welcome such criticisms, I assert that they are unfair. The unique geographical situation of the *Mean Fish* means that, as yet, questions of weather and navigation affect us little, and Bridger handles the crew so deftly that I should spoil the soup by meddling. Also, any future readers shall doubtless find more of interest in my various adventures attending to our project, than in whether it rained upon such-and-such a day, or if sailors A and B were punished for engaging in fisticuffs over a dice game. I aim to record matters of import.

That said, an event occurred in the early morning hours of this day which, whilst somewhat embarrassing to relate, must rank amongst the most dramatic to yet take place aboard the *Mean Fish*. Though it involves neither navigation, nor weather, nor crew discipline, I deem it worthy of my log.

It must have been about two hours past midnight when I felt the need to use my personal lavatory. Having done so, I would normally, of course, have proceeded straight back to bed. In this particular instance; however, owing perhaps to the lateness of the hour, the utter darkness of the lavatory, and the comfort of the padded privy seat, I fell back into a state of slumber.

I am certain of having gone completely to sleep in the lavatory, due to my experience of a remarkable dream, vividly recalled even now, in which my lovely ship sailed over the downs of north Yorkshire. Up she went over the fells, down into the dales, a fresh southwest gale filling her purple sails and her prow cutting smoothly through the sea of grass and moor, as if it were water.

I stood at the wheel guiding my *Mean Fish* on this incredible voyage. On my right stood Nelson, hand upon my shoulder, nodding as he remarked that this had been our plan all along and look how magnificently it now unfolded. Standing on my left, Bridger expressed apprehension each time we bottomed out in a valley that the next towering swell of limestone was sure to not only swamp our vessel, but also crush her. I was very careful to steer straight up the ridgelines, however, so that we never ran the slopes obliquely nor turned broadsides to one, and all remained well. Our destination, I knew somehow, was Newcastle, where we would slip into the River Tyne, and thence out to sea.

In the midst of this euphoric journey, a sight caught my eye which sent a dagger into my very heart. Out on the downs I beheld Thistle, clad in her shepherdess' garb but with the floral garland she had worn, upon that fateful day which encompassed both the alpha and omega of our courtship. She stood amidst a flock of sheep, about a mile distant from our course, and as she caught sight of my ship sailing by I observed her hands go to her hips, and her face turn aside, in clear gestures of disdain.

How desperately I wished to join her! Preferably on board the *Mean Fish*, of course, but if she would have it so, out on the dales where her family flocks roamed. I felt an urge to relinquish command, dive overboard into the grass, and rush to her side, never once looking back. For I knew that where we were bound, there she was not, and never would be though ages might pass, and whilst such a wine at first brushed the palate with a sad sweetness, owing to the words and feelings which had passed between us, its aftertaste was a loss irredeemably bitter and sure to linger always.

At that moment in my dream, the ship's wheel unaccountably pressed itself against my body, surprisingly heavy and strangely

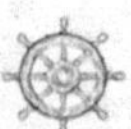

warm, as if a thing alive; a moment later it sprang away from me with a cry of surprise.

Instantly I snapped awake, for my brain gave me to understand that this weird event was not a figment of my dream, but something which had happened to my body in the waking world. Someone had sat upon me whilst I slept on the privy!

I shot to my feet, even as I heard a noise, as of someone stumbling heavily into the far wall, but in the stygian darkness of that room, which has no window, I could see nothing.

Sensing danger, I groped upon the adjacent shelf for some implement with which to defend myself, seizing a toothbrush, which I brandished in the general direction of a groan heard from the darkness. Though not ordinarily deployed as a weapon, the toothbrush could have at least poked an intruder in the eye, had it been directed properly.

All of this took place, I believe, within a mere moment of my having been sat upon, and thus my assailant had little time to react before I shouted, my voice ringing with shock and indignation, "Prepare to die! Shew yourself, knave, should you possess the courage!"

In retrospect, this was not the most reasonable demand, as it was rather too dark in the room for anyone to have obliged me, courage or no.

"Richard, it is I," came a voice from the void. "I say, you have frightened me half to death!"

In my fury I failed to recognize the voice, and countered, "Only half? Well, I stand poised to take thee the rest of the way, varlet!"

"For heaven's sake, calm yourself, and leave off chattering like the oafish hero from some asinine drama! It is I, Nelson!"

"What!"

"It is your uncle! Whom did you expect to meet in the ship's lavatory, an assassin from darkest Persia?"

"Well, and what do you mean by sitting upon me like that?"

"I mean nothing by it! I was rather drowsy and you were ruminating here in the dark. Asleep, I daresay, if you failed to mark my approach."

"Asleep! I hardly think so! But that is beside the point! How is it that you feel at liberty to enter this room, which is meant for the captain's exclusive use?"

After a moments' pause, my uncle said, in a more measured voice, "I do hope you'll excuse me, but I believe that we have hit upon a misunderstanding. It has not been my belief that this lavatory *is* for your exclusive use."

"Indeed! And how do you figure that, when it is connected to the captain's cabin?"

"The connecting door from *my* cabin, that is how!"

"What!"

I heard a few shuffling footsteps, followed by a creaking noise, and then to my astonishment a section of the lavatory wall swung away, revealing my uncle's cabin beyond, dimly lit by a guttering candle.

"How … how came that door to be there?"

"We put it there when we designed the *Mean Fish*, Nephew. I shall allow that our plans were laid many years ago, but really, this causes me to wonder what else the captain may have forgotten about his ship!"

"But how is it that our paths have not crossed here before? Why have I not found your toiletries intermixed with mine?"

Nelson, half-silhouetted in the doorway, gave a great heaving sigh which I both saw and heard. "Richard, my few implements of personal hygiene would be hopelessly swamped by your own, as you keep more such gee-gaws than your mother did. Mine are in a shaving kit in my cabin. As for why our paths have not crossed here before, I was until recently spending much of my time in the Hall, as you well know. Aside from that, I suppose it is only dumb luck which

prevented us from meeting thusly days ago. Although it still might not have happened tonight, had you not fallen asleep on the privy."

"I was never asleep just now! The very idea is absurd!" When Nelson gave no response, I went on, "I must say that had any other officer sat upon my person in the dark, disciplinary action would result, and that surprising door beside you would be nailed shut before they could say Jack Robinson! But, as it is you, and as I suppose that we must have agreed upon that door, or else it would not now exist—for those reasons I shall think upon the question of your using this lavatory, and I shall give you my decision in the morning."

My uncle gave a bow which, even in the dim light, I saw to be sarcastically exaggerated. "How very magnanimous of you, Nephew. I humbly await your judgment. And now, since my cabin, like yours, lacks a commode or chamber pot, I shall sally forth to the main deck, there to take aim at the fishes, as some say in His Majesty's Navy." He turned to go, then paused. "Oh, and Nephew ..."

"What?"

"Do pull up your pants."

I saw that we had indeed carried out this conversation whilst my night breeches lay about my ankles. Doubly thankful that the intruder had been my uncle, I restored my attire and returned to my cabin.

After a modicum of reflection, I decided that Nelson shall be allowed to share my lavatory, on the conditions that he never enter without a prior knock, and perhaps a hullo as well, and that he not allow his toiletries to mix with my own—little to ask, I think, in return for the privilege.

(Sunday, June 14, 1795)

Nothing to record for this day, save that I attended Sabbath service for the first time since my plunge into melancholy. I found the music, the sense of fellowship, and even Whitehand's gloomy sermon (upon the topic of Saul's treachery to David) surprisingly uplifting.

(Monday, June 15, 1795)

Jolly well nothing to report for this day.

(Tuesday, June 16, 1795)

The officers' meeting which took place on this day is of note, due to the timing and manner of Bridger's arrival. Whilst he is normally so punctual that one could set one's watch by his comings and goings, on this particular morning he was not only three minutes late—enough that it crossed my mind in half-jest to dispatch a search party—but he also arrived in a state of agitation so great that his usual sense of officerly decorum was entirely overcome. Rather than excusing himself for his tardiness and taking his seat, he stormed straight up to me and said, "It's too bloody much, Cap'n! Ferget the plank, I'll heave the bugger over the railings meself! Something's got to be done!"

I had been speaking to my officers about our upcoming dinner menus, and so was utterly unprepared for such a violent turn in the conversation, and could only manage to reply, "Where in heaven's name have you been, Bridger?"

"In folly-land, floggin' a dead bloody horse, that's where! That bloody fool Mustardhead don't hardly have sense enough to breathe wi'out bein' reminded, and as fer trainin' him up to any useful task, I'd just as soon teach a hipper-potamus to fly!"

"I see. Please do take your seat, Mr. Bridger, and since this seems to be a matter of such grave importance, I suppose that we may set aside for a moment the question of our menus. Thank you. Now, I take it that our newest sailor is presenting difficulties?"

"Difficult ain't the word! Impossible more like it! Beggin' yer pardon, Cap'n, but since you saw fit to employ this dunderhead, you've had no dealin's with him whatever. Sir, it's like takin' a viper fer a pet then never attendin' to the nasty beast yerself. Would you treat yer people in Stonesthrow that way? I think not. Yet me and some of England's doughtiest sailors are bein' asked to babysit a snot-nosed idiot from Birmingham!"

"Surely he can't be *so* hopeless! You've started him off too fast, I'll wager, with knots and constellations and whatnot. Shouldn't he be, say, swabbing the decks for a while?"

"Indeed he should, Cap'n, but the oaf can't even manage that! He trips over the mop, then gets his foot wedged in the bucket, then trips over the mop again, then starts mopping the fo'c'stle door, then claims he's forgotten altogether what he's meant to be doing. All that before swabbin' a space big enough to dance a jig on. Froth an' damnation! *This* boy learn knots and constellations? Next you'll expect your second mate to command the weather!"

This was troubling to hear, as I had retained Mustardhead on board with the reasonable expectation that he would be able to make himself useful, if only in some small manner. Seeing my steadfast second officer thus discomfited, I announced my determination to take on Mustardhead's education myself, finishing with the remark, "Perhaps we are barking up the wrong tree, Bridger. If the boy is so physically inept, it may be that intellectual pursuits are his arena."

"Huh!" Huffed Bridger. "It may also be that the Earth is a giant goddamned sweet-biscuit!"

"Hmmm, well, such theories aside, I shall see if we can get him going in letters and maths; perhaps confidence thusly gained may enable him to better help with chores. Mustardhead shall begin in my tutelage tomorrow."

Bridger seemed highly dubious about this plan, but also pleased with my intention to instruct Mustardhead myself; his spirits seemed much improved for the remainder of the meeting. As for myself—I had made the assumption that Bridger, through a combination of frustration and his natural contempt for non-sailors, must have exaggerated the boy's uselessness and therefore a fresh, patient approach was sure to produce improvement. It has taken the clarity of hindsight to shew me how wrong I was.

However, I shall not get ahead of myself; my conference with Mustardhead did not occur until the 17th, and there was another significant development on the 16th.

At just after two bells in the afternoon, as I paced upon the plank preparing for my role as tutor by perusing an elementary grammar from my own schooling days, I was informed by a sailor that Rugby stood on shore, requesting to come aboard and confer with me upon a matter of some urgency.

Rugby has handled the routine business of the hall so very adroitly, that only something exceptional could have caused him to seek me out in between our regular meetings. I was filled straightaway with foreboding that this had something to do with the Loose Stone: either a second instance of its recent odd behaviour, or perhaps yet another demolished footstool.

I ordered that Rugby be admitted on board; by the time I arrived on deck myself, he was already seated at our customary table on the forecastle. As he rose to greet me, I said, "So, my good man, what brings you aboard the *Mean Fish* on this fine day, with such a clear air of puzzlement about you?"

"Well, My Lord, it is most curious. An event we have not anticipated, and upon which I must consult Your Lordship right away, as your decision is awaited by persons of apparent respectability."

"I say, out with it, man—you have me on tenterhooks!"

"A party has arrived unannounced at the Hall … Actually, two parties I should say; they claim to have met whilst en route here, discovered that they shared in common a destination and reasons for traveling, so then went on together … and their intention is apparently to view the *Mean Fish*."

"I see. And what credentials have they presented?"

"None, My Lord, although I will allow that they are well-dressed and seem reasonably well-bred."

"But what business have they here?"

"They seem to have no *business* to speak of, My Lord. I am given to understand that each party, one from York and one from Hull, has journeyed here on a sort of pleasure trip, their objective being to view the *Mean Fish*, about which they have heard splendid things."

"Heard splendid things? From whom?"

"I am sure I don't know, My Lord."

Suddenly I recalled that strangely quiet little man on the turn-pike Commission, and the suspicions I had entertained on account of his taciturnity. "Do these appear to be county officials?"

"I wouldn't say so, My Lord. They appear to be two prosperous city tradesmen or professionals, traveling with their wives—the couple from Hull accompanied by a child, the other by an older gentleman. Both men apologized for being unable to present us with calling cards, but as they did not understand the *Mean Fish* to be upon the property of a great house, they misanticipated the nature of their visit here, and left such fineries at home."

"And you are quite sure that you have never seen any of them before? Especially the older fellow?"

"Quite, My Lord."

"Hmmm. And they wish to view the *Mean Fish*. But they could do that from the public road."

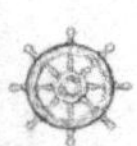

"Indeed they could, and I made that quite clear. I was told that they did in fact take in the view from the road on the way. However, they wish to beg your indulgence for a rather closer look than may be obtained from the road."

"Where are they now?"

Rugby shifted uncomfortably in his chair. "In the foyer, My Lord. I hope that their waiting there does not meet with your disapproval, but as these are none of our locals, and turned up quite unannounced, I could not feel comfortable shewing them into the new parlour— and yet I hesitated to leave them standing about in the driveway."

"Quite so, Rugby. And may I add that your manners become less Cornish and more English with each passing year. There was a time when you would have simply advised the whole lot of them, in no uncertain terms, to bugger off!"

Rugby made a sour face. "Er—quite so, My Lord."

"Hmmm. Well, I can think of no reason to deny their request, yet damned if I don't wish for more time to mull it over."

"My own feelings exactly."

"Seeing as how they've traveled all the way from York, and even Hull, with women, and a child, and an elder in tow, it seems ungracious to flat out refuse them, and the nearest possible lodging I could recommend, were I to think upon their request overnight, is clear down in Richmond. Very well, then. The terms of their visit are that it is not to exceed fifteen minutes, and they are not to be allowed onboard. Let's take them out the front and around the hall to that lawn there, off the starboard side. I shall greet them from the ship. Would you be so good as to present those conditions, and bring them round should they agree?"

Rugby rose with a slight bow. "Yes, very good, My Lord." And with that he hurried down the gangplank and back towards the

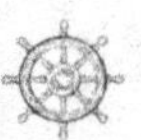

Hall—seeming relieved, as servants usually shall, to have had a logical course of action placed before him.

This development was indeed, as Rugby had said, most curious.

During the process of building the *Mean Fish*, and shortly after its completion, it had not been unusual to see gawkers from our environs pass by on the fells, taking a few minutes to admire this nautical spectacle in their midst, but the novelty of our ship in its pool seemed since then to have worn off for the locals. I had even overheard one of the ladies' delegation from Keld—Miss Cartwright, I believe—remark during her visit that how strange it was that a tall ship could have become a taken-for-granted feature of upper Swaledale, and yet she felt that this had, for the most part, come to pass. This day's visitors, however, had journeyed from some of the farther reaches of Yorkshire, apparently for the sole purpose of viewing our landlocked vessel—something which it had never occurred to me, that anyone might wish to do.

For the first time I thought to question their motives. Had they traveled so far to admire a graceful ship situated in a scenic and surprising location? Or to ridicule a mad viscount's folly? I wished that I had thought to have Rugby sound them out further before bringing them around, but by then it was too late. If our visitors' manners proved poor, I would simply have to eject them from the estate, as I was not about to have my crew subjected to a shew of disrespect.

Rugby had not been gone for five minutes before I spied movement beyond the plane trees by the east wing, and moments later our six visitors came into full view, my steward leading the way. It seemed plain at once, from the enthusiastic astonishment writ upon every face, that these two gentlemen and their families regarded my *Mean Fish* as a wonder to rival the pyramids, rather than a monstrosity to be mocked. Rugby brought them to the designated spot upon the

lawn, where they all stood for several long moments admiring the ship, their exclamations of esteem never ceasing.

At that point, Rugby pointed out my person at the railings of the forecastle and introduced me as His Lordship Viscount Keld, Captain of the *Mean Fish*. He had since our interview learnt the names of our visitors, and presented them as Mr. Tristram Williams, a barrister of the law courts in York, and Dr. John Graham, a surgeon at Hull General Hospital, along with their families.

There followed a pleasant exchange between myself and our visitors, albeit carried on with voices raised rather higher than ordinarily tactful, given the distance between us. The travelers were keen to know all kinds of things about the *Mean Fish*: by whom she had been built, why the masts were not rigged, how we provisioned ourselves, and whether we had yet sailed across the equator all being topics touched upon. That last was obviously a jest, and seeing how Dr. Graham offered it up in a smiling, lighthearted manner, as a clear absurdity given our situation, I parried it in the same jovial spirit.

Of course, the question was also brought up of why the *Mean Fish* had been built in this particular spot rather than, say, a shipyard in Newcastle or Liverpool, as is rather more ordinary for sailing vessels. It has been many years since I have heard that question frequently; back then it was put to me by neighbours in Swaledale during the early stages of the project (my officers and crew seem surprisingly incurious about this detail, so long as they are paid). To these travelers from outside the valley I gave the same response as before: I desired to have a ship close by my ancestral home, and building her beside the Hall had been, all told, rather less complicated than locating a seaside property both pleasing and available, managing to purchase it, and then moving Stonesthrow Hall along with all its contents to some location possibly difficult of access and at least a hundred miles distant.

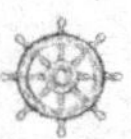

For my part, I managed to make a few inquiries, as well. Some were in the vein of polite conversation, to wit: where did your wife find that adorable hat, how fares the bright-looking lad in his studies, have you ever been called upon to amputate a limb, *et cetera*. But of course the chief nugget of knowledge I wished to pry from our visitors, if I could, was how they had come to hear of the *Mean Fish*. In this way I learnt that my ship has become a topic of conversation amongst gentlemen in at least their two home cities, although how the subject had been introduced into such circles in the first place, neither of them could say. Mr. Williams offered his additional opinion, that we would very likely see newspaper men shewing interest in the near future, if we had not already.

Just as it was time for our visitors to depart, the young lad, who had remained silent during the conversation, blurted out a question which I had certainly anticipated but which his elders may have considered too absurd (or else too tactless) to ask. The group was turning away to start back towards their carriages when the youngster's voice rang out: "But Captain, sir—will she ever *go* anywhere?"

This inquiry, too, I had heard from neighbours in the beginning, and I had laughingly told them: no, of course not. But now, with our project so very much farther advanced ... and given the look of hope, almost yearning, in the lad's eyes ... and given that he hailed from the port city of Hull, upon the Humber estuary—under such circumstances I could hardly resist shewing a card, as one might say, giving an answer undoubtedly more daring than well-advised.

Striking what I hoped would appear a cocksure pose, I gave a wink and said, "Laddie, you keep a sharp lookout on the Humber!"

In reply, the boy favoured me with a gleeful grin, and a sort of half-baked salute, as he turned to follow his parents.

May it indeed come to pass, before many more moons have waxed and waned, that this boy and his fellow citizens of Hull may

indeed behold the *Mean Fish*, purple sails unfurled, blowing a kiss towards their fair city as she makes for the open sea!

(Wednesday, June 17, 1795)

This morning I tried my hand as Mustardhead's tutor, and the result must surely rank amongst the least successful such endeavours in history.

Things began well enough, with a knock upon my cabin door at the appointed time. I found the boy standing without—looking cleaner and better-dressed than before, although retaining that atrocious bird's-nest of a hairstyle. However, the hopes elevated by my pupil's timely arrival were instantly dashed by his admission that he had been searching for my cabin for some time, down in the hold. What could have given him the impression that a captain would abide in that portion of his ship, is beyond me. Fortunately, a sailor working down there had given the boy directions, which he followed with only a couple of further detours, so that he had managed to present himself punctually through sheer chance, rather than any iota of proper planning on his part.

Mustardhead and myself took chairs on either side of my chess table, from which the board had been removed, as I deemed it premature to confuse him with the proper movements of horses, castles, queens, *et cetera*. Having heard more than once that the boy could not read, yet hoping that this might not be entirely true, I opened my old elementary grammar to a page which spelt various simple words, and invited him to read one of them.

He looked at the word blankly for a moment before saying, "Cannon."

"Ah. Well. That is actually the word 'cat', but it seems that you have correctly identified the initial character, which is the letter 'c'.

Very good. Far too many persons in this world cannot manage even so much. Now ..."

"Anchor," said Mustardhead. To my confusion, he again pointed at the word 'cat'.

"Um, no, that is 'cat', as I thought we had established." Seeing the complete lack of comprehension in his expression, I felt a sort of dread begin to creep over me as I asked, "Tell me, Mustardhead, what letter does this word 'cat' begin with?"

"W", said Mustardhead.

"All right. All right. Well, I see that we shall have to back up a bit and begin with letters. Let's see, where has that page got to? Letters, letters, letters. Ah, here we are. The letters of the alphabet. Read them off, if you can."

Mustardhead and I spent the next few minutes reviewing the alphabet of the English language, during which time it became clear to me that he not only recognized fewer than ten such symbols, he had also somewhere gained erroneous knowledge of a letter 'blee' which "looks like an upside-down x", and a letter 'double m', which "can never be written down because it is too long."

Finding written language too lofty an aim for this initial lesson, I turned to matters of basic geography, few things being more pertinent to gathering knowledge than this marvelous framework on which everything else may be hung. "So, Mustardhead," I went on, "let us discuss the world in which we live and our place in it. What is the name of the planet we live upon?"

"England," said Mustardhead.

"Er, well actually, England is a nation, of which there are many on our planet, although you and I do have the good fortune of dwelling in England, which is without question the mightiest and most enlightened of nations. Our planet is called Earth."

For the first time since my becoming acquainted with him, Mustardhead shewed signs of mirth—a crooked grin, and an odd wheezing sort of snicker. "Earth! That's the brown dirty stuff in me auntie's radish patch," he said.

"Indeed—and how very insightful of you to make that connection—but Earth is also the name of our planet. England, our nation, occupies something like three-fourths of the island of Great Britain, which is amongst the larger islands on Earth."

Mustardhead's brows knit tight and his eyes narrowed, in what appeared an Herculean effort of thought. "England is on an island," he said, slowly.

"That is correct."

"So … there's water all round us. We're surrounded by water."

"Yes! Islands are surrounded by water," I said, feeling ludicrously pleased to have had a breakthrough at last, however feeble.

My joy was shortlived, for Mustardhead began to repeat the phrase, "We're surrounded by water," over and over and over again, more loudly and rapidly each time, with a look upon his face which I may only describe as mounting panic.

"Now look here," said I, rising to my feet as the boy jumped to his, "there is nothing to be upset about! Millions of people are surrounded by water, and suffer no ill from it! As a matter of fact, we are standing on board a ship sitting in water, so that we are *doubly* surrounded by it!"

This remark was meant to shew the harmlessness of being surrounded by water, but unfortunately, it may not have been the most helpful thing to have said in that moment. As I spoke, Mustardhead fell into a frenzy of sheer terror, the likes of which I had never before witnessed. His rapidly repeated words having smeared out into an incoherent ululation of dismay, he proceeded to flail about

my cabin in a fit of aimless confusion, upsetting the chess table, my robe stand, and other expensive furnishings.

This behaviour so shocked me that several moments passed before I could muster a reaction, which was to command that this foolishness discontinue at once. When the boy failed to obey, I girded myself to fly at Mustardhead and restrain him, but before I could act he saved me the trouble, by running headlong into a bedpost, so smartly that it knocked him out cold.

I had Mustardhead removed to the sick bay. I then summoned Lampson and informed him that he was forthwith to be Mustardhead's tutor. Let the university graduate deal with this pupil; it is not, I now see, a captain's place to do so.

(Thursday, June 18, 1795)

Of note on this day at the officers' meeting, Dr. Converse informed us that Mustardhead had awakened shortly after arriving in the sick bay on the 17th and has since been doing remarkably well there. Previously, whether in the brig or in crews' quarters, he has shewn discomfort with his surroundings, and has frequently expressed this in a manner irritating to those nearby. According to Converse, however, the boy has seemed quiet and contented in the sick bay.

The doctor remains undecided as to whether this behavioural change is a result of the blow Mustardhead sustained (which has left a nasty welt on his forehead), or the sick bay's soothing ambiance. Whilst this is an intriguing question, and surely of interest to medical science (Converse contributes articles to *Zeitschrift Für Unheimlich Medizin Bayern* on occasion) I ordered that we defer, for the time being, any experiments which would involve moving the boy about and then observing his reactions. Mustardhead seems content for the first time since coming aboard, the crew are gladdened by his

absence, and so altogether this strikes me as an opportunity to let a sleeping dog lie.

Later in the day a messenger from Rugby informed me that another party of sightseers had arrived at Stonesthrow Hall for the purpose of viewing the *Mean Fish*—this time, a dozen persons from Sheffield, representing three generations of a family which owns that city's largest bank. I sent back word that they should be brought round to the lawn as we had done with our previous visitors. Then I enjoyed a brief parley with them from the ship's railings, answering many of the same questions their predecessors had asked, and found that they had gotten their information in much the same way—word of our ship has been making the round of professional circles in their city, as well.

And why, I asked myself following our visitors' departure, should such a thing be occasion for surprise? Had I expected that a marvelous tall ship, at anchor in a breathtaking location so distant from the sea, would attract no attention whatever from the world beyond our little valley? The answer, upon reflection, was that I had never fully considered the possibilities to start with, and therefore had entertained no expectations either way.

The more I considered it, however, the greater a boon it seemed that our project should stir curiosity and admiration amongst respectable persons throughout Yorkshire. Events shall soon be in motion, which shall sorely test the standing of a viscount who promises his duke and his county a turn-pike then fails to furnish one, and in the controversy certain to ensue, such public good will may prove an advantage.

And so, visitors of the sort we have so far encountered are welcome. In anticipation and hope that more shall soon appear, I instructed Rugby to follow our now-established protocol with any arriving sightseers whom he deems fit for admittance to our estate,

so that he need not bother me for permission in each particular instance. Thus may my *Mean Fish*, already the vehicle and chief embodiment of my dream, become also a worthy ambassador in helping to ensure its own success.

Friday, June 19, 1795

Factum est nihil.

Saturday, June 20, 1795

This day began, as so many seem to do of late, with a rather astonishing fact coming to light during an officers' meeting—in this case, an announcement from Lampson that the crew have nearly finished their play, which they shall soon be ready to present.

"Mr. Lampson," said I, "there may still be bathwater in my ears, for I seem to have heard you imply that the crew of this ship are engaged in theatrics. What was it you *actually* said? Perhaps that the few have nearly finished their clay? That would seem *less* nonsensical and could have something to do with the turn-pike diggings near Reeth."

"But you heard rightly, sir," said Lampson, wearing a bemused smile. "The crew have collectively written and directed a play which is to be presented upon the stage of the Cat & Cabbage within a fortnight or so. And a decent job they are doing, too, based on rehearsals I have glimpsed."

"And how is it that the captain has not been informed of this? What other pretentious artistic fripperies am I not privy to? Is that fool from Chelsea composing us an anthem? Are the sails to sport appalling murals?"

Lampson appeared genuinely taken aback. "Begging your pardon, sir, but the crew's desire to create a play was mentioned at this table some weeks ago, prior to your unfortunate absence, and the notes I left you from the meetings chaired by Mr. Nelson, made several mentions of their progress."

"Confound it, Lampson, 'twas never so! I'd swear by the King himself, this is the first I've heard of it!"

Nelson gave a mildly derisive snort. "From the man who was unaware of our cabin boy's existence for over a month."

"From the man who wields absolute authority aboard this ship, if you please! Now. As captain I am indisputably the artistic director

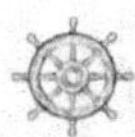

of this vessel and all works of art must be approved by myself beforehand!"

"Mmmm," said Nelson. "There was the plank. You didn't approve *that* work of art beforehand."

"Well, yes. Quite so!"

"And then there's been some fine scrimshaw done by our sailors up in the fo'c'stle, hasn't there, Mr. Bridger?"

"Aye, that there has, Mr. Nelson."

"And you didn't approve that either, Nephew?"

"Indeed! Well, I have heard quite enough and unless my first officer relents in this distasteful teasing, I shall declare a complete moratorium on art, for which the blame would rest entirely upon his shoulders! Right! Well then, isn't it about time we discussed the cannon logistics? That is going to be a bloody lot of weight to heave around, wheels or no!"

Following the meeting I remained in a cross mood, due to this annoying impertinence on my uncle's part, and the lapse in communication on Lampson's. Whilst I do not object to the crew putting on a play—indeed this is precisely the type of wholesome, camaraderie-building activity which I hope to see onboard—a captain must be informed about such enterprises at all times, in order to ascertain the prevailing mood of his men. How I may be expected to lead effectively, when furnished with shoddy information, is beyond me. Alexander himself could not have made it across the Dardanelles, never mind all the way to the gates of India, had he been burdened with such forgetful officers as I.

However, during mail call at eleven bells, an event caused me to quite forget the play, the cannons, and in fact everything which had been discussed at the meeting.

I receive a good deal of mail each day, most related to business of the Hall and estate (the lion's portion of which I pass to my uncle).

But on this day as I sorted grimly through the usual assortment of bills, petitions, and legal claptrap, my eyes of a sudden beheld an envelope addressed to myself in a lovely flowing hand, the origination upon the back reading: *Mary Ashwood, Keld*

Instantaneously I flung the rest of my mail upon the deck and rushed to my cabin, very nearly falling down the gangway in my haste. I sat at my desk, well-lit by daylight through the great windows at the stern, and feasted my eyes upon this, the first sample ever I had seen of her writing. How like her it was, how elegant and assured! How thrilling to hold in my hands this envelope, this object caressed by her pen and sent hither by her wish!

And yet ...Until I opened the envelope, and read the letter within, I could not know whether this thing of beauty I held brought into my life a delight, or a disaster—and it seemed certain to be either one or the other.

My hands trembled as I opened the envelope, taking utmost care against damaging the precious item inside. I pulled out and unfolded two sheets of decent paper, neatly covered with more of that splendid writing, and with my heart in my throat, scarcely able to breathe, I read the following words:

My Dear Lord Keld,

As leader of the delegation from Keld, which visited My Lord's ship on the occasion of the venerable archdeacon's arrival, I have been remiss in not writing before now, in order to express the humble gratitude felt by my fellow delegates and myself, and indeed all Keld, for the magnanimous hospitality shewn us on that day. It was unexpected, and marvelously gracious of My Lord, to have not only welcomed us aboard the Mean Fish, but to have also provided us with chairs, shade against the sun, very fine tea, and a sailor to shield us from impertinent behaviour (although based upon what I observed, this crew are better behaved than novels of seagoing adventure have led me to expect).

That said on behalf of the delegation and village, I must now beg My Lord's leave to speak solely for myself, upon a subject which has caused me a good deal of distress since the day of our visit, and which I earnestly hope has not brought any remotely similar affliction upon My Lord's person for one single second.

If my departure from his estate was precipitous and ill-mannered, I hope that My Lord may, in his gracious nature, find it possible to forgive me for this slight, which I wish him to understand was brought on by the extreme surprise which his words caused me, rather than by anything objectionable I found in the words themselves, either at the time or upon further reflection. I was never offended by My Lord, as he may have concluded. There has simply been nothing in my young life, which could possibly have prepared me to answer in a proper manner, and upon a moment's notice, such warm and flattering words, from such an august personage.

In the heat of that moment I accused My Lord of perpetrating a jest in speaking so to a poor shepherdess. Again, this was due rather to surprise than conviction, and I beg pardon for it. I must allow, based upon My Lord's life-long reputation in our village, and his personal conduct towards me, and the dreamy manner with which he uttered the words in question, that I believe him to have spoken in earnest. I trust that it is not in My Lord's nature to trifle with Swaledale's upstanding ladies, whatever their station. (How earnestly I pray to be right in this, for if I am not, then my hasty speech in that moment proves true, and I am bound to be disappointed by such treatment from one whose power over me should move him to noblesse oblige.)

In addition to the shock of being thus addressed by a man of noble family, my agitation was increased by the knowledge that nothing may ever come of such pleasant fancies as My Lord murmured, even were they spoken in all sincerity. The reason for this is the doctrine of my father's, which has been a constant throughout his life, that the one truly unpardonable sin which an Englishman may commit, is to rise, or even contemplate rising, above one's allotted place.

My Lord may, understandably, take it for granted that his interest in a common girl such as myself, would be received with joy in her family, as a sort

of manna from heaven, but I must assure My Lord that my father would find the wooing of his daughter by a viscount, or a baron, or even a city gentleman, to be cause for humiliation, as in his eyes it would shew every villager within ten miles, that Benjamin Ashwood had forgotten his principles or, almost as bad, had failed to instill them in his daughter. No amount of land, nor money, nor even affection is likely to overcome this persuasion of my father's.

It is true that I have resisted his efforts to interest me in sundry bachelor shepherds of good standing, on account of my not fancying any of them in the least. But for that reason, too, I cannot for an instant contemplate the possibility of disappointing this kind and worthy father, who has ever been loving to my mother, and has never bade me marry against my wishes, even though it would be within his rights.

Upon my return to Keld, I was as My Lord must imagine in a state of very great agitation. As there was no hope of concealing this from my family, I was compelled to explain it. I did not wish to implicate My Lord for my upset, after what a kind host he had been, so I told my family that I had misspoken before the archdeacon, in an embarrassing manner, and was therefore vexed with myself. Of course, Miss Cartwright and Miss Smith know fully well the true cause of the emotions I could not fail to shew, but be assured that they shall speak of it to no one, as I am privy to certain facts about each of them, which they would not wish to be generally known, and we three have therefore entered into a solemn agreement on the matter.

One last thing shall I say. I have traveled and seen little in my life (save through the pages of books), sadly never having been farther from home than my uncle's in Ripon. So perhaps it is a symptom of my inexperience, but I must exclaim that My Lord's ship seems to me amongst the very wonders of the world, and I count myself fortunate to have trod her deck. Whatever My Lord intends for her, may it become reality, and may he always remember me as I was that day, a loyal shepherdess doing her utmost for Keld. I beg to remain, My Lord. Your most humble and obedient servant,
Mary Anne Ashwood

Upon finishing this letter my amazement was so complete, that I could have been knocked a mile with a feather. How very bold of Thistle—Miss Ashwood—to have written thusly to a man of my eminence, and yet given what had passed between us, I could find no impropriety in it. On the contrary, her words on paper proved every bit as germane and well-bred as had her words in person.

I read the letter through thrice, from beginning to end. I then read it five times more. I concluded by reading it another four times.

What a storm of clashing emotions tossed my heart this way and that, through these repeated voyages down the page! Relief swirled into sorrow, and sorrow into relief, until I scarce knew them apart. Relief at receiving word from her, whom I had thought never to hear from again, and finding that my damnable slip had miraculously not caused her offence; sorrow at learning of this intractable axiom of her father's, which I could hardly flout without shewing myself indifferent, if not hostile, to one of the most upstanding villagers of Keld.

Hovering above this maelstrom of moods, I glimpsed through the tumult a shining star of joy for the question which had weighed upon me most heavily had vanished. "Especially when I could never..." she had begun, and my imagination had finished that sentence in countless unpleasant ways. Now I gathered that this mysterious thing she could never do, was give any consideration to such "pleasant fancies" as I had murmured, on account of her father's disposition.

How very sweet of Miss Ashwood to wish that my person had suffered no similar affliction to hers these past weeks, and yet I would wager that my torment had worsted hers, having been woven from a web of uncertainties which troubled her not, as she had known (and now shared with me) the very answers I had agonized over.

The most unpleasant news in the letter, aside from her father's intransigence, was how she had wrongly shouldered blame in order to protect me from censure. She, who had spoken so eloquently that day, claiming to have shamed herself before the archdeacon, when it was *my* ill-timed speech which had sent her home all topsy-turvy! How noble of her to have fallen upon that sword, so to speak, for my sake, and yet, if only she had found some other way to preserve my character (if indeed I deserved such) than by doing herself an injustice.

As for her hope that I always remember her as she was that day— heavens, how could it be otherwise? I shall sooner forget which way is up, or how to breathe, or my very name sooner than the grace and aplomb with which Mary Ashwood led the delegation from Keld.

And so, did the letter prove a delight or a disaster? Both at once, if one may believe such a thing. I shall reread Thistle's letter every day, and think upon some gentle means of circumventing her father's prejudice, as a woman of her quality and station shall find it difficult to continue deflecting unwanted suitors for long. There must be some way to make a viscount's interest acceptable to her entire family— short of renouncing my title and becoming a shepherd myself.

Tuesday, June 23, 1795

Saturday's letter from Thistle sufficiently dispelled the gloom which had afflicted me, that I have resumed current keeping of my log—with the improvement that I shall no longer record an entry for each and every day. As I have noted, the pace of events has slackened recently, but also my experience as captain has taught me to better distinguish between that which merits inclusion in this log, and that which does not.

My uncle shall no doubt approve that the first observation in this resumed record of our adventure, is of a meteorological nature. After several weeks of unseasonably warm, dry conditions, today dawned cool and rainy. Nelson had predicted this himself two days ago, as he is fortunate enough to possess an arthritic condition, which informs him of coming wet turns in the weather by dint of searing pain. In this case my uncle predicted an especially strong storm due to the intensity of his discomfort, and our ship's barometer concurred. As of sunrise today, a heavy rain had indeed been falling for at least an hour.

The crew found the timing of this deluge quite unwelcome, as today had been designated for the hanging of our lovely purple sails from the yardarms. Getting the great swaths of heavy cotton-duck secured aloft would be no easy business in fine weather; slippery conditions and squally winds made it even less so. We heard some grumbling from a few of the sailors, but of course, we may brook no delay due to a bit of harmless water, as Bridger made clear to everyone.

I spent the day warm and dry in the library and in my cabin, making a study of all things related to sails and sailing, as lack of such knowledge would be unbecoming in a ship's captain. There turns out to be a good deal to learn about propelling a ship with

what amount to gigantic sticks and sheets, more than one might suppose; I found the jargon alone exhausting to absorb. I persevered, however, and may now discuss such things as jibs, tacking, and heaving-to without sounding entirely the landlubber. Meanwhile, our crew toiled through an unrelenting downpour, and by evening the sails were in place. I decreed that every sailor involved receive a horehound candy with supper.

Of course, the sails may not be unfurled yet. Only during a period of dead calm could we venture to do so; otherwise we risk being dashed into the flagstone sides of the Mare Jacobum, even with our anchor-chains deployed—and conditions remain quite gusty at present. More than likely we shall have to wait until the broad waters of the Humber estuary lay beneath our hull, before shewing our ship's full magnificence to the world. In the meantime, it is stupendously satisfying to see that at long last, her masts and crossarms no longer stand bare.

June 23; Nearly Midnight

An event occurred less than one hour ago, which I would never believed had I not witnessed it with my own eyes. I waste no time recording it on paper, should it presage some terrible fate which may befall me, afore I have the chance to write of it tomorrow.

I lay abed and soundly asleep when a knock upon my cabin door roused me to attention. I recognized a pattern used by Nelson, to signify that it is he knocking, so I fell out of bed and answered.

Upon opening the door, I found my uncle in such an unexpected state, that I wondered for a moment if I might be in the throes of a dream. His countenance ashen, his jaw slack, Sir James Nelson looked as if he might have seen a ghost—or as if halfway to becoming one himself. Never in all my life had I witnessed such a look of dread

upon his face. Such an impression did this make, that I found myself swallowing hard before he had spoken a single word.

"Nephew," said he, with a gravitas to match his appearance, "you had better see this." He gestured towards the gangway with a lit chamberstick and added, "We should go up that way."

I allowed Nelson to take the lead. At the foot of the steps he set the chamberstick down on a table, snuffed the candle, and said, "We'll be better able to see without it." In the dim light which remained, I followed my uncle up the gangway, through the ceiling hatch, and into the strategy room.

The chamber lay dark and empty at that hour, the regular rounds of whist having been concluded some time before. Nelson led me to the windows looking out upon the main deck and gazed outside, wordlessly inviting me to do the same.

The reason for leaving the candle behind now became clear. It was only slightly less shadowy without than within; a flame brightening the room, and reflecting from the windowpanes, would have made it quite impossible for us to see anything outside. As it was, I could make out fairly well the familiar outlines of the middeck, and glancing above, the marvelously novel sight of our furled sails. A pelting rain persisted, everything in sight thoroughly soaked by a day's worth of downpour.

I looked carefully about, but saw not any spectacle which could have so shaken my uncle, compelling him to bring me there in the middle of the night. Pirates climbing aboard? Mutinous sailors with muskets? Dr. Converse transformed into a vampyre? No such dramatic scenes greeted my eyes. Indeed, there was no one on the main deck (though I trusted that our night watches manned their posts elsewhere). Everything visible through the window looked in its proper place and in good order, albeit rather wet.

I began to ask Nelson what on earth I was meant to see, and a syllable did indeed escape my lips, but before I could finish the word, I saw it.

A stone sat upon the deck, not fifteen feet from the window. I squinted and peered more closely. This was not just any stone. An involuntary shiver racked my body.

The Loose Stone of the Hall had lit upon the main deck of the *Mean Fish*. There was no mistaking it. Ancient, rough-hewn, missing a bit off one corner, a weathered block of limestone cut from the very fells rising invisibly all about us.

It sat near the top of the gangway leading down to the officers' quarters—in one sense a very typical place for the Loose Stone to appear, as its favourite trick over the years (even more so than smashing footstools) has been causing members of the Jacob household, family and staff alike, to trip and fall at the most inopportune moments.

But to find the Stone *outside of the Hall*—this was beyond atypical, it was absolutely without precedent, not only in our own lifetimes, but also in the centuries' worth of lore which has come down to us. Of course, my uncle knew this perfectly well, so when I turned to him, unable at first to speak, he nodded in complete understanding.

I looked back outside. The Stone was still there, pelted by fat raindrops, somehow in spite of its modest size looking as unmovable as Gibraltar.

"How long?" I whispered.

"Can't say. At least three, four minutes," said Nelson, also speaking in a whisper, as if the thing out there might be able to hear us and comprehend. "I was up here fetching my pipe. Came over to have a glance at the weather, and there the little devil sat, right where you see it now. I went to you straightaway. How dearly I'd hoped it would be gone when I returned."

"Perhaps it is a trick, played upon us by the crew," I said. "They have heard the stories, surely. In fact, the strangely persistent Stone which Rugby and other staff witnessed in the Hall a few weeks ago could have been a similar hoax."

"That crossed my mind. But how could anyone onboard have come up with such a perfect replica, down to the chipped corner?" He shook his head. "You and I may have only glimpsed it before now, Nephew, but the Loose Stone's physiognomy has been well mapped by our family's collective memory; you and I know its features as well as those of the "Man in the Moon". There before us lies our phantom Stone, Richard, and no mistake."

Nelson and I exchanged the briefest of glances. When we again turned outside, the Stone was gone.

This settled the matter. We had looked away for a single second; it was impossible that a trick stone could have been moved away, without any sound whatever, in that time. The thing had simply vanished, as the Loose Stone invariably does.

Nelson and I shared another look, this one grim and protracted. We needed not speech in that moment to wholeheartedly agree, that such an apparition must surely bode ill for our project, and possibly for ourselves.

Wednesday, June 24, 1795

Slept poorly last night. Spent hours awake, fruitlessly theorizing what it might signify to have seen the Loose Stone aboard our ship. With every bump and creak (and these were legion, for it was a blustery night) I imagined that the Stone's curséd form had materialized somewhere in my cabin—perhaps even atop the canopy of my bed, where its weight would rend the fabric and send it plunging down upon my defenseless person.

Never before had I cause to fear the Stone; I have been raised to regard it as an integral, if annoying, feature of the household. But now that its customary mischief seems to have been replaced by something else—a mute warning, perhaps, or so feel those of us who have seen it—I know not what turn its behaviour might take next, and I pray that its former impishness is not now evolving into some manner of devilry.

Naturally, the topic dominated this morning's officers' meeting. In order to better discuss the matter, I required Rugby to attend; along with my uncle and myself, he has had the longest experience in Stonesthrow Hall.

I began by describing what Nelson and I had witnessed. By the conclusion of my brief tale, poor Rugby looked every bit as discomfited as had my uncle the previous night. Two others in my audience knew firsthand of the Loose Stone: Whitehand—whose lips had set into a grim line by the time I finished—and Converse, who shewed an uncharacteristic amount of interest in the discussion (which is to say, a noticeable amount).

My other officers have had no personal experience with the Stone. Bridger and Wheelwright both appeared lost in concentrated thought, as if carefully comparing our situation to strange apparitions in their own vast experience. The latter also nodded sagely during my tale,

as if this were merely the latest in a long series of enchanted stones with which he has personally dealt, and its behaviour, so amazing to me, surprised him not in the least.

Then there was Mr. Lampson. Alone amongst those assembled, he listened to my story with a raised eyebrow, and a curl of his lips which resembled a smirk rather too much for my liking. He was the first who spoke up when I concluded.

After a moment's pause during which no one made a sound, Lampson said, "I do beg your pardon, Sir, if I am not getting the drift, but the effect is really quite good. I felt shivers as you spoke, imagining the diabolical Stone and what its appearance may portend. This could be developed quite readily into a novel, or perhaps a play. It would please me to assist in such a worthy endeavour, but it does seem as though you have the thing quite well in hand. Bravo!"

Before I could say a word, Nelson thundered forth. "*Mister* Lampson ... your captain is hardly an aspiring novelist, and this is no literary trifle he speaks of. The Stone is as real as the nose upon your face; I myself have fallen victim to its machinations on many occasions. Referring, of course, to the Stone. Not your nose."

Lampson appeared at a total loss. "I ... I am afraid that I do not understand," he said, looking back and forth between my uncle and myself.

"Do you mean to say," said I, "that you have lived amongst us for months now and never heard tell of the Loose Stone of the Hall?" When Lampson agreed that he had not, I said, "Damn it all, Lampson, you have been spending far too much time in the library! It is vital that every officer onboard be familiar with the particulars. Mr. Bridger, Mr. Wheelwright, I believe that you both have some knowledge of the Stone's history, but it appears that a review is in order, to ensure that we are all drinking from the same well, as it were." I then related the legend of the Loose Stone for the edification of my

officers, and I record it here, as well. To the best of my knowledge, no portion of it has ever before been written down.

When my grandfather, William Jacob, was made Viscount Keld by George II, and moved into the ancient pile already (for obscure reasons) known as Stonesthrow Hall, he and my grandmother Anne were the first to dwell there since the reign of Elizabeth, something like two hundred years before. The main house was essentially a ruin, having lain abandoned for so long in the wet weather of the downs; a family of foxes had to be evicted from the parlour, after which the building was stripped to a stone shell and entirely rebuilt in the best Palladian style. The west and south wings were added as an extension of this process, as in size the original hall had amounted to little more than a glorified cottage.

Early on, my grandfather noticed a stone missing from the front façade, a few feet to the right of the door as one faces it, leaving a hole through which the second layer of stonework lay visible. This struck him as peculiar, as there was no clear manner by which a single stone could have simply fallen out, when the work around it remained entirely sound. Neither were there toolmarks to shew that the stone had been pried free, although ages of weathering could have made such clews difficult of detection.

Naturally, William had his stonemasons repair this hole. Next morning, the replacement stone had vanished, an event for which no one could account. The masons provided a second replacement. Again, it was gone without a trace next morning.

Later on that day, my grandfather welcomed a delegation of elders from the village of Keld. Many locals were involved in the rebuilding efforts, and news of the vanishing stones had by this time reached every ear in upper Swaledale; these old-timers professed knowledge of an event over two centuries old, which was locally held to explain the mystery.

The original inhabitants of Stonesthrow Hall, who built the place in the middle fifteenth century, are only ever referred to by villagers of Keld as "the old ones." This is supposedly due to the family's name having been literally forgotten over the intervening generations, but it is my belief that local memory *does* in fact preserve the name, and that superstition rather than forgetfulness forbids its use, as it is thought cursed.

These old ones, though noble in title, were no paragons of chivalric behaviour. Ugly tales of their debauchery, vice, and malfeasance circulate yet in Keld. The particular story which the village elders shared with my grandfather, tells how a traveling Scot—perhaps the worse for drink, yet clearly of means, and styling himself a laird— was, along with his retinue, refused food and shelter by the old ones on a stormy winter's eve. In retaliation, the Scot bellowed a terrible curse upon the house and its inhabitants, before finding warmth and respite for the night amongst the welcoming cottages of Keld.

Of course, the old ones mocked this gaelic tirade and gave the matter no further thought. But the next morning their chief steward fell downstairs and broke his collarbone. The fellow swore having glimpsed a rectangular Stone upon the step, whose unexpected presence had caused his accident, yet moments after the disaster no such object was to be found there, or anywhere nearby.

Shortly thereafter, it was discovered that a stone had gone missing from the façade, and that it was, inexplicably, impossible to replace.

Having heard this tale from the elders of Keld, my grandfather's chief mason proposed making the repair for a third time, then setting a watch overnight, in the expectation that the villagers themselves had removed the previous replacement stones, as a kind of antic. But William Jacob forbade it—he put stock in the old story and feared that anyone undertaking such a vigil would risk witnessing the Devil himself at work, a sight which no mortal man could hope to survive.

At that point in my narration (which was, at any rate, essentially finished) I found myself interrupted by Bridger, who said, "The Devil his own self hasn't the time fer movin' stones about—if the priest may allow me to muse upon theological matters—but that Scots laird was a warlock, or sorcerer, I believe so wholeheartedly."

It was difficult for me to read Lampson's pinched expression, which may have been of a sort learnt at university, and therefore outside of my experience. However, he sounded genuinely intrigued as he said, "So, if I understand correctly, there is a stone missing from the façade of the Hall, which has become supernatural through the curse of a drunken Scot, and it periodically manifests itself as a sort of harbinger of doom?"

"The harbinger of doom part is admittedly speculative," said Nelson, "It is this change in the Stone's routine, if you will, which worries us. Normally, the Stone is a mere annoyance, coming and going in an eyeblink, causing spills, minor injuries, and the like."

"And crushing footstools," I added.

By this time I was able to classify the evolving look upon Lampson's face as the grimace of someone at a complete loss to ascertain whether or not they are being led on. "I say … you all seem so earnest about this, and it's jolly well fascinating, but heavens … are we seven grown men really holding a serious discussion about a phantom hunk of limestone?"

Whitehand's reaction was immediate. "Are you a Christian, sir?" He asked of Lampson, in his most acidic tone. "Because if you are, I should not need to remind you that our faith is built upon the fact that the world we perceive is but a passing illusion, and that deeper truths lie beyond, in the realm of the spirit. I have seen this Stone myself, and barked my shin upon it rather badly, yet in spite of its transient physical reality, I have no doubt that it is a fixture of the

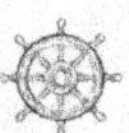

spiritual realm, controlled by forces beyond our ken. And such things, sir, are very appropriately discussed by grown men."

Lampson honoured our vicar with a slight bow. "I am indeed a Christian, Mr. Whitehand, and as a trained botanist, I recognize that the creator has endowed our world with wonders, spiritual and otherwise, which do exist quite beyond the surfaces we perceive with our eyes. Science uncovers more of these on a daily basis, thanks to such manmade miracles as mathematics and the microscope. I have no doubt that the ministrations of spiritual men like yourself contribute at least as much to the betterment of the human race."

Lampson turned to me and went on, voice rising. "But perhaps we have here a phenomenon which might be explained in some other way. I intend no offense, captain, but as you yourself have said that seeing the Stone outside of the Hall is without precedent, perhaps you and Sir James have fallen victim to some skylarking of the crew's, or some trick of the dim, stormy light."

Now, I shall without hesitation state in writing that Mr. Lampson has proven a loyal, efficient, punctual, intelligent, and congenial officer and companion. On many occasions I have found him a treasured peer with whom to discuss various fields of knowledge (Nelson and I share many interests, but after a lifetime of intimate association there is little we do not know about one another's views; as for Wheelwright, his vast erudition is tainted by a penchant for dubious hyperbole). Furthermore, I agree with Lampson's opinions on the merits of science, making our rapport that much more strong.

However, in this instance the young man's reflexive reliance on Baconian thought, which normally I would find admirable, instead filled me with fury. How dare he cast doubt upon what my uncle and I had witnessed with our own eyes—and by extension, upon this ancient curse, the results of which, whilst we may not subject them

to controlled experiment, have nevertheless been as observable and repeatable as any phenomenon in a laboratory!

"Mr. Lampson, I believe that you mean well," said I, "but you must learn to recognize when you are out of your depth and know not that of which you speak! Perhaps that is not a talent which they teach at Cambridge! An officer must also shew proper respect to their captain's well-documented family curses, if any! This is not a problem which we shall solve with a sketchbook and a slide rule!"

Face flushed, looking as if stung by my words and scarcely able to contain himself, Lampson retorted, "Sir, I do hope that you shall forgive me if I speak my mind in a blunt manner, as I do so for your own good! This entire myth of the Stone is utterly ridiculous! It belongs in a collection of fairy tales, not an officers' meeting at this table, and the man of knowledge whom I have come to admire should know better!"

I stood to my feet and shouted, "I should, should I? Utterly ridiculous, am I? I shall shew you the meaning of the term ridiculous! For the period of one week, commencing immediately, you, Mr. Lampson, are to be not only Mustardhead's tutor, but also his servant!"

I must confess to feeling a good deal of satisfaction, with the look of disbelieving horror which my pronouncement of doom threw across Lampson's features. Pressing my advantage, I continued, "Yes, that is right! I shall personally ensure that the boy understands —insofar as he is able—that you are to cater to his every need, and indeed his every whim, for a period of seven days! Perhaps that shall teach you to never again scoff at enchanted stones, which you have never even seen!"

Mr. Lampson appeared so infuriated, that I fully expected him to rise and storm out of the room; however, to his credit he kept his seat and held his tongue, digging no deeper the hole into which he had already got himself.

There was little further discussion of the Stone, as it was agreed upon by all (excepting Lampson) that the only rational action to be taken at this point was for Whitehand to anoint the spot where the Stone had been seen, and other key locations around the ship, with holy water, in hopes that this might deter the hall's curse from further spreading to the *Mean Fish*. Meanwhile, we shall all of us remain especially vigilant for further appearances of the Stone, or other signs of nefarious activity, although at Bridger's recommendation the crew are not to be informed about any of this, as yet.

Turning to other business, Wheelwright informed us that the crew's play, for which he and Lampson have been acting as advisors, is to be performed in five day's time, should this please the captain, and that it has been titled, *The Bench and the Bishop*. I declared myself very pleased indeed to witness this production on the day proposed. (Having recovered from my indignation at not being informed of the play promptly, I now find the idea entirely charming, and furthermore its title seems to promise hilarious mischief.)

The meeting concluded with a review of how the cannons are to be managed, for all sixteen of them are to arrive tomorrow. We must bring them aboard using the crane, as we dare not rely upon the gangplank to bear their weight; even so, Bridger estimates that once the weapons are assembled on shore, they may all be emplaced with four to five hours' work.

Afterwards, Rugby remarked to me that he had never expected our officers' meetings to be quite so entertaining, and asked if he might be allowed to drop in to them more often. Alas, I was bound to inform him that today's shew of high spirits was far from an ordinary occurrence, and that he was certain to be disappointed with the usual humdrum nature of our business. I was compelled to deny his request, which judgment he accepted with a minimum of Cornish grumbling.

In the afternoon, a brief respite in the rainy weather brought me above decks on a lark, and I found myself standing at the great wheel which turns the rudder. Normally a focal point of activity on a ship's deck, our wheel has been hardly paid attention to, as there is no occasion to steer a ship which lies at anchor in a pool. I myself have hardly touched the wheel in waking life; I have only ever used it in that marvelous dream of some days past in which the *Mean Fish* had gone sailing off across the downs.

Today I surveyed the scene from that spot with satisfaction—the furled sails, the activity on deck, the play of light and shadow across the green fells as clouds went scudding by overhead. Damp left by the rains added a vibrancy of colour to the scene, and I fancied that I could even hear the swollen River Swale roaring along its rocky bed at the bottom of the hill.

As I stood there, I watched Rugby escort yet another party of tourists from afar, this one armed with umbrellas, around the corner of the Hall and into our designated viewing area. Such parties have become so commonplace that no one onboard pays them attention any longer. My participation is no longer required, for which I am thankful, as the inconvenience of being repeatedly drawn away from captainly duties was burdensome. Also, each party tends to ask identical questions; addressing these again and again had become frightfully tedious, however admiring the askers. Rugby is now equipped with a sort of informational pamphlet, of which we had several dozen printed in Richmond; between this and his own knowledge, he is able to satisfy our visitors' curiosity—even if his overall mien is perhaps not quite so welcoming as one might wish in a tour guide.

Although at that distance I could not hear everything Rugby told the tourists, it was clear enough when he pointed out the ship's captain standing at the wheel as if deliberately posed for their edification. I gave a slight bow and a hearty wave by way of greeting, which was

returned with enthusiasm by the tourists—I even heard something like a brief cheer from one of their number.

I was puzzling over this level of élan, which according to Rugby has increased amongst our visitors, but which I find difficult to understand, when I felt a hand clap down upon my shoulder.

"Hard to port, Captain," said Nelson, "lest we run aground on the reef of the fawning public, who would no doubt prefer that our ship never budge from this spot, so they may leer at her between breakfast at Richmond and a picnic luncheon at Kirkby Stephen."

Waving once more at the happy tourists, I said to my uncle, "I am convinced that the admiration of these city gentlemen and their families shall be a boon to us, although I cannot say how. I still marvel at their appearance here in Swaledale, but then, travel for leisure is no longer the exclusive domain of our class, you know."

"Oh yes, did you not hear Fitzhenry the other day when he was here? Complaining bitterly about having to rub shoulders with *bourgeoisie* in places like Venice and Vienna. You'd have thought the man spoke of rats or fleas, not people."

"Sorry to say, I somehow missed that portion of the fascinating speech, with which he regaled us for the entire duration of his visit."

"Ah well, you need only pop down to Langthwaite one of these days and request an encore. However, I am not here to discuss "His Loutship," but to congratulate you most heartily on a job well done this morning."

Past experience led me to feel wary of what my uncle might aim for when setting out upon such a trajectory, so with some trepidation I replied, "I see. And what job might that be?"

"Why, putting our university man into his place," said Nelson. "A more apropos judgment you have never meted out, Richard. It was all I could manage to hold back a great guffaw, when you condemned our skeptic to an entire week of what I expect shall be the most vexing servitude. I could almost see your father nodding in approval, up there in the heavenly hunting-chase."

"Hmmm. Well. Of course I do appreciate your approbation, but must own that I spoke in anger and am not now entirely pleased. I would wish to retract or commune Lampson's sentence, if possible. Yet I dare not now, and appear irresolute."

"Indeed? Tell me, Nephew, what sort of archer repents of striking the bullseye? Do you, too, now question what we both witnessed right *there*"—and here Nelson pointed out the very spot where the Stone had been—"not fifteen hours ago?"

"Well, no, of course not. The Stone *was* there, sure as we stand here now."

"Exactly. Now let us be honest, Richard. We both of us admire Mr. Lampson's intellect and wit enormously, and unless I am very much mistaken, you are like me somewhat envious of his academic achievements, the likes of which might have been ours as well, had circumstance differed. But you know full well that here we deal with something quite beyond his experience, and possibly due to his youthful zeal for science, he failed utterly to recognize it."

"That is true," I said.

"Nephew, God help us, you are gradually becoming a leader of men. At one stroke this morning you crushed an insubordinate argument in the presence of all your officers, assigned the arguer to a task which should have the salutary effects of tempering his pride and reenforcing your authority, *and* set up a week's worth of what promises to be bloody good entertainment. You have killed three birds with one stone; I should like to see David himself manage *that* with his little slingshot." Nelson nearly knocked me into the wheel with another clap upon the back. "One should never wrestle with success, Richard. One should embrace it."

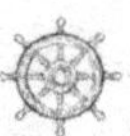

Thursday, June 25, 1795

Early this morning a convoy of wagons arrived, bearing our cannons. These sixteen long-guns have been salvaged from HMS *Warspite*, a Dublin-class, third-rate being broken up at Newcastle. Nelson's naval connections, together with the fact that this particular model cannon has been supplanted on His Majesty's newer vessels, enabled us to purchase these doughty old weapons for a song. Gunpowder and ammunition we have had in the hold since our provisioning days, some weeks ago.

Many of our crew enjoyed a sojourn ashore, assisting the teamsters in unloading the cannons to a staging area within reach of the crane. During this activity, which took place beneath a fresh wave of pelting rain, I invited the chief teamster to join me for a cup of tea in the officer's mess. In response to questions of mine, this worthy old fellow reported that their journey from the Newcastle shipyards had been uneventful, and that our cannons were not so imposing a burden for him and his men as one might imagine, as he has overseen the movement of far heavier goods (to give one example he mentioned, a steam engine nearly half the size of our ship), and over far longer distances.

"Oh," said the chief teamster, after a long sip of tea, "but there was *one* oddity along the way. Down around Reeth, we ran into a sour ecclesiastical on horseback. I'll swear, M'lord, this fellow gave us a glare so unfriendly it might've lit our wagons on fire, if not for the rain."

"That would be the Rector of Reeth, and no mistake," said I. "The scowl you describe is a permanent fixture; it casts a frightful pall over every christening and marriage his poor parishioners dare celebrate. Tell me, did the rector say anything to you?"

"He certainly did, M'lord. He asked—well, demanded, more like it—to know what we had under the tarps and where it was bound."

"Ah, naturally he would. And what did you tell him?"

"I politely informed the fellow that it was not his business to know."

"Ha! Capital! You've earned an extra guinea, my good man!"

"Why, thank you indeed, M'lord. We were not bound to secrecy, as you know, and a friendly fellow I might've answered in kind, but such a disapproving scarecrow as that, I am not inclined to gratify."

The chief teamster went on to add how very enthused he was —along with many others of his profession—about the Swaledale turn-pike under construction, and the great ease it shall introduce, to the movement of goods between lowland Yorkshire and Cumbria. "We marveled at it all the way up from Richmond, M'lord—the steady grade, notched into the hillsides up above, smooth and regular as if some great machine had furrowed the land. And it's even to be covered against the weather! For my money that's a road of the future, M'lord, the first nineteenth-century highway, built here in the waning years of the eighteenth." He shook his head in wonderment. "That caliber of road-building would make the Romans themselves wet their togas in astonishment—if you'll pardon the vulgar reference, M'lord."

The vulgar reference, as he thought it, bothered me not a whit, but his misguided enthusiasm cut me to the quick. My conscience is troubled enough at the prospect of hoodwinking the honest residents of Richmond and Swaledale (not to mention our beloved duke) with the regrettably necessary fiction of our turn-pike, without a host of hard-working teamsters also entertaining hopes which our success must inevitably dash. I smiled and politely accepted his praise, but then excused myself, citing business to which I must attend, but in actuality, feeling unworthy to sit face-to-face with him in that moment.

After popping above-decks long enough to see that the first cannon was ready to be brought onboard using the crane, I retired to the library for research into the currents of the North Sea. There I remained some time later, comparing a treatise on the subject with various nautical charts, when a knock upon the doorframe arrested my attention, and I looked up to see Lampson.

"Oh! I say, nice to see you! You shall find this jolly well interesting, just look here," I began, stopping short when I remembered that my third officer, whose presence was always so welcome in the library, was in fact serving a term of punishment, and likely not at the liberty to study charts with me. "Er, well, actually, it surprises me to see you here by yourself today, Mr. Lampson. Is there not a young man to whose needs you should be attending?"

"Indeed there is," said Lampson, his tone rather more formal than I was accustomed to hearing from him, "and I am in fact sent here on an errand. Mr. Mustardhead has instructed me to deliver this note into your hands."

His cheeks visibly colouring, Lampson handed me a sheet of paper which had been folded into quarters. The exterior surface presented to me was marked with a single, large letter M, done in respectable calligraphy.

"This is a rather fine M," I said. "Surely the lad himself didn't ..."

"No, sir, I rendered the M, at his behest. I also wrote the note. If you would be so good, sir."

"Oh, of course!" I unfolded the paper and read the following words:

From: Mr. Mustardhead

To: The RT Hon Viscount Keld

My Dear Lord Keld,

It would please me greatly if you were to honour me with your presence at luncheon today, at twelve bells, in the Cat & Cabbage, for lunch. I fear that we

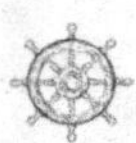

have gotten off on the wrong feet and would like to meet you properly. There is a bar here, with beer. I look forward to your reply most regrettably and remain, Your humble servant,

Mr. Mustardhead of Rag Market, Birmingham, Nation of England, Planet of Earth

Having finished, I looked up at Lampson, who said, "Written exactly as he dictated it, sir, with the exception of the manner of address to Your Lordship, which I found it necessary to correct. What reply shall I give, sir?"

"Well, I am certainly not accustomed to taking my meals in the pub, but it seems a friendly enough invitation. Hmmm. Yes. I shall have my luncheon served there, rather than in the officer's mess. I … er … I expect that you shall join us?"

Lampson heaved a sigh. "I too expect that I shall, sir. I expect that I shall." And with that, he bowed slightly and left the room.

There was at that point more than half an hour before my *rendez-vous* with "Mister" Mustardhead, so I went back to my charts; however, the import of Lampson's visit left me unable to devote the same attention to my studies, and I paused to reread the note several times. What exactly had been my expectations for Lampson's servitude I was not certain, except that they had *not* included Mustardhead styling himself some sort of gentleman and issuing *faux*-formal invitations to his captain. Improving the lad was one thing; encouraging him to put on ludicrous airs, quite another. It was with trepidation that I finished my work in the library and strode over to the pub.

I arrived there punctually, which is to say, at exactly three minutes after noon. The first thing which struck me was how surprisingly empty the pub was, for that hour; only four of the dozen tables were occupied. Although I have rarely visited the place myself, I have been informed that luncheon is its busiest time, as everyone

not on watch takes a meal at noon, whereas the crew's suppertimes are staggered out. I realized that on this particular day most of the crew were assisting with the cannons and would be taking their noon repast elsewhere, in order to expedite that work.

The second thing which struck me was Mustardhead's appearance. Never had I seen a more striking transformation in a human being. It is true that since his arrival onboard, he has been furnished with clean clothing and encouraged to practice personal hygiene, and yet his posture, hair, and general demeanor had previously changed very little since that day when he had cowered wretchedly in my presence, fearing that I would bid him eat grass in purgatory. In that moment, however, I found myself looking about the room, reflexively certain that Mustardhead must be slouched at one of the other tables farther back, before realizing that the fellow seated there beside Lampson was actually he.

Mustardhead's hair was the greatest change. Although still the colour of rancid butter, it had been neatly parted and combed. The effect was pleasant, if not exactly attractive. His face, whilst far from handsome, had a sort of honest quality about it, now that it was no longer half-hidden by a cascade of greasy yellow locks, a quality reenforced by the silly grin he wore in place of his customary expression (which is to say, the look of someone about to vomit). The lad seemed to have grown several inches, as well, surely due to his sitting up straight, instead of flopping about like a rag doll.

Lampson, very properly, stood to his feet as I approached the table. Mustardhead, very *im*properly, did not. Lampson tugged at the boy's collar as a signal that he too should rise, but Mustardhead brusquely brushed away his servant's hand, giving Lampson a cross look before returning his attention, and his idiotic smile, to me.

When Mustardhead spoke, I found that his voice had changed no less than his appearance. In place of his usual cross between a croak

and a whine, he sounded open, cheerful, even very slightly educated. "Captain! Lord Keld! Nice to see you! We've just been wondering if you were going to shew up on your own, or if we'd have to hunt you down and lead you here by the earlobe!"

Lampson gave me a look which very clearly indicated, that *he* had just been wondering no such thing. As for myself, I was for a moment too dazzled by the spectacular impropriety of Mustardhead's words to say anything, before the lad went on, "But I forgive myself, My Lord. Please, sir, have a seat with us and partake in beer and food. I have arranged a sausage for you!"

"Er … I appreciate your thoughtfulness very much, but my meal shall arrive momentarily, from the galley," said I, as I took the chair which Lampson pulled out for me.

"Very good, Your Lordship! Lampson, you lucky duck! You get the second sausage!"

"Thank you, sir," said Lampson.

At that moment Penywern arrived at our table with two sausages, some bread, two draughts of beer, and my meal sent from the galley (consisting of a modest leg of mutton with gravy, salted green peas, and a spot of bread pudding). Penywern had apparently overheard the conversation on his approach, as he straightaway served Lampson the sausage which had been ordered for me. The other sausage he set before Mustardhead, who instantly fell upon it with knife and fork, shewing no more table manners than a lion ripping into its prey.

Had I not refused the sausage, would Mustardhead have furnished his servant, an educated gentleman, with *nothing* to eat, as well as no beer? The possibility disturbed me. Not being certain; however, and wishing to hear more of Mustardhead's newfound voice, as it were, I chose to hold my tongue for the moment.

Very little listening on my part sufficed to hear more from Mustardhead, a good deal more in fact, as the boy did not hesitate

to speak with his mouth full of sausage, or bread, or beer, or all three, and he proceeded to hold forth on a great variety of topics whilst I ate my meal.

"Why so many cannons, Captain? Will the French armada attack us here? Ha ha! Well, there *are* highwaymen, and sea serpents may live in a lake or pool—one does in Scotland. Although cannonballs are no good against sea serpents! My uncle says so, and he sells shoelaces. Keld is a strangely small city! Does anyone live there? It must have a very small dump, though I can't see one from the ship. May I visit the dump? There are not nearly so many sheep in Birmingham as here, and the ones there are dead. It rains too much here, because the sky is so large. The sky is smaller in Birmingham. Lampson says that he's been to school! He learned about plants! I don't like plants. Some of them are radishes, and some are poison, and I lost a tooth biting a stick. I'm glad that no one makes me eat plants. Or grass. Do you know what purgatory is? Most people there are pagans and babies, which is awful."

I hereby laud Lampson in this log for exemplary behaviour, for he bore this asinine monologue with a patience befitting Job. Throughout, he methodically consumed his sausage, maintaining an air of calm resignation which I never could have mustered, had I found myself in his place. I could have expected—and perhaps even deserved—looks of reproach from an officer for having subjected him to such a bout of torture, and yet Lampson kept his gaze down, and his face remained impassive. I felt pangs of regret at having doomed an intelligent gentleman, whom I consider a friend, to wait upon this great fool, consoling myself with the knowledge that the injustice was to last but a week.

In the meantime, Mustardhead's mindless prattle rolled on. "I am back in crew's quarters, now that I have a servant, but I liked living in sick bay. Doctor Converse talks in a strange way, but he isn't very nice. I heard him talking while asleep, to someone named Benny, or Denny. And making kissing noises. Girls are very strange, but I don't really like them. Girls punch me a lot. I think they're all crazy, except my auntie, who is a fish because she was born in March. She says I'm a bugger. Do you like witches? I'm afraid of them. In Bbirmingham there's a dog that is a witch. It has three legs and can fly. It hexed me and my toenail fell off. I'm worried that it might find me here. Please, Captain, don't let any three-legged dogs onboard, in case one is a witch."

This much did Mustardhead spout in the course of thirty seconds. The full extent of his musings, whilst I ate my meal, I have neither ink nor patience enough to record, nor do I believe that my doing so could benefit humanity in any way. So it shall suffice to say that during the ten or so excruciatingly long minutes which it took me to wolf down my food, the boy touched upon such diverse subjects as Voltaire (whom for some reason he believes to be an Old Testament prophet), rocks (he opined that rocks are made of stone, not the other way round) and a mole on the inside of his thigh which he claims is shaped like an angel. I declined his generous offer to have a look at the mole— with some difficulty, as he was unaccountably enthusiastic about shewing it and at one point had his trousers halfway undone.

By the time I wiped the gravy from my lips and rose to my feet, the lad *still* droned on. Again, Lampson stood respectfully, and Mustardhead shewed not the slightest inclination to do so. Indeed, the boy did not even stop talking, but only switched his topic in midsentence from some nonsense about keeping flies as pets, to the exceedingly ill-conceived farewell, "So happy to dine with you, My Lord, your conversation shines like the sun! In the daytime. At about three o'clock. We really must meet again soon, and when we do, I want what *you* had to eat. Well, ta ta! Give my love to your lady friends!"

This last was altogether too much. Had I, in fact, any *lady friends*, I would never dream of sullying their lives with any manner of salutation, let alone *love*, from the likes of Mustardhead. Finding myself literally unable to speak, I favoured Lampson with a nod of acknowledgment—and a look intended as a sincere apology—then retreated to my cabin. It took a good fifteen minutes of walking the plank in my stocking feet in order to regain my composure, and dispel a strong desire to maul something, anything, any destructible object which might come to hand—Mustardhead's face, to give one possible example.

It is fortunate that I was able to calm myself, for I had a ceremony to preside over at three bells. By then the cannon had all been brought onboard, the teamsters had bid us *adieu*, and it was time to officially retire the musket tied to a pole, which has served as our ship's sole armament since her completion.

Whilst a contingent of the crew stood at attention in the pouring rain, the musket, which has been mounted upon the forecastle, was ceremoniously fired into the air. This was, I believe, the only time it had been used, aside from the occasional sailor on watch taking a potshot at a grouse.

Moments later, this delicate crack of gunpowder was answered by a *basso profondo* boom from one of our newly mounted starboard-side guns—fired without ammunition, of course, as we had no desire to send a cannonball into the midst of some local shepherd's flock. A spontaneous cheer went up from the assembled sailors, as the robust voice of our eighteen-pounder echoed back from the fells.

'Twas a proud moment indeed, tempered only when I caught sight of Mustardhead. He and Lampson stood on the poop, well apart from the sailors; the "servant" kept an umbrella over his "master" and held a platter containing more sausages, one of which the boy grasped with his bare hand, then devoured with a few hoggishly large bites.

Fearing that the lad might approach me and attempt to resume his moronic chattering, I hastened to my cabin, there to read Cato until suppertime.

Later this evening came a knock which I recognized as Nelson's. He asked if he might have a word, and relaxed into one of my chairs, as I perched upon the plank.

"This rain," he said, "has been remarkable, indeed. I have dwelt in Swaledale all my life, excepting my time in the navy, and cannot recall seeing the likes of this … This *bout* of precipitation. The combination of persistence and volume astonishes me."

I agreed that it had indeed been quite wet lately, then waited to hear what my uncle would say next; he is not one to make small talk about weather, so I reckoned that he must have begun in that vein, as the preface to a topic of more import.

"Well of course, the Swale rises fast when there's a good rain. 'Tis famous all roundabout here for it. But I've had Rugby talking to old-timers in Keld, and casting about for news from farther afield, and the consensus is that our little river has scarce if ever flowed this high in living memory."

He paused for a moment, as if to let this sink in, before going on, "And it isn't the Swale only. Rivers all around Yorkshire are at or over their banks. We have it from the postal clerk in Richmond that rising waters have impeded the Royal Mail to an extent not seen since the time of the first King George. The Ure, the Ouse, the Trent, all are in flood." Nelson leaned closer and added, with clear emphasis, "The Ouse Bridge at York is presently *closed*, as the south approach is under water."

I could hardly have failed to see what he was driving at, and the implications caused a tingle of elation to creep up my spine.

Leaning back into his chair, and appearing satisfied by the effect of his words, my uncle said, "Richard, I need not explain the significance

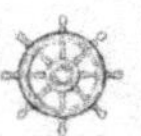

of all this, not to mention how uncanny the timing is, since we have *just* gotten the guns aboard."

I cleared my throat, and heard a surprising quaver of emotion in my own voice as I said, "And the ditch upstream?"

"It has been extended, and may now take in the Birkdale Beck as well as the Sleddale. As you know, when we filled the pool, we had but a trickle, less than fifteen percent of the ditch's capacity. We could go full-bore now, should we open both gates."

My heart beat faster. "And our workings at Reeth?"

"Miss Smeaton tells me that they are serviceable, if a bit rough. The builders have wrought a miracle, in more ways than one. I never would have dreamed that our project might be this far along, before July. And good heavens—Miss Ssmeaton is rechecking her calculations, but with this much water, she tells me that we might not need to use the locks, or at least not all of them."

For a few ticks of the ship's chronometer, we simply looked at one another, my uncle and I. We had both been working towards just such a moment as this, for so many years, that for it to have finally arrived, and in such a seemingly flawless form, was difficult to assimilate.

It was my uncle who spoke next. "So. Shall we open the gates above? And below? God's blood, Richard, we could wait another century and not see such excellent conditions as these."

I thought of our duke, and the turn-pike he would not get. I thought of Thistle, and the Hall, and the fells, and the prospect of leaving all these behind, for the foreseeable future. I thought of the Loose Stone, and what it might have been trying to tell us. I thought of Fitzhenry and the rector, through whose territories we must pass, and their not-so-veiled threats. All these things whirled through my mind in a flash, but the time for careful consideration, for deliberation, for worry and the wringing of hands—the time for all these things was past. The project was built. The water was here. The ship could soon move.

I swallowed hard, and said, "Open the gates above, and once we have inflow, open the gates below. Ready the passage; we may uncover it once the flow is deemed sufficient—I expect that it shall take a few days, even blessed with such an abundance of rain. And then …"

Sir James Nelson nodded as I spoke, and a broad smile spread across his face. He rose to his feet and said, "Aye aye, captain. It shall be done." With that, he swept from my cabin, a spring in his step which I have rarely seen—and which I interpret as the *joie de vivre* of a sailor who knows that he shall soon, at long last, return to the sea.

Friday, June 26, 1795

𝕴n the wee hours of this morning, I sprang suddenly awake, to a perfectly dark and quiet cabin. Thinking that some loud but transitory sound must have startled me from the arms of Morpheus, I lay inert for several minutes, listening for some such to occur again—alert, yet unwilling to quit the comfort of my bed.

No sound came to my attention, but as I lay there, I gradually became aware that something about my cabin was subtly *changed*, in a way oddly disorienting, and which I could not quite lay a finger upon.

Puzzled, I propped up on my elbows and looked about in the dim light. Everything seemed in its place—the furnishings, the plank, the paintings—and I saw nothing which did not belong. I sniffed the air but smelt no smoke, and felt no draft nor unusual temperature. What could this strange difference consist of?

Finally, it struck me—the ship's motion had altered.

Yes, the *Mean Fish* sits in a pool, secured by a triad of anchors, but this does not mean that she has been entirely immobile. There have always been delicate reminders that our vessel lies suspended in fluid, whether it be a wobble brought on by wind, or a bump as the ship pulls an anchor-chain fully taut, before starting a gentle drift in the opposite direction. These effects have normally been so slight that I best noticed them whilst prostrate in bed. Hence it should have caused me no surprise, that the onset of novel motions, however subtle, should have alerted my slumbering mind, to a change worthy of my waking attention.

The wobbles I now felt were more pronounced, regular, and rapid. The straining against anchor-chains had become similarly amplified. The reason for this could not be in doubt. As I had ordered, the pool's inflow and outflow gates must have been open. Water diverted from the swollen Sleddale and Birkdale Becks, more than a mile up-valley, now poured through our ditch and into the Mare Jacobum; the outflow followed our passage towards Richmond. The *Mean Fish* lay at anchor in a current.

The delightful satisfaction of this knowledge would be difficult to fully describe to anyone who had not shared the long road with my uncle and myself through many years of toil, both mental and physical, which have led us to this point. May it suffice to say, that sensing this new life in my ship filled me with joy, and that I lay awake for some time glorying in these motions before the same lulled me back to sleep.

Some hours later, I found myself awakened rather earlier than I deemed pleasing by a loud and insistent knocking upon my cabin door, accompanied by exclamations which gave me to understand that it was Bridger who stood without. I fell out of bed and opened the door with the greeting, "I say, if 'twas my wish to wake before the crack of dawn, I would keep a rooster upon my desk! You'd bloody well better have a good reason for this intrusion, Mr. Bridger!"

"Sir, this ship is in moving water!"

"Indeed it is! I gave orders last night for the gates to be opened."

"Well, this orderin' about of gates and water is surely the cap'n's prerogative, but neither I nor the crew knew a damned thing about it until watch-change this mornin'! I respectfully suggest that yer boatswain and second mate ought be informed of sech alterations afore they take place, as it makes a diff'nce for ships' operations, whether we're anchored in flat water, or in a five-bloody-knot current!"

"Well put, Mr. Bridger. Please accept my assurance that I have not deliberately snubbed you. It is even possible that I may owe you an apology, as I assumed that Mr. Nelson would have informed you about this decision yesterday evening." Reaching for the peg upon which my dressing-gown hung, I went on, "But now, have you a

few moments to join me topside? I should very much like to have a look at this myself."

Bridger had no objection to accompanying me, so he and I made our way to the poop. The sun had by this time barely made itself known; only a thin glimmer of onrushing daylight gilded the dark, rounded outlines of the fells to our east. Yet the deck was a good deal busier than normal for that hour, as curious sailors crowded the railings to gawk at the spectacle of water sliding past our hull. I led Bridger to the stern, and shewed him the ditch, which even in the dim light clearly brimmed with water flowing in from up-valley. I explained how we had utilized this same ditch (albeit with a far more meagre flow) to fill the Mare Jacobum in mid-May.

"Very well, the source of the water 'tis plain, Cap'n," said Bridger, "but I'll be blowed over if I can make out where it's going. At that rate, the pool ought be filling up fast enough fer us to watch the rise. In ten minutes we'd have overflow, and seeing how Stonesthrow lies downslope from us, that'd be no boon to yer fancy carpets and furniture in there. But the water level's hardly changed, and there's nary an outlet, only flagstones all the way 'round. What manner of magic's at work here, Cap'n?"

By way of reply, I smiled and led Bridger forward, until we stood at the very bow. I asked him to examine the water surface in that direction, and tell me what he saw.

"Well, the current's passing our anchored vessel, and I can see where it's piling up just a bit against the flagstones, there straight ahead. But there's nothing past the pool in that direction, except one of yer big lawns."

"And what lies beyond the lawn?"

"Part of that turn-pike yer diggin'."

"And what if I were to tell you, Mr. Bridger, that it is not a turn-pike at all?"

Bridger gave a little snort of derision. "Come now, Cap'n, I can only s'pose it's thirty mile of curvy bowlin' lane, if it ain't a road."

"Oh, it is no bowling lane, Mr. Bridger." I paused for a moment, collecting my thoughts, then went on, "Tell me, Mr. Bridger, you and your fine crew were brought aboard with the understanding that you were to man a stationary ship, in a pool, one-hundred sixty-three river miles from the sea, and over twelve hundred feet above high tide. But would you—or, in your estimation, any sailor aboard—possibly object to the idea of receiving the same generous pay to man a ship at sea, captained by myself, with no admiral or governor-general dictating our bearings, our keel steered not by profit or politics, but by whimsy, and the prospect of adventure?"

Bridger had the incredulous look of a pauper in squalid lodgings, who stands awed by a description of heaven's glittering, gold-paved avenues. "By all that's holy, Cap'n—a swearin' that's proper enough since the priest ain't here—there's not a one of us wouldn't revel in the chance to serve aboard sech a ship. Pray tell, sir, where may we find her?"

"My good man," said I, "you stand upon her." And with that, I left Bridger at the bow of the *Mean Fish*, his look of dawning wonder having collapsed into a grimace of puzzlement.

Saturday, June 27, 1795

This morning's officer's meeting, as yesterday's, was largely concerned with ensuring that our *Mean Fish* is, in every particular, ready to move. Bridger still seems to regard the concept as a sort of jest, but as he observes that the rest of us are in earnest, he manages to set aside his skepticism quite admirably, although it is clear enough that he bursts with curiosity as to how, exactly, this shall happen, and when. For the moment, I am content to leave him in the dark; he shall know what he needs to know, when he needs to know it.

As for my other officers, being members of the Jacob household, Whitehand and Converse have for many years anticipated the events now unfolding; like my uncle and myself, their excitement is palpable (albeit in the doctor's case, barely so). Lampson has not been present for these meetings, as his attendance would require Mustardhead to join us, which is utterly out of the question. As for Wheelwright, he seems to accept as a matter of course the idea that the *Mean Fish* shall soon be underway; I could probably inform him that the ship was going to sprout wings and fly to Sicily without eliciting the slightest surprise from this gentleman, who has— as he never tires of boasting—seen it all.

During this morning's discussion, I could not help but notice Whitehand looking grim and preoccupied, in a manner which suggested to me that he brooded upon an unpleasant subject which he would raise at his first opportunity. And indeed, I have not learnt nothing from my many years of association with this worthy, as once the floor was opened for other topics, he did instantly indicate a wish to speak.

"Captain, it is this business with Mr. Lampson and the boy, Mustardhead," said our vicar. "It offends me to witness the degradation of an educated officer, in having to follow this oafish young fellow about and do his bidding, which seems to consist of the most frivolous and ignoble tasks. As for the boy himself, far from gaining moral instruction, he drifts farther from propriety with each passing day of this nonsense. He seems to think himself very fine indeed, and he addressed me in an intolerably familiar manner yesterday afternoon. The situation has become insupportable."

My uncle beamed broadly. "Yes! It is all magnificently entertaining, is it not?"

"I am serious, Sir James. Captain, I understand the spirit in which you meted out this sentence, but I wish to suggest that it cannot possibly continue for an entire week. Surely Mr. Lampson has long since learnt his lesson, and at any rate, he cannot deserve this continued impingement of his dignity before the entire crew. It does none of us good for any officer to become a subject of the common sailors' ridicule."

This was an excellent point, and I myself was, of course, uncomfortable with the turn things had taken. However, my decree had been that Lampson's servitude would last for one week; every soul on board is aware of that, and to commute the sentence now might not only appear to the "common sailors" as an unfair favour conferred upon an officer, but would surely shew my decisiveness in an unflattering light.

So I thanked Whitehand for his advice and informed him, truthfully, that I would think upon the issue. Having done so, my decision is that Lampson shall be released from Mustardhead's service on Ttuesday. That should hopefully provide our young scholar with an early reprieve without seeming biased to the crew, and without cutting short too precipitously my uncle's source of amusement.

Despite the continued wet weather, today saw the largest assembly yet of travelers from afar, here to admire the *Mean Fish*. No fewer than eight parties arrived at the Hall for this purpose, one having journeyed all the way from Bath, and one consisting entirely of

Calvinist clergy from Glasgow. At one point midafternoon, five such groups stood upon the lawn at once. I have observed that these gatherings become as much social events as sightseeing ones, with a good deal of introductions and hand-shaking amongst the various mingling parties. However, I still limit travelers' visits to fifteen minutes, so any further hob-nobbing must take place elsewhere; my lawn is not a fairground.

At just after four bells, I received a message from Rugby, informing me that a lone visitor from York was, in fact, the vanguard of the newspaper men which one of our earliest admirers had advised us to anticipate. This fellow writes for the *Gazette*, and naturally enough, our brochure did not satisfy his appetite; he approached Rugby to request a personal interview with me. I sent the reply that I would speak to him from the port-side railings of the forecastle, and would reply to five questions.

This fellow seemed well-dressed for a newspaper writer, and his youthful face appeared earnest enough, and yet I found myself rather put off by his interest in our ship, motivated as it was by questions of getting paid, and selling newspapers, as opposed to the wholesome curiosity and wonder which has been the hallmark of our previous visitors. So I must admit that I hailed him in a manner not quite so gracious as I might have shewn.

"You, there! You are the man from the *Gazette*? Very well, then, let's have it. Five questions, no more. Also, no questions within questions. And no leading questions. All right, then, fire away."

Huddled beneath an umbrella and consulting a notepad, the fellow began, "I have the pleasure of addressing Lord Keld of Stonesthrow Hall, who has built a most impressive ship in the wilds of the Yorkshire downs, and my first question for Your Lordship is, how was this vessel built?"

"Hmm, well, any shipbuilder could tell you that. I may cause ships to be built, yet I am not a shipbuilder; talk to someone in Newcastle."

To the young man's credit, he wisely chose to take this clever answer on its own terms, rather than grapple with its unassailable logic, and he went back to his notepad. "The question on all Yorkshire's lips, Your Lordship, is my next one. Why here?"

"Simple, because of the sheer impossibility of building her anywhere else."

"I see. And would Your Lordship care to explain to our discerning readers, why this ship is fully rigged, when she is clearly unable to sail more than a few rods in any direction?"

I felt myself growing more vexed by the moment, due partly to the disappointingly unimaginative nature of the questions, and as this one in particular bordered upon impudent, I said, "To your discerning readers, I answer with another question: Why is it that some York dandies dress as if for an audience with the King, when they are merely going out for a hunt, if one may indeed call it that when one is ushered into range, then handed a loaded gun, and needs merely aim and pull the trigger?"

This gave the fellow pause. He gave me a long, measuring look, an uncertain half-smile upon his face, before going on, "Well, such sentiments from a country viscount shall certainly interest our readership, which I daresay includes more than a few of the gentlemen to whom you refer. Your Lordship may wish to keep an eye on our letters column in the near future, if you do not already, for possible parries in answer to so bold a thrust. So. My fourth question: Why such a grotesque figurehead?"

"My good man, you may have noted that my ship is called *Mean Fish*, rather than *Aurora*, or *Elizabeth Jane*, or some such vapid nicety. This writhing, fanged fish came to me in a dream, or vision, and that form of inspiration no mortal is worthy to question."

"But why not a mermaid?"

"How in blazes should I know? I would bloody well rather have dreamt of a lissome mermaid, but instead, I got an ugly fish! One cannot pick and chuse visions, you know, as one would select a waistcoast from the wardrobe!"

"I suppose that is indeed so, Your Lordship. And so, finally, about the new Swaledale turn-pike, which I understand your estate to be …"

I cut the fellow off. "Tsk-tsk, you have had your five questions! Besides, I am not taking inquiries about the turn-pike at this juncture. If you wish to write a story about that, try coming back in about … oh, say two week's time. Meanwhile, it has been a pleasure to speak with you, and as you can see, my steward waits to shew you back to your conveyance."

The newspaper fellow wrinkled his brow and consulted the contents of his notepad before appearing to realize that his question about mermaids, which I took to have been reflexive rather than scripted, had in fact been his fifth one. He gave a resigned nod, muttered a rather unconvincing thank you, and allowed Rugby to lead him away.

Taking my customary walk upon the plank this evening, I thought back upon this interview, and found myself hoping that I shall not regret the stridency of my words. Until now, our interactions with curious visitors from afar has been entirely salutary, likely to disseminate good tidings about ourselves and our ship throughout Yorkshire and beyond. However, I may have allowed my annoyance with the newspaper man to make my answers overly flippant, and my remarks about foppish hunters could even be considered offensive by some. All of this may appear in a newspaper with a large regional circulation, presumably including persons of importance. With no clear means to moderate my hasty utterances, I can only hope that they shall not in some way damage our cause, or outweigh the good reports which previous visitors have borne away with them.

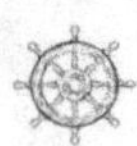

Monday, June 29, 1795

Today was a special day aboard the *Mean Fish*. At two bells in the afternoon, all ship's work ceased, and every soul onboard (save a minimal watch) assembled in the Cat & Cabbage to witness the crew's play, *The Bench and the Bishop*.

Wheelwright assures me that it is no misnomer to credit this production to the crew at large, as it is truly a child of their collective wit, with Wheelwright himself (and Lampson, prior to his recent indisposition) offering only minimal guidance.

Nelson and I arrived at the Cat & Cabbage ten minutes prior to curtain time, and found the place transformed.

The tables had been stowed elsewhere, and the chairs deployed into neat rows with an aisle down the centre, mimicking the appearance of a *bona fide* theatre. The stage, though equipped from the outset with curtain, footlights, and proper proscenium arch, has in the past stood open and unlit, ambient light having sufficed for the musical performances there. On this day, however, our stage glowed with glamour, its drawn purple curtains brilliantly illumed by flickering footlights and stirred by the rustle of unseen activity beyond.

More noteworthy than the physical change to the place, however, was an aura of excitement in the room, such as I had never before experienced aboard this ship. The pub packed with sailors … chatter loud and congenial … beer flowing freely… an air of anticipation even more palpable than that prior to the great occasion of Mustardhead's not-walking the plank.

Naturally, this ferment was due in part to the imminent debut of the play. However, there can be no doubt that larger events amplified the sense of *esprit*. The forecastle is abuzz, I am told, with rumours about the new phenomenon of water flowing around our ship, where

the water is going, and what this portends for those who serve aboard the *Mean Fish*. A hundred times, over the past few days, have I met with questions on the subject from excited sailors, and always my answer has been: have patience, lads, and soon you shall see. This has fed a delicious sort of perplexed fervour amongst our crew, which is very much to my purpose; joining streams with the advent of their very own stage production, these twin titillations could hardly have failed to make this day the most ebullient yet aboard the *Mean Fish*.

The front-most row of chairs was, of course, reserved for officers; a courteous sailor ushered Nelson and myself to seats front and centre, in between Bridger and Whitehand. With our arrival, the roster of officers in attendance was complete.

Unfortunately, we could not under the circumstances have denied Mustardhead a place amongst us, as Lampson was not to be banished to a row farther back, and yet he was still required to wait upon our former stowaway. In order to minimize adverse effects of this regrettable necessity, I had given orders that Mustardhead be seated at the far left side of the officer's row, with Lampson on his right, hoping that any disruptions caused by the boy would thereby have little effect upon the performance, or the audience's ability to appreciate it. Further, I had spoken to Mustardhead myself shortly prior, assuring him in no uncertain terms that a gentleman should never require anything of a servant during the performance of a play, and that failure to observe this rule would certainly be grounds for banishment to purgatory when his time *did* come. Judging from the manner in which the boy's face had blanched at these words, and given that a spark of his former fear had reappeared in his eyes, I felt satisfied that my point had been made.

After a few minutes of pleasant conversation, during which Nelson and I speculated upon the nature of the play we were about to see, there came a sudden and jarring sound of breaking glass.

The room fell silent at once. I looked over my shoulder to see that Penywern had broken a bottle upon the bar. Apparently this had been a prearranged signal, for he went on to say, "Gentlemen, thank you very much for your attention. Without further ado, may I present for your edification and enjoyment, the debut of a theatrical production by and for the crew of the *Mean Fish*: *The Bench and the Bishop*. There followed a few moments of lull, broken only by scattered coughs and throat-clearings in the room. Then, the curtains parted—their progress rather more jerky than graceful—revealing a most interesting tableaux.

The scene was a wood, as could be inferred by a painted sylvan backdrop and several large plaster trees which stood about on stage. In addition, the stage itself had been festooned with patches of grasses and underbrush, which I supposed must have been collected from the near vicinity some days before, as they now appeared quite desiccated—so much so, in fact, that I feared some of the patches nearest the edge might be set alight by the footlights' open flames. Once the play's action was underway, however, I became sufficiently engrossed that this distracting concern was forgotten.

Into the forest scene stepped Mr. Bigg, clad in a strange species of nautical dress-uniform, which must have been assembled from cast-off parts of several such outfits. He stood atop a large rock— an imported specimen of our local limestone—and in a reasonably impressive voice, delivered the following monologue:

"Good people who are here today
We hope most dearly that our play
Shall bring to heart, and mind, and soul
Both drama high, and humour droll.
Recall that we are common men
Ne'r understudies have we been

So here's our effort, come what may
Here is our best; here is our play."

Having spoken these lines, Bigg quit the stage, amidst a thunderous outpouring of applause and enthusiastic whooping from the audience, such as one might expect to follow a famous actor's thrilling rendition of Hamlet. I found myself a bit put off by this at first, for whilst I appreciated the effort which my crew have put into this production, a reaction of such magnitude seemed rather like bowing to a wagon-driver in thanks for the simple courtesy of not having run you over. However, by the time the cheers began to subside, I realized that such feelings should be set aside, as if would be difficult for me to fully fathom the effect a production of this nature must have upon a group of men, who have possibly never attended a dramatic performance, and certainly not one which they and their peers have created.

During the last scraps of applause for Bigg's monologue, a sailor hurried across the front of the stage to extinguish about half the footlights, and the eerie call of a hoot owl sounded from offstage. From these cues, I gathered that we now gazed upon a forest at night.

And then, a bishop appeared. The fellow's occupation was clear thanks to both his garb—consisting of papish robes, a mitre, and a staff—and the title of the play, which naturally led one to expect a bishop sooner or later. I am a great believer in the power of costume to reveal character upon the stage, and therefore felt pleased to learn from this fellow's manner of dress, that he held the bishopric of a rather impoverished region with poor tailors. As for which of our sailors had captured this titular role, I could only say that it was one of the many whom I see about the ship daily, or nearly so, but whose name I unhappily have not come to associate with their face.

The bishop began to poke about the stage, as if methodically searching for something. This carried on for so long that I thought

he might be hoping to find a copy of the script, but finally he gave a huff of displeasure, sat upon the stage, and began to speak.

"Here am I, a proper bishop," quoth the bishop, "properly meeting a proper friend in this wood at past midnight, and I'll be damned if this bosky dell furnishes a single proper spot for a bishop to sit. This ground is so damp that it shall moisten my bullocks, and no mistake."

Naturally, such language from a bishop struck the audience as comical, and laughter went up from the crowd. I could see, however, that Whitehand was rather less than amused, notwithstanding that the clergyman depicted was clearly Romish; our vicar crossed his arms, and his face assumed a sour look. As for myself, I felt assured that the good bishop was for certain a city dweller, as experience informs countryfolk that forests shall not normally afford a plethora of good places to sit.

At this point, there came a strange sound—somewhere between a lamb's bleat and a bout of flatulence, to my ears—and the bishop looked all round in trepidation. "Who's there?" he cried.

As if in response, ten enchanted trees shambled onto the stage. I took them to be enchanted since they were capable of movement— hardly a quality of ordinary trees—but must add that they did not resemble trees, so much as persons thrust into stiff, cylindrical sheaths (adorned with leafy branches) which covered their entire bodies save their feet, and which must have bound their arms to their sides in a most awkward manner. Somehow, the intrepid actors within these ungraceful costumes managed to shuffle into position (although three of them very nearly toppled over in doing so), and at that juncture they broke into a song:

"As trees, we've been splendid
But here's a sad bit:
Our guest, the good bishop,

222

Has no place to sit.
If word of such outrage
Should spread from this place,
The name of our fine wood
Would fall to disgrace."

The trees sang this straight through once, then began to repeat it in the form of a round. Unfortunately, the interlocking parts got muddled rather quickly and the entire musical edifice collapsed into a cacophonic mess, with trees warbling what sounded like random lines at random times. They would have done well to recognize this and stop, yet they soldiered on, only falling silent when Penywern shattered another bottle back at the bar. That must have been some sort of emergency signal, and to everyone's relief I am sure, put the crippled song out of its misery.

In the silence which followed, the largest tree yet ambled out onto the stage. This giant made straight for the bishop and only stopped about three inches short of him, causing the Man of God understandable discomfiture, as no one would wish to be trod upon by a tree.

"I am Woody, King of the Trees!" said the very large tree, in a properly majestic voice. "And who might you be?"

"I am Simon, Bishop of Bluebury," said the bishop.

"Simon, Bishop of Bluebury," said the tree, "I have heard your complaint about the lack of seating in our wood, and I am very sorry for it. It is not our wish that guests be uncomfortable here."

Simon stood to his feet. "'Tis a fine sentiment, Woody, King of the Trees, but it shan't make my arse ache any less." This remark sent another flutter of laughter through the audience.

"Bishop, it is a bitter embarrassment to all trees in the wood, and I am sorry indeed that your grace has had to sit upon this damp, rocky ground."

At that moment, an object appeared above the players—dangling from a visible string—and began to swing to and fro over the trees' leafy crowns. Judging by its size and appearance, I took it to be a chicken which had been rolled in gunpowder and fired from a cannon, but with a voice coming from the crawlway atop the stage, the thing introduced itself as Art the Dove.

"Art the Dove," said the bishop, "I am Simon, Bishop of Bluebury. Might you be able to fly high above this wood, and espy some comfortable location for me to settle this pampered bottom of mine?"

Instead of favouring the bishop's question with a reply, Art the Dove said, "Woody, King of the Trees! Have you considered summoning the bench for this good bishop to sit upon?"

At this, a gasp went up from the assembly of trees.

"Bench?" said the bishop. "What is this bench you speak of?"

"Ah, my good bishop," said Woody, "It is a magical bench, wrought of nature's dark magic, which appears in this wood when we trees summon it."

"And how did this come to be?" asked the bishop.

"Legend amongst us trees tells that, long ago, a man came to this wood with the intention of building a house here. Unhappily for him, he had miscalculated the amount of stone he would need, and only had enough to build a bench. Embittered by the unfairness of it all, he laid a curse upon the bench, then left, never to return. It has been so ever since."

"Bring the bench here," snapped the bishop. "I want it."

"But my good bishop! It is a bench of dark and accursed magic!" Woody cried.

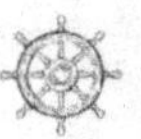

"I don't care if it's the seat of the Devil himself, I wish to sit upon it!" said the bishop.

I noticed Whitehand lean close to Nelson and remark, "Huh! Fresh out of seminary, I see."

As for the bishop, he had scarce finished speaking when the trees converged into a circle around him, obscuring his person from view, and appearing to jostle him about rather roughly with their trunks, as in low voices they chanted something like, "doo … Doo.… Dooooom … Doo …," and so forth. I felt at a complete loss as to what the trees meant to accomplish by this, my confusion compounded by an eerie fog rolling onto the stage, and plaster objects suddenly flying about, which had been shaped and painted so as to resemble rocks. The rocks originated offstage, some striking the trees, but many bouncing along the ground, and although I wondered for a moment who hurled these missiles and what their motives were, I quickly concluded that the flying rocks and the fog were meant to convey that a sort of general upheaval was taking place.

Amidst this chaos, the trees herded the bishop off to one side of the stage, and left off mobbing him. The rain of rocks also subsided, although one final plaster chunk, the size of a pumpkin and cunningly aimed, bounced right off the bishop's head, doing him no visible harm save knocking off his mitre, much to the amusement of the audience. I took this particular insult to be unscripted, for as the bishop collected his mitre and put it back on, he shot someone offstage a pointedly vexed glare.

Moments later, as the fog began to clear, I saw that a bench had appeared in the centre of the stage. Apparently, the alarums and confusion had been the incantation required to summon it. It looked the sort of simple, backless bench one might find in a garden, though normally such furnishings are fashioned of stone, whereas this one was obviously wood which had been painted grey.

The bishop went to the bench and examined it closely. "Hmmm," he said, "I had expected something more noble—more fitting for a prelate of my standing. Well, having seen your bench, I do not believe that I wish to sit upon it, after all."

At this, the trees began to moan ominously, and again they converged into a circle, this time surrounding both bishop and bench. More fog rolled across the stage, and a few plaster rocks were flung about (in what looked to me a desultory sort of way).

Moments later, as the trees waddled back into an arc across the stage, and the fog again cleared, we in the audience saw that the bench had undergone a marvelous transformation. Some sylvan alchemy had converted its grey stone to shining gold, and its every surface now gleamed with enormous gemstones.

The bishop's attitude towards the bench changed accordingly. Mouth agape, he gingerly lowered himself onto it. He caressed its gilded surfaces, a weird gleam in his eye as he sang a song which began:

"O bench for a bishop!
O seat for a King!
O glorious arse-rest!
O beautiful thing!
If with my own eyes
I did not see thee shine,
I would never believe
How I wish you were mine!"

Subsequent lyrics followed, but struck me as redundant, the gist of the song being that Simon very much wished to take this bench home with him, upon the conclusion of his meeting in the wood. As he sang, however, it became clear that this desire of his was upsetting to the denizens of the forest; the trees wavered about uncertainly

amidst a renewal of their disapproving moans, and Art the Dove began to pendulate even more rapidly than usual, as if agitated.

"Good bishop!" Quoth Art at the end of the song. "We beg of you to not even consider taking the bench! Part of the dark spell is that, should the bench be removed from this place, the wood and all creatures within it shall perish!"

So now our protagonist, as in any good drama, found himself upon the horns of a dilemma. He launched into a monologue—meant to be stirring, I daresay—debating the merits of the choices before him. On the one hand, he could seize as his own a bench worth a fortune, then either sell it and give the proceeds to the poor, or else install it in his own quarters, where he could sit upon its beguiling surface whenever he wished. On the other hand, he could forego the bench and spare the lives of his new friends, consisting of a few sick-looking talking trees and a badly burned chicken calling itself a dove.

Simon still wrestled with this—a moral quandary worthy of Saint Augustine himself—when a second person appeared upon the stage. Based upon the bishop's reaction, this must have been the friend whom he had arranged to meet in the wood. Much to the bishop's professional discredit, this friend was clearly a she.

Having no ladies on board, the crew had naturally reverted to the Elizabethan tradition of placing a man in this role, relying upon such contrivances as costume, wig, and cosmetics, to shew the character's gender. They had also employed padding to imitate the shapely contours of the fair sex, although the resulting proportions were rather unrealistically exaggerated (whether for comic effect or from a sense of lewdness, I cannot say). The appearance of this actor in such habiliment solicited a wave of bawdy laughter and catcalls from the audience, which the fellow had composure enough to ignore.

Simon sprang up from the bench and ran to embrace his paramour. "O! My daisy! My sweet lovely maiden, Daisy, flower of my life!" cried the bishop. "How wrong it is for us to meet here in this manner, and yet I can contain no longer my burning love for you, nor my frozen hatred for your evil uncle!"

Daisy opened her rouged lips as if to speak, but before she could utter a sound, one of the trees broke rank and roughly barged in between the lovers, nearly knocking them over. This rude tree proceeded to blurt out, seemingly to no one in particular: "You know, I did think it a bit strange, a bit peculiar, that this bishop, being priestly and all, would be out here in the middle of a wood, past midnight no less, waiting to meet a friend; it's enough to make you wonder what's up with the ol' bishop, eh? And so this friend, being a lady and all, I mean, it seems a mite inappropriate! Now I'm really wondering about the ol' bishop, having this liaison in the woods and all—being a talking tree and all, I just wonder about it. We talking trees can wonder and think, you know, that's how come we can talk. But then, it also strikes me as a might strange that this bishop would be out here chumming about with us talking trees, seeing as how we're animated by pagan spirits, and …"

This soliloquy must have been unplanned, for during it another tree drew gradually nearer the one speaking, informing it several times, with increasing emphasis, to shut up. When the tree failed to heed this advice, two of its fellows pushed it over, silencing its ruminations. Daisy again began to speak; this time she found herself interrupted by the fallen tree informing the room, in a loud voice: "I'd like some help, seeing as how I'm not able to get up and all!" And "I'm from Chelsea!" Simon gave the prostrate tree a sound kick; it went rolling towards the back of the stage, as several of its colleagues moved nimbly aside to avoid being bowled over by it.

Able at last to deliver her line, Daisy said to Simon (in a voice not quite convincingly feminine), "O Simon, my love! I know that others, and even the whole of Europe, would never approve of our meeting like this, but how, O how, can it be wrong? Let us rest here upon this lovely bench, and speak of our admiration for one another, and our future together."

Daisy moved as if to sit upon the bench. Simon stopped her doing so. She made another attempt. Again Simon prevented her, rather roughly. Daisy tried a third time. The bishop slapped her full across the face (drawing hisses and angry exclamations from the audience for such ill-treatment of a lady), and in a voice filled suddenly with malice he said, "Foul woman! 'Tis my bench, and no one else may sit upon it!"

After a moment expressive of utter shock, Daisy exited stage left, weeping as she fled, declaring that the slap had hurt far less than her beloved's unwillingness to share the bench with her.

The bishop made as if to run after her, yet he was clearly loath to leave behind the bench. So he sat upon it and proceeded to verbally agonize over what he had done, expressing his love for both Daisy and the bench. This noble speech on the choice before his heart was, I am afraid, somewhat impaired by the fallen tree, which continued to roll about the rear of the stage in a noisy attempt to re-erect itself.

At length, Simon reached a decision. Standing to his feet, he bid a tearful goodbye to the friends he had found in the forest, especially Woody and Art. Then, turning upon the bench, he angrily reproached it for its "strange and malign power over men." With that, the bishop left the stage, saying, "Fly, my feet! May there be time yet for me to marry my Daisy, and lay low her evil uncle! Yoiks and away!"

The bishop had scarcely vanished stage left, when Mr. Bigg reappeared from stage right. He adroitly stepped over the rolling fallen tree and stood beside the bench with a sign reading:

Fifty years later

Bigg shewed us this sign for such a length of time, that I began to wonder if perhaps, in order to enhance the play's realism, he was actually going to stand there for fifty years. When he at last quit the stage, however, it was immediately clear why so long a delay had been necessary—Simon and Daisy returned to the forest wearing a good deal of cunningly applied makeup, causing them to appear elderly. The effect was truly impressive.

Arm-in-arm, the ancient lovers strolled to the bench, gladly greeting their old friends, Woody and Art. Now, whilst a tree may easily live for fifty years and more, one may not say the same for a dove; this, together with the fact that the bird's appearance and flight habits had changed not a whit during that time, led me to speculate that Art was no ordinary blackened chicken, but the accidental product of some sloppy enchanter.

The ensuing dialogue between the lovers gave us to understand that Simon had renounced his bishopric on that very night long ago, in order to wed his Daisy, and that the two of them, now in failing health, had returned to the bench after many happy years together, to peacefully shuffle off their mortal coils in this fondly recalled place of rendezvous. I heard more than one melancholy sniffle from the audience as Simon and Daisy sat upon the bench, clasped hands, leaned their heads upon one another's shoulders, and blissfully passed into the next world. The blessed transition was made plain by the appearance of two wingéd angels, clad in white and crowned with golden haloes, who took our hero and heroine by the hands and led them offstage, presumably to paradise.

As these players left the stage, the curtains closed, and such an outburst erupted from the audience, that the term "applause" utterly fails to describe it. Beyond a thunderous tide of clapping and cheering—which I had anticipated, given the warm response to

Bigg's prologue—many sailors leapt atop their chairs and stomped with great enthusiasm, accompanied by such hollering as one might expect from a tribe of howler monkeys. Surely nothing of the sort has ever been seen at the Drury Lane!

Moments later, the curtains again parted as the entire cast performed a walkdown; this they did with admirable style (although the trees' costumes did not allow them to execute anything like a bow, so they turned circles in place). It alarmed me to see several beer mugs hurled upon the stage, their shattered fragments fanning out across the boards, but I quickly realized that this was a sign of approval, as the sight of it caused the players to bow their bows and turn their circles all the more delightedly.

The curtains closed again, the delirious ruckus slacked off into a hum of excited conversation, and I rose to leave, in order to personally congratulate the players backstage. Nelson chose to accompany me on this happy errand. As we made our way amongst the throng, edging past Mustardhead and Lampson, I heard the boy ask his *ad interim* servant if any of that had been real. Lampson's eyes briefly met mine before he laid a hand upon Mustardhead's shoulder, and in his most grave manner, said, "Oh, yes. Much of it was real. Art the Dove and the trees dwell aboard this ship, and woe to any man who incurs the wrath of our captain, for these magical beings do his bidding, and have the power to send a person not only to purgatory, but also ... to the bad place."

I had only a glimpse of the boy's profile in that moment, but even so I could see, it was as if a mask was pulled away and the old, cowering Mustardhead revealed underneath.

As I moved past, Lampson again caught my eye; I favoured him with a slight nod. The boy has become far too familiar and cavalier in his attitude towards everyone, but especially myself, and so however disingenuous this statement of Lampson's, I could not help but

approve of the check it should place upon Mustardhead's unseemly swagger. Hoping that here, at least, Lampson's bout of servitude might prove to have a salutary effect upon the boy, I led my uncle through the crowd and out of the pub, towards the backstage door.

After supper this evening—a festive event in the crew's mess, I am told, given the success of their play—a letter passed into my hands, which was addressed to myself in the unpleasantly jagged handwriting of the Rector of Reeth. It was with a sense of foreboding that I paced along the plank to read this note:

The Revd Simon Wright, Rector of Reeth
Wormwood House, Reeth, Yorkshire

My Dearest Lord Keld,
It has come to my attention, and to the attention of the Rt Hon Earl of Arkengarthdale, that a number of fully functional cannons have been mounted upon your ship, the Mean Fish, *which lies at anchor in the pool behind Stonesthrow Hall, near Keld. In addition, His Lordship the Earl and myself were made aware, during our tour of your fascinating vessel, that a considerable amount of gunpowder was already at that time stored in the ship's hold.*

Taken together, these facts imply that anyone bent upon causing injury to the lands and villages of Upper Swaledale, which lie within range of these guns, or anyone determined to hold in thrall the villagers of that area by the threat of ruination, lacks only ammunition to make fully operational these engines of war, and such matériel may in fact already be stowed aboard the Mean Fish.

Neither the earl nor I mean to insinuate that you yourself, nor any of your officers, would even contemplate such heinous offenses to the peace of our valley. Your Lordship, in particular, enjoys an unimpeachable reputation as a lifelong friend to one and all in our neighbourhood. However, it has also not escaped our notice that there may be amongst your crew certain elements supportive of a seditious and revolutionary order, which desires the overthrow of Great Britain's

benign government, in favour of an unchecked rampage of so-called liberty, the likes of which is currently consuming the erstwhile Kingdom of France.

It is therefore the intention of His Lordship Arkengarthdale, and myself, to ensure that His Grace the Duke of Richmond is made fully aware of this perilous situation, so that he may act accordingly to secure the safety of his lands and the King's peaceful subjects in Upper Swaledale.

The earl and myself are confident that Your Lordship shall do everything in your own power to forestall even the possibility of a violent plot, by at once disarming your vessel (as we can imagine no legitimate reason for her being armed to begin with), and by ensuring that any groups or individuals disloyal to the King of Great Britain are at once turned out from your employment, and handed over to the proper authorities in York.

His Lordship Arkengarthdale, and myself, remain admirers of your accomplishments in Keld and,
Your most humble and obedient servants.

This hateful accusation posing as an affable missive, was signed with the indecipherable scrawl which Reeth terms a signature.

I summoned my uncle at once and bade him read the note. This he did with a visible souring of expression, and such a tightening of his fingers upon the paper, that he appeared poised to rend it into a thousand pieces. However, when finished he merely handed the letter back to me and said, "Well, Nephew, what may we expect from a serpent? And yet you appear caught offguard, unless I read you wrongly. Did you hope that the rector would perhaps publish an ode singing our praises, in every newspaper from York to Hong Kong? Of course he wishes to cut us off at the ankles. Let us thank the heavens that he has forgotten himself and shewn his ill will in this letter, for this gives us the opportunity to fire a return volley, sooner than we otherwise could have."

Nelson's artillery metaphor caused me to envision, for a sweet moment, the guns which so discomfit the rector laying waste to his residence as our ship speeds past Reeth, but of course, such vindictiveness would do me no credit and, what is more, would only confirm the nefarious motives which certain idiotic locals clearly attribute to us, for the entirely natural precaution of arming an ocean-going sailing ship. So with a grit of my teeth I laid aside this pleasing fancy, and said, "Uncle, you told me four days ago that the works downstream are very nearly complete, and that given the volume of water on hand, we may not even need to use the locks for our inaugural voyage, once we have diverted enough flow. What news have we of conditions down-valley?"

"Nephew, we have been putting the lion's share of the swollen Swale into the project for almost ninety hours now, and with these rains continuing to blow through, I am assured that the flow is more than adequate for our needs."

"And the transition at Richmond?"

"Well, that is going to be a very tricky part, even with this much water. Miss Smeaton has assured us all along that such would be the case, unless we wished to make our intentions all too clear with a lowermost lock feeding straight into the Swale."

"Which we do not have time for now, even should we wish it. Well, Uncle, it sounds as if there shall be no time better than the present, even if we did not have this letter from that wicked Reeth to goad us." I took a deep breath and let it out slowly, before saying, "Uncover the passage tonight. We set off in the morning."

Four days' past, when I instructed my uncle to begin the diversion of Swale water into our project, his reaction had been an almost childlike sort of glee. Now, as we two stood upon the verge of the next great step, he received my orders with an air of gravity. Then, had we both felt positively giddy at the thought of river water

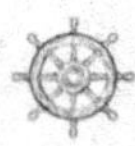

flowing beneath our keel; today, it is I suppose the magnitude of our undertaking—both logistically and politically—which tempers our enthusiasms.

This is truly the point of no return. Until now, any local observers have hopefully attributed the flooding of the Swaledale turn-pike to the recent incessant rains, together with the fact that weatherproof roofing has yet to be erected over the "road." As dawn breaks tomorrow, no one viewing the upper end of our project shall any longer doubt its true purpose.

Nelson, of course, understood this as well as I. With a grim sort of smile and a firm nod, he said, "I shall oversee tonight's operation myself. Tomorrow the *Mean Fish* begins her migration to the sea."

He turned as if to go, but paused, looked back, and faced me again. "Nephew, I have something to say," he began, in an uncharacteristically sheepish manner. "That business a few weeks back, of me carrying out most of my work in the Hall, and not sleeping aboard ship ... I didn't realize it then, but looking back 'tis as plain as the cliffs of Scarborough Head, that my heart was no longer in any of this. It had been damn well exhausting to keep up my belief in our barmy ambition for all those years, even as we made such splendid headway. Once the ship was here, why, she sort of seemed fine right where she was, and our project would have made a profitable turn-pike, after all, and as for you, you seemed not to notice nor care how much I'd been drifting back to the Hall. And then also, I'd had a bit of a falling out with miss ... well, let's not go into that. Suffice to say that I'd laid aside the idea of this ship's keel ever touching the sea, in sentiment if not in word.

"But then that night ... seeing that you had marked my absence, after all, then troubled yourself to steal after me, wrapped in a tablecloth ... damned if I can say exactly why, but that rekindled my faith in the whole enterprise. And naturally, the sight of my nephew

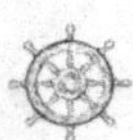

knocking about in such a foolish getup shewed once and for all that he'd never manage to pull the bleeding thing off without me."

I stood speechless for a moment, caught, as I occasionally am with my uncle, in between gratitude for a compliment he has paid me, and resentment at some affront which he has woven into the same breath. I finally stammered something to the effect of how gratified I was, to hear that my actions had brought him back to the ship in spirit as well as in body, but before I could object to his low opinion of the tablecloth disguise, Nelson held up a preemptory hand and said, "Ah—ah—there shall be ample time for talk later, one way or another. For now, I must be off on the moment. There is a great deal to be done before the sun rises, and it shall be a short night. Heaven help us, Nephew—and the Romish saints, if they can, and the Bodhisattvas too, should they lend that sort of assistance. I would refuse no supernatural help, save perhaps the Devil's, with what lies before us." And with that, my uncle gave me a vague sort of salute, and quit my cabin.

Heaven help us, indeed! We grapple now with a challenge, next to which our years of preceding work have been but the merest prelude … nothing more than the tuning of instruments before an overture's first bold notes are struck.

Tuesday, June 30, 1795

Although it has been only fifteen hours or so, since last I set pen to this paper, it feels as though far more time has passed. How much more? A week? A fortnight? It is hard to say, but one thing is sure, this day has proved more eventful than any previous day of my life. This morning now seems the distant past, and yesterday, possibly a dream I have awoken from.

Sunrise this morning—the day being so near summer solstice, and Keld being rather far in the north of the world—took place at a time which would have perplexed a rooster from Rome. Three-forty-two, to be exact. I fell out of bed at three-thirty, dawn light already visible around my curtains, and myriad exclamations of astonishment audible from the decks above. I knew—or rather, hoped that I knew—what spectacle inspired those enthused cries.

Dressing myself more hurriedly than usual, I rushed up onto the deck, and into yet another morn of driving rain. It looked as if the entire crew stood assembled along the forecastle railings, their attention fixed off to the southeast. I myself made for the rails, anxious to learn how Nelson's work had progressed overnight.

I was mere steps away from gaining a vantage point when Bridger came charging up to me, looking so alarmed and disheveled that one might have supposed the *Mean Fish* under attack by cannibals with cannons. He grabbed my shoulder, pivoted me about to face him, and said, "Per'aps there's a thing or two more you ain't informed yer second mate about, Capn'? Like per'aps this here ship has wings, and tomorrow we're unfurling 'em and flying to London?"

I failed to resist breaking into a broad grin, even though this shew of satisfaction clearly irked my trusty boatswain. "Did I not furnish you with a clew just a few days ago, Mr. Bridger, when we discussed

the water flowing here from the forks of the Swale, and why it had not caused our cozy little pool to overflow?"

"Truth, you did, sir, and it was plain enough to me that some sort of tunnel must be carrying water out of the pool, and probably on down into the Swale. But this … this…" He trailed off, seeming bereft of words, gesturing in the direction which held the crew's attention.

I took this opportunity to unclamp Bridger's hand from my shoulder, and go to the railing, for my own view of the wonder which had appeared off our bow during the hours of darkness.

What yesterday had been a broad, featureless expanse of manicured lawn, was now bisected by a passage of water, arrow-straight and bordered on both sides by stacks of wooden pallets topped with green grass. The near end of the passage emerged from the Mare Jacobum, water flowing into it from our pool betwixt piles of removed flagstones.

"You were right about the tunnel," I told Bridger. "But it was a tunnel made to be unroofed. Our chief engineer designed a series of wooden pallets to cover it, which could be pulled to either side in manageable sections, by teams of horses. You see those handles atop each set? Those were unearthed last night, and the teams hitched onto them. The lovely lawn which we grew atop the whole assembly succeeded, I venture you shall agree, in concealing the tunnel's presence entirely."

"I bloody well do agree! How long's that water course been there, for Pete's bloody sake?"

"For a rather long time. We built the passage, then covered it with pallets and grass, several years before starting construction on the ship—lest anyone make an easy connection betwixt the two."

"So water from the upper Swale's been feeding into this here fancy ditch for days, now," said Bridger.

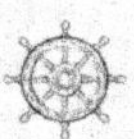

"Actually, we filled the passage with water at the same time as our pool, back in mid-May, as it was a covered extension of the Mare Jacobum. Since then, it has lain concealed below the grass. Nelson and his men did an admirable job of uncovering it last night, although it does look as if the horse teams muddied the lawn in places, as they pulled the pallets aside. Pity, that, but I suppose there was no getting round it."

"But then ... if the Swale water's flowing into the pool ... then into the fancy ditch ... where in bloody blazes is it going from the far end of the ditch? There's nothing over there save the uppermost cuttings of your not-a-turn-pike!"

By way of reply, I favoured my second mate with a grin of genuine glee, so wide that I felt it must split my face. Bridger's answering expression, most satisfyingly, blended a dawning realization with complete and utter awe.

"The turn-pike ... the whole bleedin' thing ... is a ditch?"

"It is a canal, Mr. Bridger! Hence the sunken grade following the contours of the valley slope, the steady gradient, and the so-called toll gates, which are built to function as locks. Given the great hydraulic head—nine-hundred and twenty feet of drop between here and Richmond, or fifteen feet per lock—it is all designed to work by gravity, under normal conditions."

What an unspeakable joy did I feel, at being able to freely speak of our canal. For so many years had my uncle and I held close this magnificent secret, assiduously concealing it from county authorities, who had approved a turn-pike in such a remote and topographically challenging location only after years of persuasion from us. Seeking approval for a canal along the same alignment would have been a hundred times more difficult; even if a waterway in Swaledale were to confer the same economic advantages as a turn-pike (and it would not), the technical hurdles involved would have been considered insurmountable by those small minds down in York. And unfortunately, the small minds' approval had been an absolute necessity; only with the establishment of a county right-of-way were we able to build our project across the multitude of properties betwixt Keld and Richmond—including lands belonging to both the Rector of Reeth and His Loutship Arkengarthdale.

For fear of our true intentions ever reaching the wrong ears in York, Nelson and I had never been able to tell anyone, save Whitehand and Converse, who had been sworn to secrecy, and of course, our engineer, Miss Smeaton. I have not heretofore felt able to be honest even within these pages, should they have fallen into unfriendly hands before our aim was accomplished.

How many times had I rehearsed in my imaginings, the pleasure of finally divulging the truth about our project, then savouring the exclamations of amazement sure to follow. At long last that moment had arrived, and I must say that Bridger's reaction did not disappoint. He had the look of a man who has just witnessed every tree and blade of grass in sight change colour from green to purple, and he seemed scarce able to speak.

"So, the *Mean Fish* … we are going … sailing … no, to be towed by draft animals. . . all the way down to Richmond?" he managed to ask.

"Mr. Bridger, in these past couple of weeks my leanings towards deism have been shaken, as I nearly believe that the almighty himself looks with favour upon our plans. The unprecedented flooding which plagues our fair Yorkshire is for us a positive boon, enabling us to do away with locks and towpaths for this inaugural journey down the canal. We're able to put enough water down the gullet, so to speak, that we'll be carried right along, with every lock-door standing wide open."

"And who says this'll work? You?"

"No—our engineer, who has designed the entire project. She assures us that we shall have ample water beneath our keel under these conditions, all the way to Rrichmond."

Poor Bridger. As our conversation progressed, he had been overtaken by a look of thunderstruck amazement not once, but repeatedly, and his astonishment appeared to reach a pitch nearing all-out desperation as he blurted, "She? This whole bleeding tower of nonsense rests on the ciphering and words of a *woman*?"

"Aye, Mr. Bridger, a woman whose ciphering and words I would stake my life upon … which is fortunate, since that is in fact what we are about to do. I have complete faith in her determination that we shall have plenty of water from here to Richmond, and in the rivers below there, owing to the widespread flooding in all this part of the country. Although I daresay it's going to be quite a ride."

"And just who is expected to pilot the ship down this narrow sluice of water?"

With a hearty slap on the back, I told my second mate, "Why, you are, Mr. Bridger! You are!"

At that very moment, Nelson's best nautical voice cut like a musket report through the dull rumble of rain. "All hands! All hands to stations! Prepare to weigh anchor!" I spotted my uncle ascending the gangplank along with several members of our road crew—or should I now properly term them the canal crew—who had helped un-roof the passage. He met my gaze and gave a cheery wave. "The way is open, Captain!" he declared, reaching the main deck and heading our way, through a throng of suddenly active sailors. "Is Mr. Bridger ready to take us down-valley?"

"I am ready to do no such thing!" said Bridger. "There's no man alive could outmaneuver me on the open sea, but taking a tall bloody ship down a bloody log flume is not something any sailor should bloody rightly be asked to do, on a moment's bloody notice!"

In hindsight, it *had* been unfair of Nelson and me to have kept our second mate so in the dark—and yet, Bridger being a newcomer to our inner circle, we had felt obliged to do so. In that moment, however, I was so buoyed up by excitement that I did not, perhaps, shew sufficient respect for his misgivings. "Nonsense!" said I. "You'll have the rudder, and the sides of the canal have been made smooth, to minimize turbulence. It should simply be a matter of keeping the bow pointing downstream as we are whisked along. I feel absolutely certain that you are up to it!"

"Your background does include river-piloting," said Nelson, who had by then joined us.

"That was the Severn, not a bloody spillway!" spat Bridger.

I noticed my uncle subtly, but certainly, take a half step to his left—a sure sign that he is about to switch tactics. "Well, by the King's Colours, Mr. Bridger! I never would've credited the idea that you, of all men, should confess yourself unfit for such a task."

"What's that, then? Well y'see, it's just that ..."

"No, no, it is all very well, Mr. Bridger. Although my nephew and I have harboured the highest expectations for your piloting abilities, we do respect your wisdom and self-knowledge in this matter, and so it looks as though we shall have to go with our second plan, after all." Turning to me, he went on, "Captain, shall I send into Keld for that pilot we have held in reserve—the Liverpool fellow ..."

"Liverpool? Bite yer bloody tongue! I'll not have sech dregs lay one pinkie-finger on the wheel of this here ship!"

Blinking in false confoundment, my uncle said, "But you have expressed doubts in your own abilities, and we ..."

"Bloody hell an' bastard bones!" Bridger snapped. "I've no bloody doubts, and I'll bloody well flay any man dares get between me and that wheel! Er ... which I state with all due respect fer present comp'ny! Cap'n, there's no better sailor on God's Earth fer the job

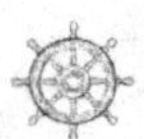

at hand, and I'd pilot this here ship straight through the Maelström into the bowels of Hades, were sech an extremity called for! So as fer this here flat-water gambol on down to Richmond – pah! I could steer it with one hand, blindfold!"

"Good man!" said I, giving Bridger another clap upon the back, and favouring my uncle with a surreptitious nod of thanks.

"Now," Bridger went on, "If you gents'll leave me to it, I've got a thing or two to say with my bosun-pipe which—no offense to Sir James—will light more of a fire under a crew, than brave shouts from a first mate ever shall. What time are we shoving off, Cap'n?"

"Six o'clock," said I.

"She'll be ready," said Bridger, and then he launched into a veritable symphony of bosun-pipe calls, so numerous and rapid that with my still-rudimentary knowledge I could only half-follow them. All along the topside of the *Mean Fish*, sailors mobilized by my uncle's call to stations did indeed appear to redouble their efforts in response to the hypnotic warble of Bridger's pipe.

For my part, I proceeded to busy myself in the hold, the library, the galley, and a half-dozen other places, ensuring that our ship was ready to move.

How the mood on board had shifted—a transformation every bit as complete as the metamorphosis from lawn to waterway which had so impressed everyone. The excitement over the play was as nothing compared to this; sailors hurried hither and thither with a sense of purpose which I had never witnessed aboard the *Mean Fish*, and their manner of greeting their captain, which I must admit had often been rather perfunctory, was all of a sudden far more enthused. Even the galley cooks, who have seemed always to consider it a requirement of their positions to behave in a surly manner towards everyone, shewed a modicum of respect for their captain which I had never before enjoyed.

Amidst this whirlwind of activity, as I checked my wine racks in the hold, in order to ensure that the bottles would not be easily damaged by movements of the ship, I was startled by the sudden appearance of Nelson. "Captain," said he, "I believe that you wish to deliver a speech prior to our launch? The crew are now assembled on deck for that purpose. Heavens, I have looked for you everywhere!"

Thanking Nelson for his timely reminder, I made haste to the poop deck, determined that at long last I should enjoy the pleasure of delivering a proper speech to the entire crew, free from the ridiculous interruptions which had spoiled every previous attempt.

I found the entire ship's compliment gathered on the main deck; my officers stood smartly in a line across the poop, facing the assembly. It especially pleased me to see amongst them Mr. Lampson, released at last from his vexing indenturement to Mustardhead. My joy was compounded when the young man favoured me with a respectful bow, which I took to signify that his lesson had been learnt and that no ill feelings existed between us.

The rain had slacked off to a mere drizzle. Given prevailing conditions over the previous days, such weather seemed fair by comparison. Still, it could have been a torrential downpour and I would not have cared a whit; the gravity of the occasion trumped all considerations of personal comfort.

I stood there looking out over that sea of expectant faces, and felt a swell of pride within my bosom, the likes of which I had never known. There was no mistaking the fact that this crew now looked to me, in a manner which they had not before.

"Sailors of the *Mean Fish*!" I called, my words echoing back from the walls of Stonesthrow Hall. "Moses, that great prophet of old, led his people on a dry path across the Red Sea—or at least some respectable inlet of it, if not the main part, which *is* rather wide—by dint of a miracle wrought of God. On this day, we witness a sort of

secular counterpart to that story in Exodus. Through the application of foresight, cunning engineering, and horses, we have caused a watery path to appear across a flawless lawn! Beyond lies a canal, which shall launch our ship on her journey to the sea!"

A hurrah went up from the crew. Caps were tossed into the air, along with various other objects less well-suited for safely hurling skywards above one's head. More thoroughly pleased by this reaction than I may easily describe, I pressed on as soon as the cheer had died down. "Gentlemen, within two day's time, I fully expect that our keel shall ply the saltwater of the North Sea! And yet I must caution and admonish you! Our journey shall not be without its perils! I ask every man amongst you for your utmost ..."

In the midst of that last sentence, a piercing bosun-pipe whistle split the air. Instantly, a loud ratcheting sound arose from some indefinite location, and at the point when I stopped speaking, the ship gave a great lurch. There must have been sailors standing ready at the windlasses below decks, who had responded to a call from Bridger, to weigh anchors. Another great hurrah went up from the crew as it became clear: the *Mean Fish* was no longer held fast in the waters of the Mare Jacobum. She was underway, pushed by the current flowing through the pool!

My ship was moving! Torn between ecstasy and indignation, I swiveled round to face Bridger, who had stepped out of line and stood at the wheel, already making adjustments as he aimed us for the uncovered passage. "I say, Bridger! What is the meaning of this?"

"Why, the meanin' is, it's six o'clock, sir! Time to shove off and get this beauty moving!"

"I can see what is happening! But I was not through with my speech! In fact, I had a good deal of it left, including the best parts! Why on earth could you not have held off until I had finished!"

"You did tell me six o'clock, sir," said Bridger.

"Yes, but … confound it! I did not realize what the time was!"

Bridger shrugged. "Good thing I did, Cap'n, otherwise we'd be laggin' right out o' the gate!"

"But look here, Bridger, I …"

"Beggin' yer pardon, Cap'n, but we are underway, and I'll need every scrap of attention I can spare to steer this lovely lady! Your Lordship's most esteemed person is hinderin' my view! And might I suggest, before you turn any more shades of purple, that here's a moment we should all of us savour! Whatever happens next, this we'll remember all our lives! We're moving, Cap'n! Don't neglect the moment! We're moving!"

I looked about, and realized that Bridger was right. This was no occasion to waste on bickering.

How strange the sensation of our ship's movement! I had become so accustomed to the *Mean Fish* being fixed in place, that it initially felt to me as if she must remain so, whilst the entire world around us had somehow been set in motion and now slid slowly past. Already our bow entered the upper end of our passage, the south wing of Stonesthrow Hall slipping by to port. I spotted a gaggle of Hall staff assembled near the orangery, waving and calling "Godspeed!" Rugby and Gertrude front and centre amongst them. I heartily waved back.

The entire crew seemed every bit as wonderstruck as I; they stood at the railings all along the forecastle and main deck, sending up spontaneous cheer after cheer as our proud vessel passed between the stacked pallets of turf which had concealed our watery passage.

I found that my officers still stood round about me, no longer in a line, but forming a sort of halo around Bridger and the wheel. My uncle appeared immeasurably proud in that moment, so much so that I would not have wondered to see a tear course down his cheek. Wheelwright looked serene, Converse dumbstruck—quite the opposite of what one might have expected, given that the latter

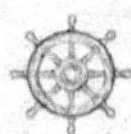

was acquainted with our long-laid plans for this moment, whilst the former was not. I saw upon Whitehand's countenance a curious blend of approval and vexation (later I learnt that he had taken umbrage with what he considered my flippant remarks about the Red Sea, and was considering the best manner in which to reprimand me).

As for Lampson, he appeared at my side in what I may only describe as a fit of overwhelming enthusiasm, craving to know more mechanical details about this marvelous passage, and the canal below, than I myself could have provided. Fortunately, Nelson was available to supplement my knowledge, but still we found it necessary to defer many of these questions to Miss Jane Smeaton herself, whose graceful presence we hope to welcome aboard ship near Hull.

The *Mean Fish* neared the end of our un-roofed passage, and the upper end of our canal loomed ahead, when Lampson asked, "Weren't all of the anchors drawn in just now? I heard windlasses running both fore and aft." When I confirmed that this was indeed the case, he went on, "But if we are to run the canal with every lock-door standing open, and given the number of bends in the canal between here and Richmond, would it not be better to proceed with a couple of anchors dragging, say one on each side? Would that not slow us enough to give Mr. Bridger more time to steer, and therefore more control, especially on the bends?"

"That it would," said Nelson, "but there is the problem of the opened lock-doors and their hinges. There is no way to ensure that a deployed anchor would not snag upon such a structure, and bring the ship to an extremely sudden halt. In such a situation, there would be no way to haul the anchor back in, against the current's persistent force upon our hull; we should have to cut it loose and pray to regain control once we snapped free."

"In sech a situation," Bridger added, "the current's force, or a collision against the canal walls, could also cause a capsize, or even

rend our hull to shreds. All hands and cargo into the swift water, cannons crushing blokes, limbs off, heads off, blokes run clean through by timbers busted into wicked shards—aye, 'tis not a reel this here sailor cares to dance."

Lampson, who had turned white as a sheet, swallowed hard. "Well then, let's leave the anchors where they are, shall we?"

There came a cry from the crows nest: "Easy to port, Mr. Bridger! Standing waves ahead!"

"Aye aye, Mr. Bigg!" shouted our pilot. He eased the wheel towards what a landlubber would term left, craning his neck for a better look at the turn ahead, where our passage met the upper end of the canal. Here lay the second highest gradient we would encounter on our journey seaward—merely a couple dozen yards of it, ending in another slight turn—yet this represented one of the trickier maneuverings we would need undertake. Should we pass through this spot unscathed, I would feel considerably less anxiety about the better-graded bends down-valley. So it was with bated breath that I stood there betwixt Bridger and my uncle, hands braced upon the poop's front railing, hearing the approaching rumble of rushing water, watching a grassy hillside loom up straight before us, then feeling the ship tip forward, ever so slightly, as we reached the downgrade.

"Saint Elmo and Saint Michael," I heard Bridger mutter.

Our speed increased noticeably, and rhythmic puffs of spray rose over the bow as it cut through a series of small standing waves.

"To port now!" called Bigg, from the crows nest.

Bridger gave the wheel a stronger turn this time. Our slide into the slower water at the foot of the downgrade was accompanied by no audible splash, but by a cessation of downward motion strong enough that I felt my feet press more firmly against the deck for a few moments. Meanwhile, in spite of our turn, inertia continued to carry the *Mean Fish* laterally towards the starboard side of the canal;

I could see Bridger watching this and making corrections. It seemed that we must inevitably graze the canal wall, and yet our pilot's expert hand kept us pointing straight downstream, and brought us up short of contact.

Making further adjustments to bring us towards the centre of the canal, Bridger let loose a laugh. "Ha!" he cried, his voice taking on a strange tone, which I took to be his attempt at a posh southern accent, although it sounded more like someone with a mouth full of marbles. "Officers and crew of the *Mean Fish*, welcome to the official opening of the Swaledale turn-pike, the wettest goddamned road on Earth! Toll fees shall be waived, for today only! I invite you to enjoy the views, but you daren't relax! This here twisty serpent we're a-riding could at any moment bite us all on the arse!"

A smattering of laughter went up from the crew. I looked at Nelson, whose expression in that moment I may only describe as joyful disbelief.

We were well and truly under way. Already, Stonesthrow Hall receded into the distance behind us. The grassy shoulder of Great Shunner Fell ascended sharply to starboard; off to port the land sloped down to Angram Bottoms, with Kisdon Hill's verdant slopes rising beyond. No amount of anticipation could have prepared me for the singular sensation of standing upon this mighty ship as she slid smoothly along the hillside. With the valley to our left, we looked down upon the cottage roofs and fields there. Our transit felt more like flying than sailing. The crew must have felt this too; every man topside gaped in open wonder at the spectacle around us.

And then, it was our turn to be gaped at. I heard a cry of astonishment, and looking towards the bottoms, saw a cottager and his boy standing stock-still in their pasture, mouths fallen open in abject awe as they watched a sailing ship glide along the hillside above them. The boy dropped a pail he held; neither he nor his

father paid the slightest heed to the fresh milk wasted as it sloshed over the rim and wet the grass. And then the boy broke into a run towards us, charging uphill, veering to his left (as we were already passing him), shouting hurrahs, begging to go with us, finally falling behind as his exertion caught up with him and we continued our smart clip down-valley.

Looking back at the spirited lad, who had by then come to an exhausted stop with his hands upon his knees, I asked Nelson, "How fast are we going, do you suppose?"

"Well, the usual measurements won't work in this case, as we are going the same speed as the water we are in," said my uncle. "And it's rather hard to judge by sight, as normally on a ship one does not observe sheep and cottages flying past on either hand. Fixed reference points at sea are scarce, and aside from the odd patch of floating seaweed, tend to be far away. But Miss Smeaton calculated a likely flow speed of seven to nine knots, with the locks open, and I'd say we are doing about that."

I did some quick mental calculating. "Four to five hours to Richmond, at that rate."

"Indeed! We would be in time for luncheon, did we plan to stop there for refreshments."

Lampson had joined us. "Speaking of the locks … I understand that they are all thrown open for us?"

"Yes," said Nelson. "The flow of water into the canal so exceeds the amount we'd normally need in order to operate it, that we may do away with gradual means of lowering the ship. We may simply ride the flood on down! It's going to cut our transit time to Richmond by ten hours, at the least."

"How merry indeed," said Lampson, "but are we not concerned about the elevation changes built into the canal? Every such structure

I know of has a stairstep construction. Are we to ride the flood, as you put it, over a series of several dozen terrifying plunges?"

"Oh, heavens, no!" said my uncle. "In order to make it appear a *bona fide* road while it was being built, our canal has an unbroken, steady grade all the way down. That means that when the lock-doors are closed, the pools they create shall be shallower at the upper end than at the lower, though this shouldn't impede movement of the small freight barges which we hope shall use our canal, moving lead and wool and whatnot. It also means that we shall have a smooth passage all the way down to Richmond. Good God, how awful it would have been, to take this vessel over sixty-two fifteen-foot waterfalls! I daresay our entire crew would have jumped ship before we got through ten such obstacles, even if Bridger could have coaxed the *Mean Fish* over them!"

"Well, that is certainly a relief to hear," said Lampson, although he still appeared anxious despite this reassurance. "But I say, that's a rather sharp turn coming up ahead, isn't it?"

As if in agreement with this remark, Bigg called out from the crows nest at that very moment, "Hard turn starboard ahead!"

"I see her!" Bridger shouted from the wheel.

Although encouraged by the aplomb with which our pilot had handled the entry into the canal, I must own to having had concerns about the section we now neared: the longest series of turns, or bends, we would have to negotiate. Our canal followed the contours of the valley side whilst steadily dropping, and here it had been necessary to veer some distance south and west, on account of side-valleys cut by two becks cascading down from the Buttertubs area. Our expectation that the ship should be able to slide along the outer sides of such bends without incident, was to be more sorely tested here than anywhere further down-valley.

I stood beside Bridger as he gripped the wheel, peering ahead. He had already begun to nudge us towards the port side of the canal, so as to be near the outside edge when it bent to starboard. He must have seen, instinctively, that there was no way to muscle our ship through such a turn whilst remaining in the midline of the canal; inertia would inevitably send us towards the outside of the bend, so our best hope was to ease gently into the wall there and ride it around the curve.

"These bends shall be a tricky business, Cap'n," said Bridger.

"You've seen trickier, I'll wager," said I.

Bridger gave a curt nod, and took a deep breath. At that moment, we entered the first bend, and the port side of the ship met the canal wall.

The ship shuddered, nearly knocking me off my feet. A deep rumble issued from the two points, one fore and one aft, where our hull now grazed along the curving canal wall. I heard Bridger curse himself under his breath; clearly, he had not met his own expectations in executing this maneuver. And yet, though I detected a slight list to starboard, and our speed seemed reduced by contact with the wall, the *Mean Fish* carried on downstream, each moment bringing us nearer the sea.

"This just might work, Nephew," said Nelson. "It might actually bloody work."

"Current's catching the stern a tad," said Bridger, making rapid and minute adjustments to the wheel, "but I'll keep her tight against the wall through the bend, so we don't drift out broadsides and get wedged."

"Yes, let's avoid wedging," I said.

"I'll give your builders credit, Cap'n, these here walls are polished shiny-smooth. I'd hate to see their effect on a hull otherwise! Still, there's friction where wood slides on stone with so much force. The

timbers'll get hot as blazes, wherever they rub that wall. We need watch fer smoke, be ready to stifle a fire if need be."

"Heavens! I hadn't even thought of that possibility," I said.

Without taking his eyes from the course ahead, Bridger gave a sneering grimace. "Not what I need to hear, Cap'n. Let's all of us at least pretend that you, yer uncle, and yer lady engineer left no stones unturned, hmm?"

Although it surely took us less than two minutes to get through that first bend, the noise of the passage, and the accompanying vibration of the entire ship, seemed interminable. At long last, the canal straightened out again. Our hull left the wall as Bridger brought us out midstream. Right away, though, Bigg called out "Hard turn port ahead!" And our pilot began to inch us nearer the starboard wall of the canal.

This second bend was sharper than the first; the canal here took its turn directly above a culvert, through which our builders had diverted the waters of the cheerfully tumbling beck which had carved out the side-valley. In spite of the challenge, however, or perhaps because of it, Bridger did masterful work here, easing us into the canal wall so smoothly that I felt scarcely a bump. I daresay we all felt the ship's inertia as we swung round that bend, however; the force caused me to take an inadvertent step or two sideways in order to keep on my feet.

But then, with surprising speed, the second bend lay behind us. There had been no cracking of timbers, and no smoke. In short order followed another bend to starboard—the sharpest yet—where the canal rounded the point of land separating the two side-valleys. Our views from there off to the northeast, hundreds of feet down to the village of Thwaite, were truly vertiginous. Minutes thereafter we slid smoothly through another bend to port, over a second culverted stream. Bridger handled these curves so deftly that one

might have thought him an old hand at this style of navigation, and never suspected that this was, all probability, an utterly novel accomplishment in all the history of tall ships.

And then, we were through the worst of the curves, entirely unscathed. A few more notable turns awaited us farther down-valley, but I felt assured that they should be child's play compared to what we had just endured.

From here the canal could be seen running relatively straight into the distance, making only minor diversions as it followed the south slopes of Swaledale. Bridger heaved a sigh of relief; however, I do not believe that he relaxed one iota, nor did I expect him to do so until our ship safely plied the waters of the North Sea. Given the way he had handled the obstacles thus far, and the vigilance which he still visibly maintained, I found myself swelling with confidence in the abilities of our pilot (and perhaps, feeling more blasé about the way ahead than was wise in that moment).

At this juncture, I became fully aware of a sort of running cheer or huzzah which had been nipping at my ears. This noise did not originate with our crew, who had by this time fallen into a sort of silent, awestruck diligence as they manned their stations. I was for a moment puzzled before realizing that the sounds were relatively distant, and coming from off to port. Moving near the railings on that side, I witnessed an amazing sight.

The cluster of cottages marking the village of Thwaite were just receding behind us, and it looked for all the world as if the entire population of that place, and then some, had forsaken their morning chores in favour of running and riding along the road below us, waving and shouting in our direction with great enthusiasm. The sight of our ship gliding magnificently along the slopes of Swaledale ought naturally have stirred such a reaction, but it occurred to me in that moment that the loud rumbles our hull had made in riding

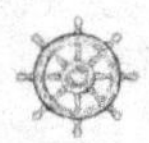

round the canal bends must have reverberated far and wide up and down Swaledale, causing many locals to turn out-of-doors and see what strange manner of rolling thunder had met their ears. This would explain why a great many of the villagers cheering us on did so in their bedclothes—not a usual custom in any part of England familiar to me.

Nelson stood at my side, grinning like a fool and waving at the crowds below. Then he caught my shoulder and pointed down-valley, where I made out three riders heading east along the road at a gallop. At such speed, they would easily reach Reeth and Richmond well before we did.

News of our approach, then, was sure to precede us down-valley. We had supposed as much, but the ramifications were not entirely welcome. It was at least possible, if not likely—given his thinly veiled threat about boating hazards in the vicinity of Reeth—that the rector might endeavour to impede our progress in some manner. My uncle and I shared a look which wordlessly acknowledged this, and he said, "I daresay our cannons could reach Wormwood House, although it would be devilishly hard to aim well at such a speed."

To this I replied, "Richard Christ sayeth in the wilderness: 'get thee behind me, Satan James!' Ha ha! I shall thank you to not tempt me with such a scenario, Uncle. We have explaining enough to do for a certain act of necessary destruction in the offing—I need not tell you what—without also pulverizing the residence of a rector, however vile he may be."

Nelson favoured me with a quizzically raised eyebrow. "Good thing Whitehand was not witness to that modification of our names, as he would surely have found it more blasphemous than amusing. 'Satan James'. Hah! And yet, I have been called worse, Nephew!"

With this, he resumed waving to the crowd below. This had already thinned, as folk on foot were unable to keep pace with the

Mean Fish, and many now milled back towards Thwaite. But those on horseback matched us easily as we sped down-valley, and fresh locals turned out from their cottages and barns with each passing minute, anxious to see what the hubbub was all about, uniformly enthused when they sighted our ship gliding past above them.

As our course had taken us along the west side of Kisdon Hill and above Aangram Bottoms, we had lost sight of the River Swale; here it reappeared round the east side of Kisdon, and I espied the hamlet of Muker in the valley far below us.

Although the canal had been losing elevation steadily since leaving Stonesthrow, we remained far above the valley floor. As a matter of fact, we were at this point higher above the River Swale than when we started. The reason for this was the nature of the canal's course versus that of the Swale; whereas the former provides a slow but steady downgrade, the latter drops precipitously just below Keld, rushing over a series of three waterfalls then into a gorge around the east side of Kisdon Hill. So, whereas Stonesthrow Hall perches on gently sloping ground three hundred feet higher than the Swale, here we cruised along a mountainside, nearly five hundred vertical feet above the river.

This great elevation above the roaring Swale, and its valley speckled with sheep and cottages, reenforced the sensation of flight. One may be accustomed to standing atop the heights of land, or riding them on horseback, looking down upon the trappings of civilization made toy-like by distance below—but to witness such a sight from a ship moving swiftly and smoothly, the steep slopes beneath us not visible unless one stood near the railings—that made for an altogether novel experience. I felt remarkably moved, in a way difficult to describe, gazing across Swaledale to the peaks of Rogan's Seat and Water Crag, where shafts of sunlight pierced the cloud and lit shifting patches of emerald green on the hillsides.

My appreciation of this heavenly tableaux was cut short by a bloodcurdling scream. I turned in the direction of the sound, in time to see a blur of yellow streak across the main deck from the portside railings to the nearest gangway, there to vanish, accompanied by a noise which suggested someone falling down the steps.

"Well, it seems as if Mister Mustardhead fails to appreciate this marvelous view," said Nelson.

"Mustardhead!" said I. "Why, I'd forgotten about the boy, these past several hours. I have not even seen him since I instructed you to release Mr. Lampson from his service. How has our budding gentleman weathered his change in status?"

"Oh, not well. Not well at all," said Nelson, fairly brimming over with mirth. "I wish you could have been present, Nephew, when I found the two of them in the pub and passed along your pronouncement. Mustardhead was terribly put out. He hemmed and hawed and sputtered on and on about justice, and fairness, and silly rot apropos of nothing, and as for these ridiculous airs he's been putting on, they shriveled up and blew away in about twenty second's time. Before my very eyes our budding gentlemen, as you term him, diminished to his former wretchedness. By the time I left the pub, he was cowering under a table, moaning about bats. I had not seen him since."

"He seemed rather terrified just now," I said.

"Nephew, I've no doubt that with a servant by his side, Mister Mustardhead would have stood right here beside us, gnawing on sausages and spouting sub-sophomoric nonsense. This outward semblance of status denied him, he crumbles into the dust from whence he came. One of us should really write to Herr Kant about this; he'd find in it a fascinating case in psychology, and probably an ironclad proof of something profound."

Philosophy aside, I found myself of two minds when it came to Mustardhead's fall—both wholeheartedly relieved that the idiotic faux-gentleman I had inadvertently created was no more, and yet crestfallen that the experiment had failed to produce any improvements in the poor wretch.

Leaving the cottages of Muker behind, the *Mean Fish* made capital progress over the next hour or so. We passed without incident through a mellower series of bends as the canal detoured into the side-valley of Oxnop Gill, above Ivelet, then a few bends more above the hamlet of Crackpot. All of these Bridger handled with an adroitness bordering upon flippancy; our pilot already looked as though he could have sleepwalked through such challenges. The weather stayed mixed, with passing showers and patches of sunshine. All along our route, the parade of admiring locals continued along the roads below us; those on foot came and went, unable to match our speed, but the number of cheery riders accompanying us down-valley grew with each passing mile, and I recognized some who had been with us all the way from Thwaite.

It was about half-past seven in the morning when the first sign of looming trouble appeared. I observed three riders making their way up-valley along the road from the direction of Reeth. These new arrivals reached the riders following us down-valley and there ensued an animated parley, of which I could hear nothing, owing to distance, although I did observe a good deal of gesturing in the direction of our ship. After a few moments of this, one of the new riders broke from the group and pressed his horse upslope, towards us.

Nelson had wandered off to the forecastle, where he stood in conversation with Whitehand; I had a sailor summon him to join me at the portside railings of the main deck, in order to receive the message which this rider apparently had for us.

My uncle met me at the railings just as the rider drew near enough to shout, "Hullo! Uh … or rather … ahoy there! May I have words with the captain of this vessel?"

"I am he," said I.

Easing into a canter alongside the canal, the rider said, "Sir, I have been sent by the citizens of Reeth, who present their most amiable greetings to Lord Keld and his crew!"

"We are very much obliged," I said, "and hope to return their greetings in person within the half-hour."

"But that is just it, Your Lordship," said the rider. "You may have rather more time for such pleasantries than you anticipate."

I exchanged a quick look with Nelson before answering, "Well, no beating about the bush, man! Let's hear it."

"The rector has caused one of your gates—the one nearest Reeth—to be closed. This shall surely halt the progress of your ship. We townsfolk have not been told as much, but we believe that the rector means to have a word with you, and that his intentions are not friendly."

"Blast it! Where is the rector now?"

"With His Grace, the Earl, and a few of the earl's men. They await you at the pool which has formed behind the closed gate."

"Are they armed?"

"Yes, Your Lordship, the earl's men carry pistols. At least one bears a musket as well."

"My good man, you and the people of Reeth have our heartfelt thanks for providing this valuable intelligence far sooner than we otherwise could have had it. Please convey our gratitude to your townsmen."

"That I shall, Your Lordship!" Here the rider appeared to hesitate a moment, before going on, "If I may be so bold as to ask, sir, are there any instructions which I might convey to the able-bodied men

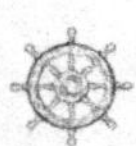

of Reeth, in the interest of—shall we say—facilitating your ship's journey?"

My uncle and I exchanged another look, and his grave expression surely mirrored my own. This offer was gallant, but to accept it would be perilous indeed. Given the rider's earnest manner, the wording of his question, and the pains which his townsmen had taken to inform us about the lock-door, thus denying Fitzhenry the element of surprise—given all this, sentiment in Reeth would seem likely to support a shew of force from the town, in hopes of causing the earl's party to stand down. The trouble was that we could not possibly have risked such a confrontation. Our project, dear as it is to our hearts, could never be worth the possibility of harm to even one citizen of Reeth on our behalf. This was our quest, not theirs, however supportive they felt of it, or however much they might have enjoyed humiliating this irksome upstart of an earl, whose presence in the neighbourhood they openly resent.

So, I thanked the rider for this spirited offer, but then explained that whilst we appreciated the support of Reeth's citizens very much indeed, strong considerations compelled us to halt where the earl wished us to, there to engage him on his own terms.

The rider seemed crestfallen by this reply, but he accepted it with grace. Wishing us Godspeed with a tip of his hat, he urged his horse to a gallop and made for the road below. Moments later, he and his two companions were on their speedy way back to Reeth.

As soon as the rider had left us, I said to Nelson, "That goddamned snake in rector's clothing! It could be the duke's place to intervene, but this puffed-up little preacher has got well above himself! That ha'penny loutship of an earl, too! Goddamn them both!"

"Richard, I agree wholeheartedly with your rough language, yet we cannot pretend to be surprised," said my uncle. "Word has it that His Grace The Duke remains indisposed—may heaven grant him

better health soon—and if for that or some other reason Reeth did not manage to bring Richmond's disfavour upon us, then naturally he would take matters into his own hands. And no wonder that Fitzhenry, with his petty army, stands beside the rector on this matter; the two of them are corrupted peas in a pod."

Peering down-valley towards the blockade which we now knew awaited us (though it lay out of sight around a bend) Nelson went on, "We must come to a halt where the lock-door is closed; there can be no two ways about that. If we deploy all four anchors, we should be able to hold fast, even against a current. Then we shall hear what our foes have to say. Where things go from there, Nephew, heaven only knows. We shall have to play it by ear, I am afraid."

Nelson was right. I instructed him to inform all hands about the blockade, as well as the possibility, however slight, that an armed confrontation might unfold. Determined that no escalation in hostility should be laid to our account, I made it clear that our sailors would only fire if fired upon, and that the cannons were not to be deployed without express orders personally delivered by Nelson or myself. My uncle nodded his assent, and left at once to spread the word.

Here I write a few words about the lay of the land in the vicinity of Reeth, so that the arena where events were about to unfold, might be better envisioned by future readers of this log (and I now believe it likely that there may be such, as our project has advanced sufficiently far that it could be worthy of at least a footnote in history books).

Approaching Reeth, we were less high above the River Swale than we had been to start with. The canal had continued its steady downgrade towards Richmond, whilst the river's rate of drop had mellowed; as a result, the valley bottom at that point lay only about two hundred feet below us and perhaps a half-mile distant, at the foot of a grassy slope partitioned into winter pastures by stone walls.

Between us and the river ran the side road called Low Lane; across the Swale lay the main road, and the village of Reeth.

Reeth is the second-largest community in Swaledale, after Richmond. It is several times the size of Keld, boasting a church, a pub, two blacksmith shops, a bakery, and sundry other businesses arranged around a proper village green. We Jacobs have long maintained a cordial relationship with the people of Reeth, a situation reenforced since the current rector and earl have proven themselves disagreeable leaders. It is an open secret that folk in that region of Swaledale feel more warmth and respect for our revered duke in Richmond, and for the Jacob family of Keld, than for the rector whose presence looms over town like a storm cloud, and the earl whose massive disaster of a 'cottage' defaces the landscape two miles north.

Given this long-standing goodwill between Reeth and my family, I had hardly been surprised by the town's offer to call Fitzhenry's bluff with guns of their own. This very same goodwill, however, made it out of the question for me to accept their undertaking such a risk on our behalf.

Mere minutes after Nelson left me to spread our news around the ship, as we rounded a broad curve to starboard, Bigg called from the crows nest that the closed lock-door had come into sight.

By that time, I had joined Bridger at the wheel, and our pilot remarked, "Aye, Cap'n, I feel the slack water. We're slowing up." Giving me a fierce look, he went on, "I hope to hear from your own lips that we shall in no wise kowtow to them bastards! We can bloody well ram the bloody lock-door! I'll be damned if they're built to stand the weight of a vessel this size, with sech a flow of water pushing her!"

Nelson and Lampson joined us at that moment, and my uncle said, "Mr. Bridger, you are right about the lock-door. Given the parameters it has been designed for, we could surely wrench it asunder using the

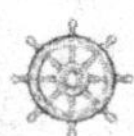

ship. But think of what would follow! Up until now we have been buoyed along by a smooth, steady flow. Ram that lock-door, and we shall find ourselves entirely out of control, riding a great surge all the way down the canal to Richmond! The odds of not being dashed to pieces would be nil. And we could no longer count on sufficient water beneath our keel. It is possible that we would feel bottom, perhaps with such violence that we would lose the rudder."

"Unless we moved slower than this here great surge," said Bridger.

Nelson's eyes narrowed. "Well, yes, if we could somehow lag behind the initial pulse of water flung down the canal, it would be easier to control the ship. But how would we manage it?"

"Why, we'd go down the rest of the way with two anchors out, one to each side," said Bridger.

My uncle blinked in surprise. There was no missing the admiration in his voice as he replied, "I say! That'd be terrifically risky, Bridger, but it would move such a gambit from the realm of insanity, into that of the vaguely possible."

Lampson cleared his throat and put in, "Begging your pardons, gentlemen, but less than two hours ago I was assured that going down this canal with anchors deployed would qualify as suicidal, given what could happen were one of them to snag upon something."

"Two hours ago, we did not expect to be waylaid by greedy idiots," I pointed out. "But fear not, Mr. Lampson. Fitzhenry and the rector may be asses of the first magnitude, but they are not immune to persuasion. On the contrary, I have found them susceptible to the right sort. I shall endeavour to not kowtow, as Mr. Bridger puts it, but there are concessions I am prepared to make, and enticements I may offer, which are, in all likelihood, exactly what our foes hope to gain. Meet those expectations, and we shall be allowed to pass."

"If they were to open the lock-door fer us, I believe we could hold steady here, on four anchors, until water filled the canal ahead," said Bridger.

"Capital!" said Lampson. "Now *that* is a plan. Captain, please do let me know if I may be of service in any way, when it comes to furthering a strategy which does not involve, as its sunniest outcome, two hours of unceasing terror."

Despite my brave words to Lampson, I felt little assurance that I *would* be able to talk our way past the blockade. Concessions Fitzhenry and the rector may indeed have sought, in exchange for allowing us to continue on our way, but I could not rule out the possibility that they acted out of mere spite, and that *nothing* I offered would satisfy them. In such a case, we would have to chuse between the humiliating demise of our dream, and Bridger's highly dangerous plan.

By this time, we had slowed a good deal. Momentum, rather than current, carried us forward into slack water. I could make out the closed lock-door ahead, and some few hundred yards short of it, on our portside, a small party of men on horseback beside the canal. "See there, Mr. Bridger," I said. "It would be ideal if you could stop us within hailing distance of those fellows."

"I could stop us atop any minnow in the sea," said Bridger. He steered us close to the portside of the canal and gave a bosun-pipe signal for all four anchors to be deployed.

Even the rumble of anchor-chains reeling out failed to overcome a waxing roar which suggested a waterfall … and yet I knew of no falls in that part of Swaledale. Peering ahead, I made out the cause, then brought it to Nelson's attention.

"By the King's Colours, Nephew," said he, "Of course, this must happen under such conditions. And yet, it looks rather worse than I would have supposed."

We were now near enough the closed lock-door to see that water had over-topped it; a modest amount poured on ahead, down the canal towards Richmond. Of greater import, however, was the fact that a sizeable quantity of water was escaping the canal entirely, and spewing down the hillside below the lock-door.

There, as everywhere along our canal, a series of evenly spaced openings perforated the top of its downslope side. These had ostensibly served the purpose of fixture-points for the timbers which would have comprised the promised 'roof' over the 'turn-pike'. Their actual function was to act as conduits for overflow, should the water level become excessively high in any portion of the project.

One possibility which we had not accounted for, however, was any of the lock-doors being closed against the great volume of water currently coursing down the canal. Under normal conditions, the locks would have operated with a far smaller flow; in the event that high flows made possible the sort of journey we had so far enjoyed, none of the lock-doors should have been shut. The result of closing one under such conditions, then, was to place upon that structure stress which it had not been designed to withstand for long, and simultaneously, to send a larger amount of water than we had ever anticipated, through the over-flow openings, and downhill towards the Swale.

"That lock-door may not hold up long enough for Bridger to have the satisfaction of ramming it," said I.

"Not only that, but look there," said my uncle. "The torrent of overflow is visibly eroding the ground! God's blood, Richard, if this keeps up, it could undermine the canal! Either way, we shall have a catastrophic failure before long. We cannot afford to parley with these bastards 'til the cows come home."

At that very moment, we heard a hullo from the group of horsemen. It was Fitzhenry, grinning like an idiot and waving his cocked hat.

Bridger had done his work very deftly indeed, and the *Mean Fish* was by this time sliding to a halt directly beside the earl's party. As we had been advised, this group consisted of Fitzhenry, the rector, and five of the earl's men. The latter qualified as conspicuously armed. One detail which had been omitted by the rider from Reeth was the fact that not far downslope from this assembly, the rector's dour coach (and even more dour coachman) sat parked on Low Lane, as if awaiting passengers.

"I say, Keld!" gushed Fitzhenry. "This ship is an even lovelier sight here at Reeth, than it was beside your mouldering old bat-haven up-valley! It's jolly well dreamy, if I do say so!"

Standing at the main deck railing, mere yards from "His Loutship," I executed a bow and said, "As they were during your recent visit, Your Lordship's kind words are very much appreciated. And now, I hope that you shall forgive me if I seem in haste, but we are en route down-valley, and I wonder if perhaps Your Lordship and I might continue this conversation at some other time, which might better suit all parties."

"You are indeed en route," leered Fitzhenry, "in a most magnificent manner, and should you accomplish nothing else in your lifetime, Keld, you have at least become the first man on Earth to captain a ship down a turn-pike!"

At this, a corner of the rector's lips turned up in a subtle smirk; Fitzhenry himself laughed aloud at his own witty observation. If the earl's men found any of this the least bit amusing, they gave no sign. Rumour has it that most of them are continental mercenaries, and certainly I marked nothing in their expressions beyond a sort of blasé lethality.

Chusing to ignore the earl's jibe, I said, "Let us be very plain, shall we, My Lord? It is rather inconvenient for myself and my crew

to find our progress inhibited in this manner, and I beg your leave to proceed."

The asinine smile remained plastered upon Fitzhenry's face, but his voice took on a notably sharper edge. "You beg my leave. You beg. I say, Keld, you may *beg* here in this remote spot until you are blue in the face, and I'll not have a word of it. Not through any lack of grace on my part, mind you, but because I wish so very strongly to welcome you once again as my guest, at Langthwaite. Consider yourself and three companions invited—in the strongest possible sense of the term—to accompany this merry band of mine back to my princely abode. There you may indeed *beg*, Keld, and as you are, after all, of noble birth, there shall I gladly grant you audience."

Only with great difficulty could any Christian have managed to maintain composure in the face of such a highly infuriating speech directed at a ship captain, in full view of his officers and crew, no less. However, it gives me pleasure to report that I maintained a civil tone as I thanked the earl for his kind invitation, and informed him that I accepted it gladly, and would be grateful for a few moments in which to assemble a merry band of my own.

Turning to Nelson, whose hands had flexed into fists, I said in an undertone, "Uncle, you shall not relish this, but I must insist that you remain here. One of us two must stay aboard the *Mean Fish*. I know full well that you wish to stand by my side in this fight—for such it seems destined to be, hopefully in words rather than deeds. But I need you here badly, given your authority over this crew and your knowledge of the canal."

He nodded grimly. "You are right on all counts, Nephew. My heart protests that you should not accompany this weasel to his den without me, and yet I recognize the necessity of my remaining on board. Whom shall you take? We need Bridger here as well, I daresay."

"Yes, the ship cannot spare him. I shall take along Lampson. And Wheelwright."

"The librarian? I am not sure *that* fellow shall be of much help."

"Well, Whitehand *could* serve as a counterbalance to the rector, should that snake presume to speak on behalf of the church. And then there is the doctor, who does tend to unnerve those who do not know him. And yet, no! I do feel that Wheelwright should go with us."

"Very well, captain, and who else?"

I was about to ask Nelson which of our sailors he thought the most physically formidable, so that I might add brawn to the brains already selected. But then I glimpsed a flash of sickly yellow popping out of, then back into, the nearby gangway … And on an utterly bizarre impulse, I said, "Mustardhead."

"What about him?"

"He is to be the fourth member of my party."

My uncle could not have looked more astonished, had I informed him that Aristotle, Caesar, William Shakespeare, and Jesus Christ were in the strategy room having a hand of whist. He opened his mouth, but appeared struck speechless.

"In the opposing camp is already a man of the church, along with more strong arms and crack shots than we could muster," said I. "In this boy is something we have, which they do not. Please do not ask me to elaborate, because it would be impossible. But the boy is going with me."

"Er … as you wish, Richard," my uncle managed at last, although his look clearly shewed that he found this choice absurdly daft.

In short order, my party was assembled. Lampson and Wheelwright looked keen and ready; I instantly felt fortified in having these two at my side in such straits. Mustardhead, on the other hand, had to practically be dragged on deck, and would not stop muttering about

the ship being up in the air, and something about wicked spells. This was the first good look I had gotten at the boy, since his demotion from the status of gentleman, and Nelson's evaluation was on the mark. With a speed matched only by his earlier transition to the muddled outskirts of propriety, Mustardhead had reverted to the pathetic, disheveled state in which we had found him.

The gangplank was let out, and so precise had Bridger's maneuvering been, that it perfectly spanned the space between the main deck and the grassy bank of the canal. Before leading my party ashore, I paused and clasped my uncle's hand in my own.

"Godspeed, Richard," said he.

"Godspeed, Sir James," said I.

With that, he and I parted, each to his own perilous role in the drama which had overtaken us.

My party and I were met by the earl's mounted men, and escorted graciously enough downhill to the waiting coach. As we passed by Fitzhenry, I said to him, "Your Lordship should know that the water overflowing from the canal over yonder, as a result of the lock-door being closed, shall sooner or later compromise the canal. It could fail entirely."

Far from seeming taken aback by this, the earl grinned all the more broadly. "Well then, once you are through begging, Keld, you shall have to send word up-valley for the water to be stopped, shan't you?"

This smug remark I favoured with no response. The earl went on to bestow the same inane smile, along with a slight nod, upon each of my party; even the unorthodox appearance of Mustardhead seemed not to stir any interest on his part. The rector, on the other hand, certainly noticed the boy—eyes narrowed, the Rector of Reeth appeared to take close measure of Mustardhead, as if suspicious about why on earth such a sorry specimen of sailor had been chosen to attend a parley of noblemen at Langthwaite.

I had supposed the rector's coach to be empty, so it surprised me to step within and find a seat already occupied by Miss Fenny Drayton of Lamb's Conduit Street, Bloomsbury. She greeted me and my officers in a polite manner, although the colour flushing her face shewed that she was not unashamed by the conduct of her fiancé. Miss Drayton did not manage to maintain the same level of composure when Mustardhead stumbled into the coach, nearly sprawling onto the floor as he did so—although to her credit, she made a valiant attempt to favour him with a civilized greeting.

The coach door was closed behind us—and locked from the outside. Without a word from earl or rector, the coach began to move.

I stared out the window at my ship—my magnificent *Mean Fish*—as we left her behind. How magical she looked, perched upon the grassy slopes of Swaledale! The canal was invisible from this low angle, causing it to appear as though she really did ply a sea of grass, as she had in my dream. A fair portion of the crew had gathered along the portside railings to see us off, but then an order must have been given for return to stations, as this assembly broke up in a flurry, each man hurrying his own way. Only two figures remained at the railing: my Uncle James, and Paul Whitehand. Bridger, I could see, had not left his post at the wheel.

The shortest route between that spot and Langthwaite would normally have involved the bridge over the Swale at Fremington, downstream from Reeth, but in that direction Low Lane lay submerged under the deluge of water overflowing from the canal. So, we followed the lane up-valley as far as the Shepherd's Bridge near Low Whita. This low-water crossing would have been impassable as well, given the recent prodigious rains, had not most of the Swale's flow been diverted into our canal far upstream. As it was, the river's waters lapped at the roadway, but our passage to the north bank was dry.

I felt puzzled at first by the presence of Miss Drayton, but it quickly became clear that her fiancé had enjoined her to entertain us with light conversation during our journey to Langthwaite—and I must allow that her honest charm, such a contrast to His Loutship's patent falsity, did have a relaxing effect, even under such vexing circumstances. With a gracious manner, no doubt honed through many an hour spent in drawing rooms and at dinner tables, she drew out from our party a trickle of polite conversation on such subjects as the very rainy weather, recent horse-racing results, and news of the ongoing Vancouver Expedition in America.

I was most impressed by our hostess, however, when she indicated the Swale—which lay to our south as we had doubled back towards Reeth on the main road—and remarked how the diversion of so much water into our canal had alleviated the flooding, which had before affected many bottom-land pastures, the hamlet of Ivelet, and several bridges. "I pointed out to His Lordship, the Earl," she said, "that Lord Keld had in that way done a great service to the people of Swaledale, whether it was his chief intention or not, and that the canal might be used in a similar way to ease future episodes of high water, making them less disruptive to the folk of our valley."

I was pleased by this gracious assessment, and struck with keen admiration at the idea of using the canal as a means of flood control, a possibility which had never once crossed my mind, but was entirely feasible. "And how did the earl react to this speech in my favour?" I enquired.

Miss Drayton, who had been speaking to me in direct earnest, now averted her gaze to the passing landscape, and her voice faltered as she said, "He … He was not appreciative, I am sorry to say." It looked as if she might have wished to say more, but instead, she fell silent.

Mustardhead, though failing to take part in conversation, seemed engaged by our hostess in a different manner, which is to say, so

271

gobsmacked by the calibre of her feminine charm, that he was able only to stare at her, his jaw hanging stupidly open. I feared that, at any moment, a string of drool might issue from his slack mouth. No less than during our previous meeting, Miss Drayton's style of dress accentuated her figure in a rather bold manner (by Yorkshire standards; I know little of those in London), and I must say that her face struck me even more than before, as pleasantly fetching. Little wonder that Mustardhead seemed to regard Miss Drayton as a vision dropped from heaven; given the gawk upon his face, together with my knowledge of his usual behaviour, it would not have surprised me to see him fall upon his knees before her, bawling thanks to God for allowing him to meet an angel. Whether I would have felt more amused or embarrassed by such a pathetic display, I know not, for thankfully it never came to pass.

Shortly after conversation in the coach had fallen silent, we found ourselves entering the village of Reeth. It struck me that the place seemed oddly quiet. Normally there should have been residents out and about, attending to the day's business, but even the village green was nearly empty, and the only people there (local merchants chewing the fat, from the looks of them) seemed to make a point of not glancing our way—this in place of the respectful interest normally accorded an earl's entourage as it moves through the chief village of his estate.

Our caravan turned north on the road to Langthwaite, and left the strangely quiescent village behind. It was then when Lampson moved to dispel the awkward silence, by enquiring of Miss Drayton on the subject of the earl's home, of which she was soon to be lady.

Whilst never deviating from the politest sort of language, Miss Drayton proceeded to express strong dissatisfaction with her fiancé's 'cottage', and in particular, the inconveniences caused by its size and complexity.

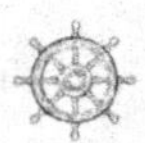

Staff were constantly becoming lost in Langthwaite's vast maze of interconnecting wings and halls, she informed us. One bewildered chambermaid had so despaired of finding the room she had been directed to tidy, or ever regaining a familiar region of the house, that she had resorted to settling down on her own in one of the more remote kitchens. She had been discovered living there days later, by a reconnaissance party sent from the central pantry to find lard. Miss Drayton also reported that she herself found it virtually impossible to know which of the multitudinous drawing rooms, parlours, banqueting chambers, or conservatories was being referred to at any given time ... And as for the innumerable bedrooms, each of which had been named for a London street, she doubted if even that city's famously adroit cab drivers could have kept half of them straight.

"Just last week," she told us, "His Lordship sent me a message by courier, to meet him for dinner in the East-South-East Banquet Hall, of Section U—an especially tricky region of Langthwaite. I waited for nearly an hour, alone and hungry, before realizing that the message should have designated the *South*-South-East Banquet Hall of Section U, a good five minutes' walk distant. When I got there, His Lordship had already partaken of dinner, and left. Oh, and the mezzanines, many of which have their own *sub*-mezzanines! Let us not even discuss the mezzanines, for that way lies despair!"

"By Jove," said Lampson, "I am terribly sorry to have brought up such a distressful topic, Miss Drayton. The place sounds rather overly large. Dangerously so, I might even say. What if, heaven forbid, some accident were to befall you or the earl, when a servant was not present? How should aid be promptly furnished?"

"Indeed, Mr. Lampson, I have expressed just such a concern to His Lordship. We have five physicians in residence, but there are disagreements about which sections of Langthwaite constitute their various territories; some overlap, leaving areas in dispute, and I fear that some areas remain unclaimed by any of them." Here Miss Drayton drew a deep sigh, and with a look which struck me as both hopeful and shy, her voice softened. "Speaking of the medical profession, Lord Keld, it does surprise me that your Doctor Converse has not accompanied you. No offense, of course, to anyone present, each of whom is obviously here for an important reason. But I trust that the doctor is well?"

"Yes, Miss Drayton," said I, "Doctor Converse is well indeed, although I have it on good authority that he pines after someone named Denny, in his sleep. Might you have any idea whom that could be?"

She gave a sharp intake of breath, her lips pursed, and an unmistakably amorous gleam flashed in her eyes. However, this crack in her comportment lasted but an instant; she shook her head vigorously, seeming only mildly stirred as she went on, "I have barely noticed him, to tell the truth, let alone become privy to his intense, mysterious secrets. Not that I believe him to have any. Intense, mysterious secrets, that is. Which is to say …"

Fortunately for Miss Drayton, the coach rounded a bend at that very moment, and the sight which came into view so absorbed my companions and myself, that the topic of Dr. Converse was forgotten.

In the days of my childhood, an actual cottage had stood on the hill overlooking the hamlet of Langthwaite, from across the valley of Arkle Beck. I remember this distinctly, as a servant of our household had retired there to be near family in his old age, and on several occasions I journeyed to that place in order to receive lessons in astronomy, his knowledge of that subject being excellent and the spot favourable for use of his telescope.

By the time the Earldom of Arkengarthdale was created for Henry Fitzhenry by our cracked King (God save him) seven years ago, the cottage lay abandoned, and the newly minted peer chose to make it the seat of his estate. Of course, such a modest structure

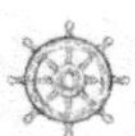

would not have served for even a baron, let alone an earl, so no one in the neighbourhood expressed the least surprise when builders and architects were brought in to expand it.

What no one expected, however, was that the builders and architects were in Arkengarthdale to stay. They finished one new wing, then two, then three, then a new hall sprang up off one of the wings, and it too began to sprout additions. The expansion has never ceased. The 'cottage' of Langthwaite now covers a good deal more ground than the settlement for which it was named, having spread mainly to the northeast up the hillside, and onto the relatively level stretch of moorland behind.

We could see much of Langthwaite from the road, though by no means all of it. Its crowded jumble never fails to remind me of an illustration in one of my childhood geographies, of a hilltop village in Tuscany—only without defensive walls, and equally lacking any trace of architectural harmony.

Fitzhenry not only claims to employ more architects than the House of Hanover, he boasts of having set these worthy gentlemen against one another, in a frenzied race to produce additions ever more exotic and spectacular. The result is a bewildering hodgepodge of styles which would have driven Inigo Jones or Christopher Wren certifiably mad.

Langthwaite 'cottage' today resembles a sprawling temple complex of Classical Greece (shewing Doric, Ionic, *and* Corinthian orders) which has, through some awful series of mistakes, become scrambled together with the Roman Forum, a cathedral in the Gothic style, and the Mohammedan Alhambra. Off to one side, gilded onion domes of Rus jostle with what appears to be a wing of the Versailles chateau; over yonder rise half-scale pyramids in both Aegyptian and Aztec styles, along with a soaring pagoda and a flurry of castle turrets too slender and fantastical to serve any purpose, save vanity.

Rising beside the still-extant original cottage is what one might take to be a partially ruined peel tower, even though no such fortification ever graced Arkengarthdale in the reivers' days; it is the only feature remotely native to Yorkshire, yet Fitzhenry himself has told me that it was added as a mere folly.

I must confess to having felt some satisfaction when the sight of this garbled monstrosity, looming upon the hillside ahead, rendered Augustus Wheelwright visibly shocked, even speechless, for the first time since I had made his acquaintance. Apparently even *he* had never seen the like, amidst all the wonders of the wide world. Lampson, too, appeared awed and repulsed in equal measure by the garish spectacle. Only Mustardhead failed to shew any reaction to Langthwaite, as Miss Fenny Drayton remained the sole subject of his impolitely rapt attention.

Through the scattered buildings of Langthwaite village the coach rolled, over the rain-swollen waters of Arkle Beck, and up the hill. We passed the original cottage on our left (looking tiny and sad perched at the southerly tip of the earl's boondoggle) followed by one of the earliest wings, which had been done in a respectable Palladian style. Beyond this rose a massive hall modeled after the Doge's Palace in Venice; here the coach pulled into a circle drive and halted before a vast entranceway.

Miss Drayton alighted, inviting the rest of us to do likewise. Before taking ten steps, we found ourselves encircled by Fitzhenry's men-at-arms. The rector and earl led the lot of us towards the entrance.

"You've not seen the inside of this area, Keld, unless I am very much mistaken," said Fitzhenry. "The best bits are uphill, really—some of the recent additions. But it would take a few minutes more to get up there, and the modest little chapel here in Section A shall serve our purpose today. Do remind me, though, to shew you around my Hindu ashram one of these days. It really is bracingly savage."

As the vastness of Langthwaite cottage, Section A swallowed us up, I glanced back at the coach and felt relief to see it sitting in the drive, as if awaiting our return, rather than heading off at once. Several grooms had appeared out of thin air and held the earl's horses. All of this bade well; it would have increased my already considerable unease to think that our host might intend this visit to be a lengthy one.

The cool, dim-lit entrance hall into which we stepped carried on the Venetian style of the exterior, with elegant wainscoting and sumptuous plaster designs gracing every surface. My own home's great hall could have fit into this chamber twice over, and yet I felt certain that in the grand scheme of Fitzhenry's Langthwaite, this peripheral place hardly rated notice, having been superseded by grander entrances elsewhere.

A quick turn brought us into the chapel Fitzhenry had mentioned. In spite of his description of it as 'modest', this place easily exceeded the size of the rector's church in Reeth, and its lavish interior seemed worthy of the Vatican itself. Every square foot of surface bristled with décor of the most violently Baroque style—a veritable blizzard of columns, entablatures, and pediments executed in a rainbow of multihued marbles, granites, and porphyries. Over the altar rose a great canopy which struck me as a scaled-down version of the *baldacchino* in Saint Peter's.

Along the chapel wall to our right, three marvelously wrought stained-glass windows admitted light; these were echoed on the opposite wall by three monumental frescoes of exactly the same shape and dimension as the windows. I hardly knew whether to feel more amused or appalled by the towering frescoes, each of which portrayed the master of the house as hero in various historic and mythologic tableaux. In the first, Henry Fitzhenry led the Royal Navy against the Spanish Armada (an event which he is obliged to have not participated in, seeing as how it took place over two centuries ago). The second fresco seemed a rather conventional depiction of Saint George slaying the dragon, until one recognized that it was Henry Fitzhenry, rather than England's patron saint, wielding the lance. And last but certainly not least, the fresco nearest the altar shewed Henry Fitzhenry presiding over the miracle of the loaves and the fishes (Christ himself being nowhere in sight, perhaps having gone into Bethesda for some wine).

Oddly, the chapel contained no pews. We were escorted towards the altar across an ornate (and quite empty) marble floor, the men-at-arms forming a hedge about us.

Our host and his ostensible Man of God stopped before the altar. They turned to face us. Miss Drayton stood at her fiancé's side. Far from acknowledging his *amour*, he paid her no attention whatever as, with an especially grimace-like quality in his perpetual grin, he said, "Keld, it pains me, it really does, to take you to task over this business. The duke, however, is feeble and unable to act, and so this disagreeable responsibility falls to me. I take it that you have received the letter from the Rector of Reeth and myself, concerning the issue of threats to public peace in Swaledale?" When I nodded, he went on, "Very good, then, would you care to verify in our presence that all heavy armaments have been removed from the *Mean Fish*, along with any seditious elements of your crew?"

I informed His Loutship in forthright language that the cannons did in fact remain aboard the *Mean Fish*, albeit with gun ports closed, seeing as how our ship traversed a region populated by friends, and had no reason to expect ill-will. Furthermore, I added, not a single member of my crew had been deemed by myself sufficiently seditious, or republican, or anything of the sort, to have been turned out as suspected future regicides.

Hearing this report brought on a remarkable duality between Fitzhenry's expression, which betrayed gleeful delight, and his voice, which sounded only the most doleful of notes as he said, "My dear Keld, it disappoints me gravely to hear you say so. I know not what maleficent influence provokes you to desert your duty to the welfare of England, but clearly some devilry is at work here. Would you not say so, Reeth?"

"Indeed," said the rector, his lips distorted by a sneer, "and we have now proof of knowing lies from Lord Keld's tongue and pen. Years' worth. Or would Your Lordship have us believe that your vessel has gone floating down the Swaledale turn-pike on *accident*?"

"Ah, yes," said Fitzhenry, "there is the matter of the promised turn-pike, which was to be such a boon to all Swaledale, and which now seems solely designed to convey your eccentric boat on down to Richmond. I need not enumerate for you, Keld, the many land-owners, including myself and the Church of England, who assented to a county right-of-way across our properties, in order that this folly might be built, with the explicit understanding that it was to be a revenue-generating turn-pike. Tut-tut, Keld, news of such a heinous deception shall not sit well with any Englishman, from the meanest stable-mucker to the King himself. And oh yes, the rector and myself do mean to make it known. Not out of any malice on our parts, you understand, but from our shared and profound sense of justice."

"With all respect due Your Lordship, and your grace," said I, "you have been premature in judging the merits of my project. Our marvelous waterway, once the *Mean Fish* has completed her voyage upon it, may be used as a toll-canal for the lucrative movement of freight up and down Swaledale. Or, it could indeed be drained, roofed, and used for an all-weather turn-pike. Either way, this boon—for such it *is*—has been created, and presented for public use, at no

expense to yourselves nor anyone else in the neighbourhood, save the granting of right-of-way which you mention.

"Today I ask only that our ship be allowed to pass on her way, as her doing so harms no one. And then there is the fact if we do not soon resume our journey, erosion caused by your ill-advised closure of the lock-door may trigger a catastrophic failure of the canal, which would not only render it useless as a waterway, but would unleash a terrible flood towards Richmond."

"Hmm, yes," said Fitzhenry, "you mentioned already the possibility. 'Tis a poor bluff, Keld; I should expect better from such an imaginative fellow as yourself.

"And so. It seems to me, and I trust that the rector concurs, that your position today is one of thorough uncooperativeness and nonrepentance for your selfish and deceptive actions and words. Whilst Reeth and I would not dream of considering ourselves your judges, in a legal sense, we are your fellow leaders in the Swaledale community, bound to shield it from harm and abuse, and therefore it is my sad and solemn duty, on behalf of the Duke of Richmond, to announce the confiscation of all ..."

"Lord Keld!" came a sudden shout, cutting short Fitzhenry's rambling stream of bullshite. It had been a woman's voice, charged with feeling. I spun about and beheld the loveliest sight ever to meet unjustly waylaid eyes.

It was Thistle, or as I should say, Miss Mary Ashwood, crossing the marble floor of the chapel in our direction, her stride and her expression equally resolute. At the moment I turned, she passed through a shaft of sunlight streaming through the stained glass, bestowing upon her matchless face and simple white dress, a riot of glorious colour worthy of the sweetest dream. Surely no being so like an angel had ever been seen upon the face of this Earth.

Fitzhenry found his voice before anyone else did. "Who is this woman," he said, "and how the devil did she get in here?"

Only then did I notice one of Fitzhenry's grooms hurrying along in fruitless pursuit of my lady. In response to his master's question this fellow said, "I beg your pardon a thousand times over, My Lord! This woman rode up, then dashed inside, without so much as a hullo. We had no opportunity to stop her!"

Thistle came straight up to me and, for an instant, made as if to take both my hands in hers. But she must have thought better of this impropriety (heavenly though it would have been) and simply stood there looking me in the face with great earnestness.

"Lord Keld ... I was riding down-valley and I saw that the ship had been stopped," she said, voice quavering with emotion. "I noticed the horsemen and coach going towards Langthwaite, and surmised that you might be a guest of the earl." Here she glanced at Fitzhenry before going on, "But I had a dark premonition of what might unfold, and the words I heard from His Lordship the Earl just now confirm my fears. My Lord Keld, is there nothing I may do to help you? At least convey a message to Stonesthrow? Or to the ship? Humble as I may be, I stand here at your service, My Lord."

This speech stirred within me a swell of grateful and admiring feelings, which I cannot possibly describe in an adequate manner. At its conclusion, Fitzhenry cleared his throat very loudly, apparently to get my attention. Turning to him I witnessed a shockingly prurient leer, which he made no effort to disguise in spite of his fiancée and rector each standing five feet away.

"So! The lass is a toy of yours, Keld! Hmm, and what a spirited filly, what a delectable morsel! How I should savour *this* charming little tidbit!" When Miss Drayton objected to these outrageous words with a gasp of indignation and a thunderous scowl, Fitzhenry added in haste, though not so convincingly, "But of course, my dear Fenny,

I should follow up with *you* for my main course! This little chickadee would provide but the merest appetizer!"

So stunned was I by the audacious inappropriateness of these remarks, that Mr. Lampson cut in before I was able to reply. "For shame, Your Lordship!" he said, with a good deal more heat than seemed wise, given the circumstances. "What sort of villain speaks in that manner to a worthy maid, not to mention his own betrothed! I might expect such slimy language at a mechanics' pub in Cambridge, rather than from the master of a great house!"

Given the look of bemused puzzlement upon Fitzhenry's face, one might have supposed that he found himself reproached by a talking dog, rather than a scholar whose intellect inarguably dwarfed his own. "My good sir—whoever in hell you are—you forget to whom you speak. I expect an apology this very instant, for I have struck men down for less."

It would be useless to attempt a description of the many warring feelings within my bosom in that moment. Had I the ability to split into multiple Richard Jacobs, I should have simultaneously delivered a stinging clout to "His Loutship's" face, fervently shaken Lampson's hand, and kissed Mary Ashwood full upon the mouth. But being so pulled in different directions by diverse passions, far from causing confusion, seemed to have an oddly clarifying effect upon me. Suddenly I glimpsed a way forward—a way which I had not clearly anticipated prior to that very moment.

"Arkengarthdale!" I said, my voice raised only slightly, "is it not true that Great Britain is an island?"

The earl appeared utterly taken aback. "Heavens, Keld, what kind of a question is that?"

"It is a clear and simple question. Is Great Britain an island, or is it not?"

"Why yes, I do believe that the last time anyone checked, Great Britain was indeed an island."

From a certain unseen person standing behind me, who had remained utterly silent throughout this unpleasant social call, I heard a sudden, desperate sort of sniveling sound.

I pressed on. "And so we stand here today, all of us, entirely surrounded by water?"

"Well … yes."

The sniveling behind me became a repeated, choking gasp.

"Completely and forever surrounded by water? Unswimmably vast, unfathomably deep water?"

"Damn it all, Keld, yes! We are surrounded by so much bleeding water that God himself could not measure it!"

That did the trick. The sounds of distress behind me escalated into a deafening wail, magnified by the stone surfaces all around us. Before anyone knew what was happening, the panicked Mustardhead had sent two of Fitzhenry's men sprawling flat onto their backs, and in a terrifying, shrieking, dervish-like flurry of whirling limbs, he made straight for the earl.

I saw Fitzhenry's eyes grow wide, and heard him exclaim, "Jesus bloody hell Christ!"

And then I was off, Thistle at my side. We clasped hands, and ran. Mustardhead's bloodcurdling cries echoed from the walls. I heard footfalls close behind which I dearly hoped belonged to friends, not foes, yet I dared not look.

Thistle and I emerged from Langthwaite, Lampson and Wheelwright steps behind us. Fitzhenry's grooms remained with the horses, Reeth's driver atop the coach. These underlings appeared startled by our appearance. We had but one moment before armed enemies would be upon us.

Before I could act, Wheelwright advanced upon the grooms, brandishing a wicked-looking scimitar. Where upon his person he had concealed this formidable weapon, I knew not, but its effect upon the grooms was instantaneous. Wheelwright made it clear without speaking a word that we were helping ourselves to the earl's horses, thank you very much, and the grooms graciously acquiesced without so much as a whimper, handing over the reins and backing quickly away.

The rector's driver appeared no more inclined to challenge the scimitar, yet he must have felt relatively safe perched upon the coach, for he dared cry, "Help! Horse thieves! Help! Stop the viscount and his rabble!"

I mounted one of the earl's horses. Thistle leapt on behind me, nimbly swinging herself up by cantle and stirrup-top, our dire circumstances arguing against the modesty of sidesaddle. As her arms wrapped around me, and her body pressed against my back, I experienced a jolt of joy, a surge of strength, and felt as if I could have driven that beast the whole length of England, and even over the sea itself, to carry her away from harm.

Wheeling about, I saw that Lampson, Wheelwright, and Miss Drayton had claimed the other three horses. What? Yes, Miss Drayton! Miss Fenny Drayton of Lamb's Conduit Street, Bloomsbury, leapt astride a saddle with the aplomb of a practiced horsewoman.

I must have given Miss Drayton a look, for she said to me, "Don't you dare give me a look, Lord Keld! Do you really expect me to remain in this awful place with such a man as that? What was my father thinking? I would sooner marry a sack of elephant vomit!"

I was very much struck by this novel and apropos turn of phrase, but there was no time to express admiration. The earl's men came sprinting out of the hall. We four urged our horses into full gallop. Within moments we had left behind our pursuers, who now lacked

saddled horses, as well as the rector's driver, who went on sitting there, shouting unkind things about us.

The Arkle Beck and village of Langthwaite flew by in a blur. Thistle held me so tightly, that I fancied I felt her heartbeat jostling with my own, or perhaps that was the pounding of hooves beneath us, as we sped back towards Reeth.

In springing so unexpectedly from the earl's clutches, we had gained a few precious minutes of head start. Even so, less than halfway to Reeth I glanced behind, and witnessed six fast horsemen crossing Arkle Beck, bent upon closing with us. I urged my horse on as best I could, given that I lacked both spurs, and the animal's trust. My companions did the same. Still, when I next ventured a look back, our pursuers had closed the gap. *They* had spurs, sure enough, and mercilessly goaded the poor beasts they rode.

By the time the first outlying cottages of Reeth lay but a few rods before us, I heard thundering hooves of pursuit behind. The earl's men were very close. There was no longer any hope of outrunning them. I had begun to feverishly cast about for some means of evasion, when I looked back again and witnessed one of the most remarkable sights I ever shall see.

Wheelwright had stopped his horse, right in the centre of the road. As I watched, incredulous, he used reins and heels to wheel his horse about into a magnificent rearing pose, facing straight at our onrushing enemies, the earl himself amongst them. One hand on the reins, Wheelwright held in his other something rectangular, something black, bringing it up like a shield, or perhaps wielding it like a talisman, between us and our pursuers.

Should I live to be one thousand years old, I shall never forget the violent reaction of the oncoming horses. Their eyes grew wide, rolling back in horror. They swerved and flailed, skidding from a hard gallop to a full stop within moments. One rider was thrown outright; the others fought to remain in their saddles, all semblance of control over their beasts lost. None of this may be fully explained by the sight of a single rearing horse in the road ahead.

A heartbeat after the horses came to this precipitous halt, three of them—including the one now riderless—turned tail and galloped back towards Langthwaite, ignoring the curses and abuse of their enraged riders. The other three horses left the road, clearly against the wishes of their masters, whinnying and wheeling about on the grassy verge, unwilling to move one step nearer the spot where Wheelwright held up the black book, his horse still rampant, its forelegs pawing at the air.

All this I saw in the space of a few seconds. Turning my attention back to the road, I let up our speed not one jot.

Within moments, we reached the outskirts of Reeth. Here I took another glance back and saw Wheelwright galloping after us, yet hanging back enough to act as a rear guard. Our three remaining pursuers—including the rector and the earl—had not given up chase, but for the moment they maintained a respectful distance.

This passage through Reeth was very different from the one we had experienced not a half-hour prior. Whereas before the place had been strangely inert, most of the town now turned out to see who passed through at such a desperate speed. Cheers went up from the crowd as we blazed past; no doubt these good folk realized at once that the we hardly took the earl's horses on such a reckless joyride by his gracious invitation. It was all I could do to refrain from waving my hat in salute as we thundered through Reeth, bathed in hurrahs. (Refraining *was* made easier when, attention thus turned to my hat, I found it to be missing; it must have flown from my head.)

Leaving Reeth behind, we swung up-valley along the main road. Just across the Swale, still several minutes' ride away, my *Mean Fish* lay at anchor. The roaring waters ovespilling the canal remained

turbid with mud as they relentlessly eroded the land; my heart nearly stopped at the thought that a breach might erupt at any moment, carrying my splendid vessel and her marvelous crew to certain doom. I considered cutting straight across the valley, and braving the swollen Swale, but the stone field-walls here were too high and too numerous for a horse to jump. We would again have to cross at Low Whita.

Towards the low-water crossing we sped. My horse shewed signs of mounting exhaustion, yet perhaps divining the feelings of its rider as good mounts undoubtedly do, it pressed on urgently. By the time we splashed across the Swale at Low Whita, our pursuers had again gained ground on us.

As we galloped up Low Lane towards our ship, I noted a flurry of activity aboard. I heard Bridger sound his bosun-pipe and Nelson bark orders. Clearly, our headlong flight back to the ship had been espied. I surmised that our crew prepared for the dire gambit of ramming the lock-door.

Despite its marvelous spirit, my horse felt near spent when we finally arrived at the lower end of the gangplank. I could spare only a kindly word for the poor beast as Thistle and I dismounted and, hand in hand, sprinted up the gangplank and aboard. Lampson, Wheelwright, and Miss Drayton followed us closely.

Even as we boarded, the two forward anchors were being drawn in; I felt the ship lurch as the current caught her. With the two aft anchors still deployed, however, the *Mean Fish* did not begin to move at once—and to my horror, I saw that Fitzhenry, the rector, and one of the earl's armed men were much closer behind us than I had thought. In fact, they had quit their horses and made on foot for the gangplank, which in the tumult of getting under way, no sailors were on hand to draw in. We were about to be boarded by a hostile party!

With our enemies mere steps away, something most extraordinary took place, witnessed by all present. A damnably familiar shape

appeared in the air, ten feet above the gangplank, where an instant prior, there had been absolutely nothing. The shape hung in midair for what seemed like an impossibly long moment. Then it plunged, straight down.

The Loose Stone of the Hall reduced the centre of our gangplank into splinters, rending it in two. Then came a deep *splosh* as the Stone dropped into the canal below, followed by lesser splashes as fragments of demolished wood fell into the water.

When the gangplank ceased to exist, Fitzhenry had been just a couple of steps away from it. Somehow, he managed to stop himself, coming to a precarious halt on the very brink of the gulf which now cut him off from the *Mean Fish*. The rector and the earl's thug also stopped short.

And then, the ship began to move … Slowly at first, but picking up speed. Our enemies were left standing there on the edge of our canal, their faces masks of wrath and disbelief.

"'Tis devilry at work!" sputtered the rector, grasping Fitzhenry's shoulder. "Devilry, all of it! The yellow-haired boy is possessed! That black book is wicked beyond all accounting! And that Stone just now—what could it be but the work of Satan himself! We must inform the bishop straightaway! We must! My Lord, why do you not answer me?"

Indeed, Fitzhenry paid no attention to his apoplectic rector, instead staring intently at me, his expression gradually fading from anger to something like his usual inane grin, only tinged with fear and revulsion. "Hang the bishop, Reeth, and shut your bloody mouth," he said aside, before directly addressing me. "I have dreamt of that bloody Stone, Keld! Oh, yes! I've dreamt of it! On numerous awful occasions! And I'll have bloody well nothing to do with such things! You keep your bloody ship and your bloody canal and your goddamned right-of-way! Oh, and by-the-by, keep that blue-stocking

bitch of an ex-fiancée as well, and let us leave things at that! You are henceforth obliged to leave me the hell alone! Do you hear me? *Do you hear me, Keld?*"

I drew myself up and said, "Henry Fitzhenry, I do indeed hear you! And since you are so very generous regarding things which I may keep, it is the least I can do to repay the favour, and so the trig young gentleman who goes by the name Mustardhead is assuredly yours in return! If you are lucky, he shall by the time you are back at Langthwaite have exhausted his fit, and be ready to regale you with no end of fair sayings! Fare thee well, Your Loutship! I very gladly take my leave of your odious person!"

With that, I turned my back on him and the Rector of Reeth. If ever I see either of them again, it shall be too soon.

The *Mean Fish* moved along smartly by this time. I could see Bridger struggling to steer us towards the centre of the canal, aiming to ram the closed lock-door; with the overflow's current pulling the ship to port, this was a difficult maneuver. Still clutching Thistle by the hand, I thought to join Bridger and render any assistance I could, but upon turning I found myself face-to-face with Wheelwright, and without thinking, I blurted out, "What in heaven's name *was* that back there? How *did* you do that? Where is the book now?"

"The books are all of them the earl's, now, and good riddance," said our adventuring librarian, with the air of a man who has felt a great burden lifted from his shoulders. He must have seen the further question about to spring from my lips, for he put up a gently warding hand, adding, "It is a story for another time, Captain."

He was right. This was no time for conversation. Scarce had Wheelwright finished speaking, when Bigg called out a collision warning from the crows nest. The lock-door loomed, dead ahead.

Every man aboard—and every woman, I must now add—braced themselves for impact as best they could. Thistle and I grasped the

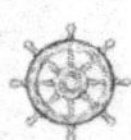

portside railings, crouching low to keep our balance. She looked at me, eyes wide, and asked, "Is this a very dangerous thing we are about to do?"

"Yes, it is," I said.

"Then even if it proves our end, I shall relish every moment!"

At that very instant, the *Mean Fish* rammed the lock-door with a great, shuddering crash. The sudden stop caused me to topple over on top of Miss Ashwood. She and I quickly extricated ourselves from this unseemly (if not entirely unwelcome) entanglement, and I stood up, to better take stock of our situation.

Bridger had steered us very skillfully. Despite the current pulling us to port, he had placed our bow very near the centre of the lock-door, where its two halves met. There the weight of our vessel—magnified by the current behind us—now mangled the lock's beams and hinges, which groaned and snapped as they gave way to more force than they could withstand. A complete breach seemed imminent.

Bridger surely saw this, as well, for in a booming voice fit to be heard over the loudest gale or strongest sea he cried out, "All hands! All hands on deck, ready to swim fer it if she wrecks! This is it, lads, this is it, 'twas child's play afore, but now we're a-heading down the bloody fluuuuuuuuuuuuuuuuuuuuuuuume!"

That last word he drew out as the lock-door, amidst final cracks of rupturing timber and shrieks of twisting iron, gave way. With a lurch ten times more violent than when we had struck the door, we rent it asunder, and were again underway, although for several long, terrifying moments, scarcely under control.

So fiercely did the great gush of water propel us forward, that it felt as if our ship had been shot from a gargantuan cannon. There came a great shock immediately, as the port stern glanced from remnants of the lock-door; through some miracle, the anchor dragging on that side failed to snag on any debris. As Bridger fought for control, the

ship fishtailed amidst the roiling surge. The *Mean Fish* vibrated awfully, accompanied by a thunderous roar, our keel dragging bottom. Spray flew over the railings as water, moving faster than the anchor-slowed ship, struck our stern in furious waves.

Terrifying though all of this was, the battering by passing waves shewed that our plan was already working. With two anchors slowing the *Mean Fish*, we spent only moments perched upon the foaming vanguard of the flood. With each excruciatingly slow minute, that tumult, which we never could have ridden safely all the way to Richmond, got farther ahead of us, and the water swirling in its wake around us grew deeper, and less turbulent.

After perhaps five minutes—though I swear it seemed an age—our keel had ceased to feel bottom, and Bridger had straightened us out. We had resumed our journey towards the sea!

One might have expected a hurrah from the crew, yet nothing of the sort was heard. All hands surely understood that danger, as well as the time for rejoicing, still lay ahead.

I tended to Thistle as soon as I could stand, helping her up and ensuring that she was well. It pleased me to find my lady far from traumatized by our long, hard gallop and the ship's brush with death; on the contrary, her fine features glowed with the elation of adventure. How strong the impulse to kiss her, then and there, in front of God and everyone, and scruples be damned!

But, before I could, my uncle physically interposed between us, grasping both my shoulders and saying, "Blow me over, Nephew, what the devil happened with the earl? How did Miss Ashwood come to join us? I saw Miss Drayton board, but where is she now? And for Christ's sake, Richard, that was the *bleeding Loose Stone* which severed the gangplank and saved our skins, or I'm a mackerel! But why on earth would …? And how did … ? Richard William Jacob, what in God's name is going on!"

"Uncle, I shall tell you all I know, as soon as I am able. Suffice it to say for now, that the earl thought to sidestep our unwell duke, and swallow our ship and canal into the belly of his own estate, but I daresay he found elements of their seasoning unpalatable. I myself know not how Miss Ashwood came to Langthwaite today, but I hope to learn momentarily. Miss Drayton did indeed come aboard with us, but someone must have escorted her below decks, for safety. She has bravely thrown over His Loutship, and she deserves a damehood for it! As for the Stone … Good heavens, Nelson, had I any inkling why it has rendered us aid, I should be wise as Solomon. We may never know. But now, if you shall pardon me, I *must* confer with our pilot."

I made for the wheel, Thistle in tow, and found Bridger as blasé about the previous hour's events, as my uncle was flustered by them. In response to my heartfelt thanks for adroitly managing our escape, he merely shrugged and said, "Cap'n, 'twas nothing to some scrapes these eyes've seen. Why, even ramming that lock-door turned out summut disappointing, in the danger department. We're back in friendly waters now, though it'll be a jostler from here on. I think we may reel in the aft anchors afore long, get up to the same speed as this current. There's no way we'll overtake the nasty part what surged on past us, thanks to them anchors."

Making a mental note to favour Mr. Bridger with extra sweets for at least one week, I waved away my uncle, who still wished to converse, and drew aside with Miss Ashwood—for it was her story which I found myself unable to put off hearing for one moment longer.

Alas, my patience on that score was to be sorely tried. Before I could utter a syllable of the questions burning upon my tongue, my ears were assailed by the jarring and unmistakable sound of gunshots!

Certain that the earl's men must be attacking us, I instantly shielded Miss Ashwood as best I could, and looked about for the ambush. With a great sigh of relief, I discovered that the shots had

not been fired *at* us, and that far from expressing malice, they were in fact celebratory.

We were by this time below Fremington, where the main road crosses the Swale. The road now ran along the valley on our side of the river, a mere hundred yards or so downslope from us. This thoroughfare I saw to be thronged with locals, following our ship and shewing great enthusiasm for its progress. A dozen riders waved, as our sailors waved back. Shouts of encouragement reached my ears, peppered with such pleasantries as "Godspeed the Viscount Keld!", And "To hell with the earl!" Apparently, our daring escape from His Loutship had not only swelled the ranks of our admirers, but had also increased their fervour, to such a pitch that firearms were being discharged into the air.

The friendly nature of the gunfire notwithstanding, it served to remind me that Thistle would be dangerously exposed above decks, should anyone bear ill-will towards us. I found Lampson at the railing, waving to our admirers, and ordered him to ensure that Miss Ashwood and Miss Drayton were shewn to the Cat & Cabbage, there to be served any food or refreshments they might wish.

"Sir," said he, "I shall gladly accompany Miss Ashwood to the pub, but I should inform you that, to the best of my knowledge, Miss Drayton's whereabouts are not strictly known."

"But she *did* board with us; I saw her come up the gangplank!"

"Yes, sir, so did we all." Here Lampson shot a sidewise glance at Miss Ashwood, and leaning closer to me, he went on in a much quieter voice. "To be candid, sir, more than one sailor claims to have seen Miss Drayton in the company of Doctor Converse, below-decks, immediately after her arrival, although their present location is, as I say, not known. However, as they were seen with hands clasped and seeming in rather a hurry to get … er … *somewhere*, we may

probably rest assured that … uh … that her safety and comfort is being attended to. If you follow my meaning, sir."

I gathered from the expression of amused shock on Miss Ashwood's face, which she tried in vain to suppress, that she had overheard and, like myself, hardly failed to follow Lampson's meaning. I felt my face flush as I cleared my throat and said to Lampson, "Very well, then, carry on, and ensure that Miss Ashwood is escorted to the pub. I shall check in on her shortly."

Turning to her, I went on, "Miss Ashwood—it delights me beyond words to find you onboard with us. Only pressing matters of command could induce me to relinquish your company, but unhappily, they do so. In the meantime, my ship and crew are entirely at your disposal. Anything within our power to grant, shall be yours immediately!" With that I executed my most elegant bow, and with strong regrets, took leave of her whose unexpected appearance was the only thing which could have improved this already worthy adventure.

I watched Miss Ashwood go, Lampson helping her down the steep gangway. They were not yet out of sight when Nelson interposed himself and said, "Well, now that Aphrodite is for a moment out of sight, I suppose that your first officer may request an explanation as to what in hell happened back there? Lampson seems bamboozled by it, Wheelwright speaks in riddles, Miss Drayton is said to be amorously indisposed, and Mustardhead, thank the heavens, appears to have gone missing."

I did owe my uncle an explanation, and so I proceeded to relate the entire story—from the moment we left the *Mean Fish*, up to our desperate flight from Langthwaite with Fitzhenry in pursuit. Nelson proved a most appreciative audience; never before had I a tale to tell which kept him in such rapt attention for so long a time.

During my narrative, I heard a whistle from Bridger's bosun-pipe, followed by the rumble of the aft anchor-chains being drawn in. Our

speed picked up noticeably, yet our progress remained surprisingly smooth, the *Mean Fish* making its merry way towards Richmond almost as if no interruption had occurred. We had, then, managed to outmaneuver the earl entirely, at least for the time being, and my heart thrilled at the thought—and yet, so much potential peril still lay ahead, that I refused to shew any exuberance.

When I finished my story, Nelson regarded me in silence for a moment. Then he said, "Richard, if I follow you correctly, I gather that Henry Fitzhenry has, in the space of thirty minutes, lost his fiancée, been frightened out of his wits by Mustardhead, and shewn himself a horrid malicious fool before all Reeth?"

When I agreed that this was a fair summary of events, Nelson nodded thoughtfully, and let slip a snicker. This he followed a moment later with a mild guffaw.

I had just begun to chuckle myself in genial agreement when my uncle burst into a bout of sidesplitting laughter, the likes of which I had never once seen from him. The poor fellow became, for some moments, helpless in the grip of overwhelming mirth; he laughed until tears flowed, and his face turned red as a beet. He was even obliged to lean upon a railing for support. My uncle carried on so loudly that the folk down on the road heard him, and sent up a responding cheer, accompanied by further festive gunshots.

When he finally mastered himself, my uncle wiped his eyes upon his sleeves as he said, "Oh, Richard, that is without a doubt the most splendid story I have ever heard. I would gladly give my eye-teeth to have been present in that chapel ... to have seen the look upon that slimy bastard's face when Mustardhead came at him. Do be sure to write every bit of that down, there's a good fellow."

Whilst that last remark felt somewhat patronizing, I let it pass. Sir James Nelson may be a cracking good first officer, but he is, after all, first and foremost my uncle.

At that juncture, it was a quarter past nine in the morning. We had been underway for three hours, and the old stone tower of Ellerton Abbey, visible off to port, shewed that we had traversed about two-thirds of the distance to Richmond. I detected no signs of hostile pursuit—and indeed, the troupe of armed supporters escorting us down-valley naturally discouraged such a thing.

Given such auspicious circumstances, it was acutely tempting to go below and indulge in conversation with Miss Ashwood. But, whereas such an impulse might at one time have mastered me, I now found myself recognizing that this was not the time for such pleasantries. My duties as captain were to remain on deck, observe our progress, encourage my officers and crew, and be ready to deal with any further crises which might arise.

Of the known obstacles which remained ahead, one loomed large in my mind, by merit of its extreme hazard. Had I assembled the crew weeks ago, and outlined in detail our plan to move the *Mean Fish* to the sea, a description of this particular peril would likely have caused second-guessing amongst the sailors, and perhaps even desertions. I had held off on telling even Bridger about it, chusing to first observe how he handled navigating our canal, before bringing this particular danger to his attention. Now that we were most of the way to Richmond, it seemed high time to finally do so. It was with trepidation that I approached our pilot at the wheel, cleared my throat, and said, "Mister Bridger, you have thus far handled every challenge thrown at you, with even more skill than I could have hoped. It is no exaggeration to say, that every soul aboard this ship is indebted to your competence and courage."

Bridger shrugged. "I do 'preciate that, Cap'n, but you may's well thank the sky fer bein' blue!"

"Yes, well, be that as it may, there *shall* be a bit of an additional bother to deal with, about ninety minutes ahead of us, and you should know about that now."

Bridger shot me a scowl. "We ain't expectin' more trouble from that mealy-mouthed earl?"

"Well, no, hopefully not. But you see, there's going to be a tough patch at Richmond. In fact, it's going to be the toughest patch yet. That rough water up at Stonesthrow, where we first entered the canal proper? Mere riffles by comparison.

"You see, just as we disguised the upper end of our canal, by concealing the passage which feeds water into it, we were obliged to disguise the lower end. We began construction of a bridge there over the River Swale, by which our fictional turn-pike was to have crossed, in order to meet the main road on the far bank. But we never could have built a direct connection from our canal straight into the river, right there, in plain sight of all Richmond. It would have made the true purpose of our project all too clear."

"Cap'n, you're not bein' all too clear, even now. Spell it out, fer Christ's sake!"

"Very well. At Richmond, this canal comes to an abrupt end twenty feet above the river, and thirty feet distant from it. In between, we must expect the water to rush down a concavity in the rocky hillside. To reach the lower Swale, our only feasible avenue to the sea, the *Mean Fish* must traverse this awful rapid. Whether or not that is even possible without our ship being torn to splinters, is the chief challenge which remains before us. God knows it has caused me many a sleepless night. I have given this problem great thought, as has my uncle, and our engineer, but given our need to beguile the citizens of Richmond, we have seen no other way."

Bridger remained quiet for a moment. How I dreaded his response! Having learnt of this horror ahead, would he now falter? Did the

same marvelous knowledge which had enabled Michael Bridger to overcome all perils thus far now inform him that what his captain required was tantamount to suicide?

After an excruciatingly long pause, during which I sought in vain to read his expression, Bridger said, "Cap'n, I've never knowed a man to say so little with so many words, as you manage every single day, from morning 'til night. What it boils down to, is that we've got a mighty bracing rapid to run. I reckon it won't be much diff'nt than that to-do in Penzance back in eighty-five, with all the eels and whatnot, and I got my ship through *that* with nary a scratch. Not to worry, sir. I'll coax this here *Mean Fish* right into that river, slick as a whistle, or die trying! The ship's a good sight longer than this here whitewater chute you speak of, which'll help with control. Why, so long as our keel don't snap from too much weight in the wrong spot, and we don't capsize from hitting the river current crosswise, 'twill be easily done!"

Whilst Bridger's willingness to pilot the ship through this danger, and his general enthusiasm, was a great relief, the parts about ways of wrecking, and possible death, were rather less than welcome. However, I did feel reassured, on balance, and so turned my attention elsewhere for a time.

The following hour abounded with encouraging sights *vis-à-vis* our progress. Swaledale becomes a gentler valley below Reeth, and to our north, high fells had given way to lower hills—thus, already, the sea *felt* nearer, despite our distance from it. The crowd of well-wishers keeping pace with us on the road grew ever larger and more vociferous, with additions arriving constantly, especially from the direction of Richmond. Our sailors carried on a congenial *tête-à-tête* with this burgeoning audience from the portside railings, swapping salutes, greetings, jokes, etc. This jolly interplay became especially pronounced below Downholme, where a narrowing of the valley

meant that our watery new 'road' closely paralleled the old one, at times just a few yards upslope from it.

Between these promising developments, and further check-ins with Bridger, and three retellings of my adventure at Langthwaite to enquiring groups of sailors, the time flew by. It seemed surprisingly soon when I heard Bigg call from the crows nest, "Richmond ho!" But sure enough, the *Mean Fish* had rounded the last significant promontory on the south slopes of Swaledale. The roofs and great castle keep of Richmond lay visible ahead.

How my pulse raced at the sight of that ancient city! Just beyond its handsome buildings, a terrifying chute of whitewater lay in wait. And somewhere in town, probably within the congenial walls of Goodwood House, lay our unwell duke, whose trust I had blatantly violated in advancing my canal project with the promise of a turn-pike. I could only pray that evil words from Fitzhenry had not preceded us down-valley, fanning flames of anger in this normally temperate man.

Flouting the earl's disapproval had been a positive pleasure—I would welcome the opportunity to do so again—but I could never behave in the same flippant manner towards the duke, whose person and authority I have ever held in the highest regard. Would his representatives, or the man himself, appear beside the canal and order us to halt, demanding that I answer for my public dishonesty? If so, how could I possibly disobey? And yet, was it not equally impossible to abandon this journey, now that we had passed through so much danger, and progressed so far towards the sea?

My heart felt stuck in my throat as we coasted through that final mile of canal. I stood lookout at the bow, anxiously watching the canal banks ahead for any sign of a scowling duke. I heard Bridger's bosun-pipe whistle for all hands to brace for impact. Some way back, the main road had crossed over to the north side of the river, since Richmond lies entirely on that bank; the road now lay some

distance off, leaving us bereft of our noisy entourage. How eerily quiet it seemed, with our supporters out of sight and earshot—yet presumably the lot of them were by then trooping into Richmond, amongst the woods to our north.

The silence was broken when my straining ears detected the low, steady roar of raging water. I felt my skin crawl as this ominous sound grew rapidly louder, heralding—so I supposed—the tumult at the end of our canal.

Why did Bigg, with his better view, not call out a warning? I was about to do so myself, when the ship emerged from a stretch of dense woods. To port, the ancient walls of Richmond Castle came into sight across the river, now a mere bowshot distant, and directly below us, the rain-swollen Swale roared over the Falls of Richmond, the final such drop on the river's course. I allowed myself a half-sigh of relief, for this was the torrent whose voice I had heard. The one we must somehow traverse still lay a few minutes ahead.

Passing the falls, we entered the final thousand feet of canal. I glanced back over the decks of the *Mean Fish*. Every sailor topside had wedged themselves into some protected spot, or held fast to some solid portion of the ship, in response to Bridger's warning. The only exception was our pilot himself, who remained at the wheel, his expression so *nonchalant* that he might have been steering a toy yacht on a tiny pond.

The sound of Richmond Falls receded behind us, only to be gradually replaced by an even more menacing rumble from somewhere ahead.

Finally, as Bridger deftly steered us through one last minor bend to starboard, the end came into view—a horizon-line where the waters of our canal fell into empty space. Beyond I saw only the trees and slopes on the far bank of the Swale.

The thunder of the violent cascade ahead grew deafening. It suddenly occurred to me that, although my position at the bow had made sense when on the lookout for angry dukes, it was not the most salutary place to be when the ship was about to tip forward down a sluice of frothing whitewater.

However, it was too late to move. I had not time to find, let alone secure myself in, any better location. So I lay upon the deck, wedging my body as tightly as possible between the railings which converged at the bow.

I heard a warning shout from Bigg—his precise words lost in the roar of falling water.

A moment later, the ship lurched forward in a most chilling way, and we seemed to slide off the edge of the world.

I knew full well that the vertical drop between the end of our canal, and the River Swale, was no more than twenty feet. This had been the point of many discussions amongst myself, Nelson, and Miss Smeaton, over the previous several years. So, I cannot account for the sight which met my eyes as the *Mean Fish* tilted out over a torrent which I would swear descended five times that far, to the foaming river below.

I had all too much time to contemplate this horrid view, as we seemed to hang there for an agonizingly long moment, hovering above a maelstrom of destruction, the bow moving farther and farther out over this watery hell, until it felt as if the whole ship must have gone airborne.

Then we reached the tipping point.

There came a second or two of stomach-twisting drop. Frothing water rushed up towards me. I closed my eyes and gripped the doughty wood of my ship's railings, so tightly that it hurt.

Sheets of spray exploded skyward mere inches away. Buffeted by violent waves of freezing water, I redoubled my hold. The ship to which I desperately clung thrummed with terrifying vibrations and shocks, as our keel slid along a jumble of rocks.

It cannot have lasted more than a few seconds, yet it seemed an eternity.

And then, abruptly, the horrific turmoil yielded to an eerie stillness.

Was I yet alive? I thought so. I felt myself still jammed against the ship's railings, which argued against my being dead, unless the whole of the *Mean Fish* had plunged along with me into the afterworld.

Venturing to open my eyes, I saw only sodden wood before my face. I lifted my head, and beheld a river ... riverbanks ... trees along the riverbanks.

The roar of the rapid already grew more faint, and I heard swelling above it a competing commotion of glee. Twisting to peer over my shoulder, I found myself looking upstream along the swollen River Swale, towards the bankside meadows below Richmond. There, with the walls and roofs of the town rising behind, stood a great throng of townspeople on foot, and countryfolk on horseback, the lot of them sending up one hearty hurrah after another. Arms waved in elation, hats were flung skyward, and a barrage of celebratory gunshots rang out. Word of our approach along the canal had surely preceded us into Richmond, so this crowd must have gathered to see whether we should be foolhardy enough to attempt that perilous descent into the Swale. I daresay that we had not disappointed them.

In the next moment, an answering cheer—even more jubilant— went up from the *Mean Fish*, as our crew realized that we had survived the harrowing drop. Our sailors whooped and hollered, saluting our supporters on the riverbank, causing an even louder outbreak of hurrahs from that quarter.

I looked all around, the better to take in our new situation. We traveled no longer upon our marvelous artificial waterway, but upon the Swale, a highway to carry us—as rivers quite naturally shall—

towards the sea. Normally, this portion of the Swale would have been unnavigable for a ship even half the size of ours; only the incessant rains of previous weeks, which have sent every stream in Yorkshire far over its banks, made it possible for us to travel there. Even so, the Swale just below Richmond seemed scarcely able to contain us. Branches from trees along both riverbanks continually raked the sides of our ship, with some rather large limbs even being snapped off, no match for the weight and momentum of our vessel.

I hurried aft—pausing to share congratulatory handshakes with knots of triumphant sailors—and joined Bridger at the wheel. My initial impulse was to throw my arms around the man, but I thought better of that, instead favouring him with a hardy clap upon the back. "Well done, sir! Well done! Surely nothing of the sort has ever been accomplished with a tall ship!"

Bridger shrugged in his usual modest manner, but both looked and sounded immensely pleased with himself as he said, "Oh, 'twas a trifle, Cap'n. I ain't even broke a sweat yet."

I was about to say something else deliriously complimentary, when the *Mean Fish* gave a lurch, accompanied by a vibrating rumble felt through the deck, and our speed slowed noticeably.

"Our keel's feelin' bottom, Cap'n," said Bridger, adjusting the wheel. "Impossible to tell where the deep channel runs, what with water so high. Keeping her between the trees is all I can do. We're sure to keep scraping over what'd be sandbars and points at normal flow. But the force of the flood should push us through, so long as we're aimed straight downstream." By the time he had finished speaking, our keel had already regained deeper water, the vibrations ceasing as we recovered speed.

Nelson joined me on the poop then, having come up from below decks. Him I *did* embrace, and I need not muddle this log

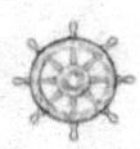

with the congratulatory words with which we regaled one another for several minutes.

We were, in truth, really on our way. Although moving more slowly in the Swale than we had in our canal (measurements shew an average speed of four to five knots here), Richmond already receded into the distance. We descried no sign of pursuit on land, of either a friendly or unfriendly variety; indeed, there was hardly any sign of *land*. We had reached the low-lying vale of Mowbray, where the engorged River Swale had spread out over fields and meadows to either side; only half-submerged trees, hedges, and farm buildings shewed where the river's waters did not normally run. Our crowd of well-wishers must have been thwarted by this situation just below Richmond, assuming that any of them had wished to keep following us. And so, we found our ship gliding through an eerily empty countryside, high waters having pushed both man and beast far from the course of the Swale.

By noon, six hours after leaving Stonesthrow Hall, we found ourselves passing the site of the bridge at Catterick. I say 'site', because the bridge is not presently there. It is in the process of being rebuilt, the coach road through Catterick served by a ferry in the interim. This absence of the bridge at Catterick had contributed to my and Nelson's conclusion, that there could be no better time to make our run to the sea. Our canal bypasses the several bridges over the Swale above Richmond, but those few spanning the river below Richmond pose special problems, as our hull could hardly fit under any of them, even if we were to take our masts down. The first of these, the bridge at Skipton, we shall deal with soon—probably within an hour of the present moment. (It is now nearly three o'clock, and I have been writing this log entry for the better part of two hours.)

Finding the *Mean Fish* traveling smoothly on the Swale, in no immediate danger, and having received a damage report which

shewed the ship very little the worse for her adventure, I left Nelson and Bridger in command on deck. And whilst I felt sorely tempted to hasten to the Cat & Cabbage, there to bask in the glow of Miss Mary Ashwood, my sun and moon wrapped in one, I felt obliged by duty to instead retire to my cabin and commit to these pages the profuse events of the day, whilst the details remain fresh in my memory. However much I desire to see her face, and hear from her lips how she came to be at Langthwaite today, the fact remains that during the past nine hours this ship and crew have achieved an unparalleled feat of navigation, and it would be slipshod of me to not record this historic exploit, to the best of my ability.

I must now return topside to supervise our passage around the bridge at Skipton. Hopefully, I may return to this log later today, in order to chronicle the outcome of that challenge.

June 30; Nearing Midnight

Seven hours have passed since last I wrote. Shortly after penning the previous entry, I returned topside to find the Mean Fish a mere fifteen minutes from Skipton. I joined Nelson and Bridger at the wheel, learning from them that our journey below Catterick had been uneventful, with even the Swale's tight curves near Morton posing no serious difficulties.

"She handles marvelous well, Cap'n," said Bridger, giving the wheel a sort of caress. "Ye did right bringin' in the Newcastle lads."

I told Bridger that it was highly satisfying to hear this, and I was about to mention a few of the individuals involved with the ship's design—curious to know if he might be acquainted with any—when a thought struck me and I blurted, "Good heavens, man! Have you been at this wheel for ten consecutive hours? I have seen you nowhere else in that time!"

"Aye, Cap'n, going by the ship's bells, that I have. Whilst you were ashore with that foul earl, I had no steerin' to do, 'tis true. Yet even then, 'twould not have been meet for me to leave this post, given that all hell could've busted out any time."

"But this is insanity! You shall surely drop dead at any moment! Bridger, you must relinquish the wheel and retire to your cabin! As you know perfectly well, we have several men aboard with experience enough to pilot the ship, Sir James not the least amongst them!"

"Cap'n, with all due respect, I won't have it! I'm not leavin' this wheel until that bow up yonder kisses the sea!"

"But … well … You should be provisioned! I shall take your order for victuals down to the galley myself; it is the least I can do for such a steadfast Prince of Pilotage, whose skill has saved our necks more than once today."

In response, Bridger held high a bottle, produced seemingly from nowhere. "Islay whisky, Cap'n. With sech nectar upon his lips, a pilot wants fer no meat, nor bread, nor water, nor even rest, whilst at the wheel. The finest goddamn tonic anybody north o' the Roman Wall ever cooked up!"

"But surely you must need at least a moment to relieve yourself?"

Bridger skewered me with a full-on scowl. "Now yer driftin' into mighty personal territory, Cap'n. I'll thank ye to mind yer own bladder, and trust yer second mate to mind his."

Thus thoroughly repudiated, I altered the subject, explaining to Bridger the means by which we hoped to circumvent the bridge at Skipton.

He frowned and stroked his grizzled chin as I spoke, then said, "So I'm to steer our ship across a *field?*"

"Yes, well, a pasture, actually. The road approaching the Skipton Bridge from the south crosses a low bottomland. Miss Smeaton's surveys shew it to be a former course of the River Swale. It takes

on water in even the lowest flood. Under such conditions as these, there should be depth for us, though I daresay we'll feel bottom much of the way."

"So we're to leave the main river channel entirely."

"Yes, but only for a couple of hundred yards."

"The trees are lined up near-solid along both banks, Cap'n. Are we to blast our way through 'em with cannon fire?"

"Why no—although that sounds terrifically exciting! But Miss Smeaton's team has preceded us. Posing as surveyors for a fictitious Yorkshire Board of Pasture Improvement, they felled any trees which might have prevented our access to the old channel, and marked our optimal course with flags upon tall poles ... hopefully tall enough that they are not now submerged."

"Aye, hopefully indeed! Otherwise, our *Mean Fish* may find a new home, and a less wet one than we'd like—stuck fast in some bumpkin's pasture 'til she rots in place!" He shook his head with a rueful smile. "Truly, Cap'n, I almost believe ye built a ship at Keld jest so ye could throw one outrageous problem after another at this old salt, 'til you manage to bamboozle him!"

"Ha ha! I surely could never manage *that!*" I returned, but my mirth was forced. I had already been uneasy about this challenge, and the idea of our ship stranded in a river-bottom pasture forever—where she would surely become a subject of ridicule to all England, if not the entire world—did nothing to alleviate my concerns.

Still, Bridger seemed as supremely unconcerned about this obstacle as he had about any previous one, and ten minutes later, when an obvious gap appeared in the trees to starboard (branches to either side having been marked with fluttering ribbons of red cloth), he steered us smoothly towards it without any hesitation.

Our keel felt bottom the instant we nosed out of the main channel; our speed slowed accordingly. The low-lying pastures ahead of us

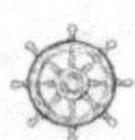

lay entirely under water. Much to my relief, Miss Smeaton's series of flagged poles were indeed visible, marking the deepest path across this otherwise trackless expanse. Better still, a significant current could be seen roiling the water's surface, extending on ahead of us in the direction of the nearest pole. But would this flow through the old channel of the Swale—our ship's only motive power, so long as her sails were furled—prove enough to propel us all the way through, and back to the river?

"We shall want to stay on the port side of the poles," I told Bridger.

"I can see that well enough, Cap'n," he replied. "I reckon I read water better than you read the King's English."

With excruciating sluggishness, we came abreast of the first pole. With each passing minute the *Mean Fish* unmistakably slowed further, even as the current visible ahead of us became less distinct, and more diffused across the surface of the floodwaters.

Our keel skimmed across these grassy pastures with far less noise than when it had raked the points and bars of the river; only the occasional rock below grated upon it, or bumped against our hull. At one point, with the Skipton Bridge visible off to port, we did cross a patch of rougher material, whose progress beneath our ship, from bow to stern, could be heard as we scraped across it; this I took to be the submerged road.

Our forward progress continued to lag until, with fifty or sixty yards to go, it felt as though we had nearly stopped. Three flagged poles rose from the water between us and the titillating spot ahead—another gap in the trees—where our course would return to the main channel of the Swale.

It was an awful moment—in some ways even worse than the raging torrent we had ridden into the Swale hours earlier. I found myself leaning forward, as if doing so might impart the slightest bit more momentum to the ship. At the same time, an odd sort of

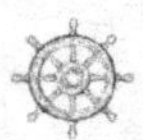

murmuring sound came to my attention—so very slight that I could not divine from whence it came. After a moment's uncertainty I ventured, "Mr. Bridger, is it you making that sound? A sound like, *en-en-en-en-en-en-en-en*?"

"En-en-en-en-en-en-en-en. Aye, Cap'n. En-en-en-en-en-en-en-en."

"And why in God's name are you doing that?"

"En-en-en-en-en-en-en-en. I'm coaxing the ship along, Cap'n. En-en-en-en-en-en-en-en."

At a speed comparable to that of an exhausted sheep, our bow inched abreast of the third-to-last flagged pole. Bridger gave the wheel a slight turn, aiming for the next.

For seemingly endless minutes, I continued to lean forward, and Bridger continued to coax the ship. The watery landscape around us felt preternaturally quiet and immobile, as if the entire world held its breath. Still, the pole we were ostensibly *passing* sat there stubbornly just off our starboard bow, its red flag fluttering limply in fitful puffs of breeze.

"Great God in heaven, this is unbearable!" I cried at last. "Bridger, should we not unfurl the sails before we lose forward motion altogether? Is there anything on board we could use as oars? Perhaps some of our sailors should jump overboard and push? We surely have doughty swimmers!"

Bridger remained entirely placid. In fact, I daresay he spoke rather more slowly than usual as he replied, "Even if we could unfurl the sails quick enough to do any good, there's hardly a breath of wind, Cap'n. Yer ideas ain't bad; I'll give ye credit fer thinkin' creative-like. But be calm, sir. We shan't need any sech help."

By this time the third-to-last pole *still* rose alongside the forecastle. At that rate, the beckoning gap in the trees ahead seemed at least a month away. "But we are practically dead in the water, man! We must do *something!*"

Bridger took a very deep breath, then said, "As ye feel so strongly about taking action, sir, you may consider closin' yer eyes, or going below decks. If ye weren't my Cap'n, I might also suggest stuffin' yer head into a flour sack—though as you are, I shan't mention it. But it does nobody no good for the cap'n to stand here losin' his mind when the pilot's got matters under control. En-en-en-en-en-en-en-en."

This flour sack remark seemed vexingly waggish, and I was about to address the issue, when a change caught my eye. Had I detected a slight increase in the speed of the pole 'passing' us? Or had I imagined it? I held my tongue, squinting hard at the pole, watching as our railings inched past it.

Yes. Yes! We had somehow gained a minute amount of speed! Moments later, the *Mean Fish* gave a soft sort of lurch to starboard, and our velocity picked up even more.

"Deeper water here, Cap'n," said Bridger. "I figgered the lower end could be a mite better."

There was no mistaking the improvement now, and from the sailors on deck there came a smattering of relieved whoops and shouts as we gained speed. What fine fellows—left entirely in the dark as to why the ship had left the main channel to start with, and yet, if any of them had entertained such misgivings as I, they had surely handled themselves with greater composure. I found myself hoping that no one aside from Bridger had overheard their captain's pitiful outburst—at the same time, feeling satisfaction that such unflappable men as these should embellish the decks of my vessel.

Only a few minutes more brought us back to the Swale, our speed increasing gently all the while. We glided past the final flagged pole at a placid but steady clip, entering the gap between trees, where our keel again met bottom with a shudder. We slowed significantly, but as our bow was by then reentering the main current, the Swale's full force caught us, and pulled us in, as it were. A couple of wheelspins

on Bridger's part sufficed to orient the ship, and we were again upon the river, the Skipton bridge visible behind us.

I doubly rejoiced—another obstacle lay astern, and with our safe passage around Skipton, I felt able at long last to resume my conversation with Miss Mary Ashwood. Remaining topside only long enough to verify that we moved smoothly upon the Swale, I left navigational matters in my officers' capable hands, and excusing myself, made straight for the Cat & Cabbage.

From the pub door, I saw *her*—Darling of the Dell, Flower of the Fell, Sweet of all Swaledale—seated at a table near the bar, engaged in animated repartee with Miss Fenny Drayton. Both ladies turned my way, and the genuine smiles which illumed their fair faces would have made any man's heart flutter —yet how much more moved was I by one of these smiles! What a miracle that this paragon of my heart—so long distant—recently sundered even further by dint of her father's disapproval—should now grace the Cat & Cabbage, her tall figure and lovely features filling the whole room with light. Still, I reminded myself that however it was she had come to be with us, her stay onboard must be brief. Mister Ashwood's prejudices would surely require his daughter's return home before we reached the sea. (It had already occurred to me that the skiff which was to bring Miss Smeaton to the *Mean Fish* near Hull, might be subsequently deployed to send Miss Ashwood ashore.)

I greeted the ladies with a bow, and voiced my profound thanks to them both for the exceptional courage they had shewn during our escape from Langthwaite. I went on to express my regret that duties had heretofore prevented me from properly welcoming such valued guests aboard, adding my hope that their time aboard the *Mean Fish* had thus far been pleasant. (At this, Miss Drayton's cheeks coloured and she turned aside slightly; I took this to signify that her

rumoured tryst with the doctor, had it indeed occurred, had been rather to her liking.)

The socially nimble Miss Drayton must have immediately divined my principal purpose in visiting the pub. The moment our initial pleasantries were done, she stood and excused herself in a most refined fashion, informing us that it would please her to take a turn on deck, should I deem such a diversion safe for a lady. I assured her that all was now well topside, then summoned Penywern from behind the bar. I instructed him to escort Miss Drayton on deck, and into my uncle's company. This he seemed pleased to do, even allowing her to precede him through the door, a gallantry which I had not expected from a barkeep.

This left only Thistle and myself in the Cat & Cabbage. Alone! Completely alone at last with the object of my admiration! Mere hours before, I would not have dared imagine it possible. But there we sat, facing one another across a plain wooden table, the very air between us seeming to shimmer with promise, to vibrate like a plucked harp string.

I cleared my throat, and said, "Miss Ashwood, I hope that you have not felt neglected in any way while captainly considerations kept me from your side. You have lingered in my thoughts since the moment you stepped aboard, and I am fairly dying to learn how you came to Langthwaite today—so far from what I would take to be your usual haunts—to intervene on my behalf, and in such a valiant manner. I am truly indebted to you, Miss Ashwood, and I long to hear your story."

"I thank Your Lordship for your gracious concern," said Miss Ashwood. "I have found myself treated with great hospitality, for which I am very much obliged. I saw little of your ship or crew during my previous visit, but must say that this public house is a perfect marvel, and every gentleman I have interacted with has made me feel

a queen. As for your preoccupations, a keeper of sheep understands perfectly well that duty comes before pleasure, so I would never feel neglected on that score.

"As to your larger question, My Lord—I find myself so amazed by what has befallen me these past few hours, that I can scarcely credit it as real, rather than some sort of astonishing dream. I shall happily explain as best I can.

"I was in the shearing shed early this morning when cries went up around Keld that the ship was moving. I felt puzzled, certain that I must have misheard, for I in no way expected that the *Mean Fish* could have budged from its pool. But when I stepped outside, sure enough … there went the neighbourhood's one and only tall ship, gliding along the valley-side as if by magic.

"My mother joined me in watching the ship. I found her looking at me in a strange way—with a sort of smiling sadness I had never before seen. She said to me, 'Mary, I have it from both of your companions, that you did *not* embarrass yourself before the archdeacon these few weeks back, as you told us you had. I am assured that you represented our village, and our family, flawlessly. Why would you have invented a falsehood about that?'

"I was thoroughly puzzled to hear this topic broached at such a moment, as it had not been mentioned in weeks, but I told my mother, truthfully, that I was very sorry about having lied, and that it would not happen again.

"She seemed to think for a moment, then went on, 'My feeling is that you must have been upset by something the viscount said to you that day. Exactly what, I have not been able to get out of Miss Smith or Miss Cartwright, and doubtless you wish it that way. But Mary, if that man, or any other, said to you anything base, or foul, I hope to high heaven that you would not remain silent on the matter.'

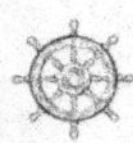

"I assured my mother that I would not remain silent, had anything of that sort been said to me. We stood there quietly then, for a few moments. Your ship had turned the corner and headed away from us, towards Angram Bottoms.

"It was nearly out of sight when my mother said, 'you know, Mary, no one who has watched His Lordship the Viscount when you are about, would doubt for a moment that the fellow admires you to the point of distraction, though I daresay he fancies himself discreet. Everyone, from the gorse-cutters to your father, has noted the way he looks at you. Why, I myself have seen His Lordship walk straight into a post while doing so.'

"I felt myself blush, but said nothing as my mother went on, 'I have studied him at such times, and found no hint of ignoble intentions. Quite the contrary. All Keld knows him as a man of good character, if a bit batty. This ship of his, you know. It *has* raised eyebrows. And yet look at this, now… Mark my words, those Jacobs have not built a mere toy, after all. They mean to get that ship to sea.'

"I agreed with her prediction, astonishing though it was, and expressed my hope that His Lordship and Sir James would succeed.

"My mother looked at me in a very fond manner, and gently said, 'You wish to observe their progress for some way down-valley, don't you?' When I nodded, she took my hand and told me, 'Take a couple of hours, then, and go. You've worked hard already today. Saddle up Emmy, and send word back if you go farther than Reeth. I'll finish with sharpening the shears.'

"I thanked my mother with delight, for she had read very well my desire to watch this lovely ship go gliding through Swaledale.

"And, as mothers shall, she had read more than that, for after I had saddled Emmy she took me by both hands and told me, 'Mary, we know not when the Viscount Keld shall return to our neighbourhood. He may be off adventuring for some while. And I hope you know,

it has never been your parents' intention that you spend all your years as a shepherdess, if you wish for some other life worthy of your gifts and your goodness. We love you too much to deny you a better place. Your father does have opinions upon certain matters of propriety, but he also loves his daughter more than breath itself, and he will be all right, whatever happens. I shall see to that.' Her eyes glistened with tears as she kissed me and said, 'Go, my love, and see marvelous sights, and when you return to Keld, may it be with an even broader mind, and a heart even more full than you now have.'

"Being anxious to catch up to the ship, I did not comprehend the full import of her words, let alone the possible outcome she foresaw. Indeed, only now do I see, and I marvel at her prescience! If I had understood in that moment all that my mother implied, I do not know if I would have had the heart to leave home, even for a few hours. But I had saddled up Emmy, and was keen to go, and so I trotted off down-valley as mother waved goodbye in the lane.

"Had I pressed my horse, I could have overtaken the *Mean Fish*, but my intention was to enjoy her majestic journey from a distance. Beyond Thwaite, I saw ahead of me the well-wishers attending your progress, but I deliberately remained behind them, not wishing to be caught up in such hubbub with a horse not accustomed to noisy crowds.

"I marveled at the apparent effortlessness of your ship's journey, even conceiving the strange notion that your turn-pike might have been built for that very purpose, rather than as a road. Hmm, and I see from your expression now that I may be near the mark! At any rate, I rounded a bend near Reeth to the unexpected sight of the *Mean Fish* stopped, and water gushing from the turn-pike, and a party proceeding by coach and horseback towards the village.

"By the time you crossed the Swale, I was near enough on the main road to glimpse you through the coach window, and espy the

earl and rector on the lead horses. Neither they nor anyone in their entourage found a lowly shepherdess on horseback worth notice. When I saw that they made for Langthwaite, I feared that your enterprise, and perhaps even your person, might be in peril, for it is well-known that the earl dislikes and resents your family, and I could hardly have missed noticing that his men were armed.

"So, I followed a few minutes behind, and saw you taken into Langthwaite under guard. Like a criminal! I found myself boiling with rage at this treatment of My Lord's person. Without thinking—it was a very dangerous thing, I see now—I dismounted and walked straight into Langthwaite, right past the earl's men. I daresay they were too dumbfounded by my sudden appearance and confident demeanor to immediately stop me. Once inside, I heard voices, followed them to that awful chapel, and strode right in. Your Lordship knows the rest."

Surely no one with even half a heart may doubt, that many aspects of this tale served to fan the flames of my feelings. Hearing an amorous quaver in my own voice, I said to her, "Truly, Miss Ashwood, your bold gambit to render me aid so fills me with admiration that I scarce know where to start in kissing you. Er, I mean, *thanking* you, of course, for your fair arms … uh, fair *aims* … and your most worthy actions today. God's truth, my lady, I would have done the same for you, and far more besides, had I thought your person or family in peril."

Thistle blushed and turned her gaze aside, yet sounded highly pleased, as she said, "I thank Your Lordship very much indeed, for so warmly commending my small efforts today."

"I am puzzled about the fate of your horse—Emmy, did you say? I did not see an extra horse about as we left Langthwaite."

"I did not see Emmy then either. I can only suppose that some groom of the earl's led her off to stable instantly, thinking that I must be a guest. She would never have wandered far on her own."

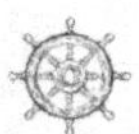

"And one other thing I find puzzling, if not quite objectionable. I have no recollection of ever having walked straight into a post, whilst distracted by any specimen of womanly beauty—not even your own, peerless though it is, if you shall allow my saying so."

Thistle favoured me with a smile so sweet, and so wholly directed at me, that gales of joy swept through my body. She said, "But good heavens, My Lord, I am quite certain that I witnessed this charming accident myself!"

O! Good heavens indeed! If the look Mary Ashwood graced me with in that moment, was to be my recompense, I would gladly walk straight into a post every hour, on the hour, all day long, for every spin of Earth's globe which remains to me.

I could have gone on conversing with her for hours, even days, and I feel certain that we would not have wanted for anything lively or important to discuss. But, I was in truth overwhelmed with emotion by that point, and no longer trusting myself to behave appropriately —feeling, in particular, a strong urge to hold Miss Ashwood's hand in an overtly fond manner. And so, it relieved me when Penywern returned to his post behind the bar at that very moment, rendering me no longer temptingly alone with this charming lady, and furnishing an opportunity for me to excuse myself, in order to collect my thoughts and feelings.

So I rose from my chair, favoured Miss Ashwood with a magnitude of bow I had been taught to reserve for a princess, and excused myself with regret, citing further captainly duties. I instructed Penywern to conduct Miss Ashwood into Sir James' care whenever she should wish to quit the pub, knowing full well that my gallant uncle would be delighted to play host to not only one, but both of our lovely guests (and, significantly, that he may be trusted to comport himself properly with them).

I bid Mary Ashwood adieu and retired to my cabin. There I remain, having had my dinner delivered, and receiving regular updates on our progress from Lampson.

What a state of perfect agitation have I found myself in! Immediately upon reaching my cabin I fetched Thistle's precious letter from my desk, and have since pored over it, line by line, word by word, again and again. Entirely unable to remain still, I at first paced about as I perused my love's epistle, until a collision with my wardrobe convinced me that this was unwise. I then tried rolling about upon the floor, but found it difficult to read whilst doing so. Finally, I struck upon the solution of pacing to and fro upon the plank, as this afforded immunity from running into furniture, and also more conducive to my undertaking than rolling had been.

Two principal thoughts consumed me as I dwelt upon the letter and recalled the minutiae of the day's interactions with Mary Ashwood.

The first thought was the most enthralling. Could it be that my feelings for her are truly reciprocated? Her letter does strongly suggest that, far from disturbing Miss Ashwood, my careless words of love during her first visit to the *Mean Fish*—my "pleasant fancies" as she put it—had stirred her heart. And yet, I have scarce dared hope that such a rose-coloured reading could really be correct. A man in my state might easily mistake civility, and the gracious language which flows naturally from a sweet nature, for the mutual attraction which he craves to discover.

But then, our conversation in the pub today had unmistakably overflowed with warmth; I had felt it not only in her pleasing turns of phrase, but in her voice, and in looks which had seemed frankly admiring.

And as for her noble behaviour at Langthwaite … I cannot overstate what it means to me. Had Mary Ashwood not interrupted the earls' machinations when she did, and in such dramatic fashion,

I might not have been afforded the mental latitude to seize upon Mustardhead's manic phobia of water as a means of making our escape. How often had I fantasized about rescuing her—from pirates, from Spaniards, from wicked elves—and yet, today at Langthwaite, it was she who rescued me.

The second thought was Mr. Ashwood's disapproval of his daughter marrying above her station, as Thistle described with such filial piety in her letter. Against this I cannot help but set the remarks reportedly made by Mrs. Ashwood this morning, as she sent her daughter off after my ship, and which seem to shew the situation in an entirely different light. Dare I dream that Thistle's stay aboard the *Mean Fish* need not be brief after all, should she by some twofold miracle chuse to remain, *and* enjoy parental approval to do so?

There is, of course, no resolving such questions merely by thinking upon them. Nevertheless, I required time in which to turn these issues about in my head, and consider them from differing angles. As a result, I have resolved upon a course of action which I shall pursue tomorrow—after we have passed the bridge at York, and prior to meeting Miss Smeaton's skiff near Hull.

How much does my future happiness thus depend upon events of the morrow! My magnificent ship nears the sea, an achievement towards which I have devoted boundless time and energy for years past … and yet, with that prize tantalizingly near, I find eclipsing it the possibility of an even greater bliss, in this person to whom I would so gladly devote myself.

Amongst the directives which I issued from my cabin during this bout of amorous hope, was that our lady guests be made comfortable tonight in Mr. Bridger's cabin. This private space has seen little use, and remains barely furnished, due to the spartan tastes and bee-like work habits of my second mate. Bridger confirmed (via Lampson) that he has no intention of setting foot in his cabin this night, so that the ladies are more than welcome to retire there. Seeing as how Bridger sleeps in a hammock rather than a bed, and that this would hardly furnish proper sleeping arrangements for two ladies, as they would find themselves rather awkwardly mashed together, Lampson and Converse have been kind enough to relinquish their own cots, which have been moved from general officers' quarters to Bridger's cabin.

I also confirmed with Bridger that he does not deem it necessary for us to anchor overnight. Given the suddenly clear weather and the moon shining just short of full, he expects sufficient light by which to steer the ship. This is a great boon, as it should get us to sea at least six hours sooner. I now estimate that we should reach the Humber estuary by early afternoon tomorrow. Bridger assures me, however, that he shall not hesitate to drop anchor and wait for better conditions, should darkness or any other danger make it too hazardous to proceed.

As for the bridge over the River Ouse at York, which we should reach in the wee hours of tomorrow morning ... a rather drastic action is, unfortunately, necessary in order to get our ship past it. I expect to record the results in this log as soon as events allow.

Wednesday, July 1, 1795

I begin my log entry for today with the inclusion of a letter, which I recently composed for several worthy recipients.

It is currently five o'clock in the morning. If all goes according to plan, hired messengers should, at this very moment, be placing copies of my missive into the hands of the following individuals, or their representatives:

> 1st. His Royal Majesty George III, King of Great Britain and King of Ireland
>
> 2nd. His Grace Samuel Lennox, Duke of Richmond, Earl of March, & etc.
>
> 3rd. The Most Revd. & Rt. Hon. Lord Archbishop of York, William Markham
>
> 4th. Sir Mark Sykes, High Sheriff of Yorkshire
>
> 5th. The Rt. Hon. William Wilberforce, member of parliament for Yorkshire
>
> 6th. Richard Metcalfe, Lord-Mayor of York

Once past the salutations, which of course differ for each recipient, the text of each letter reads as follows (I use the honorific Your Majesty in this version; of course, of the various letters only the King's was so written):

It is with the very deepest regret that I write to inform Your Majesty, that in order to secure passage for my sailing vessel down the River Ouse, enroute to the North Sea, it has been necessary to destroy the public bridge crossing said river at the city of York.

The demolition of said bridge was accomplished this morning, by means of gunpowder charges emplaced along its length by a crew of engineers. These charges were carefully measured and positioned so as to essentially vaporize the structure, dropping into the waters of the Ouse not great blocks of rubble, but fine fragments, many of which shall be borne some distance downstream by the present flood. This precaution ensures that the spot does not become a hazard to navigation once high waters recede.

I hereby pledge to Your Majesty—on my oath and to any Englishmen who may suffer adverse effects from removal of the bridge—that preparations are already made for a free ferry service to operate at York, at my own expense, until such time as a new bridge is complete. (This service shall go into operation once the Tadcaster road is no longer impassible due to the flood.) Furthermore, I fully intend to fund, again entirely at my own expense, a new bridge over the Ouse at York, to replace the one so regrettably removed. I am determined that it shall not only prove as practical as the former structure, but shall exceed it in architectural merit.

All efforts were made to ensure that no one was physically harmed by the demolition of the bridge. Although the city approach to the bridge was not under water, my engineering team cordoned it off last night under the pretense of road works. Furthermore, crewmen on our ship fired a pyrotechnic flare on our approach to the bridge; this was answered by a flare from our engineers signifying that the bridge was unoccupied and the demolition would therefore proceed. If any persons had been observed on the bridge or perilously near the charges, the second flare would not have been fired, and my ship would have dropped anchor upstream from the bridge, until the danger was alleviated.

I wish to emphasize that I personally find this act of destruction to have been not only regrettable, but even repugnant. Only a dearth of expeditious options to move my ship past York, turned such a violent extremity into an unfortunate necessity. I pledge to Your Majesty that commerce shall not suffer for it, and that the new bridge shall be in every manner superior to the old. I pledge my fealty to the Crown of Great Britain as I sail into the North Sea aboard a vessel flying its flag. And I furthermore pledge to personally address any grievances which may arise as a result of our alterations, despite my wholehearted efforts to prevent such.

Unpleasantries aside, it pleases me to report glad tidings as well. I am very much gratified to present to Your Majesty, to the people of Yorkshire, and

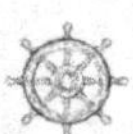

indeed to all England, a complete and functional freight canal running between the city of Richmond and the village of Keld, in Swaledale. It is my intention that the tolls on barges plying this remarkable waterway be used to recompense the various landowners who graciously consented to a county right-of-way across their properties, in order that the canal might be built. Alternatively, should stakeholders deem it preferable, the canal may be drained, roofed, and used as a lucrative all-weather turn-pike, with the possibility of extension west into Cumbria. This project has been designed and constructed entirely at my own expense, and is hereby bequeathed to the county of Yorkshire as a public boon.

I trust that in your wisdom, and with a spirit of Christian indulgence, Your Majesty shall recognize the goodwill which motivates my actions, forgive any temporary inconvenience which they may cause, and share in my enthusiasm for the salutary outcomes I have described, despite what may initially (and understandably) appear an act of wanton violence.

(These letters having been set to paper some days ago, they omit the detail of the wrecked lock-doors near Reeth, which need repair before the canal shall be of use, but heaven knows, there was no way anyone could have foreseen that unfortunate outcome.)

How shall these letters be received? I can only hope that my gift of the canal, together with my commitment to replace the bridge (not to mention my contrite and pleasing language), may deflect any outrage at the removal of a public bridge. I also hold out hope that the enthusiastic reports of my ship, which dozens of delighted visitors have been conveying to every corner of England, further mitigate opinion in my favour.

All of this remains to be seen. The deed is done; the old Ouse Bridge at York has ceased to exist. As I write this account, the *Mean Fish* cruises upon the Ouse near Naburn, several miles further downstream.

As per my orders, Nelson had me roused from bed the moment he sighted Beningbrough Hall off to port, the appearance of this structure shewing that we drew near to York. The hall remained visible by the time I arrived topside; though it must have been marooned by the flood, lights burned in its upper storey, and I hope that the Bourchiers have remained safe and dry in their handsome home, which has perhaps been protected from the worst of the high waters by its ha-ha.

The nearly full moon did indeed afford sufficient light for navigation, throwing into eerie relief each bend, each bar, each downed tree. Bridger reported to me that not only had there been no difficulties below Skipton, but also that the deepening channel —the Swale having carried us to the river Ure, and the Ure into the Ouse—meant that our keel had not felt bottom for nearly two hours.

Nelson informed me that our lady guests had retired to Bridger's cabin yesterday evening, and that they had not yet been heard to stir, although the terrific amount of gunpowder our bridge-sappers were about to set off would almost certainly rouse any somnolent being within five miles.

At the appointed moment, as we rounded the riverbend above York, one of our sailors sent aloft the pyrotechnic flare. This prodigious rocket shot skyward with verve, blossoming at an altitude of some hundred feet or so with a brilliant purplish bloom of potassium nitrate. Then all eyes watched downriver for the answering flare. Bridger held his bosun-pipe at the ready. I saw his lips move as he counted off seconds, ready to order the anchors dropped if our party at the bridge failed to respond within two minutes' time.

And then, there it was, the fiery trail and keen glow of the flare from downstream, signifying all to be ready at the bridge, the short fuses lit. We held course and speed, but remained ready to anchor at

a moments' notice, should any quandary be noted by our lookouts, or signaled by our team at York.

There were no quandaries to note. The answering flare still flickered aloft, when its brilliance was overcome by an eruption of gunpowder which turned night into day along York's riverfront.

I saw the explosions first—a string of massive orange and yellow flowers blossoming across the river ahead of us, their fierce glare reflecting from the water's glassy surface, briefly lighting nearby trees and buildings as with the rays of a setting sun. The reports reached me a moment later, and not my ears only; the deep, rapid thrum of thirty-six near-simultaneous detonations resonated through the deck, suffused the air, rattled my every atom. Surely no able-bodied person in the city of York would fail to spring out of bed at such a mighty summons; more than a few might fear the end of the world. We had never expected to pass York by stealth after blowing up their bridge, of course, but we did hope to be some distance downstream before any reflexive wrath might be directed against us.

We reached the site of the demolition about a minute later, and by moonlight it was clear that our sappers had done fine work, indeed. The only remaining traces of the old Ouse Bridge were the cordoned-off approach on the city side (now projecting into empty air), and one partial support on the far side opposite which had resisted disintegration, but which did not impede our progress. The *Mean Fish* cruised serenely right over the spot, gliding through acrid clouds of gunpowder smoke, her hull only once scraping against what may have been a submerged fragment of the erstwhile bridge.

By that time, a general alarum had been raised in York. From what I could tell, this amounted to little more than confused shouting in the streets some way back from the waterfront—Yorkers' natural assumption being that the powder magazines at the castle had somehow detonated. The idea that their bridge had been blown up

would not have straightaway occurred to them, and our handiwork was already hidden by night; our gunpowder flowers had faded as quickly as they had bloomed, and dropping the old stone bridge into the swirling floodwaters had extinguished all combustibles straightaway. The townsfolk would soon enough notice the missing bridge, but at that moment, no one on shore seemed to note our dark ship as the Ouse whisked us past the city and the doleful walls of Clifford's Tower. Meanwhile, our sappers were hopefully making their escape via rowboat across the flooded fields south of town.

The Ouse Bridge at York thus removed, no known obstacles remain between us, and the waters of the North Sea.

Exhausted by the triumphs and travails of the past thirty hours, I find that my bed beckons temptingly, yet I cannot give in. The summer sun shall soon rise over Yorkshire, and I wish to be nowhere else save the deck of my ship, during the last few hours of her journey to saltwater.

Moreover, I intend for this forenoon an interview of staggering importance with our guest, Miss Mary Ashwood, the outcome of which, one way or another, I shall dutifully record later today.

Wednesday, July 1, 1795; Five o'clock in the Evening

As the sun rose early this morning, we cruised the River Ouse near Cawood. Or perhaps I should say, we cruised the *channel* of the Ouse, for the river had spread out over this low-lying country until scarce any dry land lay visible. As along the Swale in the vale of Mowbray, only trees and farm buildings rising forlornly from the waters shewed this to be, under normal conditions, a prosperous agricultural region, rather than a vast inland sea.

Perched upon the rooftop of one marooned shed we spotted a bedraggled shepherd, accompanied by several sheep. Whilst our

approach clearly piqued his curiosity, his wave and hullo were rather more desultory that what we had heard from the crowds in Swaledale. Clearly, the fellow recognized that our ship, marvelous as it is, could be of no help to him as the river whisked it by. Before we had even quite got past him, he already appeared to have lost interest, returning his attention to the west, as if he hoped that aid would soon appear from that direction.

Naturally enough, rivers grow larger as they near the sea, and so the Ouse in South Yorkshire is a mightier waterway than the Swale at Richmond. Even since we had passed York, the Ouse had been supplemented by tributaries such as the Rivers Foss, and Wharfe, plus an innumerable number of smaller ones. Every one of these contributing streams had been swollen by the past weeks' rains to many times its normal volume. Our *Mean Fish* rode the mighty current of these combined waters, and it had been many hours since our keel felt bottom. Submerged logs had become a greater threat than running aground; our tireless pilot scanned the flood for minute signs of their presence, seeing clews in a boil of water or swirl of leafy debris which would have escaped the notice of a landlubber such as myself.

This morning's breakfast was a spirited affair in the officers' mess, thanks in large part to the novel presence of two lovely ladies. It seemed as if, with so little opportunity of late to practice the gentle art of gallantry, my officers now strove to outdo one another—Nelson, Whitehand, and Wheelwright each had a hand in seating Miss Ashwood, jostling round her chair to such an extent that she could scarcely squeeze into it. (I found myself unable to assist, rebuffed by this crowd, but I did see to it that Thistle was served first.)

A similar enthusiasm orbited the person of Miss Drayton—Lampson in particular seemed inclined to assist her in any way possible, an attitude which clearly failed to win the doctor's amity.

Those two gentlemen all but fell over one another in their deference to our comely guest from London; Converse said little, as usual, but alternated between skewering Lampson with disapproving glares, and favouring the lady with meaningful looks (which, I could not fail to notice, she returned). Miss Drayton appeared to find humour in the situation; whilst I saw her say or do nothing to encourage our charming university man, I daresay she found our taciturn doctor's discomfiture gently amusing.

This was the first meal attended by all officers (save Bridger, who remained at the wheel) since our departure from Stonesthrow the previous morning, as the intervening march of events had not allowed for such pleasantries. Talk around the table, so often in the past dominated by dull daily business, today bubbled with lively discussion of our adventures, improved by scintillating contributions from the ladies.

I was especially charmed to hear again Miss Ashwood's account of how she had come to be at Langthwaite—told to all present, in response to a question from Nelson. This version she abbreviated, leaving out most of the conversation with her mother. Despite this omission of what, to me, seemed the most significant part, she held her audience in thrall with adroit use of language and a storyteller's natural bravado. By the time she described her bold march into Langthwaite, my uncle leaned so far forward over his plate, utterly absorbed in her tale, that I feared his shirt ruffles might become soiled. I marveled—not for the first time—at how this shepherd girl, though doubtless endowed with natural intelligence, had come to acquire such poise and erudition in sleepy Keld.

Following breakfast, my officers adjourned to their duties—Nelson and Lampson topside to oversee our progress, and Whitehand to his theological studies. Converse returned to sick bay, those lonesome chambers where he has been accustomed to spend most of his

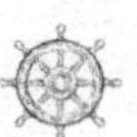

waking hours, and yet, they must surely not be so lonesome anymore. Miss Drayton accompanied him, as she went telling Lampson in a carefree voice about the doctor's fascinating tales of vagabonding in the Alps. In response, our well-bred botanist gave a slight bow— accompanied, I could not help but notice, by an equally slight grimace of disappointment.

Meanwhile, my uncle deftly drew Wheelwright above decks by inviting him to again describe his experience at Saint Louis in the Spanish War, during which he claims to have personally fired upon British troops. I had asked Nelson for the favour of some diversion, to keep our librarian occupied for a while, and of course, there is no better way to divert Mr. Wheelwright than to solicit a story, as he is ever ready to provide one in excruciating detail. Nelson gave me a look and a nod as he left, Wheelwright in tow, for he knew what I was about. As they vanished through the door, our adventuring librarian had already launched into his tale: "Since you so graciously ask, Sir Nelson, I shall, of course, be more than happy to gratify your interest! I should begin in the summer of 1779, when I had the good fortune of becoming personal librarian to Don Fernando de Lebeya, then governor of Alta Louisiana ..."

As for myself—I took a very deep breath, approached Thistle, and said, "Miss Ashwood, I wonder if I might have the honour of shewing you our ship's library this morning? It really is an extraordinary collection, if I may so boast, including much to interest a woman of your keen intellect."

Her matchless face lit up. "Ah! More than just instructional fables, cautionary tales, and treatises on proper housekeeping, then," she said.

"Er ... yes, quite. In fact, I'm not sure if the sort of things you mention are there at all."

"I see. Hmm. So, it is not a *ladies'* library."

"Um, no, well, it is *not* a ladies' library, as it belongs to me and my uncle. But I wish very much to shew it you, all the same."

"Well, My Lord, be assured that the honour shall all be mine. Unless it differs greatly from the rest of your ship, this library must be a wonder indeed!"

Relieved that this stage of my plan, at least, had been accomplished so naturally, I shewed Miss Ashwood out of the officers' mess, and down the gangway to the library. How delightful to merely walk beside her; I found myself wishing our destination farther away than a few mere steps, in order to prolong the pleasure (and, I admit in hindsight, to delay a moment of truth which I anticipated with equal measures of thrill and anxiety).

At the library, I begged Miss Ashwood's indulgence whilst I lit the lamp within, so that she might not stumble in the dark. That done, she stepped through the door, looked about with obvious delight, and remarked, "Well! In size this library surpasses any I have had the good fortune to set foot in, although there have been precious few. It fairly takes my breath away, My Lord, this many books in one place! I cannot doubt that Your Lordship's discerning eye has ensured quality as well as quantity."

Feeling myself flush with pleasure at this kind remark, I said, "You honour me indeed, Miss Ashwood, before we have examined even a single volume together."

"There is a rather large gap on that shelf over there, which I am surprised has not been beautified with a small sculpture, as I see you have done elsewhere."

The sculptures she spoke of—a nymph here, a bust of Aristotle there—were positioned upon the shelves to set off the collection's various topical sections, a practice I had carried over from the library in Stonesthrow Hall. But my guest had indeed espied an empty space which had not been there before.

What was missing? I was about to express my puzzlement, when it struck me—Wheelwright's black books were gone.

I had seen him wield only a single volume to stop the onrushing horses the previous day, and yet, I recalled his remark, once back aboard ship, that *the books are all of them the earl's now*—this spoken with evident relief, as if an onerous responsibility had been discharged. Could it be that through some unknown agency those ominous tomes had vanished from my ship, to reappear elsewhere? Were they now ensconced in some dim corner of Langthwaite's maze, there to remain unseen, oozing quiet malice, until the day of judgment? I hesitate to question Wheelwright more closely on this, as I feel somehow certain that the black books no longer burden the *Mean Fish* by their presence. And given such a satisfying end, I am content to leave off complete understanding of the means.

"Er ... well ... some antiquities of Mr. Wheelwright's had been shelved there," I said, "But I believe he has ... um ... bequeathed them to someone."

Thistle clearly noted my befuddlement, and her curiosity seemed piqued, but if she was tempted to enquire further, something on the shelves diverted her attention at that moment. "Oh! My goodness gracious! Are these volumes of Blaeu's Atlas?"

I have never, even for a moment, considered Mary Ashwood of merely ordinary intelligence. Had I done so, I could never have fallen in love with her, beauteous though she is. No, her eyes, her expressions, and her comportment have ever shewn the spark of sharp wit to even so muddled an observer as I. And yet, her casual recognition of a landmark geographical work thoroughly astonished me.

For a moment, I was struck speechless. Then I blurted out, "Miss Ashwood, you are correct—and I hope you shall not find it base in me, to marvel at how a young lady of Keld should so easily recognize Blaeu's Atlas. This is not to mention the poise and ease of speech you consistently display, and which I might expect in a lady afforded the advantages of high birth, rather than one raised in the humble household of a shepherd! Were we characters in a novel, I should think you a foundling, so wonderfully do you confound and exceed expectations!" After a pause I added, "By which I mean no disrespect whatever to your parents, or your fellow villagers, all of whom I hold in high esteem. It is just that … I have never …" Here I had to pause again, before finishing, "I really must apologize, as I fear that I am not expressing myself well at all."

How marvelous to find this verbal fumbling answered by that radiant smile, an assurance that all was well, or at least, forgiven.

"Your Lordship expresses yourself quite well, I would say, and there is no need for an apology. It is natural enough that I surprise you, for I have had the good fortune to enjoy some of the advantages, as you put it, which do not ordinarily attend my station in life."

I was dying to know more about these advantages, and said so.

"There is a widow lady over the hill, in Kirkby Stephen," said Miss Ashwood. "She fled Hanover during the Seven Years' War. She had been a tutor to the finer families of Lüneburg, who returned her years of kind service by securing her passage to our country, sending with her a substantial number of valuable books, which they feared might be destroyed by the French invaders. She has dwelt in various Cumbrian towns for near three decades, now. Although her former patrons have provided a modest living for her, she has continued to tutor young ladies, and she prefers to take on the daughters of rural families with limited means; I believe that she began life in such a situation, herself. My father heard of her during a business visit to Penrith, and he secured her services for me.

"And so, My Lord, I have enjoyed the benefit of eight years' occasional instruction, in both etiquette and knowledge, from this learned woman. In addition to my readings for her, I have for years

now carried a book in my pocket whenever going out with the flock—mostly adventuring novels, and of a silly sort, I suppose. Still, these have filled my days in the fields with interest and romance, helping me while away many an hour, and surely broadening my horizons."

"Miss Ashwood, nothing could have improved my opinion of your parents more than this beneficence of theirs," said I, "And yet I find myself puzzled. You make it eminently clear in your letter—a document which I treasure dearly, by the by, and have read a thousand times—that your father abhors the idea of striving to rise above one's place. How is it that he would take such pains to educate his daughter when, to the best of my knowledge, none of his peers in Keld has done the same? Does this not constitute, for him, a putting on of airs?"

"An incisive question, My Lord. My father has been anxious to provide me this boon, because education is to him a birthright in our family, which includes a long line of tutors and schoolmasters. An uncle of mine yet serves as schoolmaster in Hawes. My father's father only went into the shepherding business when a cousin of ours fell ill. It was meant to be temporary, but the cousin passed away, and my parents found the shepherding life to their liking. This would have happened during your grandparents' time, I believe." Her voice dropped, and she went on in a somber tone, "Your Lordship's parents were much loved in Keld, and their time with us was all too short."

Here allow me to remark that, although a reader of this log might suppose my parents to be far from my thoughts, seeing as how they have scarce been mentioned in these pages, nothing could be further from the truth. I was of age in the years of their untimely passings; I knew and loved them well, both with the uncritical ardour of a child, and the more discerning admiration of a young man. They were the finest parents in all the Earth as far as I am concerned, and I am not alone in our neighbourhood, in supposing that Almighty God may

have welcomed them into paradise at such young ages, owing to their being simply too good for this world. My father and mother linger in my thoughts continually, bless them, and my memory of their generous spirits informs my own dealings with others, especially our villagers of Keld. Matters of running and launching the ship have preoccupied my pen, but without the inspiration of my parents, who ever taught me to dream and to pursue those dreams, not two planks of this vessel would have ever been fastened together.

And so, such a tender reference to my parents from Mary Ashwood could hardly fail to swell my heart, pushing higher the already lofty mountain of my regard for her. How I longed to take her sweet person into my arms!

Yet the moment for such pleasure was not ripe. Instead I said, with a good deal of emotion, "Miss Ashwood, you honour me very much in speaking so of my late parents. I happen to know that they held the Ashwoods in high regard, and it interests me to learn of your family's background, which had somehow escaped my personal notice. Your story satisfies my curiosity about the source of your refined manners and surprising knowledge, though I suspect that no amount of tutoring could produce such a pearl as you, *sans* natural traits and proclivities of the fairest sort, which you clearly possess. I have never set foot in London, let alone in His Majesty's Court, yet I've no doubt that Miss Mary Ashwood, if dropped into that milieu just as she is, would outshine every other lady in sight."

Her cheeks coloured strongly as she said, "Your Lordship continuously says things too kind to believe, yet I feel that they are spoken in earnest."

"Miss ashwood, I have never spoken more earnestly in my life," said I. "And now, how apropos that you should have mentioned my departed parents, for there is one volume here in particular which I wish to share with you."

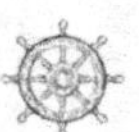

From the shelves dealing with Yorkshire history, I drew a large, heavily bound folio, the words *Familia Iacobus* imprinted upon its cover in faded gold leaf. I gently placed this upon a table and stood before it, Thistle at my side.

"The genealogy record of the Jacobs, printed at the creation of the peerage," said I. "Required study for a budding viscount, and most of it, regrettably, rather dry. My uncle is more inclined to such interests, and I have been happy to give him free rein. Here on the first leaf, our family coat of arms. In the perplexing language of the armorialist: purpure, an otter passant sable, in the mouth a fish argent."

"A lovely design, My Lord. I appreciate its simplicity. The motto, *non nobis solum* ... does it not mean, 'not for ourselves alone'?"

"Miss ashwood, at this point it would have surprised me if you were *not* able to read Latin."

"My tutor did instruct me in basics. I should be hard-pressed to read Cicero or Tacitus in the original."

Carefully turning pages and pointing out key passages, I explained, "Many centuries ago, my family followed the Jewish faith—as you might expect, given our Hebrew name. An ancestor of mine in Mecklenburg converted to Lutheranism for the sake of keeping his family's heads attached to their bodies, and we have been good Protestants ever since.

"In the late sixteenth century, my ancestors migrated to England, fleeing the ravages of the Thirty Year's War. They settled mostly in Dorset, gradually accrued land, and my great-great-great grandfather, Charles, received a baronetcy in recognition of the family's cumulative military service.

"As you see here, a Jacob perished fighting for the Crown in Ireland. ... And here, another died supporting the Portuguese Restoration. ... Another went missing at Trafalgar. Hardly a decade has passed without some Jacob giving his life for king or queen."

Turning to the back of the volume, I unfolded a large folded leaf bearing a diagram. "And here we have the family tree—the ancestors of whom we know, at any rate. You see that my uncle had the page extended and he has added developments of the past two generations in his own hand. Here am I. Richard Jacob, third Viscount Keld. The treetrunk, as it were. Odd, when diagrammed in this way—looks as if it is I producing all of these branches, rather than *they* producing *me*."

This was the moment. Turning to Thistle, I said to her, "Miss Ashwood, you should know that a skiff is to visit our ship in a few hours' time. It shall bring onboard Miss Jane Smeaton, whose prodigious engineering talents made our canal possible." I paused, and I looked at her searchingly. "The same skiff, should you wish it, could return you to higher ground. From there it would be a circuitous journey back to Keld, owing to the floods, but a manageable one. Trusted associates of Miss Smeaton's would accompany you and attend to your safety." I paused, and took a very deep breath, before adding, "The skiff would be your best opportunity to go ashore before the *Mean Fish* puts out to sea. It would be ill-mannered of me to not make you aware of it."

"Your Lordship desires me to go, then."

"I should hardly say so."

"Then Your Lordship desires me to stay?"

"Miss Ashwood, my desires are subservient to yours. I wish you to realize that the choice lies in your hands."

"And if my desire in this moment is to know your desire?"

"I would then say to you, that I very much desire you to stay."

"When would I see my parents again?"

"Whenever and for whatever duration you wish."

"And what might I expect, should I linger aboard the *Mean Fish*?"

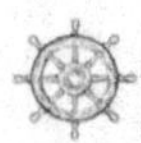

"Travel and adventure. Opportunity to peruse every volume in this library, should you wish. Every comfort and protection I may afford you, given the uncertainties of life upon the high seas. You could even walk upon the plank in my cabin."

"Please be plain with me, My Lord. In what spirit do you make such an offer to a lady?"

"In the spirit of a gentleman who loves you."

"And what would the world think of a maiden running off to have adventures with a bachelor viscount, even one who loves her?"

"The world? Good heavens, you and I together would be a world unto ourselves. Let us love one another, and naysayers be damned!"

"I feel that my heart may burst from delight, My Lord, and yet we must neither of us abandon our propriety!"

"Miss Ashwood, if you were to accompany me on my voyage, of course, I should not remain a bachelor for one instant longer than absolutely necessary! Which is to say … if it please you … Miss Ashwood, would you join me in the treetrunk? Er … not an *actual* treetrunk, but this figurative one on the page? Shall your name be writ in this book next mine? In short—Miss Ashwood, would you do me the very great honour of consenting to be my wife?"

"Yes!"

"What?"

"Yes, yes, yes, and there is no need to look so astonished!"

"You have said yes!"

"More than once, My Lord!"

"Miss Ashwood, I am over the moon!"

"Do start calling me Mary, My Lord!"

"Do stop calling me My Lord, Mary Ashwood!"

And then we were in one another's arms, and we kissed. And we went on kissing. And if it was not quite an appropriate sort of kissing for a man and a woman not yet wed, I can only hope

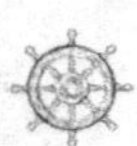

that our ardour may be pardonable. I felt enveloped by white-hot light—perhaps the very light separated from darkness at the dawn of time, for it was good.

At some point during my slide into this whirlpool of indulgent bliss, a guiding angel may have tapped me upon the shoulder, or perhaps some practical corner of my mind grew alarmed, cleared its throat, and voiced its opinion. Whatever the case, I managed to sunder my lips from Thistle's, informing her that I could wait not one moment longer to hurry topside and make our happy announcement.

She agreed gladly. In our haste to reach the poop deck, we each sustained minor injuries; I barked my shin upon a gangway-tread, and my wife-to-be, failing to duck at a low spot, received a bump upon her precious head. However, our soreness slowed us not a whit. We sped out onto the deck and up to the poop, where Bridger still stood at the wheel.

"An announcement for all hands!" I cried—but I could not possibly have waited for the entire crew to assemble. Before Bridger had even got his bosun-pipe out, I pulled Mary Ashwood to the railings overlooking the main deck, and at the top of my voice, declared, "Officers and crew of the *Mean Fish*! And any unfortunate Yorkshiremen who may be stranded by the flood within earshot, for I wish all the world should hear! This marvelous lady, who has just bumped her head, and whom I regard as the *ne plus ultra* of womanhood—for a variety of reasons too long to recite conveniently—has consented to be my wife! I hereby declare myself the happiest man upon this planet! Anyone thinking himself happier has never become betrothed to Mary Ashwood, and therefore I graciously forgive his error!"

My speech overlapped with Bridger's all-hands call on the bosun-pipe, so that some sailors arrived in the middle, and others afterwards, but there was no cause for me to repeat myself, as news of my announcement traveled like wildfire to the latecomers. A series of

hearty hurrahs went up from the crew. During these salutes, I felt moved to spin Thistle around the poop deck in a few steps of a reel, this action clearly meeting with the crew's approval, seeming to magnify their joy, as it did my own. My uncle, Lampson, and Wheelwright, who stood nearby during my speech, now extended their enthusiastic congratulations to Miss Ashwood and myself. (Only Bridger appeared unmoved, still engrossed in piloting our ship. Given the importance of not wrecking, I could hardly hold this against him.)

That miraculous event occurred twelve hours ago. Since then other noteworthy developments have occurred, and yet, have all smeared together into a sort of elated blur.

We continued for subsequent hours to travel through countryside inundated by the River Ouse, the river-channel growing ever broader. I spent this time in deliriously happy parley with my love, able at last to hold her graceful hand, the two of us making orbits along the railings from bow to stern and back again, our progress occasionally interrupted by kind expressions of congratulation from various officers and crew.

What did she and I discuss, all those hours? Particulars of our future life together, one might suppose, or the important question of how we are to handle the banns (I shall surely write more of that later!). But no, during those giddy revolutions around the deck of our seabound vessel, Mary Ashwood and I spoke of nothing and everything—birds, clouds, the husbandry of sheep, culinary likes and dislikes, teeth, Plato versus Aristotle, gardening, fabrics, the history of England, the Loose Stone of the Hall, my family, her family, the first golden light of morning upon Great Shunner Fell, the last rosy glow of evening on the craggy heights of Rogan's Seat.

At around two in the afternoon our lookout announced the flooded mouth of the River Trent visible to starboard, marking our arrival at the great River Humber. Mary and I were near the stern, but hastened to the bow, to better take in the sight.

Since splashing into the Swale at Richmond, we had passed for hour upon hour through flooded farm country. Now, at last, utterly open water lay ahead—the Humber! Though termed a river, this waterway is in fact a broad, shallow inlet of the North Sea. The ocean proper remained miles away, but here we reached its doorstep, and the sight set my heart racing.

Mary asked about the gentle swell of land visible ahead, beyond a bend in the Humber, the first substantial topographic rise we had seen below Richmond.

"That is where the Humber cuts through the Yorkshire Wolds," I told her. "The skiff shall bring Miss Jane Smeaton out to us from Welton, a town still reachable by road in spite of the floods, as it sits upon that higher ground."

"And the sails—shall we unfurl them now that we have reached this broad water?"

"Not quite yet, my dearest … although I confess that I can scarce wait any longer for it! Should we get under sail now, though, a safe rendezvous with our skiff would prove difficult. We shall continue to drift with the current until Miss Smeaton boards. We need not fear slackwater in the Humber, for we have caught the outgoing tide. Between that and the prodigious force of the flood pouring in behind us, we expect to move at a smart clip here even without sails."

Mary gazed for a moment back at my uncle, who stood at the port railings, looking expectantly ahead towards the Wolds. "You told me that Miss Smeaton has become a particular friend of your uncle's. I daresay he is thinking of her now. As Sir James is to become my uncle-in-law, I suppose it is not impertinent of me to ask, has he romantic inclinations towards this lady?"

"My darling, I am certain of it. My uncle tends to hold such cards close—as do many who have outlived a beloved spouse—but he clearly admires Miss Smeaton very much. We have spent several years working with her, and out of necessity, did so in a clandestine manner. Our meetings with her often took on an aura of adventure, convening by moonlight at the abandoned shepherds' hut near Buttertubs, for instance. Such circumstances surely enhanced the warm feelings which my uncle has expressed to me, for both our engineer's formidable intellect, and her feminine charm."

I heaved a sigh, took Thistle's hand in my own (what unspeakable luxury!), and went on, "Sir James did let slip yesterday that he and Miss Smeaton had suffered some sort of falling out. I know nothing further. I do hope that it was not serious, and that the two of them shall get on as they have in the past, if not better, now that she is to be with us aboard ship."

Mary continued to watch my uncle. "He too hopes that it is not serious. My Lord ... that is, your ... I mean, *Richard* ... How is it that Miss Smeaton comes to join us? Does not her work demand her involvement with other projects, elsewhere?"

"A penetrating question, my dove! Given her role in the bridge removal this morning, we feel it prudent to have her aboard as we are all of us already in the same *metaphorical* boat, as it were! Ha ha! But truly, we know not how the authorities may react. Miss Smeaton, Sir James, and I shall stand together until we *do* know. My uncle and I feel that Miss Smeaton, lacking the modicum of protection afforded by the family title, would benefit from proximity to us, should there be repercussions."

Over the following half-hour, as the long, low horizon-line of the Wolds grew steadily more prominent ahead, Mary and I resumed our walk around the perimeter of the ship, our talk dwelling mainly upon the adventure novels she has read. We passed my uncle on each revolution, as he remained immobile at the port railing, ever straining his eyes in the direction of Welton, as if expecting to sight the skiff at any moment. At one point, as our walk took us back towards the stern, Mary asked me about the fellow who had joined Bridger at the wheel.

"Ah, yes! This young sailor is a native of Hull. He knows the Humber as you know the pastures about Keld! All this open water is deceptive, my love! In spite of its oceanic appearance, the Humber is shallow, and strewn with shoals. Even coming off high tide we run a risk of going aground here. Hence the sailor—to act as a pilot to our pilot, as it were."

Thistle expressed interest in observing the nautical *tête-à-tête* between the men at the wheel, so we paused astern. There was no mistaking the keen intelligence in her lovely features as, head cocked slightly, she took in the sporadic bursts of jargon between Bridger and the sailor, and watched my second officer adjust the wheel. I felt my heart swell with pride as I watched her. How fortunate a man am I, to have won the heart of such a lady! I have no doubt that, with proper instruction, she could prove able to handle this ship as deftly as any man.

We remained at the stern—the green swell of the Wolds now surely less than a mile distant, as field-walls and farm buildings had become visible upon it—when we heard an announcement from the crows nest. "Skiff ahoy!" cried Bigg. Thistle and I hastened to the main deck, as did my uncle.

At first, the boat coming out from Welton appeared as no more than a mote upon the wide waters of the Humber. But gradually, as it and the *Mean Fish* both closed upon our rendezvous point, the mote resolved into a four-oared gig, with luggage and a lady in the stern. Closer still, and my ears caught the rhythmic chant of the men pulling the oars. Nearer yet, and I could make out wisps of

Miss Smeaton's long, fair hair come undone, and blowing out from under her bonnet.

I watched my uncle closely. He said not a word, yet hope shone plain upon his face. My darling Thistle had been right—surely the arrival of Miss Smeaton, and the condition in which he would find their relationship, dominated my uncle's thoughts.

Finally, the oarsmen drew the gig deftly up against our hull. Mooring lines were dropped from the *Mean Fish* and secured below. The bosun-chair was swung overboard by our crane and lowered into the gig. Never having witnessed such an operation before, I watched from the railings with great interest as Jane Smeaton perched upon the chair, signaled her readiness, and held on tightly to the side-ropes as she was hoisted up to the main deck.

I had grown so accustomed to meeting this lady under conditions which would enchant a spy, all of us sneaking about in dim places and examining documents by the light of guttering candles, that seeing her in broad daylight had a jarring quality to it. In contrast to the dark cloaks she had typically worn to our nocturnal meetings, Miss Smeaton now wore an old-fashioned (yet becoming) travel dress of a lovely blue colour, with matching bonnet, both of which would have been at the height of fashion some two decades ago, and whose hues offset her fair complexion and hair in a most pleasant manner.

I allowed Nelson to step forward and greet Miss Smeaton first. He did so with a proper bow and a few fitting words. Her reply was equally apropos. I did note between them a sort of stiffness, which I ascribed to whatever bump had jarred the progression of their friendship—and yet I saw in both their eyes, a desire for rapprochement, which gave me hope that any rent in the fabric of their amity would soon be mended.

Stepping forward, I performed a bow myself, saying, "Miss Smeaton, it pleases me greatly to welcome you aboard the *Mean Fish*!

She has found a bigger pool, as you see, and it could never have happened without your genius and persistence!"

Miss Smeaton beamed, "Your Lordship, it pleases *me* greatly that I may at long last address you as *Captain* Richard Jacob! My congratulations on your amazing journey here from Keld, which I and my associates have observed as best we could. We all knew that it was possible, on paper, but by heavens, you and your crew have brought it into the realm of the real!" Noting Mary, Miss Smeaton went on, "Captain, I am positively delighted to find that I shall not be the only lady onboard, after all! No offense to the worthy gentlemen of the *Mean Fish*, but the nature of my work surrounds me constantly with men—men, men, men!—and although that is well enough, it does cause me to cherish the company of my own sex. Captain, I take it from the manner in which you and she appear joined at the hip, that this comely lass is a special friend of yours?"

And thus was I afforded, for the first time, the delightful pleasure of introducing Miss Mary Ashwood of Keld, as my fiancée. The ladies exchanged greetings, and seemed immediately charmed by one another. Miss Smeaton was further pleased to learn that there was yet a third lady onboard, in the person of Miss Fenny Drayton. "Heavens!" exclaimed Miss Smeaton. "We have nearly enough to make an all-girls game of whist, and more than enough to pass the time onboard most delightfully. I could get used to female society for a change!"

During this exchange, Miss Smeaton's luggage had come aboard via the bosun-chair. Their mission complete, the rowboat crew cast off their mooring lines and made for shore.

Turning to Mary, I gave a nod upwards at the masts towering above our heads and said, "Now is the time, and I cannot wait another instant!"

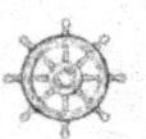

But even as I opened my mouth to give the order, a shrill call resounded from Bridger's bosun-pipe. Sailors leapt onto the rigging, and within moments the first of our glorious purple sails began to unfurl.

Not so long ago, such an usurpation would have made me furious—and for an instant, I did feel a boil of indignation rise within. But this quickly subsided. There is a time for anger, as the Proverbs of Solomon tell us, but that moment … my toes trod upon, yes, but by the truest and most capable second officer a captain could wish for … the woman I love by my side … my ship upon tidewater and her magnificent sails at last open in sunlight, filling with a fresh breeze from the west … only a truly ungracious soul could have stooped to wrath under such fair circumstances.

An increase in speed became apparent at once, and a cheer went up from the crew. Mary and I hurried to the bow. The prow below our lovely fanged figurehead sliced through froth and foam, as now, for the first time, the *Mean Fish* moved more swiftly than the waters around her. Mary and I remained at the bow for the duration of our journey upon the Humber, transfixed by the changing scenery on all sides, and by the tantalizing proximity of the open sea.

Our course was, for a time, attended upon both sides by the low swell of the Wolds' farm country, before the Humber emerged into the coastal plain.

The city of Hull slid by to port. As our local sailor guided us past the Humber's treacherous shoals, we kept well to its north side in this area; thus, our ship and Hull's waterfront enjoyed marvelous views of one another. We must have been sighted on approach, for by the time we drew abreast of the city's dockyards, a crowd had assembled, which cheered enthusiastically as we sped by. As I returned their greetings, I wondered—might there be, amongst those well-wishers, that young boy of Hull? The one who, during his visit to Stonesthrow, I had advised to "Keep an eye on the Humber"? There was, of course, no knowing.

As Hull slipped away astern, the Humber bent towards the southeast. Mary and I talked of faraway lands. I have seen little more of the world than she, truth be told, although both our minds have traveled farther afield, through books, than have our persons. But now, the seas and coastlines of the world (at least, those not French, or Spanish, or beset by pirates) beckoned, and we gave free rein to our imaginings. Might we visit exotic Egypt? Romantic Venice? Saint Petersburg, the great new Venice of the north? Canton and the Orient? The Sandwich Islands? The vistas seemed endless, the possibilities inexhaustible.

Our nautical conversation was enhanced at one point by a stirring cry from the crows nest: "Ocean ho!" We remained several miles from open water, but Bigg, from his lofty post, had sighted Spurn Head, and the North Sea beyond.

Past Hull, the Humber widened greatly. We passed near the town of Grimsby to starboard, and ahead to port, the long low sands of Spurn Head materialized from the watery horizon. Others gathered around us at the bow—my uncle, Miss Smeaton, Lampson, Whitehand, Wheelwright, Doctor Converse and Fenny Drayton—all of us watching as the tip of Spurn drew closer, and the oceanic waters of the North Sea beckoned.

Gradually, we all fell silent. Spurn head lay directly to port, the coastline falling away to either side, the flat waters of the Humber giving way to rolling swells, when the word we awaited rang out from the poop.

"Ladies and gentlemen!" called Bridger. "The *Mean Fish* plies the saltwaters of the North Sea!"

Every man and woman on board burst into a terrific, resounding hurrah.

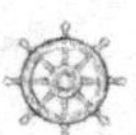

The sea! We had reached the sea! After so many years of planning and building, thinking and rethinking, my uncle and I had reached our goal! And it counted for more than I ever would have expected, that we had done so not on our own, but with the help and companionship of so many good people.

I drew Sir James into a heartfelt embrace. "We have done it, Nephew!" he said, voice choked with emotion. "We have built our ship and brought her home! Let the fates do their worst; with this alone to our credit, I could perish a satisfied man!"

"Captain!" came a shout. I looked back to see Bridger still at the wheel. "I request permission to stand down from my post!"

"Mr. Bridger," said I, "Your captain grants you permission to not only stand down, but also to feast, frolic, and repose at your whim! You are hereby relieved of all duties for a period of twenty-four hours!"

"Aye, Cap'n," replied my second officer, "You may rest assured I'll feast and frolic, as the occasion demands it! As fer repose, fie upon that! I'll take middle watch tonight, as usual."

I could have argued, but I stood no more chance of success than King Cnut refuting the tides. Instead, I faced about and kissed Miss Mary Ashwood—at that exact moment, the two of us baptized by an exhilarating mist of sea spray.

Tuesday, July 28, 1795

Now that we have reached the sea, my uncle has prevailed upon me to begin keeping a more traditional ships' log, devoted largely to matters of navigation and weather. This I have done in a separate log book. Seeing as how such things have heretofore merited little mention in these pages, to make such a change here would be tantamount to Mr. Defoe switching partway through *Robinson Crusoe* from his depiction of strange and thrilling events, to a dry recitation of chores, wind conditions, and Mr. Crusoe helping Friday conjugate verbs. The practicalities which comprise a ship's log would surely be of scant interest to most readers who have followed my narrative. To extend my previous example, I wager that few of Defoe's readers would wish to know the details of Mr. Crusoe's mundane life, after his exploits on the desert island had concluded, and that if he happened to fall into further adventures at some point, readers would expect to find those related in additional volumes, rather than tacked onto the end of the first.

I mention this by way of explanation, for I feel that the time has come to draw the curtain upon this narrative. Now that we sail the ocean, my tale of the *Mean Fish*, and her crew, and our journey from Swaledale to sea, reaches its natural stopping point. Further adventures may well lie in store, but if so they shall stand on their own as stories distinct from this one.

However, it would be unfair to my hypothetical readers to leave them hanging at the end of the previous entry, written over three weeks ago. To do so would again be like Mr. Defoe declining to inform his audience whether or not Robinson and Friday ever made it off the island.

And so, I hereby conclude this log (or *is* it a diary?) With a final entry, describing key events of the past three weeks, by which I hope to resolve what would otherwise qualify as loose ends.

One might suppose that, upon reaching the sea, we instantly set course for the destination which most dazzled our imaginings. Whilst such action was acutely tempting, Nelson and I recognized that it would not be wise for us to leave English waters until we had received an official response from His Majesty the King, regarding our removal of the Ouse Bridge at York.

To have set off immediately for parts unknown might have struck some, including the King himself, as an attempt to evade royal displeasure, or even as a tacit admission of wrongdoing. Such a flight would have made me the target of a manhunt at sea, as surely as the witless bolting of the wildebeast triggers the lion's predatory response, sealing the poor animal's fate rather than saving it. Our best course of action was to shew a spirit of submission to royal authority, and pray that the King would overlook our act of destruction, given the salutary developments (e.g., the new bridge and canal), on the other side of the balance.

And so, in order to avoid the appearance of sin (as Whitehand might say), Nelson and I decided that our initial heading would be north, along the Yorkshire coast. After a highly pleasant and satisfying sail of some fifteen hours, past Bridlington and Flamborough Head, we dropped anchor within sight of Scarborough. Anchoring in such a visible location shewed the authorities our lack of intention to flee, and made us available for the delivery, via boat, of responses to my letters. There we tarried, awaiting anxiously the King's judgment, which we expected within a few days.

Naturally enough, my main personal concern once we reached the sea was planning my wedding to Miss Mary Ashwood. Discussions on the topic began in earnest before we reached Scarborough. It was

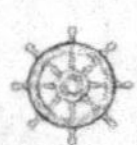

of the utmost importance to us both that our union be unassailably legitimate despite its taking place in the unorthodox setting of a ship at sea. We had, of course, an ordained minister of the Church of England on board, in the person of Paul Whitehand, but in order to meet the letter of the law it was necessary for us to either publish banns, or else secure a marriage license from the Bishop of York.

The latter course we deemed too uncertain. Even if we had sent a request to the bishop, there is no guarantee that a marriage license would have been graciously granted under the circumstances. I knew not where the bishop stood on the matter of the bridge—and regardless of his personal opinion, he may have found it politically expedient to deny such a favour to a viscount who had stirred up ill-feeling in York.

The option of publishing banns presented its own difficulties. Normally this announcement of intention to wed is publicly posted for a period of weeks at a parish church, so that any reasons against the proposed union might be brought forth prior to the ceremony. Whilst our shipboard chapel is officially recognized as Whitehand's parish church so long as he is aboard (we have written confirmation of this from the Arch-Deacon of Richmond), the only public able to read banns posted here are officers and crew who are generally not long acquainted with either Miss Ashwood, or myself. Under such circumstances, it could be argued that the banns had hardly served their purpose.

And then there was the question of consent from Miss Ashwood's parents. Mary reckoned her mother's support a certainty, and her father's likely to ultimately align with his wife's, but a bride-to-be's word on such matters is not automatically deemed sufficient by the church.

During our sail to Scarborough, Whitehand met with Mary, in order to delve into these issues. I later learnt from her that our

vicar had seemed especially interested in the circumstances of her departure from Keld—including Mrs. Ashwood's clear recognition that her daughter might not return for some time, and might be much-travelled when she did, and the implications thereof.

Whitehand spoke with me privately, in my cabin, following his talk with Mary. "It is my considered opinion," he told me, "that conditions are met, insofar as the church is concerned. As a man of conscience who knows the parties personally—you far more intimately, of course, but I *have* been acquainted with the Ashwoods, as upstanding residents of Keld, for nearly thirty-five years—I know of no reasons why this marriage should not go forward. And whilst banns posted upon this ship admittedly reach a limited population, they *shall* be public, and properly posted, just the same.

"As for the question of consent from Mr. And Mrs. Ashwood, it is not a requirement for a bride over twenty-one years of age. Mary is twenty-three; my diary shews that her christening took place in 1772, at Feetham. Only her parents' active *objection* to the banns could possibly become an issue."

"But," I pointed out from atop the plank, "someone wishing to cause mischief could argue that Mary's parents shall not have had an *opportunity* to object."

"That it so, and it is the sole chink in our armour. I can only say that I find it highly unlikely that Mr. And Mrs. Ashwood would object to their daughter marrying Your Lordship, and as for why anyone else might wish to impede this matter, that is beyond me."

"Reeth. Or Arkengarthdale."

"Hmmm, yes. You do have a point, there. Admittedly, we cannot rule out *those* possibilities. But the rector is no better respected in ecclesiastical circles than the earl is in secular ones. I feel that an attempt by either of them to stir up trouble would not be well-received by those in authority."

This opinion was comforting to hear, and I said so. "It is settled, then," I went on, "and our plans may go forward. Ah, Whitehand! I cannot express to you how very joyous the prospect makes me!"

"There is no need for Your Lordship to do so in words," said Whitehand, with a smile. "I have known you your entire life, Richard, and never have I seen you anywhere near so ebullient in word, deed, and countenance. Why, at the start of this conversation, when you stubbed your toe upon that lavish plank of yours, you seemed positively cheerful about even *that!*"

"Ah yes! What is a stubbed toe next to love? Less than nothing! And speaking of love, you and I should not neglect the matter of the *other* wedding. I take it that you have no objection to performing the two ceremonies sequentially, ours to follow theirs?"

"Oh, indeed, there is no problem with that. In the case of Doctor Converse and Miss Drayton, there is, of course, the same issue attending the banns, but she too is of age and shall not require her parents' consent. I would also expect that her father, being a professional, would not likely object to her match with a medical doctor in the service of a viscount."

"He might, could he hearken to our good doctor's muddled English! Ha ha! But such fancies aside, I understand that you have conferred with them, separately and together, and have no qualms about joining the two of them in holy matrimony?"

"I have no qualms." Whitehand leaned closer and went on in a lowered voice. "In fact, between you and I, Your Lordship, I expect that I shall find it a positive relief to have those two well and properly married."

"I see. And why is that?"

"You are, of course, aware that the doctor was baptized an Anglican, at your father's insistence. Even so, he persists in many Rromish habits, and one which he absolutely insists upon is auricular

confession. Converse fears that his soul may be imperiled should he fail to divulge his sins to me directly, and promptly. And he has always tended to be rather more detailed about such things than is strictly necessary. And so, since Miss Drayton came on board ..." He trailed off, heaving a great sigh before going on, "Let us say that I have been hearing *far* too much detail, about far too many varieties of fornication—often more than once per day, heaven help me— and I am quite ready to be done with it!"

I failed to suppress a smile. "And if the doctor believes at least some of this behaviour to still constitute sinning, even within a marriage?"

"Oh! Pray that it shall not be so," said Whitehand. "If matters took such a turn, your vicar might be driven to jump ship at our first port of call! There is only so much that even a Man of God may take!"

I know Whitehand well enough to tell that he was only half in jest, and I should have a devil of a time finding an Anglican minister to replace him in Kiel or Stockholm, to say nothing of Bombay or Buenos Aires! Hopefully things shall never come to such a pass.

And so, planning was underway for two weddings by the time we dropped anchor off Scarborough. The banns for both ceremonies had been posted on the main deck, outside the door to the chapel (and, for good measure, within the Cat & Cabbage).

The anxiety I felt two days later, on the 3rd of july, when we sighted a brig of His Majesty's Navy closing upon us, may well be imagined. Our ability to remain at liberty aboard the *Mean Fish* hinged upon what word that vessel delivered. In the extreme case that His Majesty felt our actions seditious, and my offers of bridge and canal of little account, I *could* have been arrested by royal decree. Although we felt such an outcome unlikely, it was not impossible, especially given that Our King has in the past fallen victim to periodic bouts of unsound mind.

I felt a modicum of relief once the brig anchored nearby, for both the distance she maintained and the at-ease disposition of her crew shewed a lack of intention to board us—Nelson took this as a sign that no warrants were to be served. I watched with bated breath as a skiff crossed the water between ships, and our bosun-chair brought aboard a naval officer.

This fellow introduced himself as Captain Mann, of the brig *Clementine*. He greeted Nelson and myself cordially, remarked with apparent sincerity on the magnificence of our vessel, and delivered into my hands three letters. "Your Lordship," he said, "my orders are to provide you time, within reason, to read these letters, and formulate any responses you wish delivered to their senders." With that, he bowed slightly, took a step back, and adopted an at-attention posture, clearly expecting Nelson and myself to examine the epistles at once.

One letter was from Minister of Parliament for Yorkshire, William Wilberforce. The second was from Samuel Lennox, Duke of Richmond. The third was from His Royal Highness, King George the Third, and of course, it was this I opened first, and read with pounding heart, my uncle peering over my shoulder.

What blessed relief when it became clear that His Majesty's words, far from expressing wrath, were cordial, and even touched by the wry sense of humour which, I have heard, is a notable quality of his. I dare not reproduce a royal missive verbatim, but I shall summarize it here.

After opening his letter with the customary pleasantries, the King described a rapid sequence of emotions which he had experienced whilst reading my letter:

1: Surprise that any peer of his realm would have dared blow up a public bridge for any reason whatsoever;

2: Anger at the grievously insubordinate nature of such an act;

3: Grudging admiration for the initiative and pluck required for it;

4: A sense of relief from tedium, for here was a matter of greater novelty and interest than he is accustomed to (affairs requiring his attention, he wrote, tend to be either vexingly convoluted, or distressingly grave, or both);

5: Approval of the manner in which I had ensured the safety of royal subjects;

6: Approval of my plan to provide a ferry, and replace the bridge, at my own expense;

7: Pleasure at news of the canal, or turn-pike, provided by myself to further commerce in Yorkshire, and

8: A recollection that the King had heard marvelous reports of my ship (in one case at first-hand) from individuals who had seen her anchored at Stoneshrow Hall.

All that said, after giving the matter thought, His Majesty had reached the conclusion that some form of punishment *must* be meted out, as failure to do so would set a frightful precedent. If this act of destruction were to go unpunished, reasoned His Royal Highness, then what was to discourage an earl from blowing up an absentee neighbour's manor house which he found irksome, or a duke from demolishing an entire town which happened to be causing him inconvenience? His Majesty, with regret, found it imperative that an example be made of me, in the name of preserving order in the kingdom.

Therefore, it was his royal decision that all tolls collected from the canal, rather than going to the property owners who had given up rights-of-way (as had been my intention), were to go directly to the Crown. In addition, I was to consider myself warned in no uncertain terms, that further destruction of public or royal property, for any reason whatsoever, would result in far more drastic penalties, possibly even the revocation of my title, and the reversion of my family's lands and property (including the *Mean Fish*) to the Crown.

"Thank the heavens," said Nelson, placing a hand upon my shoulder, "that our monarch seems to have been in one of his more magnanimous moods when he read your letter! This is the best outcome we could reasonably have hoped for. We are chastised, certainly—and we may expect the King's public announcement to be less delicately worded than this—yet how much worse off we might have been!

"His Loutship, though, and that despicable rector—O, Richard! They shall be gobsmacked when they get wind of this! The substantial income from tolls which we led them, in good faith, to expect—and which you graciously allowed them to retain in your letter to the King—they shall see every farthing go straight into the royal coffers, and shan't be able to do a bloody thing about it! Ha! What I wouldn't give to see Fitzhenry's face when he hears this news!"

My uncle was right. Since toll income was to have been divided up according to how much right-of-way landholders had yielded for the canal, and such a small portion crossed our own property, we stood to lose little under this arrangement, whilst the Earl of Arkengarthdale and Rector of Reeth would be especially hard hit by loss of anticipated income. How deliciously fitting! I believe this masterstroke of justice on the King's part to have been unintentional, as he likely had no knowledge of Fitzhenry's and Reeth's underhanded machinations (not to mention the physical damage they had caused to the canal). However, I shall probably never know that for certain.

As for the other letters—the one from Mr. Wilberforce was consistently (and understandably) irate, pledging to air in parliament this outrage perpetrated against the people of Yorkshire by "a petty nobleman grown far too big for his britches." I am little concerned about his ire, however, given the ruling meted out by the King— the Lords shall hardly challenge a sensible royal decree involving a peer of the realm, even if Mr. Wilberforce were to find a receptive

audience in the Commons (which I doubt he shall, given the tangle of pressing matters ever muddying the waters there). Furthermore, I know Mr. Wilberforce to be a temperate man; I believe the bluster on his part largely for shew, in order to appease his constituents, and I expect that the ferry service and new bridge shall quickly mollify any genuine umbrage he may take.

If my mind had most anticipated the King's response—seeing as how my fate hung upon it—then my heart had most anticipated the duke's. I had long felt the sting of conscience for deceiving that good man, and I opened his letter with trepidation. In it, His Lordship both scolded me for withholding the fact that my turn-pike was actually a canal, and on the other hand, praised my boldness in constructing such a waterway and sailing my ship upon it, acts which had "Enthralled all of Swaledale in their vision, daring, and majestic romance." His Lordship went on to thank me for my gift of the canal, which he felt certain would be a boon to our corner of Yorkshire. Much to my satisfaction, the duke went on to commend me for the manner in which I had "put that child Arkengarthdale into his place" and then concluded his letter with an assurance that his health was so improved, that he hoped to soon be well enough to resume his duties as duke.

Conscious that Captain Mann waited upon us, Nelson and I invited him to join us in the strategy room. There he enjoyed a tankard of ale whilst my uncle and I composed replies to the King and the duke. Each of these letters consisted largely of heartfelt thanks for clemency in judging our actions according to their salubrious ends, even if the means had not been entirely forthright. We further pledged to His Majesty the King that he may count on the officers and crew of the *Mean Fish* to remain true to the English Crown, and that we expect our voyages shall add to the wealth of scientific knowledge which sailing ships have, for hundreds of years, accrued for our Country and King.

We furnished these letters to Captain Mann, who graciously received them, bade us farewell, and returned to his ship. Both vessels then resumed sail—the *Clementine* towards the south, and the *Mean Fish* north along the coast of Great Britain.

Regarding our initial course—over the years Nelson and I had tossed about innumerable possibilities, each with its own merits in terms of geographical or scientific interest, and its own potential for adventure. Destinations we had dreamed of included the endless romantic shores of the Mediterranean, the dramatic fjord-riven coast of Norway, various ports around the Baltic Sea (including the new city of Saint Petersburg), the wild western fringe of Ireland, the exotic cities of India, and the mysterious islands of the Southern Pacific. Such speculations, however, initially took place prior to the revolutions in France, one outcome of which has been ships of the English and French navies pitted against one another in every corner of the globe. This turn of events caused us to exclude regions where the risk of running afoul of a French warship was too great—to visit such places would be to invite a brand of adventure which interests neither of us, and could well end with the *Mean Fish* finding a premature resting place at the bottom of the sea.

Seeing that this first voyage had, in essence, become a honeymoon for Mary Ashwood and myself, my uncle graciously relinquished his say in the matter, leaving it to me and my fiancée. What joyous hours she and I spent in the library, those first two days at sea, poring over atlases and histories, charts and mythologies! Her knowledge continued to astound me at every turn, even given the tutelage she had received. Were our universities liberal enough to admit ladies, my Thistle would surely exceed many an incoming young gentleman in the scope and depth of her learning.

Mary and I allowed our fancies to wander over the wide world, without the heed to revolutionary France which had coloured my speculations with Sir James—and the wonders of the rest of the world notwithstanding, we both found our attentions repeatedly swinging round to the legendary waters of the Mediterranean, and in particular, the storied isles of Greece. As surely as a compass needle points to the north, so did our mutual interest gravitate there, and we spent the better portion of the second morning consulting maps and books, contrasting various Aegean islands, and the merits of each.

We settled upon Delos, a scrap of granite which would hardly have interested anyone of strictly practical mind, but whose rich and varied mythology, along with associated ruins, captivated both my lady and myself. Delos held the added advantage of being sufficiently obscure that the odds of encountering hostile ships there seemed remote, and if this tiny speck proved insufficient for more than a few days' exploration, myriad other fascinating isles lay within sight.

No sooner had we come to this decision than my fiancée looked up from the chart we had been poring over and said, "Something is troubling you, my love. Even your excitement about these islands cannot hide that. It is the French, is it not?"

I had to admit that this was so. "Admiral Hood routed the French Mediterranean fleet last year," I added, "and yet, between remnants of that force, and the Barbary pirates, one cannot say with certainty that our passage to the Aegean would be entirely safe, regardless of how placid conditions might be around Delos itself."

She took my hands in hers. "Richard," she said, "is it not true that, even were we to remain in British waters, there would be some chance of encountering an unfriendly French naval vessel or privateer? And is it furthermore true that there is *no* course we could set, which would not involve *some* risk to the ship and ourselves?"

"That is all true, my dove, unless we were to, say, coast on down to the Thames. Gravesend would be quite safe, I'd wager, and from that haven you and I could explore London together. I have never been, and I hear that there are many interesting coffee houses."

"Interesting coffee houses! Come now! Even without that sly smile upon your face, I should see that you are jesting."

Feeling said smile grow into a grin, I went on, "There are no coffee houses whatsoever upon Delos, I fear. Apollo regards them as overly festive; Dionysus, too somber."

Mary Ashwood gave my shoulder a playful jab. "Now you are being silly, Richard, and although I find that quite fetching, I am making a serious point and you see it full well! We are on this ship to seek adventure, not to slink about avoiding it! Ten to one every sailor aboard would agree. We have already passed through perils which would have bested more timid souls. We are well-provisioned, fleet of sail, and, from the look of it, dreadfully well-armed. Why should we not follow our hearts? Why should you and I *not* wed upon the waters of the Aegean?"

"Ah, my love! When you put it that way—the French Navy be damned, and pirates, and coffee houses, as well! Delos it is, and getting there shall indeed be our first adventure!"

The journey took us eighteen days, due to the necessity of a rather circuitous route. The channel was too dangerous, so we first sailed north, around the ragged, misty crown of Great Britain, then south, through the Irish Sea. From there we made for Cape Finisterre, followed the Iberian Coastline to the Pillars of Hercules, and plotted a winding course along the Mediterranean's mid-line, which Bridger hoped would minimize our chances of quarreling with French or pirates.

Was this passage without interest or incident? Hardly. And yet, I must consider the events of this first voyage the start of a new

story, rather than contributing to the end of this one. It is likely that I shall write of those eighteen days at sea, and perhaps soon. For now, may it suffice to say that with each passing hour I reveled in my companionship with Mary Ashwood, and felt my love for her grow ever deeper.

Meantime, the banns were posted for three consecutive sundays, as specified by law. On those days the minister also verbally posed the question, during service, whether anyone present objected to the marriages proposed. These postings and readings of the banns took place on the fifth, twelfth, and nineteenth of June, and as we expected, no objections were raised.

On the twenty-first of July, the *Mean Fish* dropped anchor in the tiny harbour on the west side of that famed isle, the sight of which caused the following lines to condense in my mind, as if out of thin air:

Delos!

Navel of the Cyclades

Cradle of Artemis

Where Aeneas heard Apollo's words

And Thiasoi frolicked!

(Obviously, this 'poem' is bereft of meter and rhyming scheme. I may strive to improve it if time allows. However, it does effectively convey my mood in that moment.)

We had known this windswept speck of land to be rocky and barren, and yet it exceeded our expectations in both regards. Hardly anything green may be said to grow there. What *does* sprout from Delian ground is a wild profusion of sundered columns and rubbled walls, and of course, it was this bountiful crop which had enticed my Thistle and I. We enjoyed the better part of two days exploring the island on foot, reveling in views of sea and sky, luxuriating in one another's company, running our hands over the rough and ancient

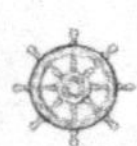

stones, speculating on whether we stood upon a spot once devoted to Zeus, or Apollo, or Dionysus, or some other deity. In spite of the greatly reduced condition of human constructions on the island, the sense of deep and profound history which I felt emanating from each and every ruin was nearly overwhelming at times, and my fiancée confessed to the same sensation.

In other respects, Delos proved a disappointment. We had expected a village, but there appeared to be no inhabitants whatsoever, not even a single solitary monk. We had expected fresh water, but there was none—and as the *Mean Fish* was by then running short on that precious commodity, I made the decision that we should limit our initial sojourn at Delos to two days. At the end of that time we weighed anchor and crossed the cerulean water—scarcely more than four miles' worth—to the island and city of Mikonos, whose lights we had seen from the Delian harbour.

We found ourselves welcomed by the Greek community there, and warmly received by the Ottoman governor, a well-bred fellow by the name of Omar Ali Pasha. We had anticipated, of course, that Lampson would act as our translator in this part of the world, and although his Cambridge Greek turned out to be at variance with the local dialect, he adjusted splendidly, and was soon conversing with the locals as if in his native tongue. What a boon shall his knowledge be in foreign waters!

Mary and I still wished our shipboard wedding to take place in the harbour at Delos, with classical ruins adorning the hillsides behind, and so when the day came for the great event, we sailed back to that empty isle, the audience for our dual ceremonies now swollen by the unexpected but welcome addition of Mr. Ali Pasha and a festive contingent of Greeks.

The weddings took place on Saturday, the 25th of July, 1795, in the harbour of Delos, Greece. After all the mishaps recorded in these

pages, readers might well expect—indeed, might even anticipate with relish—that some infuriating disaster befell me during this pivotal moment of my life. Hopefully it shall be no disappointment to such readers when they learn that no disasters, infuriating or otherwise, marred the occasion.

Yes! For the first time aboard this ship, an important event was carried off without a single vexing calamity.

The marriage ceremony preceding ours, between Dr. Otto Converse of Mittenwald, Bavaria, and Miss Fenny Drayton, of Lamb's Conduit Street, London, was brief yet poignant. The doctor appeared as happy as ever I have seen him, which is to say that the figurative cloud which ceaselessly shadows his countenance lifted enough to admit a gleam of sunlight. The fellow even smiled, full-on, as he faced his bride—Nelson could not stop elbowing me, so amused was he by the novelty of the sight.

As for Miss Drayton, she looked positively radiant in her brand-new gown. The ladies of Mikonos, upon learning that marriages were to take place, and that both brides suffered from greatly curtailed wardrobes, had insisted upon providing tailored gowns. The results of their speedy work were astonishing. Whilst I consider myself far from an expert judge of gowns, wedding or otherwise, these lovely creations of silk and lace seemed the finest I had ever beheld, and Miss Drayton's certainly enhanced her great natural beauty. I was especially struck by the contrast between her flaming red hair (braided, coiled, and stunningly wrapped upon her head by a lady of Mikonos) and the pristine white of the lovely wedding bonnet, festooned with livid greenery, which perched atop it.

As the two of them stood there on the forecastle, above the merry crowd of onlookers assembled upon the main deck, I was, of course, happy for them, and yet, I witnessed their ceremony in a dream, as it were, my heart so full of my own joy that theirs,

marvelous as it was, could only appear as does the moon when she and the sun both shine in the same sky.

The ring placed upon her finger, their vows and kiss duly exchanged, Dr. Otto Converse and—I caught myself before writing the wrong thing just then—*Mrs. Fenny Converse* made their way down the steps to the main deck, showered by flower petals and hurrahs from the gay assembly (the doctor actually *grinning*; as my uncle beheld this spectacle, he felt inspired to roughly shake my shoulder whilst repeatedly asking *do you see that*, which I certainly did).

The newly married couple took a place of honour in the front row of the crowd. It was our turn. A hush fell upon the onlookers as I mounted the steps to the forecastle, followed by my groomsman (Sir James, of course). I stood before Paul Whitehand, who looked ready to shed a tear—I imagined (and later confirmed) that he thought of my parents in that moment, and how gratified they must be, looking down from heaven upon this blessed event.

Naturally, I was well-acquainted with my bride's appearance. The graceful shepherdess, seen mostly from afar—and her matchless face, first glimpsed in church when she had worn a Thistle upon her dress—had for years embellished my dreams. Since she had joined me aboard the *Mean Fish*, I had enjoyed the very great pleasure of learning intimate details—the tiny scar in her left eyebrow (from a long ago fall in a rocky pasture), the fetching way her lips slide askew to shew skepticism, the strength in her capable hands. And yet, this growing familiarity had ill-prepared me for the vision which emerged from the gangway amidships, seeming to regally float up from below.

Here, I could have sworn, was a dark-haired, grey-eyed goddess come directly down from Olympus. Her dignified bearing, purposeful walk, serene smile—for a moment I found myself wondering: *who am I to wed this astonishing lady?*

But then she stepped up to the forecastle, and her eyes met mine, and the love in her look put that question to rest.

The ceremony was a blur. I saw little save Mary Ashwood's face, heard little save the vows from her lips and mine. I was only drawn out of this lovely spell by a sudden pain in my ribs—my uncle had elbowed me there, rather sharply.

"Ouch! Do you mind? I am being wed at the moment; we may roughhouse later!"

This remark brought a smattering of laughter from the crowd, the meaning of which escaped me until my uncle said, "Nephew, the vicar has just given you leave to kiss the bride."

"Oh!"

I wasted not one instant more before drawing into a breathtakingly lovely kiss, Mrs. Mary Jacob, née Ashwood, Viscountess of Keld. And again, I was lost to the world, only vaguely aware of a great hurrah. I believe that some of the crowd may have pelted the two of us good-naturedly with small objects of some sort, but I knew not what.

There is little else to tell, in bringing to a close this tale of two loves—for a magnificent ship I have brought into the world, and for a woman whose companionship brings me more fully alive than ever I have been.

We held a celebration following the ceremonies, of course, complete with food, wine, and the requisite lewd remarks about wedding nights (although neither couple was, by that point, rightly subject to such teasing). Amidst all the whirl and wonderful confusion, I could, naturally, focus on one person only, and the satisfaction of having her at my side could not be overstated. One image which has stayed with me was an unmistakably tender moment between my uncle and Miss Smeaton, pointed out to me by Mary, stirring our hopes that before long, this ship may host a third wedding.

Tomorrow we bid farewell to the good people of Mikonos and set sail for the famous Isle of Rhodes—and from there, who knows? The wide world awaits, with all its wonders and perils.

One last event merits mention here. It took place two days ago, prior to the weddings, whilst we were anchored at Mikonos.

My uncle and I stood upon the forecastle, soaking in the spectacle around us. The rays of the setting sun painted the whitewashed buildings ashore, and the wispy clouds overhead, the most delicate shades of rose and pink; in dusk, the sea appeared as wine-dark as any poet could wish. Mr. Ali Pasha was below decks, having a tour of the ship with Bridger and Lampson; the ladies were enjoying a reading party in the library. The deck of the *Mean Fish* lay nearly empty, with only a light watch on duty.

"I must pinch myself every hour," Nelson told me. "It seems so like a dream that we are here. The isles of Greece! In all our years of planning, nephew, did you ever believe … *Really* believe … that we would someday stand side-by-side, masters of our ship, surveying a scene like this one?"

"Yes." I said—an answer which required no reflection whatsoever.

"Well … Your faith has then been greater than mine, then, or perhaps more constant. Ah, if the folk back home could see us now! What would Rugby make of this?"

"Rugby would dismiss all this as nothing, in comparison to Cornwall," said I, "and go on to praise the unmatched beauty of the harbour at Penzance. If I have heard him do so once, I have heard it a hundred times!"

We shared a chuckle about this, but then we both fell silent at the same instant.

"Uncle," said I, "Do you see what I see?"

"I daresay that I do."

"When came it to be there?"

"This very instant, I'd swear. It was never there a moment ago."

A rectangular Stone had appeared at the very front of the forecastle, nestled into the spot where the railings from port and starboard converge—looking, strangely, as if it quite belonged there.

"Is it ... ?"

"It *must* be."

We stood there for several moments, watching the Stone, as if expecting that it might do something. It did not. And remarkably, the impression of seething malevolence which I had sensed (or imagined?) During its first appearance onboard, that stormy night at Stonesthrow Hall, seemed entirely absent.

"Uncle ... it may be that my mind has become addled from the southerly sun, but somehow ... somehow I find myself *pleased* that it is here."

"I must admit that I feel the same, Richard."

"I sense that it means us no harm."

"The Stone did in fact save us, back at Reeth."

And there it has remained, unmoving and untouched—causing no apparent mischief, and even flaunting my natural expectations by having failed to interfere with our weddings, when they took place shortly thereafter.

Already the crew, whose only experience with the Loose Stone had been a salubrious one, regard it as a good omen: a sentinel perched above our leering figurehead, perhaps ready to defend us from foes, as it undeniably did at Reeth.

And so, the Loose Stone of the Hall sails with us aboard the *Mean Fish*, a quarter-way around the globe from Swaledale. This fragment of my family's history remains a complete enigma to me, and yet in its mute presence I sense a message. Perhaps what we always presumed a curse has—in ways we never thought to consider—been a strange sort of guardian all along.

ABOUT THE AUTHOR

 Donovan M. Reves grew up in Columbia, Missouri, and was producing handwritten short fiction by second grade. While at Oak Park High School in Kansas City, Missouri, he won second place for short fiction in at the statewide UMC Writing Festival for his science fiction story "The Hatch". By that time, he had also branched out into writing poetry and novels. After moving to Corvallis, Oregon, for graduate school, he published several poems in local collections and his poem "To Do" won third prize in the Willamette Writers' Kay Snow contest in 2001. In 2008 and 2009, he published three collections of poetry and short stories: *Wombat Chow of the Damned, How to Report a Coal Mining Problem,* and *Festival at Naval Headquarters!*

He has been active in local writing critique groups since 1999 and continues to write novels while working at a locally owned independent bookstore. In 2018, his short story "Triptych" was published in the online journal *Lumina. The Extraordinary Voyage of a Tall Ship in a Tiny Pool Far from the Sea* is his first novel.

MORE BOOKS FROM GLADEYE PRESS

Follow the adventures and missteps of time-traveling PI Imogen Oliver as she recovers lost items and unearths long-buried stories and secrets from the past in this exciting series! (*The Time Tourists is available on Kindle Unlimited.)

The Time Tourists Trilogy
Sharleen Nelson

*The Fragile Blue Dot
Ross West
Veteran science-writer and journalist Ross West's collection of award-winning short fiction touches on the human aspect of living in a world on the brink of ecological disaster.

*Quilts of a Feather
Arlene Sachitano
An innocent birdwatching festival hosted by the parks and recreation goes terribly sideways when one of the event volunteers is found dead from a fentanyl overdose on the hiking trail. It's up to amateur sleuth Harriet Truman and her quilt group, the Loose Threads, to solve the mystery.

Join 19-year-old Ben Tucker for a passionate and revolutionary tale of protests, parties, trials, and a band of idealists who set out to build a countercultural utopia in the southern mountains of Oregon.

The Risk of Being Ridiculous Trilogy
Guy Maynard

*Available as an ebook on Kindle Unlimited.

All GladEye titles are available for purchase at
www.gladeyepress.com and your local bookstore.

Federation of the Dragon
Footman of the Ether
Jason A. Kilgore
Enter the ancient world of Irikara for
high-stakes epic fantasy adventure
in a mythical land filled with dragons
and demons, dwarves and elves,
magic and mages and gods.

Far Side of Revenge
Anne Dean
A tale of two brothers, bound to each other but fol-lowing divergent paths, this Booklife Editor's Pick, traces the life of Brian Boraime from his childhood as a son of a clan king until *he was named King of all Ireland.*

Coastal Coffee Club Mysteries
Patricia Brown

Five cozy mysteries follow retired poet Eleanor Penrose and her band of quirky friends as they solve mysteries along the Oregon coast.

Black & Tan Fantasy
Randall Luce
A Booklife Editor's Pick, this gritty historically accurate tale of racial identity and life in the deep South during the turbulent early days of the Civil Rights Movement is engaging and hauntingly relevant today.

COMING SOON *from*

Dying for Love
Patricia Brown

In this sixth book in the Coastal Coffee Club Mysteries series, Eleanor, Angus, and the gang investigate two murders in their sleepy little town which has suddenly been overrun with out of town treasure seekers searching for a million dollar prize hidden somewhere nearby.

Off Route
Rick Levin

From a public transit bus driver's brutally honest viewpoint, *Off Route* literally hits the pavement with a scathing look at the travails of the working class during the COVID epidemic.

I Am the Wind
Cullen Cantwell

In GladEye's first YA novel, adults as well as teens will be inspired by the journey of a young long-distance runner who receives advice and encouragement from an unlikely source.

The Kingdom Brothers
Mike Van Mantgem

Out on parole, white-collar grifter Cornelius Tayler is scraping by when his old partner reappears with an outrageous scheme and a payday to match.

So Much for a Safe Landing
Susan Solomon

With a dash of humor, action, empathy, and truth, a recently retired woman finds herself enmeshed in the polarizing and perilous world of women facing tough decisions in a post-Roe v. Wade world.

RERELEASES FROM JASON A. KILGORE
Around the Corner from Sanity: Tales of the Paranormal
Fourteen short stories of spine-tingling horror that will scare you AND tickle your funny bone!

Guide Me, O River and other poems